## PRAISE FOR
## *ARCHANGELS FALL*

"Andrew Bryan captivates from the very start. The narrative delves into the complexities of choice and sacrifice, making the characters' struggles relatable and compelling.

"This brilliant novel is a masterfully crafted tale that seamlessly blends supernatural intrigue with historical context. Andrew's narrative prowess, coupled with the unique twist on angelic lore, creates an engaging and thought-provoking story. Fans of fantasy, especially those drawn to the intricate worlds of angelic beings, will find themselves immersed in this captivating novel."

—**Alex Singh**, *USA Today* Best-Selling Author

"Andrew Bryan's brilliant debut novel delves into the blurring lines between good and evil, between destiny and will, with lyricism, intelligence, wit, and constant power. This is a singular book that twists old themes into new shapes and, at its heart, calls into question the nature of humanity, our faults and strengths, and whether our collective future holds merit. With an unforgettable narrative crafted around themes that compel an end to complacency, this splendid book merits a place on the reader's highest shelf."

—**Greg Fields**, Award-Winning Author of
*Through the Waters and the Wild*

"*Archangels Fall* is an ambitious first novel by Andrew Bryan. Filled with truly larger-than-life characters and a gripping plot, you will be on the edge of your seat and glued to every page. A terrific story with epic characters. You are going to love this book."

—**Dan Alatorre**, *USA Today* Best-Selling Author of *Six Sisters*

"What a thrill! Mr. Bryan's debut novel is compelling and suspenseful. His cast of unforgettable characters creates a world where every moment pulsates with life—leaving readers with breathless anticipation from the first to the last page and longing for the next book in this series."

—**Natacha Belair**, Award-Winning Author of the *A Stellar Purpose* Trilogy

# ARCHANGELS FALL

*Archangels Fall*

by Andrew Bryan

© Copyright 2024 Andrew Bryan

ISBN 979-8-88824-286-5

All rights reserved. No part of this publication may be reproduced, stored in a retrieval system, or transmitted in any form or by any means—electronic, mechanical, photocopy, recording, or any other—except for brief quotations in printed reviews, without the prior written permission of the author.

This is a work of fiction. All the characters in this book are fictitious, and any resemblance to actual persons, living or dead, is purely coincidental. The names, incidents, dialogue, and opinions expressed are products of the author's imagination and are not to be construed as real.

Published by

◣ köehlerbooks™

3705 Shore Drive
Virginia Beach, VA 23455
800-435-4811
www.koehlerbooks.com

LIGHTBEARER BOOK I

# ARCHANGELS FALL

ANDREW BRYAN

VIRGINIA BEACH
CAPE CHARLES

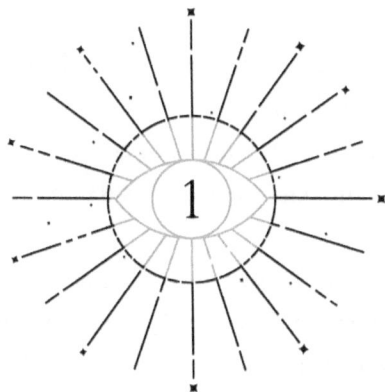

# 1

A university professor posed a question to his students.

"Did God create everything that exists?"

"Yes, he did," one student responded bravely.

"If God created everything, then he certainly created evil," the professor proposed. "Since evil exists, God must also be evil."

The student couldn't respond, and the professor was satisfied that he had "proved" that belief in God was a useless fabrication. Another student raised his hand, interrupting the professor's moment of superiority.

"May I pose a question?"

"Of course," answered the professor.

The young student rose to his feet. "Professor, does cold exist?"

"What kind of question is that? Of course cold exists. Haven't you ever been cold?"

"In fact, sir, cold does not exist," the young student answered. "According to the laws of physics, what we consider cold is the absence of heat. What we have done is create a term to describe how we feel if we do not have body heat or we are not hot. And does dark exist?"

"Of course," the professor snapped.

"Again, you're wrong, sir," the student responded once more. "Darkness does not exist either. Darkness is in fact simply the absence of light. Dark is a term that we humans have created to describe what happens when there's lack of light." The student then posed his final challenge. "Sir, does evil exist?"

"Of course it exists, as I mentioned at the beginning. We see violations, crimes, and violence anywhere in the world, and those things are evil."

"Sir, evil does not exist. Just as in the previous cases, evil is a term which man has created to describe the result of the absence of God's presence in the hearts of man."

The student was Albert Einstein.

The Damned could not be called evil. He was a dark angel, the purest embodiment of the absence of the Light, the Light being the essence of creation from which all energy and life flowed. He provided necessary balance.

Even as the Damned stood in the middle of London's Waterloo station, it was clear that the space he occupied was an energy void. Commuters bustled past him, avoiding the spot for reasons they knew not. Bearded and dressed in a tattered, hooded brown robe, his ragged dark locks knotted like rope, the pale angelic being was larger in stature than every human milling about him. His overall appearance was that of a war-wounded and weary fallen angel, cursed and betrayed.

He longed for his own oblivion.

To human eyes, the area was empty, but the celestial being had a dramatic effect on humans and the energy fields they occupied. He pulled on their will and weakened their resolve. When in close proximity, the Damned's Dark Light enveloped most mortals in a state of cold emptiness. This was of course how their senses interpreted it.

There were many more layers to the spirit world than most humans realised. The clashing energies in the spiritual realm—or etherverse, as it was known to the angelic beings that walked it—played a huge role in swaying human behaviour. Devoid of the Light, the Damned's strength lay instead in the Dark Light, a force of blood-red energy that only he and his dark-angel kin possessed. This crimson, anti-Light force absorbed pain and hatred of all kinds, empowering those who wielded it and increasing the suffering of those who could not withstand it. Most of humanity buckled under its pressure.

As the Damned stood amid the travel chaos in an ambient, removed state, his eyes closed, he sensed every whim of the confused humans around him. Obsessed with their devices, they rushed about like ants to bury their anger and fear with business, numbing their every instinct.

It was time, he decided, to begin his work.

A crimson hue appeared behind the dark angel, building to a blinding brightness in a split second. Almost as soon as the vertical hole at his back opened, its blood-red energy collapsed in on itself, taking the Damned with it. *Shhaup!*

The energy phenomenon was an ethergate, a portal that celestial beings could call upon at will to transport them anywhere on the mortal plane. The energy void the Damned had occupied quickly closed up as frantic travellers dashed through the space once again.

Meanwhile, underneath the mechanical timetable boards, a spirited nanny skipped playfully. Bobbing alongside her was a bright, handsome, five-year-old boy. The prospect of their adventure to Alton Towers theme park filled the pair with glee as they careered through the mob of disgruntled city workers. Smiling wistfully at the boy, the nanny basked in his pure innocence, drinking it in like the warm summer sun.

An abrupt buzz in her coat pocket broke the moment, making her stumble midstep. A flash of deep dread tugged at her core. She pulled out the phone, and her eyes froze solid at the words on the screen.

"Nanny, is everything okay?" the boy asked.

"Of course, sweetie pie. Nothing to worry about. I just wasn't expecting a call, that's all."

She quickly reset her upbeat exterior and guided the boy through the masses.

Elsewhere, on the upper lounge level, a suave CEO relaxed in the station's industrial-style cocktail bar. Floating above the mess of train tracks, the exclusive spot felt like his own personal office. He was intensely focused on his laptop computer screen when a call came in from his wife.

"How are you, my love?" he answered.

"Long day, just putting the girls down now. Jamie? Sarah? You wanna come say goodnight to your dad? Hang on. I'll just put you on speaker."

"I'll get home when I can," he told them. "We have a fun weekend ahead, don't we, my Power Puff Girls?"

"Yeah-yeah-yeah!" the girls squealed in unison—their ritual response.

"Night, Dad," said Jamie.

"Don't work too hard, Daddy!" said Sarah.

"I'll try my best," the CEO replied.

The polished professional returned to his laptop with a contented smirk, taking a long, satisfied sip of his triple measure of Jameson whiskey.

At that moment, on a shadowy street winding behind Waterloo station, a trendy, good-looking pair of ladies in their midtwenties bounced home from a boozy dinner. They laughed and regaled each other with stories of their raucous night out in the big city.

"Jeez, did you see how swanky that pub was? I never knew they made them that wanky. I think those red-trouser-brigade toffs were having a 'Who has the tightest jacket?' competition. I also can't believe you dared me to lick the tall one on the face."

"That was priceless," said the tall brunette. "I think he liked it too!"

"You must be way more drunk than I am 'cause your gaydar is obviously broke," the short blond remarked. "His bread was definitely buttered on the other side."

"Come on! No!"

"Yeah, for sure, you numpty."

"I do hope the waiter texts me back, though. He was gorge," said the brunette.

"For God's sake, Mills, they always text you back. You're basically a perfect human-skin-wearing manikin."

The brunette blushed.

"Shame about your manikin personality, though."

"Hey, shut up!"

The nanny continued to study her phone while she and the boy trundled along to their platform.

*Shhaup.*

The Damned warped in behind the pair, and his eyes snapped open, arresting them both in an aura of Dark Light. Turning a detached and vacant stare on the woman, he opened his mouth a crack. A powerful breath of darkness and cold landed on her. All expression fell from the woman's face. Looking down at the phone once more, she suddenly launched into action, yanking the young boy in the opposite direction, the force she applied almost dragging the child off his feet.

*Shhaup.* The dark angel was gone.

"What's happening?" the boy yelped in shock. "The train is that way. Ouch! You're hurting me!"

"Quiet now. I have a surprise for you, but we need to be quick."

The nanny dashed for a nearby station exit, which led out to the service entrance. As deliverymen went about their business in a clatter of distraction, a dark-blue people carrier screeched to a halt. The nanny headed for the vehicle while nervously checking her surroundings, then bundled the boy into the back seat. A scruffy, gaunt man turned from the driver's seat to check out the fresh meat.

"Where are we going? Nanny, I'm scared!"

The suspicious-looking man scanned the boy up and down with a toothless, hungry grin.

Suspended in the stylish environment above, the CEO studied employment reports displayed on his screen. Then he popped open another window and longingly admired the image of a superyacht and pondered his next step, a finger tapping the rim of his whiskey glass.

*Shhaup.* Phasing to the mortal plane in a blazing shard, the Damned stared down the wealthy businessman in contempt. With a breath of Dark Light, he enveloped the CEO in his cold, crimson grip.

The businessman finished his whiskey in one swift slug and proceeded to delete the employee files one by one. Left with the superyacht image before him, he licked his lips as an idea flicked into his mind. He eagerly tapped away on his phone: Fancy getting wild tonight?

The response was almost instant as his device chimed: I've been hoping you'd ask all night.

Looking on, the Damned sighed. *Are they all this misguided?* He had seen enough. It was on to the next, a red wormhole to the ether swallowing him up.

Behind the station, a strung-out teen whipped out of nowhere, confronting the trendy girls at knifepoint.

"Gimme your bags," said the drugged-up teen.

"Piss off, ya wee bollocks," said the feisty blond.

"Now, slut, or I'll cut your tits off."

Throwing her handbag at the teen's feet in a panic, the brunette stared down her friend.

"Jess, seriously! It's not worth it; just give it to him!"

*Shhaup.*

The Damned materialised behind the teen, his massive frame dwarfing the group before him. But the dark angel hesitated in his task, looking up to question the sky. His mood fleetingly flipped to a sombre realisation.

His role had become a burden in recent centuries.

Nonetheless, it was a burden he could not choose to throw off. Brushing away the doubt, the Damned inhaled a long, slow breath. He fastened his crimson gaze on the young lives before him.

The dark angel released his cursed energy over the attacking teen. A fog of pure rage poured over the boy, and he rushed the blond in a feral madness. The knife was cold and hard inside her before it was warm and wet with her blood. As soon as it had begun, the teen snapped back from his anger. Wide eyed and horrified at himself, he slowly backed away.

The brunette stood speechless as her friend's legs crumpled under her, her body hitting the unforgiving cobbles and life rapidly ebbing away.

This time there was no hesitation. The Damned was resigned to finish, warping in front of the boy in a crimson band. One final exhale landed on the drugged teen. Pulled away from indecision by the Dark Light surrounding him, the boy returned to purest hatred.

The brunette was stiff with shock when the teen pounced, knocking her down and tearing at her clothes like a wild animal. Lying in a pool of blood, the blond girl could do nothing but look on as her dear friend was violated.

The Damned's dark robes seemed to drag the energy from every living thing around it as he turned and slowly drifted away with a heaviness inside. Moans and shrieks from the rape rang out against the lonely alleyway walls.

*Thwack!* A final blow brought the silence of death. Blood rolled down the cobbled lane, glistening in the orange streetlight glow. It followed the dark angel's footsteps in an unnaturally straight line, drawn to him like a magnet.

Feeling no need to look upon the horrors left in his wake, the dark angel opened a crimson portal and stepped off into the etherverse.

The Damned had forever stood as an adversary to humanity, though he did not force their hand or influence their minds. It was not within his power to do so. His prison sentence on earth was marked only by asking the question, over and over and over again, offering them the darker choice. This had been the way of things ever since humans were gifted to the earth and the earth gifted to them. In the same way the sea could not be called evil for wiping out entire villages in one sweep, the Damned could not be called evil for playing his part in the balance of life. Neither force had the power to choose their path, and both moved within their nature. Death and decay were just as much a part of the earth's cycle as life and growth, after all.

The Damned and his angelic class resided in the lower ether, a layer of spiritual existence that was both within and outside of the physical realm. The laws of the etherverse as a whole kept the Damned chained to the dark realms below. The Fall had initiated the Damned's imprisonment in the lower planes of existence—changing the nature of his Light, changing his class.

Changing everything.

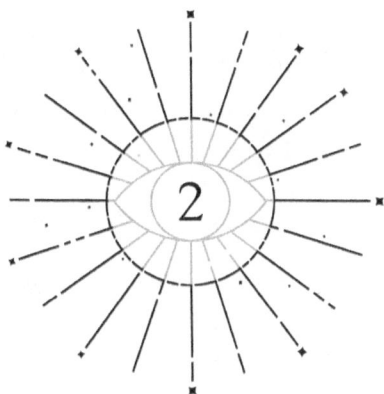

## 3.8 BILLION YEARS AGO

The earth was a churning collection of gases and solids circling an unstable core. A formless mess of magma comprised its growing crust. As the lava moved and cooled over millions of years, a huge amount of moisture condensed, and the oceans began to form. This final phase of the planet's genesis saw the bombardment of the earth's crust with numerous asteroids. Volcanoes erupted and released gas as extraterrestrial bodies smashed into its surface. The planet was a fiery death trap, not yet able to sustain life of any kind. The earth in this state almost resembled a vision of hell as was later invented by humankind.

Over the coast of what would be known as Ireland, a small meteor burst through the atmosphere in a blaze. Gathering phenomenal speed as it hurtled towards the surface, the rocky mass began to splinter with red cracks. The cracks expanded and retracted erratically like something inside was struggling to emerge. The burning entity seared hot, sealing the mass together as it morphed into a humanoid shape.

In an explosion of flame and dust, the body crashed into the planet's surface. The remainder of its rocky shell crumbled away, uncovering a lithe being that staggered to stand. An alluring, indefinable beauty arose from the debris, holding her chest in pain and hyperventilating. Her features were chiselled and her hair a flowing mane of black. Eyes ablaze at the appearance of her once-glowing hands and robes, Beel pawed at her face. Its drained appearance and her now deep-red eyes represented a palpable shift from her former splendour. A pulsating crimson energy emanated from her, a form of energy she had not known before.

The Dark Light.

Whipping her head around, Beel sensed another member of her class hit the earth further up the fiery landmass. In a blinding blade of scarlet, the celestial being dashed through an ethergate to her kin's position, exiting the wormhole 300 miles north to witness a male of her species splayed atop a heap of jagged rocks.

The hostile landscape before her extended further into a vast plane of burning rocks and spitting sulphur. The sky was grey and thick with ash. The wiry, angelic man at Beel's feet wheezed, struggling to stand. Clocking Beel's arrival suspiciously, he froze, and as Beel offered a hand in aid, her angelic counterpart recoiled at the sight of her burning emptiness. He clawed at his own darkened form in horror and awakened to his spirit's loss of the Light.

Coming to full height, the bald and bearded Abaddon exhibited an intense intelligence. His eyes looked like they could pierce through stone. Inspecting each other warily, Abaddon and Beel came to recognise that they were indeed allies.

Changed. Cast out of the upper realms.

Another portal to the ether appeared abruptly. The growing ball of the Light moved with a different energy, shining with a stunning hue of pure gold. The spinning sphere whirred and spat out sparks as the handsome, golden-haired archangel Gabriel emerged. His commanding aura and large, muscular stature befitted the leader of the guardian angels. He wore robes similar to the celestial beings he confronted, though his garment stood apart in an immaculate white, bordered by brilliant red-and-gold trims, its high, peaked collar bestowing a regal look.

The noble celestial held within him the power of light and dark energy in perfect balance. As he ruled over his class through love rather than fear, Gabriel's guardianship of the etherverse drew much adoration from every other angelic class; he was a fair and magnanimous leader whose wisdom could slice through the most corrupt of hearts.

Enraged at the audacity of Gabriel's arrival, Beel and Abaddon drew back, ready for a battle to the death.

"What have you done to us?" Beel screamed at the archangel.

"Please, you must know I had no part in this," Gabriel responded.

"I'll rip your self-righteous head off!" Abaddon roared as he lunged for Gabriel's throat in a blur of crimson.

Holding his position with a stoic glare, the archangel opened his palm and flipped his hand. Two humongous golden chains clattered out of the ether, locking around Abaddon's wrists. Lifting him off the ground, they violently slammed him back down.

"Don't," Gabriel warned Beel, recognising her rage ready to overflow.

"Traitor!" the lithe female barked. Her fists clenched.

Before she could blink, a second pair of glowing energy shackles materialised. They snaked around her body, holding the indignant angel upright and helpless.

"Where is our lord?" Abaddon sneered. Gabriel's eyes shone gold for a moment as the mighty celestial moved his senses through the physical and spiritual planes.

"I . . . do not know," Gabriel responded.

"Liar. How is it that the all-knowing Gabriel is at a loss for words?" Abaddon said. Flexing his palm, Gabriel pulsed three waves of the Light through it. The archangel twisted his head to the sky. An uncharacteristic loss of sensation had overcome his spiritual sight.

"His Light. It is somehow hidden. Distant."

"We are resolved to find him. You, however, shall find it was a mistake to let us live." retorted Abaddon. Without warning, both angelic beings began to disintegrate into burning, crimson ash, their Dark Light consuming them from the ground up.

"There will be a reckoning," Beel croaked. Holding on to one another in solidarity, Beel and Abaddon locked eyes as they disappeared. Piece by piece, their forms scattered downwards, to somewhere beneath the physical plane. Gabriel looked on in trepidation and disbelief.

This was as ruinous a day as he had ever witnessed. He could not understand its meaning or its justification. All he could do was accept the plan of the Universe. Still, he could not help but think what a loss to the upper realms this was. A new balance would need to be set. There was much work to be done in the turbulent ages to come.

It was in this fashion that the Damned's entire class of angelic beings were condemned. Thrust down to a deeper, unknown plane, robbed of the Light, they could no longer move as freely as the divine celestials above. They faced a new world of exile, bound to earth and the realms below.

Every other angelic class turned against the Damned and his companions. Each would go on to champion the human race in its own way: warrior, guardian, restoration, visionary, commandment, judgment, and death. All had their role to play in the dawning world of human existence. Humans were to be a new, more gifted species and one blessed with mortality—something that angelic beings longed for, as they, on the other hand, could never die. Blessed also with free will to choose their own path and create of their own accord, humans would become the higher species. These mortal beings, with the power to visualise the vast realms of the etherverse from earth, were to be the great intercessors between the angelic planes and the physical world.

*Were to be.*

It was a hopeful expectation that had failed to realise. Instead, over its comparatively short existence, humanity became corrupted by its own greatness. Ego and pride became the masters of these mortal beings. Their gift went to waste. With each passing age, humans lost more of their otherworldly sight, a loss that weighed heavily upon them, poisoning their species with a slow, degenerative madness. They thought themselves gods of their own small lives, and this brought them much pain. Their inability to control the uncontrollable blighted their minds with frustration, leaving them in a perpetual state of clinging, fixing—tortured by the need to figure out their physical existence.

This frustration manifested a hell on earth, and not a hell of fire and brimstone but one of small-mindedness and self-obsession.

Angels had no such freedom of choice, instead bound to the spiritual etherverse. An ancient celestial species made long before the earth, they felt no such pain. Their strength was in acceptance of the path. Their role had been set, their class chosen, their mission clear. Unclouded with details outside their own control, they saw clearly and fully. That was, until the Damned and his class became the first victims of a war between divine celestials and humanity itself.

Just as too much freedom had become chaos for the humans, too many rules had created the walls of a prison for the angels. Prison walls that were bending under immense pressure, ready to burst.

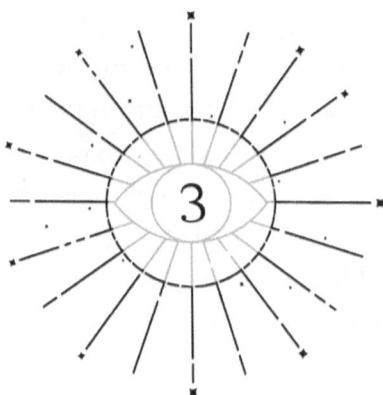

# 3

Mr. Patel lay on his back, giggling in ecstasy. His wailing filled the large room as his rubbery, aged face contorted. Snapping his head back and gritting his teeth, the man suddenly winced at the acute sensation in his lower limbs.

"Yeow!"

A pair of full, luscious lips whispered in his ear, flipping the Indian man back to an elated state. His laughter became deeper and warbled strangely. Grace peered up quizzically from between the man's bare legs. She was an earthy beauty with wild brown curls tied into a top bun. Her full, oval eyes glinted green like forest dewdrops in the hard light whirring above. It was the kind of look that could melt the toughest of exteriors.

The seductive lips next to the delirious man's head belonged to Beel, who of course went unseen by the mortals in the busy hospital ward. The dark angel's provocations were all fun and games to her, a sentiment far removed from the heartache and misery hospitals represented for humans. Beel's tatty brown hood covered a lustful amber glare as she whispered another playful suggestion.

"Again, my love?"

"Oh yes. Yes, please!" the old man begged.

Grace's head popped up once more. This time, she shouted to the junior doctor over her shoulder, "Will? How much morphine did you give Mr. Patel?" *This man should not be so deliriou*s, she thought.

With a sharp yank, she pulled a large shard of glass from Mr. Patel's foot.

"Wowie!" the man exclaimed in an odd sadomasochistic outburst.

"Fifteen milligrams," Will hollered back from the waiting area of the accident and emergency department. Busy with crowd control, the junior doctor wasn't having much luck with a clamour of irked inpatients.

To make matters worse, the scheduling system was woefully outdated. Mile End Hospital was a dilapidated, understaffed site in North London that suffered the same funding problems as most British healthcare institutions. As a result, Will almost had a barroom brawl on his hands.

"Fifteen?! I clearly wrote five on his chart!" Grace cried. Mr Patel sat bolt upright and stroked Grace down the side of the head repeatedly as if petting a horse.

"Shiny. Soft. Soft head!"

"Please, lie down, Mr. Patel," Grace snapped, pushing the patient flat on his back. Beel lurked at the edge of the room with a sultry smirk. Feeling something warm stirring inside of her, Grace settled her gaze on where the dark angel was standing, her senses taking control of her conscious mind for a brief moment. Beel's vibrant force brought a consuming heaviness to the room that was far from anything familiar.

Beel tilted her head down to shield her Dark Light from drawing too much attention. *This human woman is obviously gifted*, she mused.

This "giftedness"—if it could be called that, considering the pain it brought—was something Grace had grappled with all her life. Her extrasensory perception constantly pulled her away from her own mind and sense of reason. Monstrous migraines and sensitivity to light often followed. Grace had used medication—both legal and illegal—in the past and was passed around by doctors as a child. Nothing seemed to alleviate the symptoms of her undiagnosed condition, and so she had learned to live with it, though her naturally kind and nurturing disposition became more suffocated by panic attacks and blackouts with each passing year. Thankfully, she hadn't had one recently.

But the painkillers weren't working anymore, and she was wary of venturing further in that direction. Maybe she needed a different approach to her circumstances, but for now she was at a loss. Instead, she did her utmost to focus on her strengths: helping and healing those in need around her.

Wild rantings from the waiting area brought Grace's attention back to the main ward.

"I need someone to see my little Johnny!" yelled a middle-class Chelsea mum, Sarah. Sarah was giving both barrels to Will in the A & E waiting room. She wasn't going to let her precious child get anything but the best care possible, if she could help it.

Perched next to Sarah, a young couple full to the gills with prosecco and obsessed with their phones pinged away on social media. The scantily clad girl had a swollen ankle and twirled one of her high heels in her hand. Beel found the couple in a crimson dash and breathed a whisper of lust. Absorbing the cold wisp of Dark Light, the girl's boyfriend began to suck on his companion's high heel. The two of them started firing off a barrage of selfies, lost in ego. The impromptu photo shoot completely captivated little Johnny, whose jaw flopped open like a broken drawbridge.

"I have waited thirty minutes for someone to see my precious darling," continued the mum, quickly turning the boy's head away from the drunken couple with a grimace.

"I do understand that, madam. We will get to him when we can," Will said apologetically. In the ether, Beel zipped past Sarah, giving rise to a fierce outburst.

"Don't call me madam. I'm only thirty-three! Mind you, that's probably old enough to be your mother!"

Grace darted into the room just as the intoxicated couple moved their friskiness to the next level, kissing each other sloppily in front of each smartphone flash.

"Can I help at all?" Grace said. Sarah's laser glare was on the couple, who continued chewing each other's faces, oblivious to the entire room.

"I just want someone to look at my love. He has hurt his little finger. And can someone please tell these two that they are being completely inappropriate!"

*Pssssss.*

Out of nowhere, a golden stream poured all over Sarah's lap. Mr. Patel had wandered over to the waiting room and was relieving himself in earnest. Sarah slowly stared down at her lap in horror as urine pooled in her designer dress. She looked up at the old man, eyes ready to pop from their sockets.

"Weeeee!" Mr. Patel cried.

"Stop!" Sarah cried out, bursting into tears. Grace rushed over and turned Mr. Patel away, holding him at arm's length. Will sniggered uncontrollably, unable to muster any more self-control in his exhausted state. Grace shot Will a look that only a disapproving mother could master, immediately putting a stop to his boyish reaction.

"Will, can you take Mr. Patel to bed seven and stay with him there." Grace directed her attention to the intoxicated pair. "And can you two give it a rest!"

The couple looked up disinterestedly, and Sarah continued to sob as Will moved the wobbly Mr. Patel off.

Grace rolled her eyes, hands on hips.

All in a Saturday night's work, and it was only 12:30 a.m. In any British A & E, things could always get dramatically worse, and they usually did.

Grace set about cleaning Sarah up. Sarah watched as Grace adeptly wiped and pat down her dress. Strangely meditative, the nurse's movements brought a calmness over Sarah that she hadn't felt in a long time. She fixed her focus on Grace and now saw the tiredness weighing down the beautiful, kind nurse tending to her. The deep drain was a natural consequence of Grace's extreme sensitivity to the emotional energy of strangers, which often thrust her into an overwhelmed state. The useful side of Grace's sensitivity was that she immediately knew where someone's pain was located and how to treat it. The problem came when there were too many people in pain and she felt she didn't have the capacity to help. Considering how strained the United Kingdom's national health service was, that seemed like most days.

"Now, how about I take a look at your son? He seems to be a strong little man if you ask me," Grace said. Sarah gazed down at her son with loving eyes.

"He really is. Thank you so very much." Finally, the real Sarah shone through the wall of negativity she had built around her heart. This was Grace's greatest strength: breaking through the barriers of ego and healing people's inner pain with a word and a tender touch.

"You're welcome," she said. Turning to Johnny, Grace spoke to the boy in an exaggerated cartoon voice. "Now, how about we strap up this wonky finger of yours?"

Johnny remained silent but softened a little. Then his mind seemed to change, and he pulled his hand away from Grace as Beel's toxic Dark Light pulled on his temper. Moving closer to the situation, the dark angel lurked for the perfect opportunity to pounce.

"Give the nice lady your hand, Johnny," Sarah asked. Behind the mother and son, Beel breathed her power over Johnny, spiralling the boy into a fit of rage.

He roared. Swiftly raising her hand to slap him out of it, Sarah eyeballed her son in anger. Grace stepped in with her steadying force.

"Stop this madness!"

On the physical plane, the A & E ward seemed to slow in time as all the latent energy in the room was sucked towards Grace. In the etherverse, where Beel stood, a sharp sliver of the Light rippled through Grace from the ground up like a golden lightning bolt snaking in reverse.

A deep-orange glow emanated from Beel's pupils under her hood. The tilt of her head and widening eyes signalled a recognition of Grace's strength. This woman was more than just a little gifted. Mustering the power of the Light took immense focus and will for any human, and Grace wasn't even trying.

*Phenomenal, but unnerving. This could be the dawn of a new power.*

The bright-yellow energy still lingering within her, Grace went about her business to manage the emotion of the room.

"Listen, I am here to help you, so you both have to let me help you. I have a little boy just like you, and his daddy isn't around anymore, so I need him to be a big man for me. Do you think you can try and do that as well?"

Sarah immediately released her aggression, and Johnny nodded sheepishly at Grace, lifting his hand for her. As Grace studied the boy's injury, she felt Beel's oppressive glare on her and snapped her head up, scanning the room on high alert. Grace soon levelled her gaze directly at the celestial's position.

Caught off guard by her exposure to the human realm, Beel held her breath. *Can this woman see?!* An intense warmth came over Grace as she touched the edge of Beel's aura with her acute spiritual awareness. A split second later, Grace felt the air leave her lungs.

"Are you okay?" asked the young boy, recognizing the nurse's discomfort.

Beel whipped down her hood to shield her amber glare once more and vanished briskly in a shard of Dark Light. It was imperative that she retreat to the waiting room, away from Grace's sensitivity, or there could be serious consequences.

With no more dark energy present in the ward, Grace's anxiety subsided. Yet a glimmer in her eyes still seemed to question the space where Beel had once stood.

Shaking off the daze, Grace turned her attention back to Johnny. "I'm just fine. Let's fix you up." Beaming widely, she returned to the present moment and resolved to maintain a positive disposition.

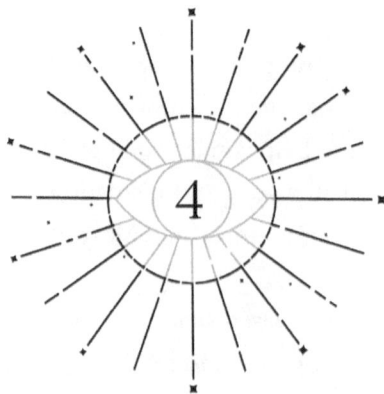

At the back of a dockside warehouse on London's Isle of Dogs, two drug traffickers armed with AK-47s unpacked their fresh cargo. The huge building had fallen into disrepair, evidenced by its cracked upper windows and the swelling numbers of seabirds nesting high in its steel rafters. It was only fit for use as a storage area, plain and simple. The multitude of crates within varied in size and shape, some piling up over seven feet high. Their arrangement created a long and winding path through the cavernous place.

The pair of East End gang members sorting the huge cocaine shipment were making a dog's dinner of a menial task. The gangly one had anxiously pulled open the delivery crate with a crowbar, smacking himself square on the shin. As he groaned and hopped in circles, his musclebound compatriot swigged large mouthfuls of vodka, enjoying the show.

Observing from a distance, his face obscured in a technical stealth mask, Jack Causer crouched patiently behind a crate. The tall, fit prowler screwed a silencer onto his tranquilliser rifle and, raising his weapon onto the crate, found his line of sight. And waited. Having been undercover with the gang he now stalked for months, Jack relished the knowledge that the completion of his efforts was fast approaching. The degenerates up ahead belonged to the lower ranks of the Wraiths, a ruthless, violent bunch who preyed on women and children to leverage money and power. The most despicable of all London's gangs, they championed chaos and bullied the weak.

Jack hated nothing more than a bully.

To amuse himself and pass the time, Jack whispered a narration of the gangsters' movements in his best nature-documentary voice.

"In the vast and rich animal kingdom of this planet, there is one species that fascinates us most, because we are one of them."

The gangly gangster poked a hole in the top brick of drugs and snorted it aggressively. Grunting like a gorilla, he bared his teeth. His musclebound companion leapt into action, clattering him around the head like a schoolboy and yanking the drugs off him.

"And that is, of course, the primate," Jack continued as he slunk towards the gangsters in his covert ops gear. "This charming duo populate the lowest ranks of the vicious and temperamental baboon species."

Jack deftly slipped forwards to a better vantage point just ten metres from the two meatheads, well hidden.

"Unbeknownst to the squabbling pair, a lone gibbon from a neighbouring tribe moves in."

The muscular thug turned to the crate he'd been sitting on and reached for the final slice of pizza from a nearby box. He brought it to his mouth with a salivatory grin.

*Thwack!* His counterpart batted it away in spite, slapping the juicy slice to the floor.

"At this time of year, food is scarce," Jack continued. Both drug traffickers leapt for the pizza slice and wrestled each other in a ball of flailing limbs.

"The hapless creatures jostle for power with wild aggression."

The gangly thug gained the advantage and thumped his compatriot's head into the concrete floor with a loud crack. Picking up the pizza, he smugly observed the muscular thug lying in a heap and holding his aching head. Jack levelled his weapon and carefully took aim.

"In position for the ambush, the wily gibbon strikes."

The gangly half-wit lifted the pizza to his mouth, admiring its beauty and anticipating a large, satisfying bite.

*Shup!*

The tranq dart lodged in the gangster's neck. With eyes rolling back into his head and his legs folding, he dropped on the spot.

*Shup!*

A second dart protruded from the muscular thug's arm. The reprobate had blocked Jack's clear headshot in the midst of rubbing his bruised head. Jack grimaced. The split-second mishap would make everything that followed a lot more complicated.

At the hitch in Jack's plan, the remaining thug went on the attack. He sprang up full of adrenaline and sprayed bullets in his concealed enemy's direction.

"The element of surprise lost, the advancing gibbon must act fast," Jack sighed.

Picking up a stray piece of wood, Jack lobbed the debris to his left and dove from cover to his right. He landed on his side several feet from his distracted target.

"Confused and enraged, the baboon is an easy target."

*Shup! Shup!*

Landing two expert shots in the thug's femoral artery, Jack waited as the drugs in his darts were transported from the main leg vein directly to the brain. The thug fell face-first, stiff as a falling tree.

"Through adversity, our heroic gibbon is victorious and moves in to survey the scene."

Removing the darts from both bodies, Jack casually pulled off his mask to reveal a charming grin. His square jaw and striking features were perfectly balanced by his razor-sharp wit and cheeky demeanour.

Hearing rushing footsteps from the next room, the cavalier joker knew that he was about to be boxed into a tight spot.

"Unfortunately for our courageous friend, the alpha male appears to be in close proximity."

Jack's breathing quickened as he stared at the door, his brain scrambling. A bold smirk signalled a solution to his conundrum. Bolting towards the nearest discarded AK-47, he scooped it up and spun on his heels effortlessly.

"The nearby alpha baboon rushes headlong to his fallen tribe's aid."

*Jugjugjug!* Jack sprayed a few rounds into the air and then rolled back next to the unconscious gang members. Finding the perfect position behind the drug shipment crates, Jack concealed his tranq gun in one slick movement and went down on one knee.

*Juggajuggajugga!* Jack fired continuously in the direction he'd originally entered the warehouse to set up the illusion and prepare a trap for his would-be attacker. The nearby door slammed open with a clang, and the head thug bounced in, armed and snarling.

"What the hell took you so long!?" Jack shouted as he fired a hail of bullets at nothing.

"Stones?! How did you— What? What the frig is going on?"

"Don't just stand there, you big dope! Gimme a hand!"

In a panic, the head thug dropped next to Jack, in cover, and began firing in the same direction.

"Is it police?" the thug yelled. The thug's attention now locked on the phantom threat in front of him, Jack switched his voice back to documentary mode and turned to the thug brazenly.

"And the penny drops with the primate."

"Huh?" the confused criminal said, turning to face Jack. He stared down at the tranq gun coolly aimed at his throat and then back up at Jack's face.

*Shup! Shup!* Two darts, right in the jugular. Lifting a finger, his open mouth ready to speak, the thug collapsed backwards and passed out cold. Jack rounded up his commentary.

"Against all odds, the wily gibbon has infiltrated the group and subdued their fearless leader." Jack grabbed the pizza slice and dusted it off. Inspecting it, he shrugged. "To the victor go the spoils."

Jack took a huge, fulfilling bite. Realising that the food was stone cold and furry, he spat it out in a hurry. *You can't win 'em all, I guess.*

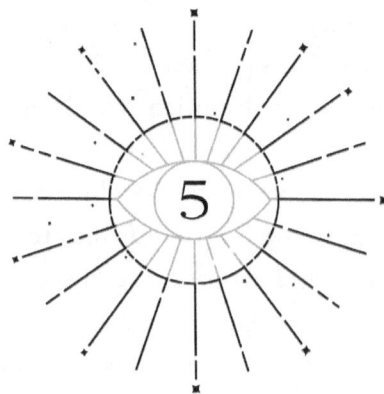

The mayhem at Mile End's A & E eventually settled into a dazed calm. Most patients awaiting treatment had been placated by strong drugs or the long night of wakefulness. Grace monitored the sleeping Mr. Patel's vital signs as she checked for other discrepancies in his chart. She stroked the frail man's head, giving thanks that his overall condition was markedly more stable. Will's mistake with the morphine dosage could have cost the man his life.

Nevertheless, Will was learning, and some of the smallest errors in the job often created life-or-death situations. It was one of the hardest things the medical staff in any emergency ward had to accept and a fact that pained Grace every day.

Moving to the next cubicle, Grace found Will nervously talking himself into lancing a throbbing abscess on a sleeping woman's foot. He was a deer in headlights.

"I, eh, I was just about to . . . oh dear. It's monstrous," he said.

Grace sighed and shook her head.

"How long have you been staring at it?"

"I don't know. It's like it's looking right back at me—taunting me or something!"

"Lancing your first abscess is kind of like birth, death, or marriage, Will. You're never really ready for it," Grace said cheekily.

"Funny."

"Go on. You've got this."

"Okay. Here goes." Will shook off the doubt and went in for the kill. Readying his scalpel, he gingerly popped the surface of the abscess, his mouth slightly open in deep concentration.

In a mighty spurt, the abscess exploded into his face, some of the spray escaping past his lips. Grace covered her mouth to contain her reaction. Will, however, was unable to conceal his terror in response to his worst nightmare becoming a reality.

"Gah," he moaned, rushing past the cubicle curtain with his hands flapping at the wrist. Grace sniggered, covering her mouth again and raising her eyebrows. The female patient Will had attempted to treat awoke, oblivious to the kerfuffle. Grace shifted back to a more professional comportment and moved to finish treating the woman's abscess.

"What just happened?" the drowsy woman said.

"You must have nodded off. It's okay; it's all taken care of."

In the next cubicle, Will desperately washed fresh puss out of his mouth over a sink.

"Oh, I see. He was taking his time," the woman whispered in an attempt to spare Will's feelings.

"Yes. He was," Grace said.

Bent double over the basin, Will gagged. He reached for a nearby bottle and emptied it into his mouth without looking at the label. The young doctor's calamity soon escalated as the harsh chemicals of disinfectant burned past his tonsils.

"Good God Almighty!" he yelled, his exclamation filling the ward.

"Oh dear, the poor boy," the patient said, looking over her shoulder.

"He's learning, that's for sure. Sometimes suffering is the best teacher," Grace said with a knowing look. The patient nodded in agreement.

Falling into a contemplative mood, the woman found herself studying Grace, struck by the young nurse's wisdom. At that very moment in the spiritual realm, a radiant oval burst open behind the patient, and a hooded angel stepped forwards to place a reassuring hand on her shoulder. It sent a pulse of emerald life force through the woman's body.

"There's something very different about you," the patient said to Grace.

"Oh really?" Grace questioned, suddenly flushed.

"There's this intense glow about you—a unique yet familiar warmth."

Grace struggled to take the compliment. "Oh. It must be from all this rushing about!"

"No, that's not what I meant. You have so much light within you," the patient remarked.

These words landed on Grace like a one-ton weight as an emerald illumination leapt from the patient and connected with the nurse's spirit. Grace's eyes welled up.

"You really think so?" she said.

The woman nodded at Grace lovingly, and the imposing angel's eyes glowed gold beneath her crisp hood. The dazzling green trim of her cream cloak denoted her as none other than a restoration class angel. These resilient and ever-present celestial beings harnessed the Light to bring and sustain life of all kinds. Akin to the guardian class, restoration angels lived in a symbiotic relationship with humanity, stepping in to correct the balance when too much death had tipped the scales. Also known as healing angels, they were the most benevolent and peace loving of all celestials.

In the shadows of the waiting room, Beel swivelled her head towards this new energy fluctuation in the etherverse; she had no doubt it was an angelic presence. Back in the ward cubicle, the patient looked Grace square in the pupils.

"You should trust in your own power more."

*Zummmm!* Entering the space in a gleaming red arc, Beel lunged at the healing angel. The angel of the Light lifted her hand. Before Beel could land her slicing blow, the mysterious angel had vanished, leaving a trail of emerald sparks.

"Coward," Beel muttered.

Feeling something of this spiritual clash, Grace blinked and rubbed her eyes. *Am I losing my mind?*

She tucked the patient in and left her. They both needed sleep. Yawning and wobbly, the nurse made her way through the back corridor of the A & E to the supply room, where she could find a bed and perhaps get some shut-eye. Even twenty minutes would be a great refresher for her brain.

Walking into the white, fully tiled room, Grace found fresh linens and threw them on the bed behind the door. She flicked off the light and settled her head on the plastic hospital pillow.

*Peace. Just a few moments of peace.*

Beel phased into the room without warning, anxious to test the boundaries of this woman who had reacted so acutely to her Dark Light not once but twice. That was a rarity. Grace absorbed the dark angel's cold presence immediately and snapped into a sitting position. The change in atmosphere pulled Grace's gaze to a medical cabinet door on the opposite side of the room that was slightly ajar. Beel stood next to it, locked seductively onto Grace.

Fighting the urge to move towards the shelves of medication, Grace closed her eyes and centred herself. Beel stood her ground and called on her power. In the ether, a crimson mist of lust and longing roiled from beneath Beel's feet and encircled Grace. The mist stacked up to the ceiling like a wall behind the nurse and began driving her towards the cabinet. Gasping, Grace jumped up and collided with the counter on the other side of the room. The wall of Dark Light closed in tighter, its fearsome energy suffocating her resistance.

"You deserve it," Beel whispered. Grace's eyes were drawn to a pill bottle of Oxycontin in the cabinet. Closing her eyes to search for strength, she simply could not find the willpower to resist. Grace turned and took a step towards the medicines.

Darting into the room, Will closed the glass medicine box he had mistakenly left open earlier in the shift.

"Whoops! Silly me! Sorry about that, Grace."

"What?" Grace said.

Seeing that Grace was dazed, Will rambled on to keep her off the subject of the open cabinet and usher her away from the scene of his crime.

"I've got this. I think it's about time you got home to your family. You sure have earned the rest."

Will's entrance stunted Beel's advance, and the swirling red mist released its hold on Grace.

"Yeah, I think I have. Thanks, Will."

"Anytime. You're always covering for me. Especially when I've got other people's bodily fluids sloshing around in my mouth."

"True."

"God, why did I even bring that up?" Will looked a bit green around the gills. "Anyway, you get yourself outta here. Doctor's orders! Ha."

Grace gave Will a wry smile as he left the room. Looking back to the meds cabinet, she gritted her teeth. Beel's mist of temptation resumed its advance, attempting to latch on to the gifted nurse and squeeze the remaining hope out of her. However, the red cloud flinched and evaporated with a hiss when it came up against an unseen barrier. Stunned, Beel recoiled, her confidence shaken.

She now recognised Grace's power as one she would rather not confront alone. From what the dark angel had observed, it was increasingly likely that this woman could be a seer.

A scarce subset of humans that had not fully walked in their power for thousands of years, seers were spiritually heightened beings that communed with the guardian angel class. It was possible for any human to sense and connect with celestial beings if they focused their minds; this was their heritage and greatest ability. However, actually visualising and being able to affect things within the etherverse was a skill reserved for seers, especially when working in balance with guardians.

So great was their rapport with the spiritual realm that they could physically see any angelic presence and even control an angel's movement if channelling the Light effectively. Seers mobilised the true potential of humankind, unlocking the ability to wield the power of the Light in all manner of ways. This was a truly awesome sight to behold and something that Beel had not witnessed since the era of the Holy Roman Empire.

Needing to gather herself away from Grace's powerful affinity with the Light, the dark angel warped out in a flash. Her mission now was to reconvene with her celestial kin and find an approach to this new threat.

Grace wearily dragged herself from the supply room to the foyer and headed for the A & E's main exit, bidding a fond farewell to the receptionist on shift.

"Night, Georgie."

"Night, love," the receptionist replied.

Grace stumbled into Johnny. "Oh my gosh, I'm so sorry!"

The young boy twirled to the side and grabbed her by the hand.

"What's your son's name? Do you think we could be friends?" the boy asked eagerly.

"His name's Andy, and I'm sure he'd like that."

"I don't have many friends. My mum doesn't let me."

"Well, I know your mummy loves you very much. You know why?"

"No. Why?"

"Because Andy is my whole world, and your mum looks at you the same way I look at him. Maybe you just need to tell her that you'd like to make some new friends. Can you try that for me?"

"Yeah, I can. Thanks." Johnny grinned as he dashed off to his mum with a sense of purpose. Grace watched from a distance as Johnny asked Sarah the question. Hearing his plea, Sarah pulled him in for a big hug with tears brimming.

"Thank you," the grateful mum mouthed to Grace over the boy's shoulder.

The beautiful nurse nodded back and exited the building with a refreshed perspective. This was what motivated her in her work every day: being able to bring a little healing to real families in a tangible way.

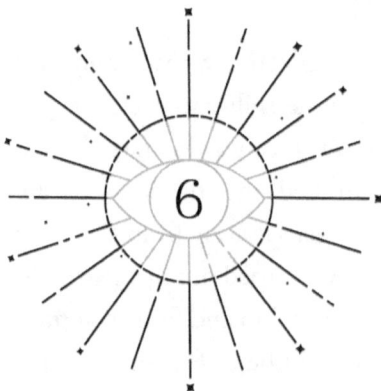

# 6

In London's Soho, a tall, well-built soldier marched purposefully towards his target. A dark hoodie with a baseball cap underneath concealed his appearance from lingering eyes. It was 4 a.m., and the city was grinding out its first waking noises as a small remainder of drunken revellers navigated home. The smell of stale beer and crawling rubbish trucks wafted about the cobbled lanes. Carrying a duffle bag down one of the area's main arterial routes, the soldier checked his surroundings for a tail.

He veered onto a brightly lit side street and found himself slap-bang in the middle of London's red-light district. The usual suspects hoping to fill a need ogled sex workers on the doors of massage parlours.

Taking this route was high risk; it could alert those who might follow him to his position. It was, however, a necessary risk as it was the only way to access his rendezvous point. *This idiot wants to get caught, choosing this meeting site*, the soldier thought. The drop-off location was every covert outlaw's nightmare and a disaster of distractions. Not only this, but the sights he witnessed en route disgusted him at the very pit of his being.

Walking past a lone door girl dressed only in latex underwear, the soldier was interrupted in his movement.

"Well, hello, big boy. Fancy a little of this?" The door girl reached out and slithered a hand over the soldier's bulky arm. Swiftly batting the hand away, the imposing serviceman eyeballed her. His tone was empty of emotion.

"Do. Not. Touch me."

"Fine, dickhead."

Briskly moving on, the soldier crossed the neon street into the murky alleyway he had been searching for. He checked his surroundings for anomalies, a flicker of gold passing across his irises. A black Range Rover nestled in the shadows opposite him blinked its headlights once, and the military man continued towards it. Then he stopped dead in his tracks.

Something was not right.

Taking a moment to again scan his surroundings, he brushed off what he thought he felt and resumed his approach. A burly, rough-edged individual with a shaved head and facial piercings stepped out of the Range Rover. This was Dio, the top general in the Wraith gang's hierarchy. He sported a long leather jacket and wore enough chains around his neck to anchor a small ship. Dio wasn't in the mood for this assignment, having missed out on the Wraiths' yearly shindig, but pulling off this gig was vitally important to the boss and could earn him major kudos.

He stood by the car warily, having never met the hefty brute pacing steadily towards him. He sensed that this professional operator could handle himself in any situation. The way the fellow seemed to glide through the alleyway suggested someone with training and raw power.

The soldier stopped at a safe distance.

"What you after, mate?" Dio said.

The soldier lobbed his duffel at the gangster's feet, where it landed with a weighty clang.

"A gift."

Dio looked the soldier up and down suspiciously. He didn't like surprises, and everything about this scenario was abnormal. When he unzipped the bag, Dio's shocked face reflected the brilliant gleam of bullion. The unexpected contents were worth at least five million. How this man had swung it over like it contained nothing more than his gym gear was also a mystery. Dio's confusion quickly turned to anger. *This is way too good to be true.*

"What the feck? Where did this come from?" Dio barked. The soldier remained motionless and silent. "Someone cut out your tongue, freak?"

"Take it. Then we shall discuss what you might offer."

"Na na na, I don't think so, mate." A realisation dawned on the gangster. "Crap. You're police, aren't you?" The soldier sighed as Dio yanked a handgun from his belt and trained it on the soldier. "You made a big mistake comin' here, GI-mutant-Joe."

In a blur of gold, the gangster was lifted from the ground, propelled by an unseen force. His weapon drifted from his hand and bobbed by his side in midair. Suspended two feet off the ground, Dio gawked down in bewilderment. The soldier studied Dio curiously and, with an opening of his palm, manifested a band of blue Light around Dio's neck. The floating handgun was likewise smothered in wisps of blue, then gradually dissolved, leaving only a sprinkling of illuminated spots behind. The soldier's eyes glowed a brilliant yellow.

This was no human but rather a soldier of the upper ether, a warrior angel trespassing in the physical realm. By taking human form and using his mastery of the Light on earth, the angel was in clear breach of the laws of the etherverse. The abuse of power would carry a heavy cost if he were discovered.

Alerted to another presence, the soldier vanished in a shock of blue. Dio crashed flat on his back on the bumpy cobblestones and sputtered, grabbing at his neck. After a pause to regain his bearings, he rolled over and heaved at the duffle's handles. It didn't budge. The bag's contents must have weighed over a hundred kilos. He dragged the bag towards the Range Rover, huffing and puffing, making a real meal out of his escape.

Having warped to the now vacant main street, the soldier braced for his next move under the neon lights. The door girl blinked and squinted at the inexplicable discharge of Light. Snapping his head around his neck like a flustered bird, the soldier sought to catch a glimpse of his pursuer. No luck. The soldier then attempted to phase through the physical plane and escape as far away as possible.

He was glued to the spot. Looking down at his feet in trepidation, the soldier realised the situation was as he had feared: his feet were clamped to the ground by a swirling mass of the Light.

"No, no, no, this cannot be!" he muttered, tugging at his limbs. Only a few metres away, the door girl remained aghast at the phenomenon unfolding before her.

A ball of pure white luminescence began to grow before the soldier. Larger and larger it expanded, soon bursting and revealing a stone-faced Gabriel. His eyes burned white hot.

"You should not be here," the archangel snapped.

"Please, I know we must not tamper with the physical, but I—"

With a twist of Gabriel's open palm, two flaming beams shot up from within the sphere of the Light at the soldier's feet. The beams locked onto the soldier's wrists and began to pulse energy back and forth.

"I was only doing as commanded!" the soldier pleaded.

Another twist at the wrist initiated a drain on the soldier's life force. His eyes shifted through the spectrum from bright gold to orange and then to red as his Light body steadily darkened. "No, please!"

"I am sorry, my friend, but you know this is the way it must be. It has been decreed."

With Gabriel's last words, the Light drain was complete, the soldier's irises now a blood red. Lost in hopelessness, the angel was yanked down into the rippling pool of radiance.

The door girl watched, paralysed in awe. Her mind could not form the words to speak. Suffused with an aura of peace, Gabriel drifted towards her and took her by the hand, and the door girl felt her world fall away as she surrendered to the archangel's gaze. She found herself weeping uncontrollably at the magnificent sight of this being towering above her. In an instant, a golden burst surged through the girl's spirit, imparting a sense of utter calm.

Stepping off the physical plane through a flaming ethergate, Gabriel left the woman stunned and alone on the empty street. Her frozen features reflected the lane's fluorescent glow, her mind now oblivious to the experience she had just had, though her soul felt at ease.

Meanwhile, back at the rendezvous point, Dio was still struggling with the duffle of bullion. Having almost heaved it into the back of his car, he stopped and panted.

"Screw this," he muttered, changing tactics. Opening the back door of the vehicle, he swivelled his stance and threw the gold bars in one by one. "Not just a pretty face," Dio said smugly.

Without warning, a gleaming force bolted past the Range Rover, transforming every ounce of gold into pure white energy as it went. Gabriel was leaving no evidence of the angelic infringement. In astonishment, Dio watched as the dissolving gold was absorbed within this formless version of the archangel. A faint siren wailed in the background. Taking this as his cue to disappear, Dio jumped back into his vehicle and sped off with a screech of rubber on road. He clamped his jaw tight and slammed his fist into the dashboard. He was going to experience a painful retribution for this almighty screwup.

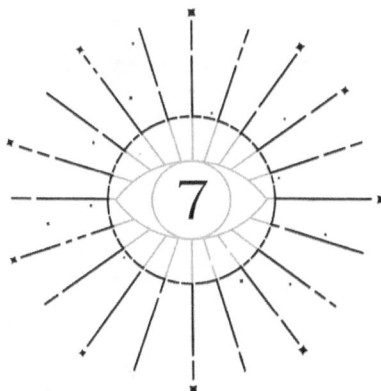

# 7

Lolloping towards her usual bus stop, Grace lined up with a gaggle of sleepy commuters. London's morning rush hour was in full swing. Chugging traffic jostled with indignant cyclists swerving to avoid near-death situations at every turn. Grace's phone pinged in her pocket. Taking it out with a flutter of excitement, she was greeted with a vibrant image of herself and her son together at the fair. The text attached read WHEN CAN WE GO AGAIN MUM? A warm feeling of love and wholeness spread through Grace. Andy was everything to her, her heart and soul.

A colourfully clad Nigerian preacher woman bellowed from the end of the bus queue, breaking Grace's tender reverie.

"Jesus, that is his name. God-given to us to save us from our sins."

Unnerved by the preacher's presence, Grace begged the ground to swallow her whole. She had always struggled to connect with religious sorts. Seeing herself as a spiritual, open-minded sort of person, she tended to grate on those in organised religion. If she had to put a name to her belief system, it would probably be closest to neopaganism, a term that most conservative types scoffed at; they either didn't understand it or thought the word "pagan" referred to devil worship.

This gross misinterpretation largely came down to negative rhetoric in the Christian Old Testament. Paganism was in fact the ancient practice of worshipping the sanctity of creation in its entirety—rivers, forests, animals, insects, fish, birds, humans, and even the earth itself—

as an interconnected ecosystem. Paganism's core belief was respect for harmony and peace among all living things. The preacher woman currently banging on about sin and retribution was frankly offering anything but that.

"Sent by Holy God to die for our sins, Jesus came with a great purpose," the Nigerian Christian went on.

Her blunt energy made the hairs on the back of Grace's neck stand on end. She disliked how hard-line religious folks often pretended to know everything about God and the afterlife. How could they? No one had come back from the afterlife to tell the story—except, conveniently, Jesus, a fact that Christ's so-called followers felt entitled them to a toxic "all-knowingness" or omniscience. As if their small human brains could possess such unfathomable knowledge. It was pure lunacy to believe that they could be as omniscient as the very god they worshipped.

Of course, not all followers of Christ let their pride get in the way of connecting with others of differing beliefs. Many were kind, humble, and respectful people. In the current instance, however, it was clear to Grace that this preacher woman had disappeared much too far down the Jesus rabbit hole.

A well-dressed commuter glanced over at the preacher and rolled his eyes. The other travellers merely attempted to ignore the scene she was making, but the situation grew awkward very quickly. Still, the atmosphere didn't seem to faze the bus queue. Londoners were, after all, expert tacticians in avoiding public transport crackpots.

"He came to heal, to teach, to love. Many did not listen then, and still mankind is blinded by greed," the preacher blared.

In a jagged blast of crimson, Abaddon materialised in the ether next to the preacher, grinning mischievously under his tattered hood. The Lord of the Pit and housekeeper of the lower realms relished a good Christian zealot. They were far too easy and too prevalent in the current age to pass over.

A shiver of cold took hold of Grace. Her instinct signalled danger. Abaddon leered in wait, ready for a little sport.

"We must learn that love is patient, love is kind. It does not envy, it does not boast," the preacher said. Cheek to cheek with the preacher, Abaddon landed a goading whisper.

"Judge."

Another shiver shot through Grace's core. Shifting her view towards Abaddon, she made out an indistinct grey figure shimmering in the morning air. She tried to shake off the impression. Rubbing her temples, Grace turned away.

*This isn't the time or place for a nervous breakdown, Grace.*

At Abaddon's word, the preacher's delivery morphed.

"We are in the end of days, people. If we do not throw off all lust, all violence, all greed, we will know the Lord's judgment!" the preacher shouted, her tone markedly more cutting.

Commuters reacted to the preacher's erratic turn with raised eyebrows. Abaddon slipped in another whisper.

"Hate."

Triggered again, Grace whirled around, her spiritual radar flaring up. The form standing next to the preacher had become more distinct as a tall, cloaked being. The Nigerian evangelist launched into another vicious attack.

"And when his judgment comes, those who have not repented shall rot in the squirming pits of hell!"

Grace snapped. Before she could stop herself, a dragon-like voice that was not her own tumbled from inside her. "Leave her be!" the voice boomed.

Stunned, the preacher jerked her head back and blinked as if snapped out of a trance.

"What? Leave who be?" she said to Grace.

"Not you. Him!" the voice within Grace demanded. Aiming a finger directly at Abaddon, Grace stared down the revealed dark angel. Abaddon winced at Grace like an animal caught in a trap and phased out in a flurry.

The bus pulled up with a screech and a hiss. The interruption knocked Grace back to reality, leaving her short of breath, her hands shaking. Commuters eyed Grace warily. As the line parted a path to the front of the queue, Grace shuffled onto the bus, head down. The city workers kept their distance. The fear that she had begun the inevitable descent into madness dragged on Grace with every step. It felt inevitable because she had known madness before—specifically, the madness of addiction.

Over half a lifetime, Grace had inched her way out of the pits of drug abuse. For this she was thankful every day, but the thought of going back still hadn't lost its appeal. Addiction's appeal lay in its ability to bury the mountain of overwhelming feelings Grace experienced every day. It had made life easier to cope with—that was, until the casual numbing became almost as necessary as breathing. The drugs suppressed all anxiety and worry, cocooning her brain in a warm blanket of chemical nonfeeling. If left unchecked for too long, any addiction could rewire the brain's synapses, making recovery an almost impossible journey. Grace, however, had battled her way back to sobriety through groups, therapy, and several near relapses stunted only by sheer luck.

It had been the hardest thing she had ever done.

Sitting now on the bus's upper deck, looking out over the buzzing city, Grace knew that if not for her precious son, she simply wouldn't have made it.

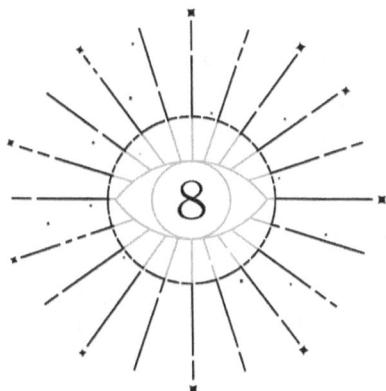

Jack crept through a vast plane of narrow, silver birch trees. Disorientated by the uniform surroundings, he navigated cautiously. He was uncertain how he had ended up here; the last few days were a blur due to the sleep deprivation that came with surveillance and reconnaissance, the tradecraft of his younger days in the Special Air Services unit, or SAS for short.

Jack had spent almost ten years of his prime bouncing from continent to continent in covert operations. He and his team were tasked with infiltrating government structures and military outposts in order to suppress war efforts. It was a thankless job, but it gave Jack the great satisfaction of knowing he had been part of moulding the bigger picture for good, ultimately bringing about peace through an efficient, shadowy strike.

Jack's time in the SAS came to an abrupt end with an aborted desert recon mission. He had failed his country and his squad. The guilt ate him from the inside and still sucked the hope from his bones. Unable to face rebuilding a team and going back to life as a ghost, he moved into law enforcement on home soil. It felt like a clear fresh start, allowing him to distance himself from his past. Undercover policing was certainly a place where his unique set of skills carried over and gave him a definite advantage.

Hearing a faint voice behind him, Jack spun around and crept towards the sound. Against his better judgment, he called out. He had to find this person fast.

"Is someone there?"

The voice returned, this time louder but still muffled and indistinct.

"Nanhnei ahey hey."

The voice clearly belonged to a female. Listening intently, Jack was unable to make out the words. He broke into a jog towards the woman's location.

"I can't hear you!" he said.

The unintelligible words returned, this time echoing from the opposite direction. "Ahey hey nanhnei."

Whirling to face the stranger's new location, Jack engaged his trusted sense of logic to solve the puzzle laid out before him. *A female. Crying out in obvious distress. The voice moved. At speed. Faster than a normal person could move. She is in a vehicle. Most likely captive. Also, the voice was young. A girl, maybe very young. Child traffickers.*

*Bastards.*

Breathing heavily, Jack ratcheted up his pace. A glimpse of a white dress and a flutter of short, dark hair ducked behind a tree in the middle distance. Flooded with terror, Jack recognised the girl he was now chasing.

"I'm coming for you!" Jack shouted.

Another rustle from the opposite direction caused Jack to swivel again. He saw the young girl running, disappearing out of sight. "Please wait. I'm here to help you!"

Running with all his might, Jack raced towards the girl. No matter how hard he tried, he couldn't seem to catch her.

*No girl under the age of twelve is this fast. Nothing makes sense.*

Pumping his arms and almost out of breath, Jack looked down to see that he was sinking.

"No. I . . . I can't find you. Please wait!" Jack only sank faster the harder he wrestled. Clawing at the ground, Jack was nearly up to his chest in the mud. The young girl unexpectedly appeared in front of him—more like an apparition than a living person, with translucent skin and floating, lifeless limbs.

"You lost me, Daddy. Why did you lose me?" the girl said, staring at Jack vacantly and sinking along with him. Jack scrambled to reach out and touch his daughter, desperate to save her.

"It wasn't my fault. You must know that! There was nothing I could do!"

Powerless, he could only watch as his little girl was enveloped by the thick mud.

Jack catapulted from his nightmare, jolting upright from his mattress in a cold sweat. After a few deep breaths, he lowered himself slowly and attempted to regulate his heartbeat. The nightmare was the same one he had endured for years. Reaching for the glass of water on his bedside table, he took a long, slow gulp to calm his nerves. He finished it off and picked up the photo frame next to the empty glass, adrift in longing. After several minutes alone with his thoughts, he discarded the frame on the floor like it was a piece of rubbish. Rolling back flat on the bed, he stared at the ceiling with one word bouncing around his head: *Why?*

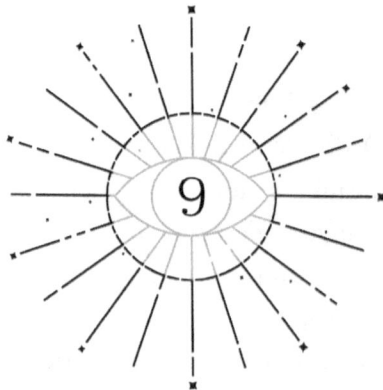

# 9

London's Wandsworth prison was a megalith of stone built in 1851. Its unique design consisted of one protruding central tower and four monstrous wings. The ingenious architecture allowed guards to look down over the four wings without inmates seeing them, an element that came in handy during a power outage or technical failure of the camera system. One of the UK's largest prisons, it had the capacity to hold over 1,800 inmates, a frightening prospect unknown to most of Wandsworth's civilian residents.

Eddie ignored the thought of the daily grind ahead as he hurtled towards the building in his beat-up 1997 Volkswagen Golf. He wasn't late; he just liked to drive fast. He also liked to play his music loud, even though his taste in music would be best described as dubious. Eddie was nothing but a bumbling clown to his mates at the pub, but at work he stood out among his colleagues as a selfless, stand-up guy. His man-child sensitivity had made him vulnerable to abuse from a few inmates as of late, but he kept going and put a brave face on things. He was, after all, an eternal optimist and believed that he really could make a difference in an increasingly violent world. After all, everyone deserved a second chance, and redemption wasn't a hopeless crusade. This was a motto Eddie lived by. Whether it had grown to be part of his belief system through nature or nurture, his strong sense of empathy, even for the most despised criminals, was a special quality.

Screeching the car around the corner into the staff parking lot, Eddie sang along to Britney Spears's ". . . Baby One More Time" behind the wheel. "Show me how you want it to be. Tell me, baby . . ."

Pulling up to the prison's side entrance, he found a parking spot and continued warbling like a teenage girl, shuffling his shoulders to the beat as he jammed on the handbrake.

He threw his arms out to his imaginary fans in preparation for the high note—"Still believe!"—and promptly knocked over the full takeaway cup next to him. His crotch was flooded with scalding-hot coffee.

"Feck. Ow, ow, ow! Feck me!"

The illusion now broken with his lap on fire, Eddie leapt out of the car and grabbed the nearest rag to pat down his soaked trousers.

*What a truly magical start to the day, dipstick.*

Hobbling to the back of the car while drying himself off, Eddie opened the boot in search of his tie. The contents of the Volkswagen's rear storage area made it look like he was living out of his car. Takeaway boxes, clothes, bottled water, and even a dirty old toolbox filled the space. Finding his tie under the collection of rubbish, he threw it on haphazardly and made his way into the foreboding building.

In the prison's central office, Jade was chatting away on the phone to an old university friend at maximum volume, adorned with glamourous hoop earrings and a shovelful of makeup. Contrary to her appearance, Jade was one of the lads deep down. Not one for formality, she judged her life by how much fun she could squeeze out of every minute, whatever came her way.

"God, it's been so long since I had a holiday, babes!" Jade exclaimed excitedly as a disgruntled Eddie entered the secure control room.

Throwing his keys down on the desk, he collapsed in the office chair next to his exuberant colleague.

"I can't wait to get away from these morons and get my slut drop on in Mykonos!" Jade quipped, swinging her free arm above her head in a techno dance move.

"God help whoever has to endure that up close," Eddie snarled.

"Shut up, twat," Jade snapped back at Eddie and returned to her call. "Demi! Oh my God, have you heard Johnny is going? He's sooo good looking, but O-M-G, he has such a horrid-looking . . . you know. He's just sent me a pic of it. I mean, I just don't get why guys think we're gonna be interested in seeing that." Jade turned the phone sideways and angled her head. "It looks like something hanging out the side of a shark's mouth."

"I've heard Johnny has a horrid amount of herpes as well. I wouldn't go near him unless you want your downstairs turning out like cauliflower cheese," Eddie said. The vile image now in Jade's head, she shot Eddie a scathing look.

"I'm off, babes. Eddie is being a top-class wank, and we need to get the morning checks over and done with. See you at the airport, woot woot!" Pumping her fist in the air, Jade finished the call.

"Can we get on with the rounds now that you've planned your holiday? You take cells one through six. I'll take seven through twelve."

"And good morning to you too!"

"Sorry. Morning," Eddie conceded. Jade nodded at Eddie's coffee crotch.

"You don't have to live with incontinence, you know. There are several daytime infomercials that can help you deal with the issue," Jade jested, dripping with sarcasm.

"It's. Coffee."

Jade ignored Eddie's comeback as she left the room and sauntered down towards the cells. Arriving at each one, she knocked her baton on the unforgiving steel doors. This section of the east wing housed the most dangerous and depraved offenders London had to offer. Eddie and Jade were well familiar with the nasty bunch, and the precision of their procedures kept most unwanted behaviour at bay.

"Rise and shine!" Jade called out.

"Morning, sweet cheeks," Prisoner 5 growled, his upper lip curling back to reveal a depleted set of wonky and stained British teeth.

"That's enough out of you."

On the opposite side of the wing, Eddie moved through his cell checks and wake-up routine.

"Wakey wakey, boys and girls! Breakfast in ten."

Prisoner 11 clocked the wet patch in Eddie's trousers.

"Poor little boy piss his pants? Ahahahaha!" Prisoner 11 laughed maniacally.

"Laugh it up, Eleven. No breakfast for you."

"Oh, come on!" Prisoner 11 moaned.

General grumbles of discontent echoed about the wing as each inmate struggled to their door. Cell 7 showed no sounds of movement. Eddie rolled his eyes. Ambling up to the cell, he appealed to the inmate once more.

"Come on, Seven, stop faffing around, and let's go."

Eddie slid open the hatch to see Prisoner 7 convulsing violently on the ground. Rushing to unlock the door, Eddie fumbled through his keys and shouted for assistance.

"I need some help here. Seven is having another fit!"

He eventually got the right key in the door and jumped on the writhing prisoner, attempting to hold him down. The inmate flipped and tossed with his eyes closed. His moans were wild and filled with pain.

Suddenly the moans turned darker, exhibiting a three-toned, otherworldly quality. The prisoner's eyes snapped open, and his hands were at Eddie's throat, grabbing him in a vicelike grip.

"Stop!" Eddie yelled. Twisting his head to try to break the prisoner's suffocating hold, he discovered his efforts were futile against the inmate's almost superhuman strength. Black cracks had formed around the man's eyes, growing outwards like worms as he jumped up and pinned Eddie to the back wall. He spat an angry warning in Eddie's face.

"Soon he will come to set us free."

As soon as the words had landed, the prisoner collapsed to the floor, motionless. Eddie fell sideways onto the concrete next to the inmate, trying to regain his breath. Two guards barrelled into the cell with Jade in tow.

"Jesus Christ! Are you alright?" Jade said.

"His voice. It . . . it burned," Eddie muttered, squinting and holding his head tightly.

"Come on, let's get you looked at, babes."

The two guards crouched to help Eddie up and out. Staring back at the unconscious prisoner, Eddie shivered. A crushing weight in his chest carried the pervading anxiety of a merciless evil on the horizon.

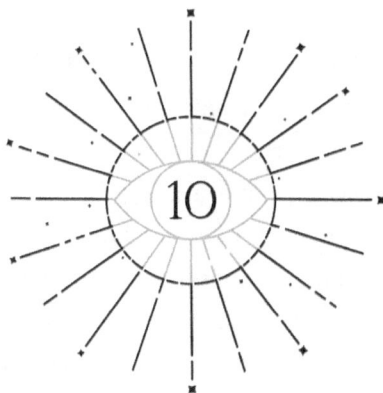

On the spiritual plane, the Damned sat overlooking the ornate York Gardens Cascade in London's borough of Twickenham. Having no need to sit or rest as such, the dark angel nevertheless enjoyed mimicking the position. It gave him a more human perspective on earthly existence—something the Damned found himself searching out a lot more as of late. He had begun to appreciate the study of the mortal beings he once enjoyed tormenting, learning what made them tick and growing closer to understanding their inner battles.

Bringing his attention to the fountain, the Damned contemplated the water feature's potential meaning and purpose. He had always admired the humans' ability to create enchanting pieces of art from nothing but their imagination. It was a gift breathed into them by the Universe that he and his kind did not possess. This collection of sculptures in particular was a favourite of his, and he liked to visit every decade or so since it had been arranged. It depicted the Greek deity Venus riding on two mythical winged horses at the very top. On the two levels below, seven female nymphs were scattered about in a variety of contorted positions, all carved in marble.

*It is glorious. As I once was,* the dark angel thought.

The Damned looked down at his hands with a burning crimson glare, pondering the splendour of his former incarnation. Now bound and twisted into fists by the unbreakable golden wire around them, his hands were crippled and covered in deep, black cracks. The shackles that contained his power were all he had known during his aeons in the lower realms.

Looking back towards the fountain, the Damned settled his gaze on an old Japanese woman throwing bread to a family of ducks in the pond below. Wisdom and kindness seemed to ooze from her pores. She was accompanied by a sleek black Labrador that roamed the nearby bushes curiously. The ducks in the pond frolicked and fought for scraps of food as they paddled in connected circles.

The dark angel watched on like a stone gargoyle.

Wandering over to the empty bench where the Damned was situated in the ether, the dog sniffed out the space. The old woman was distracted, enjoying the ducks' flapping dance on the water.

The Damned observed the dog with a sense of longing. How blissful it was to be a lower life form, without a care in the world but what was under its nose.

Sensing darkness, the dog growled defensively, its ears pinned down and stance wide. The woman's kind gaze transformed into a blank stare of dread as she felt the dark angel's heaviness behind her. Whirling, the woman gawked at the empty bench in the physical world, her eyes wide with indignation.

The dog started clawing at the ground, barking incessantly. The woman rushed over and pulled the animal by the collar.

"Come away from there!"

The Damned made a hopeless effort to connect. His cracked fist moved closer, about to touch the dog, but the animal yelped and jumped back, scampering over to its owner. The old woman scooped up the Labrador and wrapped him in her arms. Lowering his head and flexing his trapped fingers, the Damned examined his monstrous appearance once more.

"Take your rotten stench away from here," snapped the woman. At this, the Damned tucked his hands away to shield his energy from causing any more upset. The skittish pair tottered off while the soulful woman stroked and reassured her whimpering pet.

From among the thick section of bushes behind the Damned, a bedraggled homeless man stumbled over to the bench and waved a can of cider over the dark angel's position before slumping down next to him. Looking directly at the Damned, the homeless man motioned erratically with his hands and blurted a string of garbled words at varying volumes.

The Damned remained still, unfazed.

A male jogger ran past the bench and threw the homeless man a glare that could wilt a bed of roses. The homeless man went quiet, dropping his head to avoid eye contact and waiting for the jogger to pass.

Arriving from a connecting path in the other direction, a young mum passed the bench with a pram and a baby. Suddenly, the homeless man stood to attention, blabbering something unintelligible while cupping his hands for food or money.

"Ugh! Get away from me," the young mum exclaimed.

Shoving the homeless man away from her, the woman accidentally knocked him off balance. The man flailed his arms as he fell, his head caroming off the side of the park bench with a crack.

The dark angel watched this without emotion.

Looking around nervously for witnesses, the young mum made her escape. It was obvious she didn't care to face the consequences of her actions. Meanwhile, the homeless man lay crumpled beside the bench, bleeding from a large wound on his forehead.

The Damned sighed, his blood-red glare faintly visible under his ripped hood.

*So separated from each other. Sometimes I wonder why they go on living when it seems so pointless.*

With the homeless man now slipping from consciousness, the Damned felt strangely conflicted, but it was not his place to step in. Not ever.

*Whoosh!* A sharp, bright beam shot past in the foreground, crossing over the injured man. The Damned's head snapped to where the searing glare seemed to have emanated from. The homeless man began to regain consciousness and sat up delicately. A force from the upper ether was certainly present.

Another beam whirred past as the same being travelled from the opposite direction. In an arrival too timely to be a coincidence, a young girl in blond pigtails ran up to the homeless man, seemingly ignited from the inside by the sweeping angelic illumination. As she reached the poor fellow, the glow around her chest faded and drifted off mysteriously with the wind.

The girl beckoned her father. "Daddy, he's hurt. We need to help him."

In a bursting sphere of gold, the archangel Gabriel appeared before the group on the spiritual plane, face shadowed by his hood and his eyes gleaming like dying stars. The mighty celestial being's Light power uplifted everything around him. The Damned sneered at his ostentatious entrance.

*Why does he always have to make such a song and dance of it?*

"Oh my goodness. Yes, sweetie, let's help this man into the warmth," the father said as he and his daughter helped the injured man to his feet and off towards the nearest hospital. The Damned's expression greeted his brother Gabriel like a brick wall. It had been at least a millennium since they last met.

"Have you come to care for them? You are changed, brother," Gabriel goaded.

"Time is a great teacher, and all I have is time." The Damned gazed up at the sky, leaving a gaping silence between the impressive pair. Finally turning his attention back to his brother, the Damned asked, "Why are you here?"

"Something has triggered the power of a new seer. The alignment of the physical plane and the etherverse has begun to shift."

"Guardians and their obsession with gifted ones. They all turn to ash in the end, same as the rest of their kind," the Damned scoffed.

"This new power is different, more ancient. If you care for humans, why not help them?"

The Damned stood in a flash of crimson and held up his marred fists, facing off with his brother. "Because I am of the damned, and you most of all should know that I do not have a choice!"

"We may not possess free will as the humans do, but certain liberties are afforded us."

It was a leading statement that the Damned ignored, knowing full well that Gabriel was referring to the possibility of his redemption—a fantasy of the righteous.

"If only you would step out from your fear, things may be different," Gabriel continued.

"Leave me alone!" the Damned bellowed.

The two powerful celestials fell silent again, locked in the same stalemate that arose every time they met.

"So be it. But know this, old friend. I have always been your defender, even when others sought to drag your name through the mire."

In an explosion of brilliance and a trail of stars, Gabriel disappeared back to the upper realms of the ether. His unlimited energy blew away with the summer's breeze. The Damned could only watch in envy as his archangel brother returned home.

Back on the pond in the physical realm, the small family of ducks eerily swivelled their heads towards the Damned. Trickling water in the split-level pond became motionless, defying gravity. A blinding vision hit the Damned like a train.

He roared.

In his mind's eye, a giant figure of gleaming, solid gold unlike any other angelic being glided steadily forwards. A white radiance emanated from behind it, shafts beaming through its eyes and hands. The Damned staggered and held his head as pain ripped through his temples. The vision continued with the figure drawing closer, holding a thunderous musical chord as if sung by a hundred-person choir. The harmonious notes moved in a gloriously uplifting progression.

"Why? Why now?" the Damned wailed, doubled over and staggering to maintain his balance.

The golden giant halted its advance. Raising its hands above its shoulders in one smooth movement, it unleashed a final deafening note from its mouth.

The sharp pain stopped as quickly as it had begun. Stillness and quiet returned.

Coming back to his full height, the Damned glared towards the upper ether with a resentful, twisted brow, his mind drifting to the past.

### 3100 BC, WINTER SOLSTICE, IRELAND

Gabriel stood atop Newgrange's burial chamber, gazing over three funeral pyres blazing fiercely below. The domed Neolithic structure had been erected in specific alignment with the sun, moon, and stars to create a mystical relationship with the sky above, favouring a soul's safe passage to the next world. A host of Druid worshippers from three separate tribes gathered around each ceremonial bonfire with stoic expressions. The fires burned like beacons of hope in the night. The moon's sacred position at this time of year was a necessity for the consecration of the bodies of three important tribe members.

The archangel always admired the humans' passion for their lost loved ones. They had such an immense emotional capacity and sense of togetherness when expressing their faith in a higher power. As their guardian, he had loved them from the beginning, a feeling that several of his kin did not share. Still, he had hope that over time, his celestial brothers and sisters would grow in their understanding of the gifted species.

Gabriel smiled wistfully at the thought.

He took a deep breath, mustering his strength for the difficult task ahead.

"I stand as guardian," Gabriel shouted towards the sky, calling the meeting to order.

At these words, seven of his angelic kin warped in one by one, forming a circle around the top of the monument. Each was dressed in regal, cream-coloured robes, with their diverging trim colours denoting their class—all except for one, whose brown, tattered robes told of his exile.

"I stand as vision," Uriel said softly. A lean, black-haired archangel whose arcane mastery of the Light produced a sharp pink aura around her, Uriel was an archangel of great wisdom.

"I stand as judgment," bellowed Raguel, a heavy-set, bald archangel whose cracked and bearded face resembled that of a battle-hardened Viking king.

"I stand as commandment," Sariel trilled in a condescending tone. His purple-trimmed robes floated outwards as the bronzed, aloof archangel glared down his nose at every other being present. The shaman of the group, he held an ornate staff of dangling jewels.

"I stand as death," Samael croaked. As the largest archangel of the group by some degree, Samael's huge frame was surrounded by grey energy tentacles of decay. His skin, dark as pitch and hairless, made him appear more like a monster forged in the deep than a heavenly being.

"I stand as restoration," declared Raphael, a blond archangel who embodied purest perfection and confidence. Her enriching green glow brought positivity and life wherever she went.

"I stand as war," Zelda snapped. The only lower angel of the collected group, this feisty upstart was heavily branded in war paint with a closely shaved scalp.

"I stand as the damned," the dark angel mumbled furiously.

Incredulous that a lower angel was present at the gathering of the upper celestials, Gabriel barked at Zelda, "Where is Michael? He must be present for these proceedings, and you have not the nobility to stand here!"

"Do tell us, worm. Are we not worthy to hold court with your noble lord?" the Damned boomed.

Insulted by the dark angel's outburst, Sariel nodded to Raguel, who, with a flick of his hand, sent searing pain tearing through the Damned's whole being. Raguel's power illuminated the dark angel's eyes with a blast of golden brightness.

"Your presence shall be tolerated as decreed, but you will not speak," Sariel scolded.

"Enough!" Gabriel roared in a three-tone modulated voice. Like a spooked mouse, Raguel recoiled and immediately released the Damned.

"I ask you again, why is Michael absent?" Gabriel said to Zelda.

"My lord has sent me with a message: humans have become a stain on the earth's once majestic planes, corrupting anything good, like a parasite feeding on its host."

Each of the angels turned their attention to the tribes below, acknowledging the truth of Zelda's words. While some of the Druid worshippers were respectfully watching the fires and praying, others danced and drank alcohol, rubbing each other in acts of fornication. The sight made Sariel and Raguel—as the most self-righteous of the celestial group—sick to their stomachs. They expected nothing but excellence from humanity and, like Michael, were weary of the mortals' many indulgences.

Zelda continued, "Visitations from the warrior class shall be limited before humanity's carelessness taints our divine bodies as well. I call on all other classes to consider this same course of action, that we may be saved from the humans' inevitable fate."

Finishing her master's words with a flourish, Zelda wasted no time in zipping from the meeting in a blue blur.

"Wait! Please, archangel lords, do not leave. There are important matters—" Gabriel was unable to finish before Samael, the Angel of Death, disappeared in a cloud of grey.

Following suit, Sariel and Raguel exited without a farewell.

Gabriel hung his head and exhaled despondently.

"That's it, run and hide!" the Damned shouted after the fleeing group, ready to explode.

"Please, brother, do not make it worse," Gabriel interjected.

"The restoration class and I will stand by you, Gabriel," Raphael said in a steady, righteous tone.

"As will I. This is what my legions were destined for," Uriel of the visionary class pledged. The Damned, on the other hand, was out of patience, his aura aflame.

"You all stink of weakness. Together we have the power to crush those other fools if you would only set me free!" the Damned shouted.

"Dearest brother, you know it is not within my power to make that decision, and we must stand united, not torn apart," Gabriel replied.

"Mark my words: I will face Michael once more, and there will be a reckoning," the Damned snarled as he disappeared, warping out in a sweeping red arc.

Meanwhile, in the forest next to the Druid ceremony, a battle-worn tribe dressed in torn clothes emerged from the wall of trees. Brandishing sharpened flint axes and baring teeth, the small army was hungry for blood. They crept towards the fires in the dark.

Alerted to the approaching clash, Gabriel, Raphael, and Uriel all looked down as the maniacal leader's scream cut through the night. The tribe charged the funeral ceremony in a wave of brutality.

"Man's free will does begin to weigh heavy on this mortal world," Gabriel conceded, the sadness likewise weighing heavy on his immortal energy.

Axes swept through the crowd, cutting down innocents left and right. Wailing cries and spurts of blood sailed through the night air as women and children were dragged off to be raped and killed.

On the sacred corpses burned as weapons sliced through bone—faith and unity meeting death.

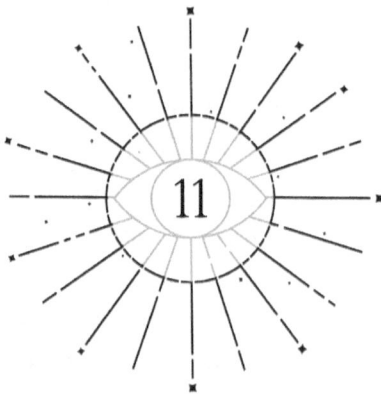

Jack Causer's house was a typical terraced, Victorian, redbrick abode just off Putney High Street, a rather well-to-do area south of London's River Thames. The neighbourhood wasn't really Jack's style. A little too twee and horsey for his liking, it nevertheless kept him at a safe distance from his East London undercover work. Putney was full of yummy mummies navigating small, double-parked streets in their child-carrying tanks—or SUVs, as Americans called them, this being an acronym for "sports utility vehicle." It was a ridiculous term for a vehicle that had less to do with sports or utility than with status and luxury. Jack's preference, at the other end of the spectrum, was for the practicality of a souped-up Mini Cooper: lethal speed and expert handling with the reliability of German engineering under the hood.

Jack stepped out of his front door and headed for his sleek black Mini parked in the white-gravel driveway. The small car wobbled strangely on its back axis, indicating a stowaway bouncing around in the boot. Jack arrived at the back of the vehicle, set his travel mug on top of the car, and unlocked the doors with a beep. As he pulled the boot open, sunlight poured in on the thug Jack had subdued at the dockside warehouse. The thug, gagged and squashed into the foetal position with his hands and feet bound together, recoiled. Jack grinned broadly with a mischievous twinkle in his eye.

"Good morning, princess!"

"Mnnmnnmnmnn." The head thug squirmed, trying to speak through the gag.

Jack leaned in a little. "What was that?"

More muffled words, this time louder.

"I'm sorry, but you're really going to have to speak up a little."

"Mmmnnn!" the thug shouted through the gag.

"Oh, I see. You need to go wee-wee." Jack pinched his cheek like a doting grandmother. "Well, why didn't you just say so before? We really need to work on your e-nun-ci-ation, darling."

More shouts through the gag.

"But didn't you realise? I put your big-boy nappies on last night when you were out for the count."

The head thug gawked down at his lower half with a dawning sense of violation. An elastic nappy protruded above the drug dealer's belt.

A muffled yelp pushed through the gag.

"There's a good big baby!" Jack said, patting the thug on the head and slamming the boot shut.

Jack took a slow sip of his warm coffee with a little something extra mixed in. It was the only way he could blow off the cobwebs these days, his lifestyle beginning to blend with that of the very criminals he was stalking. The two shots of whiskey thrown into his double espresso would see him through the morning, but that was about it.

Settling into the driver's seat, Jack started the engine and flicked on his hard rock playlist, admiring his well-styled hair in the rearview mirror in the process. It was off to Wandsworth prison to drop the criminal scumbag at his new home for the foreseeable future.

*Catching bad guys with me, myself, and I. There are definitely worse ways to make a living.*

The thought helped to cement a thick layer of denial over his insecurity and fear. There was a humble, thankful person buried under the bravado of his default setting: ego. In truth, this deeper, repressed part of Jack Causer did not feel at ease. Rather, it longed for a heartfelt connection with his family and loved ones.

Sitting in Wandsworth prison's east wing office, Eddie looked down at his trembling hand as he relived the altercation with Prisoner 7—the burning evil in the prisoner's eyes, the impossible strength that propelled him across the room, and the vicious voice spitting out a warning like a demonic serpent.

He reached into his jacket pocket and pulled out a pill bottle. Staring at it for a moment, he hesitated, then shook a couple out into his hand. He checked the door before swiftly knocking the medicine back, swallowing hard. Seconds later, Jade strode into the room with a steaming-hot cup of tea, the suspicious cylinder now concealed in Eddie's pocket.

"Here, muggins, this'll sort you out," Jade said.

"Thanks," Eddie mumbled into his chest.

"You're good, babes. You've seen this crap plenty of times before."

"He threw me up against the wall like I was a rag doll. And his voice. Did you hear his voice? It wasn't human," Eddie recounted with a shaky tone.

"What do you expect with the nutters in here? Don't let them get inside your head; that's exactly what they want. Life is one big game to them."

"I know, I know. But this was different. Something dark came over him." Eddie drifted to a morose place in his head. "Like a fever of evil, and pain. So much pain."

Jade stepped in close and tilted Eddie's face up by the chin.

"Listen, you've gotta snap out of it, mate. If they see you like this, they'll never let you live it down."

"You're right. You're right. I'm good," Eddie said, deciding to steel himself against the trauma and put a brave face on things.

"And look at it this way: it could've been way worse. At least you weren't raped."

Eddie let out a bark of laughter at Jade's unexpected comment. This was the exact reason why he secretly loved having her around: she was a master of black humour, and in a job like this, if he didn't laugh, he'd cry—and crying was not an option. If he let one tear slip, the inmates would sense weakness.

"You probably would've enjoyed that, wouldn't you?" Eddie retorted.

"Maybe just a little," Jade said, sending her good mate two tacky finger guns. "Oh, by the way, I grabbed you a bacon bap with brown sauce to cheer you up." She pointed to his desk.

"You are an absolute star, you know that?" Eddie said brightly.

"Oh, I know it," Jade said with a smirk before exiting.

Scooting across the room on his wheeled office chair, Eddie tucked into his favourite snack with great relief. *That girl. She really is my angel. Thank God for her.*

Outside the stone fortress, Jack careered into the prison car park and pulled up next to the processing entrance. It was time to get the ape in the boot off his hands for good. Stepping out of the Mini and opening the back, Jack dragged the thug out onto the pavement with a thud. This giant sack of potatoes wasn't in the mood to go anywhere, which was obvious from the way he glared up at Jack, defiance aflame in his pupils. It was time to give the thug a sobering ultimatum.

"Here's the deal, big nuts. Either you can be dragged in by your bootstraps, scraping the skin off your arms and face, or you can stand up, I'll take that gag off, and you can walk in with me like a civilised human being. How does that sound? You can nod once for the second option."

The thug nodded reluctantly with a heavy sigh. Jack moved to take off his gag and then paused.

"Oh, and one more thing. Any lip outta you, and I'll be going back to the Wraiths with news of your decision to disappear into witness protection. They know there's a rat, after all, and I'm more than happy to point them in your direction. Got it?"

The thug nodded again, and Jack untied his gag. He released his prisoner's foot bindings and pulled him to his feet as promised.

The thug squared up with Jack and growled, "Your story ain't gonna hold for long, pig."

"We'll see, princess, we'll see. I'll give you a free pass on that one. Now, not one more peep outta you." The thug remained silent, full of rage. "Well done. That's the smart play."

Leading his captive towards the entrance, Jack paused for the camera to ID them both and allow access to the building. A few seconds later, the giant steel entrance gates shuddered open, screeching and grinding as they went.

Eddie had a mouthful of bacon bap when Jack appeared at the security screen door of his office, and his mouth popped open like a party streamer, chewed-up food slapping his keyboard. Eddie couldn't believe his eyes. It had been years since the two childhood friends had seen each other, and warm feelings from the past rushed through him. Jack had always been the coolest guy, and effortlessly so.

"Every time I see you, you're stuffing something in your cake hole," Jack joked.

"Causer! What are you doing here? This isn't usually your run."

"Bottom feeder for transfer, and I couldn't resist the opportunity to see your gorgeous, moon-shaped face."

"Aw, lovely to see you haven't stopped being such a thoroughly condescending narcissist. Let's get this one comfortable, shall we?" Eddie said, motioning Jade to unlock the next gate in the processing corridor.

"Is he . . . wearing a nappy?" Jade asked, tilting her head to the side.

"You know me. Fail to prepare, prepare to fail."

"Fair enough," Eddie said. "Stick him in holding cell two until we get him sorted, will ya, Jade?" Coming back to Jack, Eddie continued, "So, I hear you're still undercover with Narcotics? What's the gossip?"

"Well, we did have a good one the other night."

"Go on then," Eddie said eagerly. He absolutely loved Jack's stories. It was like being at a stand-up show.

"Are you sure? It's not very PC, and you're in the middle of breakfast."

"Spit it out, Causer."

"Okay. A male prostitute we had eyes on tried to smuggle crack in his exit hole and got into a spanking contest, of all things, on a night bus at 3 a.m."

"What the hell?!" Grinning like a schoolboy, Eddie hit top pitch.

"Having disturbed the precious cargo in his anal canal, his body started going into involuntary fits. Thing is, you watch the bus CCTV recording, and all the other passengers think it's a new flash mob dance, being that they are all completely hammered. So the whole bus starts gyrating en masse as one guy starts up the Ibiza-style club noises: *bwoop bwoop waka waka waka waka, bwoop bwoop waka waka waka waka!*" Jack mimicked the music while shaking his hips to the pretend club beats. Eddie quickly joined in.

"Bwoop bwoop waka waka waka waka!" Eddie sang along for a bar before the pair burst into raucous laughter. The head thug looked on like a gorilla who'd had his banana snatched from him.

"That is brilliant! I wish I had some of that comedy value here. Secure wing guard duty is totally grim, every single day," Eddie said.

A siren suddenly blared, shifting the mood into high alert.

"I had to open my big feckin' mouth, didn't I?" Eddie sighed, rubbing his temples and dragging his fingers down his cheeks. After hurriedly checking the monitors, he clicked on the public announcement system to sound a rallying call. "All available officers to the mess hall. Fight in progress!"

"You want me to jump in? I could use the exercise," Jack offered.

"Are you kidding? I'd be drowning in paperwork for the next month if you got hurt. You stay here. We've got this covered," Eddie said, pulling out his baton. Jack stood back and studied the monitors while Eddie darted off to control the unfolding mayhem.

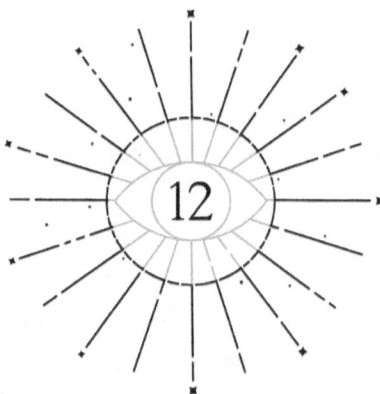

# 12

In a meagre North London flat, Haylene cooked up scrambled eggs while throwing shapes to seventies funk music. Kickboxer by day and dancing queen by night, she could best be described as a muscular goddess. The twenty-something bopped around the kitchen in sleek fitness gear as her shoulder-length red-dyed ringlets bounced to a groovy bass line.

As the best friend and longtime roommate to Grace, Haylene was Grace's rock, especially when it came to looking after her little man. Haylene's favourite way to spend downtime was with Andy, expanding his learning with exciting day trips and watching a shedload of comic book movies. She and Andy were almost identical in their love for animated movies and superhero fandom, so when they got together, there was some serious banter to be had—two wisecracking warriors against the world. Quite simply, Haylene was Andy's hero and protector.

Behind the kitchen, perched at the dining table, Andy was swept up in his imagination as he danced two colourful action figures through the air. He loved doing wacky character voices and was currently simulating a classic superhero standoff from his favourite cartoon. Haylene's massive fish tank in the middle of the large dinner table made for a dramatic backdrop to the climax of Andy's story. A beat-up Barbie doll dressed in stylish evening wear lounged atop the tank. The villainous figure in Andy's left hand was a tall, spindly character with a forked tongue and yellow, snakelike eyes. The young boy bobbed it up and down while speaking in a high-pitched, upper-class English accent.

"Hyperion! So nice of you to finally join us. We were just about to go for a dip. Well, when I say we, I really just mean her. And when I say dip, I really mean drowning amongst my deadly fleshfish. Hahahaha!" Andy mimicked, booming an over-the-top laughter.

Haylene shouted over her shoulder towards the open-plan living area.

"Do you want bacon, buddy?"

Lost in his creative flow, Andy failed to register the question and continued in his epic standoff. Andy wiggled a muscular, square-jawed figure in a tight red bodysuit in his right hand. He gave the character a cheesy standard American dialect.

"This city has suffered your madness long enough, Lizard Lord! Let her go, or I'm sending you back to the swamp where you belong."

Haylene popped her head around the kitchen doorframe, pointing the spatula in her hand like a weapon. Using a cartoon voice of her own to break into Andy's world, she emulated a grave priestess.

"We must honour this pig's sacrifice! Shall the bacon pass your lips?"

Haylene's rather impressive attempt at an animated voice snapped Andy out of his superhero trance. He stared at her for a moment before bursting into laughter.

"Oh, sorry. Yes, please!" Andy said. He immediately turned back to his toys, shaking his Lizard Lord figure up and down. "Sorry, Hyperion, you know I can't do that. She looks far too tasty, and I'm afraid my little darlings did skip breakfast! Don't you know, you just can't get any gains by skipping breakfast." Andy made as if Lizard Lord were stroking the fish in the tank beside him as he continued the dialogue with Hyperion.

"Fine, slimy and ugly. Have it your way," Andy bellowed. He moved Hyperion's arm up, using his other hand to lift Lizard Lord off the dining table towards the fish tank, mimicking telekinetic powers.

Sauntering into the room with plates, Haylene nodded Andy over to the sofa and coffee table area to eat.

"Breakfast's ready! Come on before it gets cold, bud."

As Haylene set the food on the table, the front door clicked open. Grace tottered through the entrance with a bag of groceries and her work backpack, her dishevelled hair and clothes matching the dark circles under her eyes.

"Just in time, lovely one," Haylene said.

"You are an absolute gem," Grace responded.

Still in his own world of make-believe, Andy continued with Lizard Lord's demise.

"How is this possible? I took your powers from you. No! Stop!"

Andy switched to his Hyperion voice: "Apologies, Lizard Lord. That's only what I let you believe."

Switching back to Lizard Lord, he finished his story in style.

"Nooooooo!"

Andy raised Lizard Lord over the fish tank with the imaginary telekinetic powers and plopped him into the water.

"Glug, glug, glug, glug, glug."

"Oh, Andy, what have I said about putting your toys in the fish tank?" Grace moaned.

At this, Haylene roared with laughter, and Grace couldn't help but giggle at Andy's sheepish expression.

"Sorry, Mum," Andy said, following up with a deliciously cheeky grin.

"Alright, sweetie. Come and eat, okay?" Grace said.

Dashing over to the sofa, Andy leapt onto his mum's lap and gave her a tight squeeze.

"That was just what I needed," Grace sighed.

Andy rolled next to her on the sofa and picked up his knife, imagining it as a mighty claymore sword in the hands of Hyperion.

"Time to meet your fate, egg beast!" Andy announced in his American accent.

"Please, let's have a break from the superheroes while we eat our breakfast, okay, Andy?" Grace asked.

"Okay," Andy grumbled, setting his action figure to the side.

"So, have you two had a good morning?" Grace asked.

"Yes, we have! We got lots done, didn't we, buddy?" Haylene chimed in.

"Boring cleaning. But then some wicked cartoons," Andy said.

"Oh, thank you so much for doing the cleaning, guys. That's a big help."

"We missed you, Mummy. Did you save any lives?"

"It wasn't a great night, my love, but we were able to help some."

It was obvious to Haylene that Grace was badly shaken beneath her attempt at an upbeat exterior. She had not seen her best friend this unsteady in a while. Back with his breakfast, Andy wolfed down cheek-bulging mouthfuls of bacon.

"Grace, are you okay?" Haylene asked.

"Just a little spent. That's all."

"Are you sure? You seem rattled."

"You know you can share with us, Mummy," Andy sputtered through his hamster cheeks.

"Well, I had this odd feeling at the bus stop. It was like I could feel this . . . *see* this dark energy gripping a woman behind me . . ."

Andy and Haylene were utterly captivated as Grace recalled her experience.

"Before I knew it, I was speaking to it, telling it to stop. But the words just tumbled out, like instinct. The most frightening thing was it wasn't even my voice. It sounded . . . It's going to sound really silly."

"Go on," Haylene said.

"Well, it sounded like a lion's roar forming words."

"Wow! That's so cool," Andy said, his eyes lighting up.

"What exactly was it you saw?" Haylene asked. Before Grace could answer, Andy jumped in, his imagination running wild.

"Was it a ghost? Or like some kind of evil spirit?" Andy squirmed like a *Scooby-Doo* ghost.

"Andy, let Mummy finish her story," Haylene said as Grace turned to her son.

"I don't know, sweetie. I couldn't physically see anything other than a grey, shimmering shape that somehow seemed alive."

"Sweet!" Andy added.

"Andy, go and pack your things for the zoo tomorrow. Mummy and I need to talk, okay?" Haylene said, taking control of the situation.

"But I want to hear the rest of the story!" Andy moaned.

"I'll tell you all about it later, okay?" Grace said.

"Promise?"

"I promise. Now go."

Giving his mum a knowing glance, Andy grabbed his action figures, fighting and smashing noises trailing behind him as he scampered off to his room. Grace took a few satisfying bites of breakfast before realising that Haylene was sitting back and staring at her, arms crossed.

"Haylene, I'm fine. I'm just exhausted," Grace said defensively.

"You know I have to ask, as your friend."

"Ask what?"

Haylene shifted in her chair, mustering the courage to approach the touchy subject.

"Well, don't take this the wrong way, but you're not using again, are you?"

"No! God no! I'm upset that you'd even ask me that."

"Okay, okay! Don't harden up on me. You know I'm only looking out for you."

"I know, I know. Sorry. It's just all a bit overwhelming."

"Look, let's settle into a proper rom-com to take your mind off all this heavy stuff, shall we?"

"Good God, am I that predictable?" Grace said, laughing at herself.

"Ryan Reynolds is gonna get ya every time!" Haylene said. She grabbed the remote and clicked on the smart TV, and the two fast friends grinned and wiggled back into their seats with glee, ready for the romance roller coaster ahead.

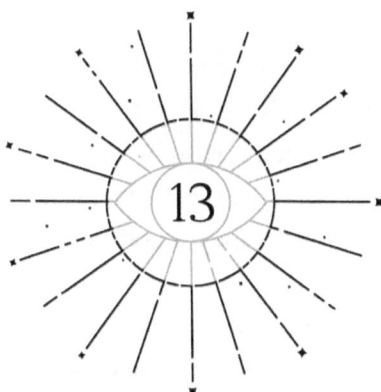

# 13

In Wandsworth prison's mess hall, a full-scale brawl was underway between the prisoners from cells 1 through 5 and the three guards on duty. Prisoners 1 and 2 were trading heavy blows as Eddie burst into the room, wide eyed and panting heavily.

*Thwack!* Blindsided by Prisoner 2's meaty fist, which had gone off target, Eddie reeled back against the door he had just come through and shook off his dizziness. He took a moment to assess the evolving havoc in front of him as his vision steadied. With no clear vantage point presenting itself, Eddie circled behind the mob to back up the outnumbered guards at the far end of the room.

Looming by a quiet corner in the ether, Beel pushed the violent mood of the room to the brink with her presence. Clouds of Dark Light billowed about the clash of bodies as a blood-red vibrancy pulsated from her eyes.

Back in the surveillance room, Jack witnessed the ferocious downward spiral and swiftly recognised that things were getting out of hand. He bolted from the control centre and rushed to the scene, secretly excited to get his hands dirty. He couldn't remember the last time he'd enjoyed a tussle of this calibre.

Arriving in the mess hall at the same entry point as Eddie, Jack was immediately confronted by a burly guard being knocked to the ground by Prisoner 1. The nearby Prisoner 2 darted through the space and kicked the guard's head like a football, rendering him unconscious. As Prisoner 1 lifted a leg high to stamp down on the defenceless guard's head, Jack snapped into action, rushing the prisoner and thrusting an arm under his rising knee. Jack used his free arm to drive a lightning-quick elbow into his target's jaw. It knocked Prisoner 1 out instantly.

One down, four to go.

The lethal efficiency of Jack's fighting style was trademark SAS, an engineered combination of Chinese wing chun and Israeli special forces krav maga. Jack's attacks came in fierce bursts with technical positional movements. The blend of using an opponent's weight and attack against them while homing in on the enemy's weak spot enabled any opponent to be incapacitated with one or two connecting blows. This was how Jack had always been taught: finish the fight before it started.

Enraged at his compatriot's fall, Prisoner 2 swung a wild, right-handed haymaker at Jack's head. Jack ducked instinctively and shot back up with a sharp uppercut, dazing the inmate. Grabbing the back of Prisoner 2's head, Jack smashed it over his knee with a dull clunk. An explosion of blood from the prisoner's shattered cheekbone turned out the lights.

Two down, three to go.

Meanwhile, on the other side of the hall, Eddie and a wiry bald guard defended their position back-to-back. They were holding their own against Prisoners 3, 4, and 5, but then Prisoner 4 scooped up a stray baton and clattered Eddie square on the kneecap. Going down in a blast of pain, Eddie launched his baton at Prisoner 3's head, hoping for a lucky hit.

*Thunk!* The baton unexpectedly battered Prisoner 3's eye socket; Eddie could barely believe his good fortune.

Coming to the rescue from behind Prisoner 3, Jack sliced a sideways hammer fist into the reeling inmate's ear. The expert strike knocked the attacker flat to the floor. He wasn't moving, and he wasn't getting up anytime soon.

Three down, two to go.

Prisoner 4 had used his monstrously superior size to manhandle Eddie up against the wall and grapple his arms into a hold behind his back. Having flattened the wiry bald guard with a vicious headbutt, Prisoner 5 was pumped up to the eyeballs with adrenaline. As Prisoner 4 swivelled Eddie to face the room, the pug-ugly Prisoner 5 slammed repeated heavy blows into Eddie's exposed midsection, relishing every moment.

"How does it feel now, pig?" Prisoner 5 snarled.

Wheezing to regain his breath, Eddie composed himself and replied in a cool, conversational tone, "If I'm being honest, like your granny on a hot day. Soft, easy, and ready for a good—"

*Thud. Crack!* A left hook hit Eddie's ribs, followed by a shuddering right straight to Eddie's face. The prisoner's blood was boiling. "Shut it!" he hollered.

Casually loitering unseen in the background, Jack seized his moment to chime in, "Oh, Eddie, you really don't play well with others, do you?"

In confusion, Prisoners 4 and 5 whirled around to see what wisecracking dope had interrupted their fun. Using the distraction, Eddie flung his head back violently.

*Crack!* Eddie's thick skull connected conveniently with the bridge of Prisoner 4's nose, sending the sweating ogre staggering backwards. Without a break in motion, Eddie launched a powerful forward kick at Prisoner 5's solar plexus, forcing the air from the toothless inmate's lungs. Eddie hurled himself on top of Prisoner 5.

Still standing, Prisoner 4 shook off his daze and zeroed in on Jack, who grinned, inviting his advance. Jack had seen Prisoner 4's type before. A mindless brute whose overconfidence stemmed from sheer size and lack of worthy opponents, the lumbering Frankenstein's monster was about to find out how skill and hard training trumped both. He lunged to grab Jack by the throat. Sidestepping the attack, Jack popped a rock-solid jab to the inmate's ribcage. Annoyed rather than injured, the giant wheeled on the spot with an immense elbow quicker than expected from a man of his size. Blocking the blow on instinct, Jack was unnerved that it had come at such speed. He had to end this violent exchange, and fast.

Responding in a breakneck flurry, Jack exposed Prisoner 4's weak spots. He grabbed the inmate's trailing arm and twisted it, putting his target off balance, and followed with a right-slicing elbow and a rapid left downward punch, each strike targeted to the prisoner's already bleeding nose. With the mutant now toppling backwards and his eyes awash with blood, Jack didn't let up. Pincering the brute's exposed armpit and shoulder joint, he gripped the nerve bundle there. The inmate winced and froze. Jack finished with a sweeping knife-hand strike, the built-up force of Jack's twisting hips landing squarely on the prisoner's jawline.

*Thud!* The lump of a man crashed to the ground, out cold.

One to go.

Spinning around to see how Eddie was faring, Jack was reassured that his friend had everything under control. Eddie knelt on Prisoner 5's back, steadily squashing the inmate's face into the concrete floor with his forearm.

"It's over. Stay down," Eddie blared in the inmate's ear.

Suddenly, in a blitz of Dark Light, Beel manifested beside the anger-fuelled Eddie to whisper a suggestion in his ear.

"Embrace your rage."

A glint of desire passed over Eddie's eyes, and out of nowhere, he began repeatedly hammering Prisoner 5 in the face. Eddie was bewitched by the dark angel's spell, lost in fist after bludgeoning fist. Shocked at his companion's switch in behaviour, Jack raced in and pulled Eddie off the beaten inmate.

"Stop! If we give in to our base emotions, we become like them."

Eddie blinked and shook his head, coming back to himself. "You're right."

"Think. Engage your sense of reason."

"You've always been best at knowing what's right, Jack."

Beel looked on, perplexed. Not one to take no for an answer, the dark angel moved in to try her wiles on Jack instead. "Pride," she whispered.

Feeling the sentiment land on him, Jack grounded himself in his breathing and batted away his selfish thoughts.

"We all have the power to withstand fear and anger if we choose to," Jack said with a stoic glare. "Now, how about we clean up this mess? This place looks like O'Brien's pub after Chelsea lost the FA Cup last year!"

Offering an outstretched arm, Jack pulled Eddie to his feet. The pair surveyed the carnage and went about helping the battered guards.

As this was the second time in a single that day Beel's advances had been resisted, the dark angel was certain of a connection between both events. The Universe offered no coincidences.

*Clunk. Crack. Thunk!*

A shift sounded above, signalling powerful tectonic movements in the upper realms. The etherverse was destabilising. Speeding from the scene in a cascade of crimson, Beel navigated the spiritual world to learn more about these strange happenings.

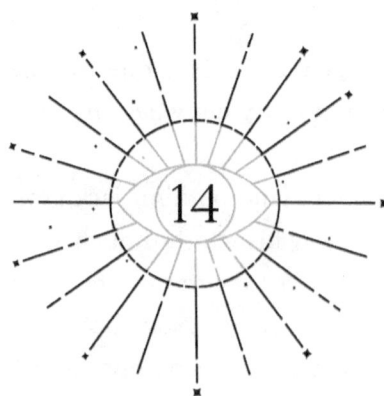

## 14

As the credits rolled, Grace pulled a final tissue from the box between them. The two soulful women wiped wet eyes and blew loose noses in floods of happy tears.

"Ah, nothing beats a good cry, does it?" Grace said.

"You're right there. I feel so clear and lighthearted after that," Haylene agreed.

Grace's mind switched track, and a cloud of worry descended over her.

"Andy's gonna be okay, isn't he?" Grace erupted into a flood of fresh tears.

"Oh, honey, that's it; let it all out." Haylene pulled Grace in close for a warm hug. "Of course he is. He's got us, hasn't he?" Grace nodded. "Plus, he's a pretty fierce little man with a lot of wisdom himself. You shouldn't forget that."

"Thanks. I guess I just needed to hear someone say it to me."

"Well, I'm always here to tell you everything's gonna be okay," Haylene said as Grace smiled.

The shadowy figure of Abaddon materialised in a blast of Dark Light behind them. Refusing to be made a fool of by this spiritually enlightened female from the bus stop, the Lord of the Pit had arrived in pursuit to tighten the screw of fear and assert his dominance. A shiver of cold emptiness streaked through Grace's being. With shock setting in, she sharply retreated from the embrace, and her breathing quickened. Abaddon loomed motionless.

"Woah, woah. You're okay. You're safe here," Haylene reassured her.

"I feel a strange void inside again. What's wrong with me? Am I losing my mind as well as my family?"

"Grace, stop beating yourself up. Andy and I are your family now. His dad chose to leave, remember?"

"I know, but maybe I could have done more to make him stay."

"Forget about that. Let's do your cards to give you a little extra guidance in this tough time."

Grace balanced her breathing with a few concentrated inhales and exhales and conceded, "Sounds good."

Taking her angel cards from underneath the coffee table, Haylene shuffled the colourful pack. Not to be confused with tarot cards, angel cards helped the user to seek guidance and meaning from spiritual forces above. They did not attempt to predict the future of the reader, a major area where tarot card readings could come unstuck. Angel cards were more open to interpretation. The unique meaning of each card came through a question posed to the divine beings of the Universe before any card was chosen, and it framed the significance of the imagery and words found on each card. Doing a reading from a single random card was a ritual Grace and Haylene performed on a weekly basis to set a positive intention.

Abaddon scoffed. *These clueless females think that they can withstand my power with some fancy words and pretty pictures. What a joke.*

Haylene placed the cards face down and closed her eyes. Moving them around the table in circles with one hand, she held Grace's hand tightly with the other.

"Universe, we ask that you give Grace peace, love, and hope as she struggles to understand her path. We ask for your direction and reassurance in this confusing time. Give her clarity, we humbly ask." Haylene flipped over a card her hand had been drawn to. The archangel Gabriel stared up at the two women. Haylene and Grace glanced at each other with a spark of exhilaration.

Fear washed over Abaddon in the ether, and the dark angel grew wary of the two potential witches. *Not possible. Surely they cannot summon him.*

Haylene went on to read the passage accompanying the beautiful guardian's image: "Archangel Gabriel is with you. His power to balance the forces of life moves through you. You must communicate at this time, as there is a power deep within you that will inspire others. You hold the unique ability to reveal truth and bring about great peace."

Spinning her head towards the space Abaddon was occupying, Grace narrowed her eyes at the fallen celestial.

"It's here," Grace remarked.

"What's here?" Haylene asked.

"That dark, cold energy I was talking about."

Without hesitation, Abaddon retreated through a collapsing ethergate, unnerved by the gifted woman's connection to the ether. Grace let out a sigh of relief.

"Now it's gone. I'm so confused, Haylene," she moaned, squinting at the revealed card. "Peace? Balance? I couldn't feel further from those things right now."

"Don't worry, lovely. Things will become clearer in time. They always do. Now, you just lie down and get some shut-eye."

"I'll try my best," Grace said, defeated.

Snuggling into the cushions, Grace found a comfortable position as Haylene threw a velvety blanket over her. It was a matter of seconds before Grace slipped into dreamland.

Early in the evening, Grace sat up, disoriented from an utterly dreamless sleep. Yet she couldn't recall the last time she had slept so solidly and awakened so energised. Lying back down to bask in relaxation, Grace focused on her breathing to find a way into a short meditation.

At the other end of the flat, Haylene pottered around in the bathroom, getting Andy ready for bed.

"Teeth all clean?" she said.

"Yup!" Andy responded, proudly baring his white teeth.

"Good man. Off you go," Haylene prompted.

Andy hesitated. "Is Mummy going to be okay?"

"Of course she will be. She has you to look out for her, doesn't she? She just needs her rest."

Andy seemed mollified for the time being.

"Off to bed with you," Haylene said, ushering the boy towards his room. Climbing into bed, Andy pulled the covers up and rolled onto his side.

"Nighty night," Haylene said as she closed the door and headed to her own room to do some reading. Passing the living room door on her way, she smiled to see Grace in a tranquil state, thanking the Universe that her friend was getting a welcome break from all the recent turmoil.

Grace came to the end of her meditation and stretched her limbs. Picking up the Gabriel card next to her on the coffee table, she studied it once again. It struck a chord within her. She had fond memories of her mum telling bedtime stories about this immensely powerful being. Grace's mum had always had a fascination with spirits and deities. Her vast catalogue of knowledge made for elaborate storytelling indeed.

Her attention wandering out the window to the approaching dark, Grace pondered how angels might be connected to her strange spiritual experiences as of late.

Grace suddenly realised that she had absolutely no idea what time it was and tapped on her phone. She was drastically late for her shift. Leaping up, she gathered her things in a whirlwind of activity, grabbed her keys, and dashed for the door.

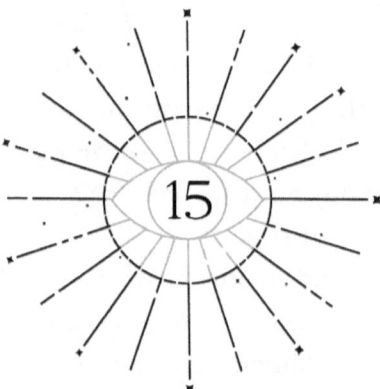

In a quiet, suburban Dublin neighbourhood, a bleary-eyed man dragged a reluctant, panic-stricken woman behind him. Losing almost every other step, the woman tumbled as the man's forceful tugs threw her off balance.

"This isn't right," the woman protested. Continuing relentlessly to his target, the man yanked on the woman's arm to keep her moving at his pace.

"Please, will you just stop? This isn't what she would want!" the woman pleaded.

"It's not about what she would want anymore! This has to be done. She didn't have a choice. Nor did any of the rest of them," the exasperated man said. Turning to face her, he raised his voice to a shout. "He won't stop until someone stops him. Don't you see that?"

The man mounted the steps of an ornate stone building, leaving the woman to stumble and collapse into a heap on the top step, defeated.

"Oh God, please," she mumbled to herself.

The furious man hammered hard on tall wooden doors. "You're going to pay for what you've done!"

"Please, let's just leave it," the woman wailed.

Roaming like a lion in front of the dark, old structure, the man glimpsed a curtain move in one of the upper rooms. He bellowed, "I know you're in there, and I'm not leaving until you answer for all the lives you've destroyed."

Inside the upper room of the church vestry, a trembling priest peered out at the couple below. He had dressed in his full ceremonial robes to prepare for this defining moment in his life. With only a single candle giving light to the plush vestry, the priest swayed back and forth, a half-empty bottle of whiskey in hand. A silver revolver on the elaborately carved desk behind him glinted in the candlelight. Sensing the dark energy of the otherworldly being that took shape behind him, he realised that the end had begun. The Damned settled calmly into position on the opposite side of the room, standing in front of the only exit.

"I was wondering when you would come," the priest slurred.

A cordless phone on the desk rang out, slicing through the heavy atmosphere. Seconds later, the religious leader's mobile blared out a ringtone from his pocket. Fate was rapidly closing in on him. The Damned's crimson eyes carried a crippling intensity as he delayed his response. *What a pitiful excuse for a human being*, the Damned thought, allowing the terrifying quiet to eat away at the misguided priest's psyche.

It was the same the world over, whether Christian or atheist, Muslim or Jew, addict or health fanatic. All tribes of humans shared the same problem: an insatiable hunger for more, a need to cling to a way of life to cover their insecurities or "not-enoughness." Obsessiveness twisted their innate goodness and corrupted the strength of humankind. Not God, not the devil. Not even dear old Mum and Dad could save them from themselves. The dark angel had seen it all before. Shifting blame was merely a trick of the mind.

When someone bent the world to suit themselves, they denied two unchanging, fundamental truths: that no one was coming to save them and that they possessed everything they needed to be free in this present moment if they could only let go.

The priest's hand shook by his side, his eyes darting around the room like those of a trapped animal. He gulped down two huge swigs from the bottle in a desperate bid for courage.

"You have done terrible things, Thomas," the Damned said, finally breaking the silence.

"My intention was always to spread God's love."

"Do not try to work me as you work your followers with your petty fantasy. People are not judged by their best intentions, 'Father,' but by how they have lived. The resentment and pain in your wake do not speak of love," the Damned goaded. The priest whirled around with a wobble and a stumble, fixing an icy glare on the imposing dark angel.

"Who are you to judge me? God alone has the power to judge. You are but the devil himself!" the priest boomed. Further displaying his indignation, the holy man snorted back phlegm and spat a slimy blob at the Damned's feet.

"Am I the devil? Am I not an agent of the divine? Do you even know what 'devil' means, Thomas?"

The priest stared blankly, the resignation of being utterly outmatched now hitting him like a train.

"It means adversary—someone or something that is set in direct opposition to the purpose of another. Is that really what I am to you, Thomas? Have I not helped you? All I have done is given you exactly what you wished for."

The priest turned his back on the Damned, fed up with listening to the truth. The dark angel had him dead to rights, and there was no escaping it. Taking another drink, the priest steadied himself on the desk as his gaze settled on the beckoning revolver. In a sudden rebellion against his inner turmoil, the priest grabbed hold of the gun and launched it directly at the Damned. It passed straight through the dark angel's chest and smacked into the wall behind him. Unfazed by the man's outburst, the Damned continued his lecture.

"I am not against 'God,' as you call it. I was sentenced here, and I continue to serve my time. Your path is merely what comes of that."

Regret finally bursting through, the priest began blubbering uncontrollably.

"You have destroyed everything I love," the priest sobbed as he dropped to his knees.

"You are not a puppet on a string, Thomas. What you choose to look at is what you become. Seeking out devils and monsters only serves to nurture an ancient evil within. You, of all people, should know better."

The priest was unable to muster the energy for a response.

"Ask yourself: what is it that you are willing to do? What is it that's best for this world and those around you?"

The Damned looked down at the gun on the floor and then back to the priest. As sirens wailed in the distance, the priest peered through the window to see three police cars hurtling towards the church.

"It was always going to end this way," the priest muttered in a subdued tone.

"Perhaps. Perhaps not. Evil exists when arrogance and resentment collide. You believed you were above consequence and above everyone else. Hatred for God took hold inside of you because you never found real love and vulnerability," the Damned said softly.

"I suppose you would know. Arrogance was why you were banished, was it not?"

"My banishment has nothing to do with the consequences you must now face," the Damned said and warped from the room in a fiery blaze. Left alone with his fear and regret, the priest quivered, glaring at the gun.

Outside the church, the fuming husband paced wildly, waiting for the police to arrive. Crumpled next to its lofty wooden doors and weeping, the man's wife had given up on life. The Damned appeared next to the indignant man in a crash of Dark Light and enveloped the husband in his blood-red power. The human was completely oblivious to his presence, yet the dark angel spoke directly to him.

"Death comes to us all, and as the light fades, so moves the hand of fate."

A gunshot rang out from the church's upper room, startling the husband and wife.

Whipping out in a flash of crimson, the Damned left the anxiety-filled couple to face the priest's corpse.

Maybe they had hoped the death of their daughter's rapist would bring them some measure of peace. Quite soon they would discover that the opposite was indeed true. The corrupted holy man's demise would fill their lives with yet more suffering and yet more questions—questions that had no answers.

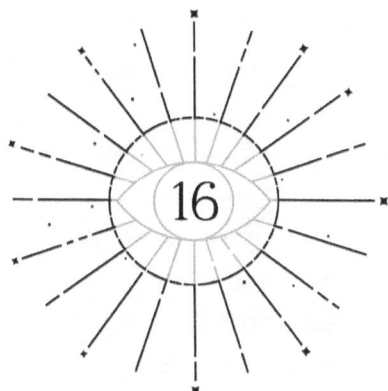

# 16

Grace clattered through the swinging doors of Mile End's ambulance port to find that the entire A & E unit had shifted into top gear, with the few staff present on the ward scrambling to reorganise the space. The managing consultant on shift, a clean-cut and slender middle-aged man of Pakistani descent, stood at the central scheduling desk and barked orders at the staff. At Grace's flustered entrance, Bhunil snapped at her in agitation.

"Grace, where have you been?!"

"I'm so sorry. I fell asleep on the sofa," Grace responded shamefully.

"Just get changed as soon as you can."

"What's going on?"

"Prepping for arrivals from a motorway pileup involving a bus. Multiple severely wounded, six fatalities."

"God help them," Grace said.

The main entrance doors slammed open. With a clamour of moans and stress, wounded people of all ages and all stations in life flooded the A & E from every direction. Two paramedics rolled in from the ambulance port with two stretchered victims.

Grace darted to the nearest sink, washed her hands, and threw her uniform on over her jeans and T-shirt. Finding herself right in the middle of it, Grace got to work separating each new arrival into critical and noncritical.

"We've got two that need stabilising here," the lead paramedic shouted through the chaos.

Bhunil pointed to the adjoining nurses' office, hollering at Grace, "Grace, try and move as many noncritical patients to the triage area as soon as possible. We have to prioritise and make some room!"

"On it," Grace replied confidently.

A third paramedic blasted in through the service entrance, supporting a teenage girl whose arm had been completely crushed. The teenager keened in pain, unsteady on her feet. Meanwhile, next to an abandoned trolley in the waiting area, a wizened old man was barking at Bhunil.

"For God's sake! My wife's in extreme pain. Can someone please help her?"

In under a minute, Mile End's A & E had descended into a cacophony of lamentations and clanging medical equipment.

Somewhere outside the realms of time and space, a huge caped and hooded figure hurtled through the firmament in the foetal position, barely conscious. This firmament was the space between the upper ether and the physical universe of space and stars—a realm that was almost impossible for the human mind to conceptualise. The falling celestial's regal cream robes billowed about his giant frame. The noise of flapping fabric was the only sound within the black void of nonexistence.

Back in the A & E, Bhunil had done his best to placate the old man with painkillers for his wife while he refocused his energies on keeping control of the room. Calling to the lead paramedic, he spoke in a commanding tone. "How many are we dealing with here, exactly?"

"We have five criticals in total and four severely injured," the paramedic responded. Grace jumped in, adding her information.

"OR two is available. Beds six, seven, and eight are free."

Bhunil nodded and continued to marshal his staff to maximise the ward's efficiency.

"Get the criticals into the OR to free up bed space. The others will have to go in here. Prioritise the severely injured. Get IVs into each and every one of them on arrival!"

Heeding his direction, the two nurses on shift rushed to organise the new setup as fast as humanly possible.

Suddenly, a midthirties male stumbled through the two-way entrance doors with a horrifying gash across his face. He was delirious and weaving left and right in a state of shock. Lunging to steady him before he collapsed, Grace propped up his chest.

Continuing to speed through space, the barely conscious angel plummeted past the moon and broke through the earth's upper atmosphere, falling like a space shuttle on reentry. Fire whipped around his body. Against the night sky, the angel's shimmering shape appeared as a blazing comet charging the planet's surface.

Directly below, Grace gently guided the spaced-out accident victim to the plastic chairs in the waiting area.

"It's okay, sir. I've got you. Just have a seat here." Grace motioned behind her to one of the nurses, who instantly jumped in to help. "Can you take him? I need to—"

A distressed shout ripped through the ward.

"This one's going into cardiac arrest!" the assistant paramedic boomed. Grace jumped to his aid, skirting around the busy room.

"Help me get him into six, and I'll use the crash cart in there," she said, rushing the convulsing young man past the screen with the assistant paramedic in tow. Placing the defibrillator paddles on the patient, Grace initiated the procedure to restart his heart. "Clear!"

The observing paramedic was totally stunned, this being the first time he had witnessed a real person in the throes of death. Clocking his bewilderment, Grace barked, "I've got this. Get out there and help the others."

The jittery paramedic nodded and dashed back to the main area in a cold sweat. Grace went again with the paddles.

No response.

*Come on, please, come back to me*, Grace thought. Sending out a prayer to the Universe, Grace tried one last time.

*Buzzzt!* Nothing.

Closer to the earth's surface now, the celestial being continued his descent at terminal velocity. The glow of the city lights came into view as his body spun through the blackened sky like a flaming pinball.

Meanwhile, in the A & E, the young man under the paddles was gone. In respect for his passing, Grace dipped her head and placed her hands on the poor soul, sending a blessing to his spirit as it went on its way.

The entire building shuddered as if a bomb had hit. Grace instinctively yanked back the curtain behind her and, in the flickering light of the overhead fluorescent tubes, spotted a massive hole in the hospital ceiling. The central control desk was completely destroyed. In its rubble, a colossal shape lay steaming.

It was as if time stood still.

Frozen, staring at the unknown entity in the middle of the A & E, Grace's senses were on fire. Every single piece of technology had been knocked out, and deathly silence hung over the entire room. Grace was oblivious to the fact that she had somehow slipped into the space between the etherverse and the physical plane as she moved closer to the impact site. Beneath the giant hole, Grace made out an impressive muscular being dressed in a cream-coloured, hooded robe bordered with a red-and-gold trim.

The being was broken and dying.

A black substance oozed from the impressive angel's eyes and mouth. His once glowing skin was now a lifeless grey, with black cracks forming around his chest and neck. The cracks were gradually spreading across his body, threatening to consume his great power. Slowly turning his head to find Grace, the perishing archangel spoke.

"I found you."

"You . . . found me? Who are you?" Grace peered through the ceiling hole into the night sky. "Where on earth did you come from?"

"None of that matters now. There is no time. Come closer," Gabriel said. Leaning in, Grace inspected the strange lacerations on the celestial being's skin.

"Your wounds—they aren't like anything I've ever seen before." Looking for a second opinion, Grace beckoned her consultant. "Doctor, do you recognise this type of haemorrhaging?" she questioned Bhunil. Whirling around, Bhunil was unable to hear or see Grace from his perspective in the physical realm. He called out in confusion: "Grace?!"

From Grace's position in the space between worlds, Bhunil's lips were moving, but no sound emerged. The fact that she could only hear and interact with Gabriel suddenly dawned on her.

"Listen!" Gabriel boomed in his characteristic divine voice. Taking Grace's hand, the archangel pulled her close. "My last message is to you, Grace. You must find the Lightbearer. This ancient power is all that stands in the way of humanity's complete annihilation."

A tall, lithe figure appeared in brilliant robes with a lush green trim. This restoration angel lunged in a panic to save Gabriel, but the guardian archangel raised a firm hand, signalling his comrade to disengage. In speaking his final words, Gabriel stared up at the sky as if trying to communicate to his celestial kin.

"War is coming. Find the Lightbearer," Gabriel croaked. With a sudden convulsion and one massive inhale, Gabriel's eyes dimmed to solid black. The healing angel gaped in horror at the mighty archangel's demise. Never before had one of his kind known death, least of all this most beloved leader of the guardian class.

Something terrible had occurred to cause this rupture in the laws of angelic existence. It was as drastic a paradigm shift as if humans were suddenly without gravity or time. Death was a reality almost impossible for angels of every kind to imagine. Until this point in time, they simply could not die. Their form could only be changed or reshaped, rising or falling based on their actions in relation to humanity. The fixed angelic order of the etherverse had been corrupted and rearranged somehow.

Ever since archangels and their clans had been breathed into existence, the commandment and judgment classes had held the ether's source of control. Their role was to keep mortals and celestials alike in check. Another archangel must have assumed control of both the commandment and judgment classes, subjugating them and absorbing their power. Only three celestials were powerful enough to attempt such a monumental feat: Gabriel, Michael, and the Damned.

Dismayed by the ramifications this moment would have for the safety of his entire species, the lone healing angel warped out in a green shard of the Light.

Meanwhile, Grace reached out and placed a soft hand on the being's cracked, grey arm, unsure of how to respond.

A jolt of energy shot from the archangel's corpse and burned violently through Grace's entire body. Her eyes exploded light as pain ripped through her every nerve. Squeezing her eyes shut and screaming to contain the surge of raw power, Grace almost lost consciousness.

With Gabriel's great life force now exhausted, his large form dissolved into ash. Grace shuddered as her body and spirit snapped back to the physical realm of the A & E.

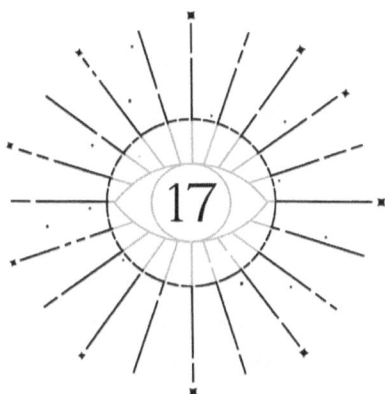

# 17

At 6:30 p.m. on London's central line, commuters were packed like sardines into a train that was hotter than a furnace and screeching like a banshee. This particular route and time of day was as bad as the Tube in London got. The oxygen-starved atmosphere was laden with body odour, engine grease, and soot particles. With the conditions putting added stress on the already exhausted and overworked humans on board, Scratitch saw it as the optimal environment to cause some delicious disorder and test the limits of the human psyche.

A gangly and hunched lower form of dark angel, Scratitch had become twisted by aeons of servitude in the Pit. The odd-looking creature was enjoying a rare break from the drudgery of torment he purveyed over in the realms below as Abaddon's right-hand gimp.

As the commuter train carriage whined to a halt at its next stop, Scratitch followed the flood of new arrivals. The contorted being observed the usual disconnect on board, every traveller's head being buried in their devices or reading material. The obvious discomfort and awkwardness that such close contact brought to British people was palpable. Waving and flailing in front of a few commuters like a muppet, Scratitch tried to break any one of them out of their mindless drone state.

With a maniacal giggle, Scratitch connected his mischievous energy to a newspaper reader's hand. As the reader flipped to another page, his left elbow came within centimetres of a neighbouring businesswoman's face. The businesswoman, unimpressed by the man's disregard for his very public surroundings, shot him a spiked glare. As the reader struggled with the broadsheets, which became more and more tangled with the turn of each page, he himself was reaching a boiling point. The businesswoman tried to avoid his erratic elbow movements, unsure if she should try to help the thrashing, antisocial moron. Discomfited glances and smirks flitted around the tube train at the newspaper reader's kerfuffle. Scratitch continued his mischievous exploration by using the Dark Light and making a beckoning motion towards the tube doors at the approaching stop. As the mechanical doors slid open, Scratitch's red darts of energy pulled a raucous band onto the train, blaring at full trumpet-tooting volume. Reactions from the weary commuters were immediate. Most rolled their eyes at their rotten luck in picking this particular carriage. Scratitch, on the other hand, danced in circles, whipping his goofy limbs through the air to the beat.

The dark angel was absolutely in his element.

Warping in through a flaming ethergate at the other end of the carriage, Abaddon stepped towards a vacant seat and cuddled up to an oblivious female passenger. Pure sex appeal oozed from the passenger's pores. Abaddon proceeded to boost the woman's ego with his presence while she went about fixing her makeup in a pocket mirror. Drowning in boredom, the sexy woman decided to make duck-lip-pose selfies for her social media profile. Several distracted commuters looked on, bemused by the display. The woman's narcissism was so far out of proportion with reality that it was laughable.

Abaddon's interest was next piqued by a fit-looking gym girl in workout gear opposite him. Flipping sides of the carriage, he perched close to the gym girl, seeping his intoxicating influence into her aura.

"Tasty, isn't she?" the Lord of the Pit suggested. At his words, the gym girl became utterly transfixed by the sexy woman on the other side of the train.

Meanwhile, Scratitch continued to dance wildly and incite chaos. The twisted celestial pulled a drunken rugby player and his two teammates in on the band's revelling. An old gentleman in smart 1920s evening wear looked on disparagingly at the display, unaware that his ensemble bore a striking resemblance to that of the Monopoly man—top hat, monocle, and all.

"Let's see you twerk that sexy booty, pops!" the hefty rugby player called out to the gentleman.

"Excuse me?" the insulted upper-class twit blurted out. The rugby player replied in a would-be Monopoly-man voice.

"Do not pass Go. Do not collect £200. Go directly to jail!"

His two teammates burst into laughter.

"I will not be made a fool of, thank you very much!"

Poking the old gentleman with a blast of the Dark Light, Scratitch prompted him to stand upright and lash out with his cane. *Crack!* The diamond-shaped head connected directly with the bridge of the rugby player's nose.

"Aaow! You broke my feckin' nose!" the rugby player moaned. Watching the variety of emotions explode all around him, Scratitch bounced with glee.

The two form-driven women on the other end of the carriage were now exchanging shifting glances. The sexy woman became increasingly irritated. Abaddon captured her mood with the Dark Light and triggered an aggressive outburst.

"Do you have something you want to say, or are you just going to stare all day?" the sexy woman barked. The gym girl blinked rapidly and turned away, her shoulders bunching into her neck.

Back with Scratitch, the bleeding rugby player stood holding his throbbing nose in shock. A teenage girl seated nearby with her friends piped up to add to the commotion: "Nah, bruv, you just got your ass handed to you by the Monopoly man, boyieee!"

Erupting with laughter, both the teenager's friends and the rugby player's teammates reacted to the hilarity of the whole unexpected scenario. Giving yet another poke to fuel the fire, Scratitch generated an overspill of emotion in the rugby player, who dove at the mouthy teenager, grabbing her around the neck. Within seconds, a brawl had broken out between the two groups. Darting about the carriage, Scratitch clapped his hands vigorously like a kid in a candy shop.

Next to Abaddon, the irked sexpot was giving the gym girl both barrels. The dark angel relished every shame-loaded word spat from the woman's mouth.

"Maybe if you took a little more pride in your appearance, you would actually be able to attract someone like me. But look at you. Just look at you. Spending all that time in the gym to make up for your face. Trying oh so hard to get all the boys' attention."

Having had enough of the insecure woman unloading on her, the gym girl jumped out of her seat and slapped the sexy woman hard on the mouth.

"Do you kiss your mother with that filthy mouth?" The gym girl calmly eyeballed the woman, who sat stunned by the brazen slap. The gym girl continued, "For your information, I take care of my body for me."

The sexy woman flew into a screaming rage, attacking the gym girl. Several commuters moved towards the entangled women to help contain the violence, but with heads cannoning backwards and several thrashing slaps meeting the helpful commuters' faces, efforts at containment only pulled them into the fight. As a result, yet another rumbling brawl evolved on the same train carriage.

Stepping back a moment, Abaddon surveyed the heightened viciousness with curiosity, then turned to see the rumble Scratitch had caused at the opposite end of the car. An insightful thought stalled the dark angel. *How has all this been allowed to happen? Usually, with this level of violence, a powerful divine force would attempt to intervene.*

Amid the unrestrained ruckus, Abaddon glanced up, sensing a significant change in the landscape of the upper ether. *It shouldn't be this easy.*

"Scratitch. Come."

"Already not, pleeeease. Me not finished jumpy jumpy time."

"Quit it. We're going!" the Lord of the Pit thundered.

Vanishing in a red blast, Abaddon dragged his companion off to consult with his kin. It was unlike Abaddon and his sidekick to retreat from such a tantalising display of aggression. There were, it would seem, much more serious matters to attend to.

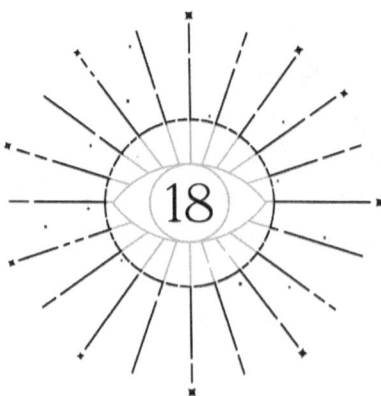

Grace was swimming in stress hormones and still on her knees, slap bang in the middle of the A & E. The laws of physics kicked back into gear as the physical world caught up and shunted her back to reality. The sensation of shifting between worlds hit her like a sledgehammer in the chest, sending her head spinning and blood pumping hard. The hole was gone as if nothing had happened. Not a single patient chart or computer terminal was out of place.

Seeing Grace again, Bhunil dashed to her aid, gathering her up. The consultant had not witnessed her rematerialise in the physical realm and only stumbled upon her after returning from the makeshift triage area to the main room.

"Grace, are you okay? Did you fall? I was wondering where you'd gotten to. I've been rushed off my feet and haven't had a moment to check in with you."

"The ceiling . . . and the desk. There was a hole . . . where he fell."

Bhunil became very concerned. "Who fell? Are you feeling okay?"

"There was this giant wounded man who turned to ash right in front of me. It felt so real. You didn't see anything strange?"

"Grace, I'm not sure what to say to you, but I didn't see anything of the sort. We'd finally got everything under control before I turned and saw you staring at the floor here right next to me. Maybe your tiredness and stress levels are so high that you were hallucinating? I thought you were in cubicle six with a patient, anyway?"

"I was, but I lost the patient. Then I heard this unearthly crash, and when I came out, there was this giant man lying just there, and the scheduling desk was completely crushed underneath him," Grace said, pointing.

Bhunil stared at Grace blankly, fearing for her mental health.

"You didn't see anything?" Grace hated his worried expression.

"Nothing like you're describing. Listen, Grace, I think you need to get home and get some sleep. The staff shortages over the last few weeks have been hard on all of us. When was the last time you were able to get more than a few hours?"

"I honestly can't remember."

"Exactly. You need to get some proper rest."

"But what about the rest of you?"

"I called in cover when the crash victims started pouring in. Two on-call doctors will be here any minute. Plus, it's my job to worry about these things, not yours. Go on to the back office and take ten minutes to gather yourself. I'll call you a taxi in the meantime, and then you can get home for some sleep."

"Are you sure? I really hate to leave all you guys in the lurch."

"You know me. I wouldn't say it if I didn't mean it," Bhunil reassured her with a kind smile.

"Alright, thank you so much."

Grace felt dazed and her limbs heavy. Bhunil was more than a little worried that she might be slipping back into her previous condition as he watched her move off. That period of her life had been terrible to witness, and he had done his best to cover for her numerous absences. It had been almost three years since her last episode, and Bhunil knew she was getting help. He had insisted on it. Since then, Grace had done a lot of work to peel back the grimy layers of self-doubt and pull her shining personality back to the surface.

Grace trundled through the ward with her head down. She was a jittery bag of frayed emotions. Again. Not wanting to burden Haylene with picking up the pieces yet another time, Grace contemplated phoning the only person she had left to confide in: her mum. Locking the toilet door behind her in the staff bathroom and pulling out her phone, she stared at the device in hesitation. Her mum, Sorchia, was a last resort in these sorts of situations and had often failed to be supportive in the past.

Grace and her mother's relationship had been fraught during her teenage years. Sorchia was controlling and a bit of a know-it-all, which went hand in hand with her career as a university lecturer, but Grace had always felt that her mother's approach to raising children didn't have to be so cold. Of course, this was an oversimplification of the issues at hand. It wasn't Sorchia's fault that she was a less emotive creature. The problems in Grace's family dynamic stemmed from the loss of her father when she was a young girl.

Jimmy Colopy. What a man he was.

Grace missed him tremendously in the deepest reaches of her heart. He stood above all other men in his truly selfless love and his endless acts of kindness. Always ready with a knowing smile and a story to break the tension in a room, Jimmy had been the soft centre of their home that warmed Sorchia's frosty edges. As for Grace, Jimmy was her one and only—the sole person who understood her sensitivity and complexity in a largely conservative society. As a police officer during the 1990s in Northern Ireland, Jimmy was a beacon of light in the darkness. Nothing seemed to overwhelm him. He took everything in stride, sucking up all the terror and violence and mustering every ounce of himself to protect the innocent. Jimmy had not once faltered in his courage, right up until the moment of his demise.

Jimmy and Sorchia had met in an explosion of passion and dancing in an Irish bar. After learning that she was pregnant with Grace, Sorchia moved from Surrey to Northern Ireland to be with Jimmy. He had been so charming and promised her the world, adamant that Northern Ireland would not be forever. A part of Grace felt that her mum resented her for causing the family's move to such a bleak place as Belfast, a move that stunted Sorchia's intellectual prime and career advancements. After Jimmy's death, Grace and her mum moved back to Southern England, and Sorchia steadily became more detached and lost in her PhD. Mother and daughter lived separate lives under the same roof—no more soft centre or heart to warm the cold.

Back in the toilet stall, Grace snapped out of her daydream and looked down again at her phone. She desperately needed to vent the crippling stress closing in around her. She was out of options, and her mum would have to do.

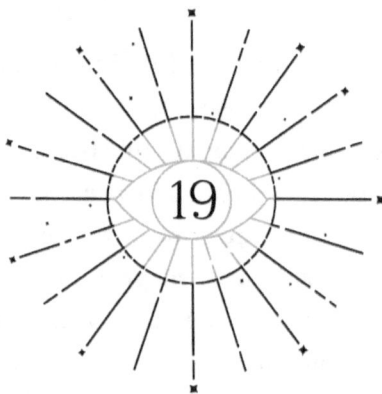

# 19

If anywhere could be called home for the Damned on the physical plane, it was here. The multitude of hexagonal stones stretching into the frothy sea at the Giant's Causeway always helped ease his torn spirit. Adding an impressive backdrop to the prehistoric volcanic formations were the dramatic cloudscapes that rolled above this part of the world. Sometimes they were stacked dense with moisture and greying against gaps of piercing sunlight; at other times, the sky shone crisp and clear, reflecting a variety of sunset colours. The scenery on the northern coast of Ireland was truly breathtaking.

It was sunrise, known as the "magic hour" in photography circles due to the special way the sun's rising light threw warm tones across the sky. The orange and pinkish hues reflecting off the sea's waters and puddles in the stone hollows provided the Damned with an even sense of calm. But what the Damned enjoyed the most was the ancient feel of bygone times the hexagonal stone shafts rising from the coastline gave the Giant's Causeway, drawing him back here whenever he sought solace from the strife of his existence.

It served to remind him of better days—the days before his exile.

The Damned had stood here many times before that fateful moment, proudly surveying the evolving creation of the earth in all its magnificence. The welcoming of the new beings to be birthed on the planet had been the Damned's chief task. He had led hosts of other celestials in worship of the coming new world. Echoing choruses had poured from his clan's mouths as the stones beneath his feet formed from molten lava in an epic scene worthy of his once awe-inspiring angelic class. This was before his class was cast out and the Damned's original name was stripped from him. Events that, to this day, he had no memory of.

The predictability of his movements before his exile had led to his eventual betrayal—a blind spot that only a select few of his angelic brethren had the courage or ability to exploit. Once they pillaged his glory, those who plotted against him saw it fitting that he should be cast out to the very spot he had treasured the most.

*A cruel gesture.*

The Damned watched the crashing waves and imagined how the sea spray and cooling wind might feel on his face. These brief moments were all that remained of his commune with the Universe. He had been ripped violently away from his celestial family, doomed to serve in the lower realms. Like an amputee with permanent phantom pain, his whole self panged with longing to be reunited with his upper celestial kin. Sadly, the Damned knew it was an impossible dream, and certainly one he had no power to achieve. The crushing irony that came with his exile was that the earthly beings he had been so excited to meet had come to look upon him with fear and disdain. His darkened form and wicked role filled them with hate. His ability to connect with them was crippled. All he could do was watch as humanity developed a numbing ignorance to the beauty and complexity of the cosmos he knew and cherished.

Alas, to them, maybe ignorance was bliss.

The causeway's primordial sense of foreboding and mystery had lived on. Other than his history here, this unique part of the planet was also a refuge from the madness that living alongside humans could bring. This madness had wearied him beyond belief. The Damned looked down at his fists—bound in golden glowing wire, throbbing with pain.

"Why do you leave us all in the dark?" the Damned questioned, hoping that for once his plea might be heard by the great spirit of the

Universe. The dark angel moved his gaze slowly upwards, at a loss as to why mankind still had to endure such suffering. He called out to the ether above in frustration. "Why must I continue on this path, making humanity doubt their goodness, pushing on their fear?"

Nothing.

"Surely it has been long enough. They need your strength now more than ever," the Damned barked. A howling wind picked up across the ocean, bringing a thick band of angry waves towards the shore. Crashing hard on the hexagonal stones, the waves sent a blast of hot luminescence rippling through him. A flash of the glorious golden being from his previous vision filled his mind. Staggering backwards, the Damned winced and pressed in on his head with his bound and marred fists.

Suddenly landing through an orb of the Dark Light, Abaddon warped in behind the Damned with Scratitch in tow.

"You still speak with the Universe after all that has passed?!" Abaddon said spitefully. The Damned straightened, responding to his exiled companion with his back still turned.

"It is only I that speaks. Though I do sense a shift of the Light, and a strange new force begins to build."

"The Universe has left us here to rot. Why bother, my lord?" Abaddon added.

"I like rot! Tasty things rotting is! Mmm," Scratitch blurted.

Ignoring Scratitch's juvenile rantings, the Damned and Abaddon continued sparring.

"Our path is with the humans, and we still must serve the balance," the Damned said, reminding Abaddon of their mandate. Abaddon lashed back at his comrade.

"You are the master of this realm! You are God here. These creatures grow weaker as they continue to hope in themselves and—"

"Abaddon!" the Damned roared in a beastly voice, finally turning to look at his right-hand man, flames dancing across his pupils. Abaddon dropped to one knee while Scratitch toppled backwards in fear and scrambled behind a rock like a scolded child.

"Enough, my friend," the Damned said in a softer, exasperated tone. The group fell silent, save for Scratitch, who intermittently poked his head out from behind his rock, his shrill and wavering lamentations resembling those of a demented goat.

"Forgive me, Lord, but they lay to waste all they have been given. I feel it is time they should all know the Pit."

Leaping out from behind cover, Scratitch launched into a Roman Colosseum death chant.

"Pit, Pit, Pit, Pit!"

"Know your place, Abaddon. The time has not yet come for us to—"
*Crack. Thunk. CRUNCH!*

A massive, unearthly noise shuddered from above, shaking the etherverse. The Damned clocked the shift suspiciously.

"Pit?" Scratitch whimpered, staring upwards in confusion.

"Quiet, fool!" Abaddon growled. Another flash of pain tore through the Damned's skull. Almost losing his balance this time, the dark angel was thrown into another crippling vision.

In the Damned's mind's eye, the glowing giant sang that same thunderous chord. Raising its hands, the power of the Light beamed from its mighty eyes in throbbing waves. The music and chorus of voices coming from the being's mouth steadily built to a deafening crescendo.

Disappearing almost as soon as it had begun, the vision released the Damned. The dark angel gasped for air as he was snapped back to the group. He struggled to regain his composure.

"What happened?" Abaddon said, a tremble of uncertainty in his voice.

"I have never felt a pull on the balance of the etherverse this strong before," the Damned muttered.

"What was it you saw?" Abaddon probed.

The Damned paused, not wanting to reveal the nature of his vision for fear of what it could mean. Taking a deep breath, he let the truth tumble out.

"A face long forgotten. My visions have returned, and a primaeval force moves on us all." Needing to address the possibility of linked events, Abaddon struggled to speak about the power he had only just observed in Grace. He opened his mouth to broach the subject but closed it firmly again in hesitation.

"You have witnessed an anomaly in the physical realm, have you not, Abaddon? You should remember that I know you better than you know yourself," the Damned said.

"I did. Lord, you . . . you should know that . . ."

"Spit it out."

"Well, there may be a new seer."

Scratitch immediately began a new chant, this time his tone more upbeat, like that of a high school cheerleader.

"Seer! Seer! Seer!"

Abaddon landed a giant backhanded slap right on Scratitch's mouth. The twisted gimp yelped as he retreated behind his familiar rock, cuddling against it like a frightened spider.

"When did you learn of this?" the Damned said.

"Only today a woman looked directly at me and spoke to me. When I followed, she was visibly affected by my presence."

"This shift may be bigger than we know. Gabriel did foretell of this, after all. What knowledge have you of my other divine kin?"

"They attempt to commune with her, but she does not yet fully understand her ability. I also have felt a movement within the humans. Their hearts become more divided, splitting under the pressure of a widespread spiritual imbalance," Abaddon said.

"There has not been a war since the infancy of this world. But the cracks are appearing." Glancing out to sea, the Damned observed that the mounting waves seemed to crash more violently against the rugged coast. "Abaddon, keep searching for others that appear gifted. This time, try to do it discreetly, my friend. It seems a subtler approach is needed with this woman."

Scratitch sniggered at Abaddon's scolding, and his master threw out a hand and twisted his ward's ear, almost tearing it off. Scratitch squirmed and cowered, fearing the anger of his master and even more so the wrath of the Damned, who was staring him down with a domineering gaze.

"Come now," Abaddon snarled as the pair vanished in a blitz of red.

Turning away from the coast, the Damned knew that something truly abhorrent was fast approaching. In his estimation and vast experience of celestial clashes, he was certain that only one force could be responsible for such spiritual destabilisation. Still, not even he could be sure of when or how such a force would materialise. This realisation presented a huge problem for his dark angels and an even bigger problem for the human race.

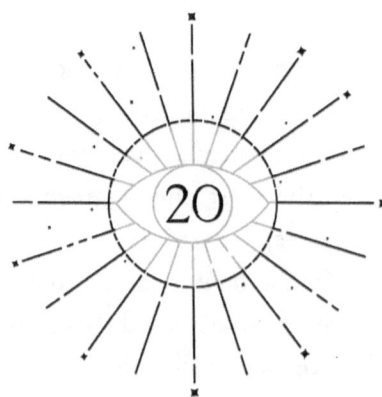

# 20

Wandsworth prison's west wing mess hall looked like a battlefield. Jack and Eddie made it their mission to get cuffs on each of the battered inmates. As they guided one prisoner after another to their feet and into their cells, the jovial pair bantered like two ladies at the hairdresser.

"Did you see my baton throw? It was so sweet! I'll have to watch that one back on the security footage to see if it looks as cool as it felt."

"You did well, matey, especially for being so drastically out of practice."

"Thanks, mate. You didn't do too badly yourself. You move pretty well for a man of your advanced years," Eddie jibed.

"It's all down to the morning wheatgrass shakes and my Pilates tribe, you know."

"Really?"

"No, ye eejit! Jeez, we do have a lot of catching up to do, don't we?"

"Yes indeedy."

Prisoner 5 was a lead weight of misery and dizziness, making manoeuvring him into his cell no small feat; nonetheless, Jack gave it his best shot. As Eddie moved along behind Jack and the inmate, he happened upon a molar that had been dislodged at the root, with a few strands of bloody gum flesh still attached.

"Oh, this is a nice one! Is this yours, muggins?" Eddie hollered towards Prisoner 5, who immediately swivelled to see the tooth and tongued the inside of his mouth in horror.

"Fuuuck," the prisoner moaned. Eddie passed the tooth over to Jack, who snickered at the sweet karma of it all. Prisoner 5 continued to check his mouth in the cell mirror and started spiralling into a frenzy at his rotten luck.

"No, no, no. My missus is gonna absolutely kill me!" the inmate lamented.

"You never know. She might be into the meth-addict-chic look. I hear it's popular with the kids these days," Jack joked.

Sharing a laugh at the prisoner's frustration, Jack and Eddie turned to each other and smugly slapped out a crisp high-five. Moving to the side of the mess hall to pick up a mop, Eddie grimaced at his aching ribs.

"I'll do that. You sit yourself down," Jack said as he grabbed the mop from his wounded friend. "You took some serious knocks there, pal. There's definitely some fight in the old dog yet."

"Well, this little fracas sure wasn't any worse than my missus dishes out after two bottles of Pinot Grigio."

"Now, that I'd like to see," Jack said. "Sit." He pointed to the nearby table.

"Thanks, Causer," Eddie said as he nodded in appreciation. Settling into a chair, Eddie watched Jack fish out the grimy mophead and swish it back and forth across the floor. It was an oddly therapeutic sight. As he zoned out to the rhythmic sloshing, Eddie was struck by how nice it was to see his oldest mate again. It had brought an unexpectedly soothing feeling of fullness. Jack, on the other hand, drifted off into the past as he dragged the wet mophead through a pool of blood on the tiled floor.

## AFGHANISTAN, TEN YEARS AGO

In a temporary medic unit on the outskirts of Basra, a tall, muscular woman paced like a roaming wolf. Sectioned off from the inner treatment tent, the makeshift waiting area was dwarfed by the special ops weapons sergeant's beastly presence. Braen was a mess of sweat and veins, searching for a target to smash.

As her commanding officer of several years, Jack knew the best way to deal with his weapons sergeant in her current state was to stay calm and avoid eye contact. Braen would find her way out of her red mist, eventually. Jack stared at the wall, waiting, nagged by guilt.

"I should have been at the front," Jack said.

"That halfwit charged on ahead. It's his own fault for not following orders and thinking he knew better. A mistake he won't soon make again."

"Still, it's on me."

"Horsecrap! Bleeding ragheads ambushed us. They did this, Cap, and don't you forget that," Braen snapped, slicing her massive arm through the air in protest. Slipping through the double tent flaps, a gaunt, bespectacled Army doctor exited the temporary operating room. Jack jumped up like a shot in anticipation.

"He's a lucky man. If you hadn't got him here so quickly, he would have bled out right there on—"

"So he's gonna be okay?" Braen interrupted loudly.

"He will be, but he desperately needs rest. You've got two minutes and not a moment longer."

"Thanks, Doc," Jack said.

Rushing in ahead of Jack, Braen was greeted by the sight of the young squaddie sitting up, looking very weak. Both Jack and Braen stalled at the doorway and took in the tangled web of tubes and machines helping the soldier recover.

"You gave us a scare there for a while, you little prick," Braen snapped.

"Yeah. I messed up bad. Guess I should have followed your orders, Cap," the squaddie conceded, dipping his head.

"Friggin' right you should have," Braen said.

"Braen, I think he's been through enough today, don't you?" Jack said in a gentle tone that immediately blunted Braen's sharp demeanour. The mountain of a woman looked down at her feet and took a step back, folding her arms behind her back.

"Sir, yes sir."

"I promise it won't happen again," the wounded team member vowed.

"I know it won't, soldier. We live and we learn, don't we?" Jack said encouragingly.

"Yes sir!" the squaddie squawked as he attempted to salute, flinching from his abdominal wounds.

"At ease, soldier. You'll be up and about in no time," Jack reassured him. Reentering the makeshift hospital, the Army doctor signalled that their time was up.

"I need to clean up in here, folks, and my patient needs some rest."

"Let me sort this, Doc. I want to stay with him," Jack stated with a cold and knowing glare that only an officer could deliver, reframing his request as an order. The Army doc nodded in acknowledgment and left to get back to his long list of casualties. Braen, on the other hand, hesitated, not wanting to leave the rest of her unit in this time of need. Jack had the greatest respect for Braen in this regard. She was loyal and fierce, a lethal combination.

Jack beamed widely at Braen, his disarming charm barely cracking a small smile from the warrior woman always at his side. Only he had the respect and connection with Braen that could force any glimmer of joy from the steely weapons expert. Other men had tried and lost several teeth in the process.

"Go on. You hit the showers," Jack said. Braen gave a curt nod at the order and strode purposefully from the medic unit. Taking hold of the mop in the corner and rinsing it in its bucket, Jack began to clean up after the squaddie's life-or-death operation. He swished it back and forth, moving through the bloodstains, water and blood mixing together in a long-streaked pattern.

Jack found himself staring at the bloody prison mop. Dragging it to the bucket, he rinsed thoroughly and watched the blood dilute into a swirling, burgundy mix of bleach and death. He twisted it dry in the draining cradle, and the mophead was fresh and ready to go again. If only it were so easy to wipe away the ruinous memories he was chained to. Wherever he went, blood had always followed him—past, present, and most certainly future.

Jack wiped the sweat from his forehead as he finished up and rolled his shoulder to loosen the tension that had accumulated there. From the mess hall table, Eddie regarded him quizzically. Setting the cleaning materials to the side, Jack turned back to the room and caught his friend's furrowed expression.

"Mate, what's going on with your love life?" Eddie said bluntly, not one to beat around the bush, especially after all this time.

"What love life?" Jack deflected.

"Come on, tall, dark, and handsome; you can't play dumb with me," Eddie persisted. Using his humour, Jack tried again to redirect from the touchy subject.

"Where's this coming from? One moment you're babbling on about your favourite meat pie, and the next you're acting like the new perma-tanned host of *Love Island*."

"Seriously, mate, you haven't patched things up with your ex yet?" Eddie said. Knowing his oldest friend wasn't going to let up, Jack paused to consider how to get out of the corner he was in. Eddie simply waited, raising his eyebrows and flipping his palms to the ceiling in expectation.

"I'm just not sure I'm ready for that," Jack finally mumbled.

"Mate, it's been three years."

"I know, but I still need time."

"That's bollocks, and you know it. You couldn't get away with this crap when we were kids, and you sure as hell can't get away with it now."

Eddie was right, but Jack couldn't bring himself to admit it. Instead he looked down at the floor in a trance.

"Look, we all make mistakes, every friggin' day, and we have to live with them. You also gotta find a way to forgive yourself in here," Eddie said, tapping his chest and searching Jack's face for a reaction. "Plus, you're a complete miserable git on your own."

"Jeez! When did you start worshipping the moon and getting on the kale juice cleanses?" Jack scoffed.

"Alright, alright! You do need to get over yourself, though."

"Do us a favour, will ya? Quit the lecture and get the kettle on."

"Now, there's an idea. A good cup of tea makes everything better," Eddie said, rubbing his hands together and grimacing from his bruises as he struggled to stand.

"I've got a wee bit o' somethin' extra special for us to throw in," Jack added as he took out his hip flask and jiggled it for Eddie to see.

"You wee beaut! Now we're talking. I think we both deserve a little tipple after that WWE-style rumble."

Jack gave Eddie a look of deep respect; he was a proper friend. Though he'd managed to escape facing some hard truths, Jack had been presented with a stark reminder of his gnawing regret—regret that no amount of whiskey could ever wash away.

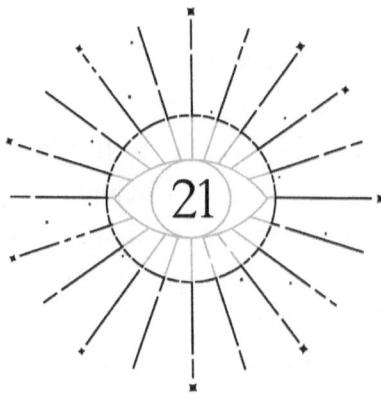

## 21

Dr. Sorchia Collopy marched up the back of Edinburgh Castle along the short, winding stretch of the Royal Mile. As usual in Scotland's historic capital city, a near gale-force wind howled under a grey sky that threatened heavy rain at any minute.

Carrying a military backpack and with her blond hair in a tight ponytail, Sorchia looked more like an ageing Army general than a university professor. Her shoulders were wider and stronger than most men her age, and the rippling sinews on her forearms spoke of a lifetime of boxing training routines and pull-ups. Contrasted by her sleek-muscled appearance were her full, soft lips and large, strikingly blue eyes that glinted behind a pair of fashionable, thick-rimmed glasses.

Even though scaling this section of the Royal Mile was a battle every day, Sorchia secretly loved it. Being fitness mad and relishing any moment to squeeze in high-intensity exercise, Sorchia welcomed the challenge of getting a better time on her regular climb than the day before.

Grinding up pavement and glancing at the stopwatch on her wrist, Sorchia turned her gaze to admire the foreboding beauty of the castle above. Any castle this size seemed somewhat unreal, as if it had been superimposed atop the hill by the wizardry of special effects. The monstrous beast of a building reminded her of a sleeping stone dragon. It almost threatened to come alive and breathe a wrathful fire of vengeance on the city below. As Sorchia reached her halfway point, she cast her mind back to imagine what it would have been like to try to assault this dominant fortress that sat more than 200 metres above the base of the hill it perched on.

Any approaching force would be seen coming for miles in every direction. If any foot soldiers survived the rain of arrows and cannon fire and actually made it to the bottom of the hill, there was still the impossible climb. A rocky and uneven wall that was too high to throw grappling ropes over made the backside of the castle a natural barrier. Even if one or two excellent climbers made it part of the way up, vats of boiling oil poured from above would melt their skin and helmets, either bringing heart failure from the pain or causing the assailants to slip to their deaths.

Thinking upon this, Sorchia was glad that she lived in the modern age and that the imposing war fortress was now a world-renowned attraction with a convenient and smooth pavement on which to make the climb.

At the top, Sorchia nipped across the bustling cobbled street packed with tour buses and excited travellers. They were of course mostly American or Chinese. The Americans loudly announced how "cute" everything was and mindlessly spent money hand over fist for any trinket with a castle or thistle on it. The Chinese visitors swarmed the streets like wild deer, smacking into locals and street vendors without a care for anyone's safety.

Tourism in general disgusted Sorchia. It cheapened the importance of every historical site in the city, and Edinburgh was a treasure trove. Quickly weaving her way to work, Sorchia passed a number of fifteenth-century buildings. A truly wondrous sight to anyone seeing it for the first time, it was old news to Sorchia. The professor ducked through an alleyway and came to her destination: Edinburgh University's New College.

Not quite as old as its surroundings, New College was otherwise remarkable for its gothic, eighteenth-century evangelical architecture, no doubt built on the backs of zealous Christian peasants. It had been designed as an eminent centre for theological studies. To this day, it continued in that same theme, with only a few more modern anthropological courses having crept into its classrooms.

Social anthropology was Sorchia's area of expertise and one that had fascinated her from a very young age. With a powerful mind and a voracious appetite for reading, it had taken Sorchia no time at all to achieve her PhD. Edinburgh University had been lucky to snap her up, a fact that she was acutely aware of. The stuffy, narrow-minded gentleman's club on the board of Oxford University had blocked her transfer to her home university. Oxford was, in her mind, where she and her unmatched talent truly belonged, but the board had denied her a place out of spite on account of her numerous clashes with influential benefactors at Oxford alumni dinners.

Such was Sorchia's Achilles' heel. She would sooner plunge her face in a deep fat fryer than suck up to rich idiots and ply a room with social graces. Even though she studied ancient civilisations and was fascinated by a wide array of historical figures, when it came to the crunch, Sorchia was not great with people. Hopeless, in fact.

As she barrelled into the college's main lecture hall, the room fell silent before her, evidence of the respect and tight rule of law Sorchia commanded from her students. Not only was she a hard taskmaster, but Sorchia had also risen above her peers in writing several famous books on prehistoric civilisations. Her published works always drew in quite the crowd, and today was no exception. Wasting no time, as was her way, the eminent Dr. Sorchia Collopy flicked on her slide projector and launched straight into her address.

"Ancient civilisations and their various iconography have depicted divine beings existing in the skies since our earliest ancestors looked to the stars for guidance. Within the first *Homo sapiens* tribes, meaning was not found within the self but rather from the perceived magic of creation. Art was also used as a way to convey abstract ideas about supernatural beings."

Flicking to the next image and pausing, Sorchia wistfully regarded the slide, which depicted a prehistoric goddess sculpture.

"As we can see here, some of our ancestors' original idols worshipped the idea of a divine feminine, mother to all creation. It is in our nature as human beings to worship something higher—to strive for an ideal, to hope in things we cannot understand."

Sorchia paused again and this time cast her gaze across the room of captivated students. She had a natural ability to grab the attention of a room by imparting her enthusiasm in an eloquent manner. "Thinking from a modern-day perspective, what are some examples of humanity's predisposition to worship something higher?" Sorchia asked the lecture group.

"Fantasy TV show fans?" a chipper dreadlocked woman responded.

"Yes, very good. People immerse themselves in a fantasy they cannot achieve, giving them the confidence to live out their own lives and empower their choices."

"Athletic superstars?" another added, this time a slender, bespectacled young man.

"Well, in a way, yes. To a lesser extent, however. Athleticism is more physical and less conceptual or spiritual. Yes, it addresses the idea of belief, but it is an ideal that can be understood and even attained with a dedicated application to training. It is not a higher worship as such but a worship of the self and something that is natural rather than supernatural."

"What about Kim Kardashian's ass? That's pretty supernatural," a snarky young man in the back row blurted out. The lecture hall erupted with laughter. Sorchia shot the young man daggers, and the whole room quickly fell silent. Every single one feared what punishment the unfortunate snarky young man was about to receive.

"Well, Mr. Smith, I'd hazard to say that if you applied as much attention to your reading list as you did to studying Miss Kardashian's rear end, then you'd be up here giving this lecture rather than me." The lecture hall filled with laughter, the cool and collected response burying the snarky student in his own hot embarrassment.

"Let's take five minutes in groups of four to discuss further, shall we? Write down your discussion points, please, and we'll bring them to the room afterwards."

The hall of students broke up into groups as instructed. Removing lecture materials from her bag, Sorchia briefly checked her phone and saw not one but three missed calls from Grace.

*It's a bit odd of her to be calling at this time, and to be calling more than once.*

"Make that ten minutes of group discussion, class," Sorchia instructed her students. Escaping into the corridor to discover what was happening with her daughter, she paused before dialling to ready herself for the worst.

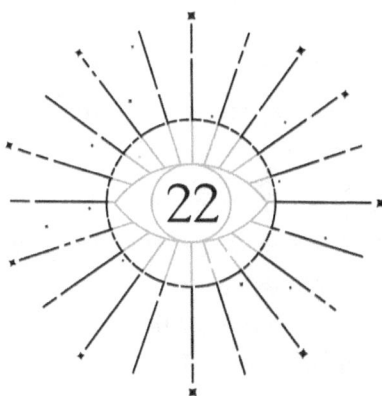

## 22

At London Zoo, Andy and Haylene were enjoying an exciting day trip, examining the spectacular array of creatures within and bopping around the colourful information boards. Currently in the crocodile section, Andy was transfixed by a lengthy saltwater croc from Southeast Asia slapping about in the water below. It was as if his evil Lizard Lord action figure had come to life right before his very eyes.

"Woah, he's massive! And pretty scary," Andy commented.

"Did you know that they are one of the dinosaurs' last living relatives?" Haylene added.

"That is so cool."

"Also, there is still a part of our human brain that is exactly the same as this crocodile's."

"What? That's mental. How come?"

"The oldest part of our brains is our reptilian brain, which signals danger and engages our emotional response to events around us. As humans developed, our brains grew, and we were able to know whether something unknown to us was dangerous or not. Instead of just reacting with fear or anger like this croc does, we can use our larger brains to think logically. Do you remember when we talked about what logic is?"

"Yeah, it's when we try to calm our emotions and see things with just the facts."

"That's right! Well remembered. Do you remember why we try to do that?"

"You said it was because anger and pain can bring fear, and fear can make us do silly things."

"Exactly, Andy. Now, do you see Lizard Lord's long-lost cousin here crawling along on his belly and snapping angrily?"

"He doesn't look very happy."

"Exactly. That's because he's afraid of creatures like you and me, so he grunts and claps his teeth. Every day we have to acknowledge the part of our brain that is like his and looks for danger but not let it rule our actions."

"But what if he wants to eat me?"

"Good question! Then you run away and hide or climb a tree and wait. The main thing is to not panic so you can see your choices clearly."

"What does panic mean?"

"It means to be very fearful, and as you said, that makes us do silly things."

"Oh, okay. I think I get it."

"Shall we go see my favourites? They have the most in common with us."

"Who are your favourites?"

"The monkeys!" Haylene jumped up and down, wildly performing her very own monkey impression. "Ou ou ah ah!" She ran up to Andy and pretended to pick nits out of his hair as a primate would. Giggling and squirming, Andy ran away laughing. "I bet I can beat you there!" Haylene shouted. Chasing after Andy and pointing ahead, Haylene raced him to the monkey enclosure.

A sudden scream rent the air as Haylene and Andy were racing past the lion enclosure's entrance.

"Mummy!" the same voice cried. A massive lion's roar followed. Changing course and darting around the corner into the viewing area, Andy came face-to-face with the mighty beast prowling behind the bars. A wailing three-year-old boy was being held in his mother's arms for comfort.

Mesmerised by the sheer power of the creature before him, Andy ogled its magnificent presence and beautiful mane. The predator sat on its haunches and eyeballed Andy. Haylene raced into the enclosure viewing area to see the boy and the lion studying each other. With no words spoken, the moment of boy meeting beast had brought a soft stillness to the enclosure, both outside of and within the cage. One by one, a female and two young male lions at the back of the enclosure moved up next to the male facing Andy.

The scared child had stopped crying, and both he and his mother were watching the exchange of respect and oneness between Andy and the pride of lions. The whole family of predators now sat together in a line, looking at Andy, all adopting a relaxed sitting position next to the adult male—as if they awaited young Andy's command. Haylene stood stunned as Andy turned and grinned.

"I've helped the lovely lions be calm, Auntie."

"Yes, Andy. Yes, you have," Haylene said.

With a wave to the lions and a skip in his step, Andy dashed to the exit of the viewing area. The mother and toddler were left frozen on the spot.

"Monkey time!" Andy said jovially as he grabbed Haylene's hand and dragged her off. Jogging up to the primate section, Andy led Haylene towards the gibbons.

"Andy, what just happened?"

"What do you mean? I just said hello to the lions. They seemed to like that, and it helped the little boy. He was scared," Andy said. Unsure of how to comprehend the event, Haylene remained speechless.

Now facing the glass of the gibbon enclosure, Andy observed the long-armed primates. His mood shifted into a sombre state as he observed a family of three monkeys huddled for warmth on a tree branch above. The male, female, and baby snoozed contentedly in each other's arms. Andy stared right through the cuddling monkeys.

"What's wrong, buddy?" Haylene said, noticing the mood change.

"Does Daddy not love Mummy anymore?"

"Oh, sweetheart, he does, and you know he loves you, right?"

"Yeah, he sends me a message every day, but he says he's busy and can't come home yet."

"Your daddy'll come soon. I know he will."

"But I miss him," Andy whimpered. Haylene moved closer to put an arm around him.

"Come here. You have to be patient and strong, okay?"

"But I'm tired of missing him. I just want it to be over."

"I'm sure you are. Listen, how about we go see the gorillas? They're big and strong and can help us be strong too!" At this, Haylene straightened up tall and made a bodybuilder pose, showing off her pumped-up muscles and pulling a stupid "sitting on the toilet face" to resemble a Mr. Universe contestant. Andy cracked a little grin.

"Yeah. I'd like that," he said and swiftly joined in on the joke by mirroring Haylene's ridiculous pose. The pair glared resolutely at each other to see who would break position first. Immediately losing her composure at Andy's funny face, Haylene let out a hearty laugh.

"And then ice cream for sure!" Haylene said.

Andy punched his fist in the air and loudly declared in his American action-hero voice, "Ice cream is surely the champion of all evil!"

Laughing and scooping Andy up, Haylene sprinted off with him under her arm, his little excited head bobbling about as they went.

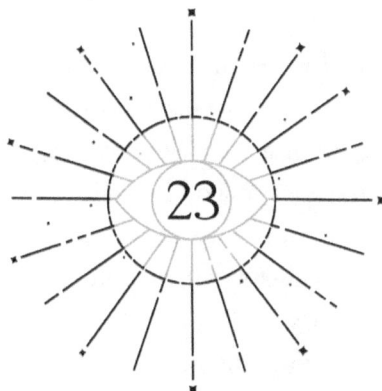

## 23

Grace glided through the streets of North London in an empty daze, moving as if outside of her own body, oblivious to the physical world around her. What happened at the hospital had left her spirit completely spun out, but taking a route home through the park was the best decision she had made all day.

Her worry having subsided for the time being, Grace strolled through the tree-lined path of Mile End Park. She soaked in each meditative step. She didn't know much about the history of this park, but on an emotional level, the weight of it tingled along her every nerve—the devastation, the fires, the immense loss of life. The sadness this piece of land had experienced was palpable. And then she wasn't merely feeling it; she was seeing it.

Grace was certain that the scenes she was suddenly visualising in real time were part of an actual historical event. In fact, the night of terror she pictured was none other than June 13, 1944, one of the worst days in London's Blitz, in which more than fifty-two bombs were dropped from a fleet of German warplanes above.

As she peered up at the sky, bombs rained down. She slammed her hand onto a nearby tree to steady herself, and through the tree itself she beheld craters of fire and dozens of screaming innocents running from factories torn open by explosions. Fleeing the buildings, the factory workers ran in all directions as their flaming bodies lit up the soot-filled sky. Grace gasped in terror, planting her feet to let the intense emotion wash over her as tears of compassion flowed down her cheeks. Unknown to her, a glint of gold flashed over her irises.

Preoccupied with the trauma of the park's past, Grace was unaware of Beel lingering at a safe distance behind her. The sultry dark angel drank in the lustre of Grace's spiritual energy. Having retreated to gather herself, Beel knew she must establish a better understanding of the threat this seemingly lowly nurse could pose to her dark angel class.

*I will watch, and I will wait. Soon she will show me a point of weakness.*

Like a slap to the face, Grace's blaring ringtone broke her out from the vision. She swiftly answered the call.

"Mum! Thank goodness. I am having the most horrifying day."

"Grace, are you okay? You sound like you're having another one of your panic attacks," Sorchia said.

"I haven't had a panic attack in years now. You know that."

"Well, when was the last time you slept? You sound absolutely exhausted."

"Mum, will you just listen to me?" Grace pleaded.

"Sorry! I'm listening."

"I know this is going to sound crazy, but just hear me out, okay?"

"Alright, go on," Sorchia said, scepticism evident in her snipped tone.

"I saw something at the hospital that I couldn't explain earlier today. This . . . being crashed right down into the A & E, and no one else could see him but me. He had black wounds that wept some kind of dark mucus, like nothing I'd ever witnessed in human physiology, and then after speaking only a few words, he just *disintegrated* right in front of me."

Aghast at this new information, Beel's intoxicating dark eyes widened.

*Could she have seen an angel fall? How did I not sense this?*

"Grace, slow down," Sorchia said.

"I don't think he was real. I mean, he could have been a spirit or a ghost or something. I don't know. Look, I know it's hard to believe, but he spoke directly to me and told me to find someone called the Lightbearer. Does that name mean anything to you?" Grace continued.

At the mention of this long-forgotten celestial force, Beel's interest was further piqued. The dark angel shifted through space, landing next to Grace to gather more information from her aura.

"Grace, are you sure you didn't just dose off for a minute, or maybe you were having a hallucination from sleep deprivation? I know how stressed you can get when your sleep pattern is broken up by your work schedule."

With this final judgment from her mother tipping Grace over the edge, she burst into tears. Beel hovered just several feet from Grace, the power of their opposing energy fields immense.

"I don't know why I bother opening up to you. It's always the same. You're never wrong, and you just can't look at something from my point of view for one minute!" Grace barked.

"Oh, Grace, please don't be like that. I'm sorry, but—"

In a rage, Grace hung up and stormed off through the park. She had been harshly reminded that the only two people she could rely on in this world were Haylene and her precious Andy.

Meanwhile, in Edinburgh, Sorchia stood alone in a cold university corridor, in sheer disbelief that her daughter had hung up on her.

"Grace? Grace, are you there?" Sorchia frowned down at her phone. Grace had never ended a call without saying goodbye before. This uncharacteristic act spoke volumes about how much her child had needed a kind ear.

*For God's sake, Sorchia, why couldn't you have been more supportive!*

When it came to humankind resolving their differences through diplomacy, it didn't matter who was right or wrong in the end; someone just needed to humbly say sorry, and the other party needed to humbly accept that apology. It really was that simple. For all her study of religions and civilisations, Sorchia had always been incapable of applying that valuable knowledge of the human condition to her own life.

Scrambling back into the lecture hall to find a pen, she scribbled LIGHTBEARER in block capitals on the back of a stack of exam papers. If she couldn't be there for Grace as a caring, listening mum, she was damn well going to get to the bottom of her daughter's cryptic vision.

Having frozen in quiet at Sorchia's return, the room full of students sat up like rows of well-trained Labradors, hanging on her every command.

"It seems that you are in luck today, class. Something pressing has come up, so I am going to give you all the rest of this session off towards reading time," Sorchia said.

The room unsettled quickly as students grabbed their belongings and excitedly filed out.

"Please use this time wisely, not forgetting that each of your dissertations will undergo their first review next week!" Sorchia appealed to the rapidly disappearing students.

Unable to put the nagging new term out of her mind, Sorchia bolted from her desk, on a mission to uncover more information.

At that moment, ensconced in the hillside of the Mound below Sorchia's feet, a vast catalogue of ancient texts sat in the darkness of the university's stacks. The entrance lay at the end of a long concrete corridor flanked by row after row of important classical texts.

A blistering beam of the Light shot across the empty corridor, signalling the arrival of an angelic being. Hidden within the archive's middle row, the regal, cloaked entity scoped out her new surroundings. The style of the celestial's robes and coloured trim was identical to that of the recently fallen archangel Gabriel and was none other than

Gabriel's right-hand commander, Chava. The brazen, wide-faced, dark-haired guardian angel did not hesitate in her objective, dashing through the underground space like lightning, moving to the final row of religious texts, marked Judeo-Christian Mythology.

At the opposite end of the long corridor, the main access door creaked open on rusty hinges. Pulling a string dangling from the ceiling next to her, Sorchia clicked on the overhead lights, which blinked and hummed. She proceeded to methodically peruse each row's category as she referred to her large notepad, which showed a full page of illegible scrawls, arrows, and underlines. Sorchia was enthralled by this fresh hunt for information—her bread and butter as a lecturer and writer. At a brisk pace, she reached the final row and glanced up to confirm the subject matter held within.

The focused professor was unaware of the divine sentinel standing within touching distance at the back end of the aisle. Quickly finding the target of her search, Sorchia reached out to remove it from the middle shelf. A dramatic twist from the watching angel's palm nudged a large red book off the top shelf to land with a thud at Sorchia's feet. Bending to pick it up, she stood just as Chava was swallowed up from behind by a blazing ethergate. For now the angel's work was done, and she would save her strength for the multitude of challenges ahead. She was more than equal to the task of avenging her dearest companion's execution. It would be a long, slow revenge. She would certainly see to that.

Back in the physical realm, Sorchia couldn't believe her good fortune. The title on the red, leather-bound book read, in an elaborate font, *Angelic Myth: God's Archangels and Their Roles in Creation*.

The quest for enlightenment had begun, and the workings of the celestial realms slowly and quietly churned on in the background.

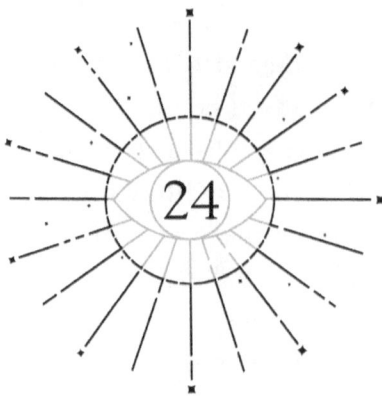

## 24

On the first floor of Mile End Hospital, bus crash victims lay recuperating in the intensive care ward after being moved from the chaos of the A & E below. The ward was eerily quiet for the night, and the steely blue glow of numerous vital-signs monitors gave the room a futuristic ambience. Mr. Patel, who had also been transferred upstairs for observation, snored softly like a purring cat next to a young accident victim, who stared blankly at the ceiling. The young man was the only one wide awake, though his appearance most resembled those in the morgue. His glazed-over look and pale complexion evidenced the distinct dread winding around in his mind. Twisting to look down at his right shoulder, the patient contemplated the horrors of facing the rest of his life under drastically new circumstances.

His arm was now a miserable, sewn-up stump ending above the elbow. Tingles in his severed nerves kept him from sleeping and sent his mind into overdrive. However, an unexpected wave of positivity washed over the young patient as he scanned the other unfortunates around the ward. Each of them was markedly older and clearly in much worse shape than he was.

Unknown to the patients, two healing angels in their regal, green-trimmed robes stood in the ether, sending regenerative waves of the Light around the room. The taller of the two stood motionless, his eyes closed as he held a hand on the crown of the amputee's head, his palm producing a vibrant green glow. The healing power of the Light was instilling a more positive sense of intention, helping the stricken man's mind recover from its negative pattern. This was the first place any healing angel began: the human mind. Once there was a solid enough shift there, the mortal's unique ability to regenerate would take over.

Standing guard on the other side of the ward, the angel's female comrade remained steadfast and alert.

*Clunk!*

A sound akin to a cracking glacier boomed, indicating that something above had shifted. Snapping her gaze upwards, the angel on guard scanned their immediate surroundings in the etherverse for anything out of place. Trepidation washed over her as she found she was no longer able to communicate with the rest of her class. Some drastic event must have occurred to disconnect her intimate sense of her divine companions.

Another movement. This time the unearthly echo sounded closer in the upper ether.

The meditating angel's eyes snapped open in terror at his sense of the shifting sound's new location. His realisation came too late.

His head spun into the air, cleaved from his neck by a long sword made of pure energy. The head burst into flames and turned to stone in midair as the dead weight of the angel's body slumped towards the ground, disintegrating into a plume of ash.

The stone head's descent was arrested by the massive palm of a chiselled warrior angel. Clothed in blue-trimmed robes, she lowered her glowing sword by her side and stared directly at the healing angel on watch as she crushed the head in an explosion of dust.

Back in the physical realm, Mr. Patel gasped a huge breath and flatlined. The young amputee screamed for attention.

"Help! We need help in here."

The remaining healing angel was a deer in the headlights, paralysed by confusion at the murder of her kin and the brash attack of those she had always considered allies in battle. Never before had a warrior angel turned on a healing angel.

Without warning, a spear of the Light burst from her chest as a second warrior angel appeared, skewering the celestial from behind. Black cracks formed around the speared angel's eyes, mouth, and the lethal chest wound. The weaving lesions of decay crawled over her skin like a spreading virus.

"Why?" the dying angel moaned.

"The balance has tipped," the warrior facing her replied.

Meanwhile, on the physical plane, the young amputee started convulsing. Foam spewed from his mouth. No longer supported by angelic energy, he became overwhelmed by the stress of something he could not see but felt lighting up his nerves.

"You don't have to do this," the angel pleaded, coughing up an oily black liquid. "Michael—he loses his way. Please, sister, do not let him drag you down with him."

The unexpected retort stalled the warrior angel's advance, but her companion twisted his spear deeper and snapped, "Do it now. Before she can heal!"

"I am sorry, sister. The allegiance of the warrior class is steadfast," the warrior said with resignation. Charging up her blades from the Light within herself, the warrior drew back to strike. The broken healing angel closed her eyes in one final prayer.

Separated in two, the celestial's body fell to the ground and dissolved into ash, just as her companion's had.

On the physical plane, Mr. Patel's flatline droned on after the amputee passed out cold. No one was coming to their aid. The new paradigm shifts within the etherverse had served to pull harder on the troubled mortal world, sending it further into decay.

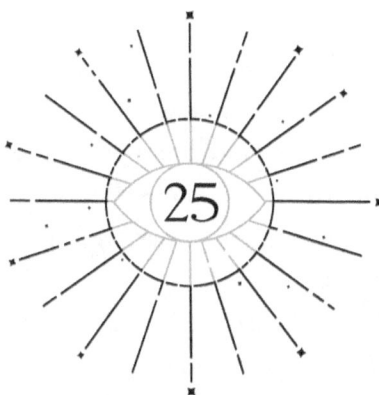

Eddie slumped on the floor beside cell 7's cast iron door, picking his nose. Mining a good one, he pulled it out and studied its size and texture. He was interrupted by three loud bangs on the door.

Eddie catapulted to his feet and heaved open the cell to reveal the prison psychologist, Patrick Lockhart. Although psychologists came in all shapes and sizes, this bearded specimen looked more like an antiestablishment hipster than a qualified clinician. He gave Eddie a tight-lipped, condescending smirk.

"I'd leave the cuffs on him for the moment if I were you," the doctor said.

"No kidding, Sherlock. He almost chewed my face off," Eddie snapped, closing the door behind the doctor. Lockhart drifted into the corridor like a woodland elf; even the way he walked smacked of someone head over heels in love with their own self-importance.

"Yes. Well, I'm sure he's not the first and most likely won't be the last," the doctor remarked.

Eddie simply returned Dr. Lockhart's pretentious smile. "Let's get back to the patient, shall we?"

"Yes, of course. It's a classic case of paranoid schizophrenia, really. Hearing voices, abnormal motor behaviours, hallucinations, etc. I've given him a heavy dose of risperidone that should keep him compos mentis for the moment. But someone will need to check on him every couple of hours or so," the doctor droned.

"Fine. Is that everything?" Eddie said.

"Actually, there was one more thing. Jade kindly informed me that you were rather shaken after the whole incident. She said it seemed to have affected you more than any other event prior that has consisted of such levels of violence?"

"Sure, it was rough. He had me round the throat, but I've survived worse, Doc. Not my first day on the job and all that," Eddie said in a nonchalant manner.

"Still, I've booked you in for a psychiatric evaluation with me at 11 a.m. tomorrow. It is a mandatory part of any incident report in the system."

"Okey-dokey, Doc. Looking forward to it!" Eddie rounded off sarcastically.

"Good. Have a pleasant evening," Dr. Lockhart said.

"Condescending twat," Eddie mumbled, seething, as the doctor turned to head out.

"What was that?" The doctor turned back to Eddie with a scrunched-up nose.

"Oh, I just said I'm betting on that."

"Alright, well, if there's nothing else, good night."

Eddie's fake smile dissolved as Dr. Lockhart left the corridor.

The prisoner inside cell 7 sat handcuffed to his bed, the medication kicking in like a hammer. Bleary eyed, he peered anxiously at the walls and ceiling of the room, his head rolling around in circles.

A tall, lean, olive-skinned warrior angel warped in front of the inmate, kneeling at his level. This was not just any warrior angel but one of the ruthless cherubim, Michael's bodyguard and elite fighting force. Zelda eyed the squirming prisoner from head to toe with a pitiless glare.

"Humans and their weakness," she said, not a hint of emotion in her voice.

"Leave me alone. Please," the prisoner begged.

"You should feel blessed. Lord Michael has chosen you and you alone."

"Forget it. I won't help you again," the prisoner said, shaking his head violently.

"I'm afraid you don't have a choice, little man; your species has been left to their own devices for far too long. Creation deserves better," Zelda said, slowly bringing a hand to his face.

"No, stop. Please!" the prisoner wailed.

"Too little. Too late." Brushing a fingertip against the prisoner's temple, Zelda transformed his eyeballs to a solid, glossy black. Dark cracks crawled in a zigzag pattern around the tortured inmate's sockets. In the familiar, unholy three-tonal voice exhibited during his altercation with Eddie, the prisoner groaned and growled.

Hearing the terrible sounds, two guards rushed from the other side of the cell and stood at either side of the cell door. They glanced at each other, eyelids pinned back, sweating at the prospect of another tussle with the vicious lunatic inside as demonic moans crept out. Nodding, they raised their batons for action and dashed into the cell.

Shouts echoed into the corridor as the guards tried to subdue the rabid prisoner. An unholy scream erupted following a vigorous scuffle that sounded like a bull bucking its horns against concrete.

*Crack!* A baton against the prisoner's skull finally silenced the moans. Across the entire block, the dangling ceiling lights flickered and crackled angrily.

Back at the other end of the wing, in the prison office, Jade had amped up the Ibiza club music and was performing some quite sensational dance moves. Eddie entered to find her mid glow sticks flow.

"What are you doing, love?" Eddie said. Her new audience only encouraged her to continue twerking as if her life depended on it.

"Getting my dance moves warmed up to dazzle the young Greek men," Jade quipped, continuing the show just for him. Eddie got right to the point.

"Can you please explain why Dr. Smarty-Pants was on my back after this morning?"

"Why do you hate him so much? He's a sound bloke, and I'd totally do him. He's definitely that repressed bookish type. I'd make sure he—"

"Jade! Please, leave out the graphic details. I'm really not able to stomach it right now."

"Just saying he could analyse me any day."

"Ugh, Christ." A shiver down Eddie's spine made his torso tremble. "Why did you tell him I was shaken up? He's only gone and booked me in tomorrow for a 'session,' whatever the hell that means. He'll probably subject me to some sort of endless 'answering a question with another question' loop. Man, I hate it when they do that, and it really is the last thing I need after today."

"He's only here to help you, doofus, and you should at least give it a try. You have to admit that you were in a complete state earlier. It'll be good for you to get some things off your chest, matey."

"I've already got some meds that are working. I don't see why I need to tell my secrets to a complete stranger."

"Oh, I hope I meet a couple of strangers on the first night in Mykonos." Jade resumed dancing, now with a moronic smile plastered on her face. Eddie couldn't hold back a guilty snigger.

"Oh God. They have no idea what they're in for, do they?" Eddie said.

Making a tiger-claw gesture, Jade swiped at the air in Eddie's direction. "Grarrrgh!"

"Okay, okay, cool your jets. Good luck with closing up, party animal. I'll catch you in the morning," Eddie said, waving goodbye. Grabbing his things, he headed out through the control room door with a great feeling of relief. He was gagging for a greasy kebab.

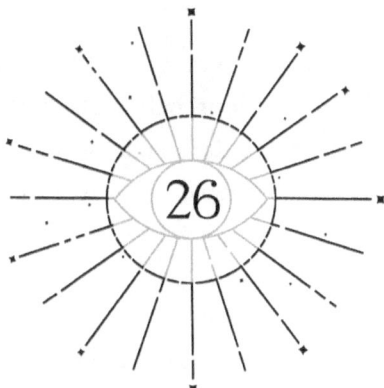

## 26

On a glass-walled dance floor, the Damned glided through the etherverse, sucking up energy from the escaping dark matter all around him. The dark matter—or the Dark Light, as the exiled celestial knew it—was fuelled by the drunken revellers writhing and shaking to the hard house beats blaring from the ceiling speakers.

Humans understood dark matter as an unseen wave of energy that could not reflect light or absorb electromagnetic radiation. Shortly put, they did not understand its significance and untapped power, nor could they conceive how it interacted with human spirituality and physiology. On the other hand, any dark angel's relationship with dark matter was as simple as breathing. The music of the club was thick and edgy, electronic tones grinding through the air like a sputtering chainsaw. These types of densely populated and emotionally charged environments were ideal for the Damned to feed, thereby bolstering his Dark Light body and strengthening his power reserves. Whether it was excitement or pain, each expression of spiritual vibrancy had the same nourishing effect on the dark celestial's energy field. It was a necessary process considering the threat looming over his angelic kin from the upper ether.

Uncertain of how great the arriving force was or where it would strike, the Damned could only wait and muster as much of the Dark Light as possible to prepare for the onslaught. It was a fight he would not back down from, a chance to exact a hefty measure of misery from those who had betrayed him long before the earth was formed. The humans might appear pitiful to the angelic armies above, but they were his humans, and the earth and lower ether were his to command. Any and every upper celestial bringing war to these realms would face the full might of his crippling power.

The Damned's mind was made up.

Next to the solid granite bar at the back of the dance floor of cascading lights, three raucous socialites were slamming back shots. A group of female twenty-somethings nursed their drinks along the booth-lined wall nearby, making their best efforts to secretly eye a stag-do group posturing against the opposite wall. These were but two examples filling the atmosphere around the seething dance floor. The Damned's hulking, dark form passed through the centre of the bubbling nightclub, his senses open to absorb what he could from the gyrating mass of bodies. A trendy girl dancing with a handsome guy brushed the edge of the Damned's blood-red aura, causing the physical world to slow down to half speed.

In an instant, the girl's expression turned vicious, and she lashed out at her dance partner, scratching thick cracks into his stunned face. He recoiled backwards. The Damned's eyes flickered orange at the rush of new energy. The Dark Light next came into contact with a nervous teen accompanied by his chubby mate, both vying for the attention of two sexy girls dancing nearby. Again time slowed. Snapping in envy, the nervous teen whipped around and shoved his chubby mate, then proceeded to batter him on the chin for cracking onto the girl he'd set his sights on. More dark matter drifted into the fallen angel's field, adding to his strength.

Turning to observe the dance floor with a more energized carriage, the Damned was content to witness the mosh pit of ferocity that broke out in his wake. Every flicker of human expression sending whisps of crimson energy towards him, adding to his Dark Light body.

He moved to the bar and stared blankly at the space in the mirror where his reflection should have been. Never again being able to look upon his image was yet another handicap of his dark angel state. The Damned did not in fact care to see his diminished self in the mirror; what angered him was that he had been erased from his own field of vision, along with several other constraints, dampening his once acute senses—senses that seemed to have lessened even more dramatically during this recent spiritual upheaval. It was a provoking new reality.

Still adrift in the mirror's reflection, the Damned narrowed his gaze on a collection of random crackles of the Light popping back at him. They sparkled and flittered back and forth over the heaving undulation of human forms. Turning, the dark angel expected the usual blinding flash that accompanied the arrival of a divine celestial. Instead, pulsing from the centre of the mirror, a bright-green orb tinged with gold grew bigger and brighter until it collapsed in an anticlimactic fizzle.

The ethergate's source energy had almost been insufficient to complete the host's journey through the spiritual realm. The stunning, lithe figure of the archangel Raphael stumbled through the gate in desperation. Taking a moment to steady herself, the leader of the healing class stood upright and breathed deeply to replenish her flowing green aura. So smooth and perfect were her muscles and skin that they looked to be made of pure silk. Her blond hair spilled about her shoulders, framing a face that was the embodiment of symmetry and goodness, offset by piercing green eyes—eyes that shone with great determination and resolve, directed at the Damned. This was an overdue encounter that the dark angel had not seen coming by any stretch of his imagination.

"Raphael?" the Damned said, clocking the massive gash in her side. The celestial wobbled before pushing her right palm against the gaping black slice in her abdomen. Warm green glowed beneath her palm, closing up the wound and dissolving the black cracks around it. Though she was able to straighten her spine and bring her power back to equilibrium, it was evident that the archangel was still recovering. She seemed dazed, lost amid images of the massacre she had just narrowly escaped.

"So, there is a war," the Damned said with finality.

"It all happened so fast. I . . . I barely escaped the madness," Raphael breathed in disbelief.

Suddenly, Beel warped in with news of the conversation she had witnessed between Grace and her mother. "My lord, the—" Upon seeing Raphael, she declared, "Step back from my master! I don't fancy your chances against both of us, perfect princess!"

"Beel! Stand down. She means no harm," the Damned commanded. The sultry mind witch eased back a little but remained on edge. Witnessing two top-level celestials of opposing factions consorting with one another was unfamiliar territory for any dark angel. Irrespective of the shock, Beel continued with her message.

"A mother and daughter I was with spoke of the fall of an angelic being. Considering the shifts in the etherverse, I felt it would make sense if this was indeed the truth."

"I believe that she is correct," Raphael interjected. Beel bared her teeth at the interloping archangel.

"There has not been a fall since our kin were damned here. But who?" the Damned said, his pensive glare dropping to the floor. Moving his eyes back up, the dark angel caught Raphael's sudden nervousness.

"You were there. You saw it happen! Who, then?" the Damned demanded. In truth, the dark angel's instinct had already told him the answer, but confirmation was needed.

Raphael stared off into space.

"Answer me!" the Damned barked.

"Gabriel," Raphael announced morbidly.

"Where is he, then? To what realm has his spirit been cast?" the Damned continued. Raphael could not answer but only shook her head and bowed it in respect, as if to pray.

"No," the Damned responded.

"I was too late to save him," Raphael muttered.

"Not Gabriel," the Damned said. The whole group shared the sombre realisation that possibly the mightiest angel to have ever existed had been ripped from the etherverse without warning. "He always balanced the Light with a fair and firm hand. There is no doubt he was the best of us."

*Shhaup!* Abaddon and Scratitch landed. Having sensed a strong gathering of the Light around their lord, they had rushed to his aid.

"My lord, I sensed— What is she doing here?" Abaddon boomed at the leader of the healing class. Losing control, Scratitch leapt at the archangel in a chaotic rage.

"Me kills!" Scratitch screamed as he grabbed for the divine celestial's throat. Phasing into Scratitch's path, Beel swiftly intervened with a lightning-fast palm strike that stopped the wiry, twisted angel dead in his tracks. She followed up with an arcing downward hammer fist, knocking Scratitch on his face in a characteristic display of brutality.

Abaddon stared at Beel incredulously. She calmly held up her free hand towards the Lord of the Pit, warning him off with steely composure. Scratitch picked himself up and prodded a large wound on his face as tears streamed from his eyes. Abaddon brought the whimpering dark angel to his chest in a rare moment of tenderness, shooting a deathly glare at Beel for injuring his ward.

"Control your worm," Beel demanded.

With the news of Gabriel's death sinking in, the Damned was livid and on the hunt for answers.

"Who has done this!?" the Damned shouted.

"You ask, but you already know," Raphael said.

The Damned paused, looking past the group with a thousand-yard stare.

"Michael."

"Of this I am certain," Raphael confirmed.

"It doesn't make any sense. Why has the commander of the divine armies turned on the creation he swore to protect?" the Damned continued.

"You were not there when he changed. It was a reversal of his core beliefs and very mandate to protect the humans. He chose to ignore the will of the Universe and plan his own agenda, corrupted by his own perceived greatness. Surely you, of all, can understand how pride corrupts, brother."

"That I do," the Damned returned.

"We must start to prepare; he is coming for the humans next. I have sent what remains of my legions to slow Michael down, but the humans must be warned, and without Gabriel . . ."

Tired of the back-and-forth, Abaddon wedged his important information into the conversation.

"Lord, the woman, Grace: she can see!"

Turning to Abaddon in surprise, Raphael added to the new discovery.

"A woman named Grace was also there when Gabriel's Light force passed. He spoke to her. One of my trusted inner circle relayed this news," Raphael exclaimed, sensing that a new power might be arising, and with it a sense of hope.

"What did Gabriel say to this Grace woman?" the Damned said.

"He told her to . . ." Raphael was reluctant to finish her sentence, knowing how the dark angel would react.

"Spit it out," the Damned said impatiently.

"He told her to find the Lightbearer," Raphael conceded.

The Damned unleashed an otherworldly roar. His outcry ripped through the earth beneath them, leaving the group stunned. Each and every celestial present had intimate knowledge of the Damned's history with the Lightbearer.

"Nevertheless, my lord, this woman may be the key," Beel said.

"Fine. I will seek her out. What of the rest of the Seven, Raphael?" the Damned asked.

"The guardians have been completely obliterated to leave the humans vulnerable. All other angelic classes have either been caged or enslaved, save Samael, who capitulated willingly." Raphael said.

"Samael is a fool, always bewitched by whatever is dangled in front of his nose. He has absolutely no foresight of what his betrayal will mean for all angelic kind." the Damned growled

"It is unsurprising that Samael has joined with Michael. The Archangel of Death and the Archangel of War always were aligned in their agenda. With Samael by his side, Michael is now stronger than he has ever been. Drunk on power, he hungers for destruction." Raphael warned.

"Do you know of any who escaped?" the Damned said.

"There are a few, but I cannot feel them, or see them," Raphael replied, defeated.

"I too am experiencing this numbness to the Light of all kinds."

Turning to his followers, the Damned began issuing their marching orders.

"Abaddon. Scratitch. Be discreet in the shadows and remain near. Beel, use your gift to feel out any anomalies on the physical plane. We will all play our part in blunting Michael's offensive against the humans. I will not allow him to destroy them."

Still unnerved by the revelation of war in the etherverse, his followers stalled for a moment.

"Go! Now!" the Damned snapped. Each dark angel nodded and disappeared, leaving the Damned and Raphael alone.

The news of Gabriel's demise had hit the Damned harder than he could have imagined. How had this come to pass, and how were he and his dark angel clan to stop Michael without Gabriel's immense strength? What now for the earth and the humans he had come so accustomed to living among? It was a symbiotic relationship he once despised lowering himself to, but in present times it had become both a useful and codependent one. If Michael was waging war, the Damned would do whatever was necessary to stop him. Death, which had become a reality for angels and archangels alike, did not scare the Damned. He longed for it and had nothing more to lose.

Michael and his wretched followers would soon know the wrath spawned by his betrayal of the Damned—a wrath that had been suppressed since the formation of the earth.

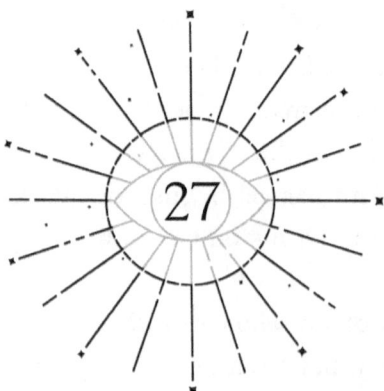

# 27

In the industrial streets of East London, Haylene and Andy walked up to a gritty-looking warehouse. The sign above the entrance read KICK'S GYM. Stopping outside to peer up at the shoddy exterior, Andy curled his eyebrows up his forehead.

"This is the popular new gym you bought?" Andy asked doubtfully as Haylene stepped up to the rusty door. Turning back, Haylene knelt beside the boy.

"It doesn't look like much from here, I know, but looks can be deceiving, can't they?"

"Sometimes, I guess."

"I want you to play with your toys and games in the office while Auntie trains, okay?"

"Aw, no fair. I never get to watch!"

"I'm not sure your mum would be happy with that. It's also way past your bedtime, and your mum made me promise that this was a one-off."

"Pleeease! I won't tell Mum. I promise."

"As long as you promise me something else."

"Anything!"

"You sit right back against the wall on the mats—and no copying! Only watching. Just this once. Promise?"

"I promise!"

Entering the gym, Andy locked onto two fit boxers skipping tirelessly in the weights area and a big bruiser pounding on the heavy bag. He stared slack jawed at the collection of human specimens on display, any one of them a match for his chiselled superhero figures. Sucked into the energetic vibe and the rock music tumbling from a monstrous amplifier in the centre of the room, Andy began to understand why the sparse environment drew in so many new fighters.

"Wow, they are so tough. I'd wanna train with those guys if I was big!"

"Now you get it, bud. It's all about inspiring people to be committed and keep fighting," Haylene replied, walking Andy to the corner by the edge of the sparring mat. "You sit yourself here and stay against the wall. Understand?"

"Got it, boss." Andy gave Haylene a tight army salute. Smiling back, Haylene dropped her bag next to Andy and started warming up with dynamic stretches and resistance bands. Haylene then focused on a sparring dummy to the side, snapping out a high kick, left jab, and right hook in quick succession. Within a minute, Haylene had found her way into a "flow state" where time disappeared and the moment became everything as mind, body, and spirit aligned into one focused task.

Trying to pretend he wasn't watching, Andy whipped out his action figures and mimicked some of the jabs and kicks. He raised the antenna of a robot figure in his hand and cheered his auntie on in a computerised monotone.

"You. Are. The. Best. All. Other. Humans. Shall. Be. Your. Slaves. One. Day. That's. What. Brainatron. Would. Do. If. Brainatron. Had. Your. Fists. And. Feet. Of. Fury."

Haylene giggled a little, breaking out of her flow.

"But. Brainatron. Only. Has. A. Brain. And. An. Immovable. Rectangular. Cube. For. A. Body. No. Slaves. For. Me. That. Make. Brainatron. Sad. Waa. Waa. Waa."

"Andy, stop!" Haylene laughed. "Auntie really needs to concentrate, okay? How about you play with your superhero cards?"

"Sorry!" Pulling out a shiny box of colourful cards depicting his superheroes and their statistics, Andy spread the cards out on the mat. Scratitch warped in next to the boy, wearing a muppet grin and sniffed and crawled around the young human. When it came to deciding upon a location of the human realm to explore, Scratitch always followed his nose.

His acute impulses went wild at the stench Andy gave off. Laughing, coughing, spitting, and feeling his fingers burn, the manic fallen angel jumped about Andy.

"Hoo, wooh. Ack. This one special. Special. Special!"

Craning his head up and around to try to spot the fly he thought was bothering him, Andy swung an arm through the air and stretched his neck and head. Scratitch darted to the side wall, sticking to the Damned's instructions to keep a low profile.

"Quiet keeping me, shush shush," the fool blathered.

Distracted again by Haylene's training, Andy was back in cheerleader mode. Haylene danced around the sparring dummy in swift, fluid movements and launched into two five-hit combinations, finishing the last barrage with a shuddering roundhouse kick. The smack of her foot on the dummy's face cracked like a whip through the cavernous space. Unable to contain his excitement, Andy shot up from the mats.

"Go, Auntie! Yeah!"

Next to Andy in the ether, eager to feel included, Scratitch attempted to mimic Andy's behaviour. His desperate attempts came out sounding more like a cat on fire. In trying to copy Andy's grin, the bent celestial further managed only a puffed-up grimace.

Walking over to Andy to towel off and get some water, Haylene smiled down in pride at her best pal and reached into her bag.

"Not bad for an old person, eh?" Haylene said.

"Yeah, totally, but you're still old," Andy giggled.

Grinning excitedly, Scratitch lunged towards them to touch the top of the bottle of mineral water Haylene pulled from her training bag.

As she opened it, the water fizzed everywhere, drenching her and Andy both, causing them to scream and laugh. Scratitch fired his legs up and down on the spot and slapped his crooked fingers together with glee.

He liked these two playful humans very much.

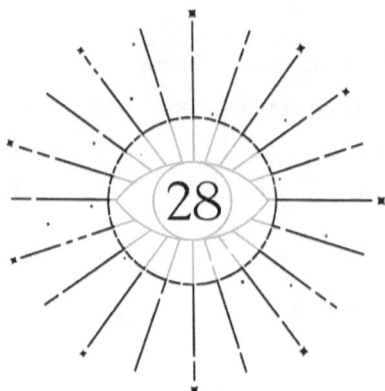

## 28

Using her mental fortitude to shake the images of the angelic massacre from her mind, Raphael came back to her present surroundings. She scanned the environment and struggled to make sense of where she was.

"What is this place?" the archangel asked.

"Let's just say it's where the humans come to blow off steam," the Damned replied.

"There does not seem to be any steam coming from their holes."

"No. There isn't, is there?" the Damned returned with a plastic smile, staring at Raphael as if she had six heads. Given to dispatching her trusted elite angelic squads to spread the healing power of the Light rather than visiting herself, Raphael had only set foot on earth on the few occasions that the Seven chose to hold council and during a handful of key historical events. Her inexperience when it came to relating to humanity's condition was painfully evident from the aloof and clumsy way the restoration angel carried herself in the packed club. The Damned knew he would have some difficulty convincing his long-lost sister to see things as they really were on the physical plane.

"The phrase 'to blow off steam' is merely an expression the humans like to use," the Damned said.

"What does it express?"

"A build-up of pain, most likely."

Raphael phased around the room with green-and-gold Light trailing after her as she observed revellers singing and dancing and falling over drunk. Coming back to stand next to the Damned, Raphael seemed pleased that people were enjoying themselves.

"They manifest the Holy Spirit and speak in tongues! Is this a place of worship, then?"

"One could say that. I fear, however, that they worship themselves more than a higher power of any description. Take these two, for example," the Damned said, pointing out a thirty-year-old male sporting a blond mohawk who was enthusiastically admiring himself in the venue's vast mirrored wall. Obsessed with his own reflection, he rubbed up and down a scantily clad girl who was also riding the narcissism train. The flashes of their smartphones captured selfie after selfie in their vain, awkward dance. Raphael warped uncomfortably close to the pair, aghast.

"These misguided souls are in need of healing!" Raphael warbled like a Las Vegas magician announcing her final act. Waving her hands in elaborate circles, she made a real song and dance of summoning her healing power. The Damned cringed at the dramatic display.

"A leprous affliction should help them find humility."

In an instant, the writhing couple's clothes vanished, exposing a tapestry of weeping sores that covered their entire bodies. A waitress delivering shots around the room who had found herself next to the naked couple screamed.

"Oh my God, they've got herpes!"

Nearby revellers froze at the horrid sight of the couple, who scrambled to cover themselves with discarded jackets in an adjacent booth. The chubby clubgoer from the earlier altercation let out a girlish, high-pitched yelp that cut through the club's bass-thumping beats.

"Not herpes!"

The outcry sparked utter mayhem. Partygoers ran for the doors, wailing in panic and clambering over one another. Witnessing the fallout of Raphael's blunt and outdated approach to interacting with the physical world, the Damned rolled his eyes.

"We don't have time for this, Raphael."

"Perhaps you are right. What is next?"

"We watch quietly and wait for Michael to act. He would not be expecting my involvement in this war, nor that our classes would dream of uniting against him. These factors will give our fallen clans a chance to take him down. However, if we are to match his experienced forces, we must also use the element of surprise."

"There is another way, brother."

"What other way? You said it yourself: the power he has absorbed will crush us all if we do not join and adopt a stealthier approach."

"There is one strong enough to stand against the power Michael has amassed. You know that the Lightbearer is perhaps the only being that—"

"Do. Not. Speak that name! That celestial is but a memory and was vanished by the Universe for a reason. It is far too dangerous to play with such a solution. For now we must be aligned, our Light and our classes acting as one. I will find the woman. If she can see, we stand with the humans."

"I admire your conviction, brother, but I fear it may not be enough."

"Have some faith in the humans, Raphael, as you used to. They hold a great spirit within them that if channelled and unleashed could right the wrongs of their barbaric history."

Gazing out at the fleeing humans, the Damned had an idea.

"It's time you learnt a thing or two about their resolve. Follow me, sister," the Damned said, shooting off in a blaze of crimson. Raphael turned her nose up at the clutter of the now empty nightclub and, shrugging at her own disillusionment, bolted off through a sparkling emerald ethergate. The leader of the restoration class was running out of hope; the Damned was all she had left.

The two enormously powerful celestials, long representative of opposing forces of the Light, now held a companionship that could not have been foreseen mere days before.

The guardian and healing angel classes had always exhibited an almost unbreakable alliance, intertwined in their roles and sensitivity to one another. This was precisely the reason Michael had targeted Gabriel and his loyal followers. The guardians were the central pivot point that balanced the opposing energies of the Universe. Their capacity alone had kept Michael's warlike agenda in check and had never once been compromised. This was not to forget the Archangel of Death, Samael, and the role his class of necrotic angels played in the great drama of existence. Death was kept at bay by healing, and the warriors had been kept at bay by the guardians. This was how it had been since the beginning.

The present alliance between the Damned and the archangel of the restoration class was one of necessity. The entire angelic species was at risk of being enslaved by Michael and his twisted vision of an evolved etherverse. But was there enough strength in their combined powers of the Light to withstand Michael and Samael's alliance—an alliance fuelled by the immense power of other great celestials imprisoned in the upper ether?

Time would tell.

The humans still had a part to play if they were to avoid annihilation. A seer was rising in Grace Collopy, and if she mastered her abilities in time, humanity might find a new champion to stand as their own guardian.

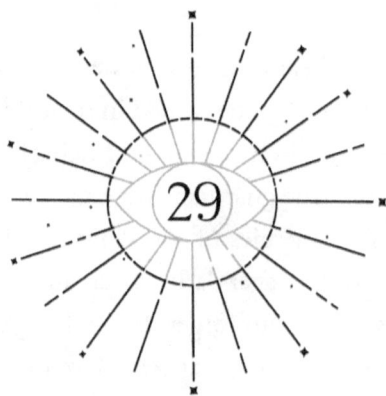

# 29

Back in Kick's Gym, a lean fighter entered the training hall to start his coaching session with Haylene. The young man stank of attitude, clumping his feet over the floor like lead weights and rocking his head side to side. Haylene read his body language instantly; although unimpressed, she decided to give him a chance to work his way into the session. Endorphins were a powerful antidote to a muddled mind.

"Hey, buddy, you ready to do this?"

Haylene's upbeat tone cut through the fighter's dark cloud.

"Guess so."

"Well, you're certainly a barrel of laughs today. Let's get you moving and outta that head of yours, shall we?"

Dropping his bag by the matted area, the fighter started shadowboxing as per his regular warm-up. Moving around the fighter, keeping careful watch on his technique, Haylene grabbed some pads and readied herself to put him to the test. The fighter soon advanced to throwing a few high knees followed by two rather sloppy-looking kicks. Haylene dashed in front of her apprentice with her pads up in challenge.

"Let's see you tighten up those kicks. Mind your through line and hip engagement to maximise power," Haylene instructed.

Warping into the gym, Abaddon leered behind the young fighter. Though he had been told to act discreetly, Abaddon could not resist the delicious torture of the human mind; it was his favourite addiction.

From the moment Abaddon was thrown from the upper realms, he had been committed to moulding his status in the netherverse, which was nothing but a void when he and his class of fallen angels had arrived there, an energy dump for all the dark matter the creation of earth had expelled. This Dark Light was a by-product of the cosmos's shifting processes. At first this new plane was a rich feeding ground for Abaddon and his exiled kin, but as time went on and its power was depleted to form the netherverse's many levels and energy portals, the Pit was created to manifest a near-endless source of the Dark Light.

Contrary to its simplistic name, the Pit was a complex arrangement of spinning dimensions where mortal and immortal souls alike were imprisoned and drained of their life force. The Light absorbed there was then used to sustain the agenda of the Damned, his class, and the netherverse itself. Abaddon took great pride in his role as the chief harvester of the Dark Light. His aptitude most certainly drew from his affinity for the one thing that defined all beings in the Universe, great and small: suffering.

Abaddon's current target was balanced on a knife edge, and the dark angel's hunger for suffering made him anxious to press in on the young fighter's pain.

"Let's start with the usual four-hit combo," Haylene suggested.

Launching a flurry of strikes, the determined fighter blinked and sweated as Abaddon forced his stifling energy inside the makeshift boxing ring.

"Again," Haylene continued. Another combo jolted into the pads, this time harder.

"That's more like it. Again."

Abaddon's dark power built up with a swirling crimson hue in the ether, enveloping the fighter. The dark celestial leaned close to the ear of Haylene's apprentice.

"And one more," Haylene called out.

"Kill," Abaddon breathed.

The fighter spiralled into a wild rage. The outbreak of kicks was so powerful that it threw Haylene off balance, each one flying astray and forcing Haylene to fake backwards to avoid any of the savage strikes connecting with her face.

"What the hell was that?" Haylene said.

"You're gonna die, bitch," the fighter sneered, firmly in Abaddon's grip.

On the street outside, Grace stomped up to the gym, relieved to be about to rejoin her best friend and son, who always helped to ground her.

Stopping midstep, Grace felt an unsettling vibration down her spine. *Is someone following me?* She twirled on the spot as a fierce wind blew across her path. Suddenly aware that there could be all manner of otherworldly beings pursuing her, Grace felt a breathtaking paranoia set in. Her new awareness of the spiritual plane—if she wasn't just going insane—was going to take some getting used to.

Back in the gym, Haylene was mystified at the fighter's explosion as she blocked his persistent attacks. Seeing his opportunity to increase the conflict, Abaddon moved behind Haylene and whispered his objective.

"Fear."

Haylene felt the urge to give in but chose instead to dig down into her emotional resilience to shake it off. Breaking her will would be no easy task, even for the Lord of the Pit. Continuing to dodge the relentless attacks, Haylene knew she had to act fast for Andy's sake. The defenceless boy had yet to realise the change in her student and might get caught in the crossfire. That was something she would not allow at any cost.

Faking to the right, Haylene found the perfect opening, rocketing a straight right into the young fighter's temple. He crumpled him to the floor.

"I think you need to work out some of that frustration with twenty minutes on the rope. We'll pick up the sparring tomorrow when your head's a bit clearer," Haylene said to the young fighter, who rolled around the mat in a stupor.

The doors of the gym slammed open as Grace burst in, hysterical and sweating with stress.

"Haylene! I think I'm losing my mind. This giant man appeared to me at work. Maybe it wasn't even a man. He could have been something more." Startled and snapping their heads towards the entrance, Haylene and Andy were both wide eyed. "Right there in the— I mean, I know it was real. I—"

Grace stopped abruptly and whirled to face Scratitch, who was darting around Andy in the weights area, trying to pick up a fifty-kilo dumbbell and making a real mess out of it. In the physical realm, Grace discerned a deep, shimmering orange glow shaped like Scratitch's figure. Her body edged towards it as if remotely controlled.

"Grace? Grace!" Haylene shouted, trying to break Grace from her strange trance. Slowly turning back to Haylene, sensing another presence, Grace beheld Abaddon clearly—and she was certain this was the very same presence she had experienced at the bus stop and in her apartment. Exposed and immobilised by Grace's sight, Abaddon glared at her.

"You!" Grace bellowed, staring back.

"Slow down, Grace. I'm here," Haylene said, assuming that Grace was having a resurgence of her panic attacks.

"Mummy? It's okay. I love you, Mummy. Please stay here with us," Andy added. Beside him, the oblivious Scratitch was still huffing and puffing in his attempt to lift the heaviest weight in the room.

"Get out of here and leave my family alone!" Grace shouted full volume at Abaddon. The dark angel vanished in a blinding eruption of the Dark Light. Looking up at Grace with a goat-like whimper, Scratitch took this as his cue to follow his master and escaped through a collapsing red ethergate behind him.

"Grace, just breathe for me, okay?" Haylene said, rushing to Grace's side. Grace was immobilised in the adrenaline rush. Encouraging her to synchronise her inhales and exhales and breathe slowly, Haylene gradually brought down the stress levels in the room. Grace's eyes softened and her lungs opened as she looked back at her best friend.

"What did you see?" Haylene said.

"He was here. The darkness I experienced at the bus stop," Grace said. "But he—"

All at once, her eyes rolled back in her head, and her body went limp. Haylene lunged towards her, catching Grace just in time. "Gotcha!"

"Mum!" Andy anxiously sprinted over, kneeling next to Grace while Haylene lowered her gently to the mat. Grace came to and squinted up at her son.

"It's all just so . . ." Grace muttered.

"Just rest, Grace," Haylene said. At these words, Grace let go and drifted from consciousness.

"Is she going to be okay?" Andy whimpered.

"It's alright, Andy. She's obviously just had a really hard night. Let's get your mum home so we can look after her."

Andy nodded sheepishly and helped Haylene gather Grace up. She was out for the count as the Light attached to her spirit slowly worked to unlock the constraints of her human mind.

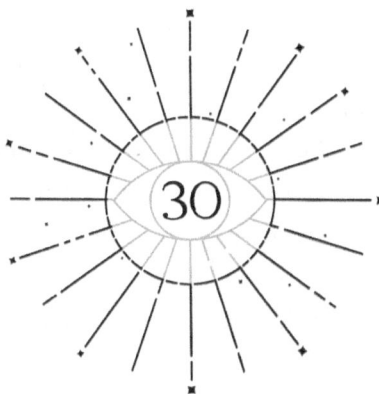

## 30

Jack chopped tomatoes on a board over a brushed concrete countertop while onions and garlic fried in a pan. Making dinner for one as usual, Jack glided around his spotless, Scandinavian-inspired kitchen. He organised ingredients mise en place, lost in the focused enjoyment of cooking. Then, opening one of the solid oak cupboards on a hunt for salt and pepper, Jack's eyes landed on a box of camomile tea at the back of the spices cabinet. The item catapulted his mind into a prison of shame, stalling him on the spot.

Three years on, his part in turning his soulmate into a stranger became clearer by the day. Jack had pushed his one true love away out of anger and built a wall around his heart. The wall of protection also served to mute the pain of the reason for their separation: the loss of their only daughter, Asha—"hope" in Sanskrit. At the time, Jack's wife was alone and without the capacity or awareness to prevent Asha's death. Jack could understand that fully now, in hindsight. As always, Jack had been stationed in some distant, war-torn place, fighting for his country but neglecting the family that was his true home.

It had been different when Jack and his wife first met; they were young and free and full of possibility. Their bright future gradually eroded over years of intermittent separation and was eventually crushed by their loss. As their hope died, so did their love for one another. Jack chose to push his agony down into a secret part of himself, but his subconscious was not so easily fooled, sending him visions of the girl Asha would have grown to be.

Removing the tea and throwing it in the rubbish bin, Jack reached for the large glass of chardonnay on the countertop and sucked it back. Immediately refilling the hefty measure, he returned to his recipe without another thought on the matter.

Over the stove on his kitchen island was Jack's happy place, where the rest of the world fell away. He had learned to cook from watching his mother's deft skills in the kitchen while growing up. Their love for food and making others happy through their cuisine was a shared passion. Similar to his mother, Jack cooked on feeling and by eye. No measuring jugs or scales were necessary. His sensitivity to making the perfect meal had been honed over years of practice, and it provided him solace from his ever-ticking mind. It was his meditation.

Lifting the board of sliced tomatoes, Jack slid them into the pan and turned to a basil plant on the windowsill to pluck several leaves. His phone vibrated against his leg. He wiped his hands on the tea towel in his back pocket and pulled out his phone to see Eddie on the line. Jack smiled and answered, stirring the pan of sauteing tomatoes with his free hand.

"Good evening, sweet cheeks. This is a surprise!" Jack said.

"Yeah, well, I wish it was under better circumstances."

"What's up?"

"Listen, I was looking at the file of the prisoner you dropped off. He's no small fish. I think he's connected right to the top of the Wraiths. You might need to watch your back, Causer."

"Right. I thought his capture seemed far too easy. The Wraiths must not have been expecting a hit on one of their generals. Moving any product of that size with so few men just wouldn't happen without the oversight of one of the higher-ups. Seems their bravado left them exposed, and my bravado might well draw some unwanted attention my way. Christ, I'm an idiot!"

"Easy mistake to make, pal. Look, I'll keep an eye on his movements and conversations in here, but if word gets back to the Wraiths, your cover's gonna be blown wide open. So whatever intel you're planning on getting out of this pack of weasels, do it quick-smart, huh?"

"I'll do my best. Thanks for the heads-up. How's things there?"

"Still pretty unsettled, but that's the nature of a bloody max security prison, isn't it?"

"Rather you than me. Best get on, but listen: watch your back, Ed."

"You too, Causer. Night, pal."

"Night."

Ending the call, Jack turned off the stove abruptly and left the half-finished sauce where it was. His detective instincts were firing on all cylinders as he made his way through the living room.

Beel blasted through a fracturing ethergate in the corner of the room, in search of the origin of a surging rush of spiritual energy. Surprised to see that it connected back to this same human from the prison riot, she thought, *The way of the Universe is unexpected and flows in mysterious ways*—a fact she had learned over her millennia as a dark temptress.

By the far living room wall, Jack flipped up a picture frame of his family to reveal an iris scanner and thumbprint entry system. Its high-tech glow lit up the dim surroundings. Several electronic bleeps and whirs later, the locking mechanism clicked, sliding open a hidden floor hatch to reveal a metal staircase. Jack descended into the darkness of the basement and pressed his palm against another access terminal at the bottom of the stairs.

Instantly, a bank of screens and electronic wall panels came to life in a stutter of shock-blue light. As the screens loaded and a hum filled the hidden control centre, Beel phased in next to the only desk in the room, which sat in front of an empty wall. She squinted at the empty wall, then at the base of the desk, aware of an incongruity in the room's arrangement. Jack flicked a concealed switch underneath the tabletop. The empty wall spun 180 degrees to reveal a pyramid of photos, with copious notes pinned around it.

Stepping back from the wall, Jack studied the connections he had already made. He took the photo of the thug he had just dropped in prison from the bottom of the pyramid and affixed it to the second row from the top, next to a photo of an even less charming specimen. This face was studded with metal, and his skin was covered in tattoos of ghosts and skeletons—trademark imagery of the Wraiths. The name underneath the photo read LAZARO.

Taking a red pen and putting a large "X" over the head thug's image, Jack stepped back again to observe how the landscape of the Wraith hierarchy had changed. His failure to recognise the head thug's importance within the group had the potential to make or break his whole operation. He had unknowingly pierced a hole in the top of the gang's well-organised command structure. This was certain to cast major suspicions among their ranks and on his undercover position in it.

The top photo on the board was a grainy black-and-white image with a blue question mark drawn over it. Looking at the grainy picture and then at the multiple screens displaying information next to him, Jack lowered his head and thudded his temple with the side of his fist. In the spirit of the gang's name, the Wraiths' leader was an absolute phantom. He had been meticulous in setting up a hierarchy that knew nothing of his greater plans or whereabouts. Jack had found his nemesis in this dangerous individual, and it was frustrating as hell.

A ping from Jack's pocket alerted him to a new message. It was from Dio, his closest ally in the Wraiths' middle ranks: BOSS IS PISSED. HE'S COMING ON COLLECTION DUTY, 9 P.M. AT BECONTREE ESTATE. DON'T BE LATE, STONES, the message read.

Stones was Jack's undercover alias, and he had worked many long, hard nights to gain Dio's trust, thereby infiltrating the Wraiths quickly and effectively. Dio worshipped the ground Jack walked on, and the lumbering neanderthal made sure everyone paid "Stones" the respect he deserved.

Jack took a deep breath. It was unlike Dio and Lazaro to break schedule like this, and it was even less likely for Lazaro to attend a lowly pickup without a savage agenda. On the other hand, this anomaly could be nothing but a show of force for the troublesome residents of Becontree. They were always late on payments and sloppy with handling distribution.

In the end, it didn't really matter if it was a trap. Jack didn't have a choice. He was at Dio's beck and call if he wanted to avoid suspicion around the head thug's disappearance, he needed to be there, bright eyed and bushy tailed.

Typing furiously on his keyboard, Jack hunted for more clues from a variety of social media accounts and web pages he pulled up on his glowing wall monitors. Racking his brains and swivelling back and forth to scour the evidence wall, Jack let out a bark of frustration and slammed his hand on the table. "Come on!"

Jack simply didn't have enough to go on to make any key connections before meeting Dio—connections that might save his skin if he was indeed walking into an ambush.

Beel's orange glare pulsed in the corner of the room. Zipping over to the desk, she brushed the polished mahogany top with her long red fingernails, washing Jack's energy in the Dark Light.

Beel was the master of temptation in the lower ether; it was her speciality, specifically when it came to the male of the human species. The lower ether's chief mind witch—Beelzebub, as she was once known, a moniker assigned to her by inhabitants of Ekron in ancient Philistine—had laid civilisations to waste by simply infesting them with lustful Dark Light. She would then sit back and enjoy the show as they tumbled down an immoral descent into lunacy. Ekron had worshipped her through vicious battles, bisexual orgies, and building great monuments in her name. In those days, of course, societies were solely governed by power-hungry men, which made her task all the easier. So much of their idiotic behaviour boiled down to one thing: an unsatisfied yearning for more. Whether it was for money or power or sex, the human male was hopelessly vulnerable to Beel's charms, and watching them squirm in torturous traps of their own making never got old.

*This Jack individual seems no different than the rest, so why has the Universe drawn me here?*

Rubbing his eyes raw, Jack removed a whiskey bottle and glass from the bottom desk drawer and poured himself a well-tipped bartender's measure. He took a swig and set the glass down, staring at the amber liquid, swishing it back and forth.

In the ambient electronic hum, a realisation suddenly hit Jack, and he fished for an object in his pocket. It was a matchbook he had found when cleaning out the back of his car after dropping off his prisoner. Jack studied it. The item was branded with the icon of two female silhouettes at the beginning of each of the two words: DARK DESIRE. Looking up at the top of the wall, Jack grabbed a green marker and wrote the words between the images of Lazaro and the head thug. Moving his gaze to a photo of Dio directly beneath those two, Jack took a red pen and drew heavy connecting lines between the three individuals. It was something to go on, but with the clock ticking on his cover being blown, even tracking down the Wraiths' mysterious leader wouldn't be enough. Finishing his drink, Jack poured another. He leaned back in his chair with glazed eyes, hoping for another shot in the dark to jump out at him.

Watching Jack's eyes grow heavy, Beel doubted there was much to be gleaned from this insignificant human's place in recent shocking events. But despite her doubts, the dark angel's core connection to the etherverse was adamant that she remain close to Jack Causer for the time being. Beel would heed its warning and obey.

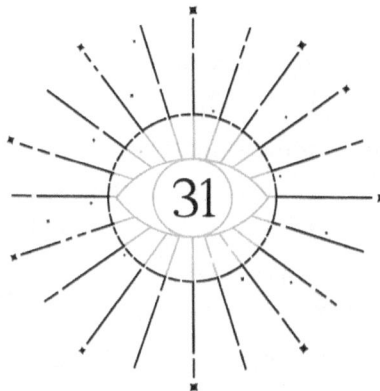

## 31

The stillness of early morning hung over the chipped concrete and rusting metal of the industrial cellblock.

Any sound made within Wandsworth prison's secure east wing was amplified by its numerous hard surfaces, so the inmates had learned to tune out most low-level noise. Clangs and scrapes of movement were ever present, making the current dead silence an unnerving anomaly. There were usually one or two inmates stirring, or the explosive flush of a toilet filling the room that was sure to wake at least one prisoner. After that, a cascade of groans and sighs would signal the rest of the wing rising from sleep.

This morning was different. All bodies present were being kept unconscious by a force willing them into submission. In the ether, at the end of the block, two large, hooded figures stood with their backs against the inner wall, embracing the peace and quiet. Their vibrating blue auras were responsible for the comatose state of the humans littered around them, a necessary stage in preparation for their commander's arrival. Both divine celestial beings wore cream-coloured, form-fitting battle suits trimmed in royal blue. Their robes and cloaks had been discarded, and only their high, trimmed collars remained. This specialist outfit was reserved for Michael's inner circle: the elite cherubim. Originally guardians of the gates to the upper ether's inner sanctuary, these hugely powerful angels were only outmatched by the archangels above them.

In recent centuries, the cherubim had been shaped into a highly effective special forces role, each a one-man army that swept into celestial—or human—conflicts and ensured victory with awesome and brutal efficiency. It was rare to see two of these lethal machines together. Such an occurrence could only mean the beginning of a major offensive.

Zelda and Ahebban had been sent as the security detail of an incoming archangel. Zelda had scouted for their arrival through her torture of prisoner 7, whom she used as a smoke screen to avoid alerting any nearby exiled angels or stragglers from the vanquished guardian class.

As for Ahebban, her lantern-jawed fellow cherub, he saw this task as beneath him and had instead chosen to aid in the execution of the captive guardian angels in the upper ether. The thrill of watching their corpses solidify and dissolve into ash was a new feeling, and he was anxious for more. His fervour for war was insatiable. Standing almost a foot taller than Zelda, he was a foreboding sight that was backed up by extensive fighting skills accumulated over generations of war.

Both cherubim maintained their positions, their fizzing energy fields filling up the room with a scattering of crisp blue beams. Between the statuesque pair, a collection of large, creeping tentacles of the Light materialised from within a black-and-silver ethergate. Unlike most other portals celestial beings could summon, this one was not spherical but rather shaped like a perfect, razor-sharp diamond. The glinting, silvery tendrils wove along the floor and ceiling in advance of a monstrous, inky-skinned archangel peering from beneath his billowing hood to survey the conditions that had been paved for his arrival.

The fearsome entity was none other than Samael, the Archangel of Death.

As the largest and most muscular of all angelic beings, his square frame dwarfed the cellblock. His sea beast appearance and shiny skin presented a gruesome sight to those who did not belong to his class. All under his leadership exhibited a similar serpentine look. Not to be confused with the Damned, as most humans did, Samael was the spiritual plane's chief agent of death and decay, the great regulator and necessary constraint on swarming populations of any species. Samael severed and simplified, serving the Universe's endless cycle of life and death. While the Damned set humans on the path to ruin, Samael stood at the end of their journey with the gift of another life, or of oblivion. Even though they worked in tandem, allies they were not. Their relationship was one of the great mysteries of the cosmos, being that they were so similar in their agenda but so vastly different in their approach.

In the physical realm, the prison wing's cells opened simultaneously as Eddie announced over the speaker system, "Alrighty, nap time's over; grub's up. Usual rules. Keep in single file, and eyes front."

The prisoners slowly formed up and fell in the line, shuffling forwards. Each and every one was zombified by the energy emanating from the warrior angels. Zelda and Ahebban grabbed the last two stragglers' skulls in icy vice grips. Both prisoners were immobilised before they could make the line, suspended on their tiptoes and gasping for air.

Their life forces shunted into each cherub through blinding, golden zigzags of energy that raced from the centre of each prisoner's chest. Their irises were left a solid, glassy black, and their skin became cracked and infected like Gabriel's at his death.

Samael glided towards the two guards on duty at the front of the line, his grey tentacles squirming in tow beneath his regal cloak. Grounding himself, the Angel of Death spread out his meaty arms and, with a gesture forward, sent two of his writhing appendages through the back of each guard's skull as they faced each other.

A silver flash passed over Samael's golden, reptilian eyes. The same creeping darkness gripping the inmates now possessed the two guards, blackening their eyes and tracing their skin with tell-tale, snaking cracks. Both sets of men began convulsing, something inside of them attempting to fight the effects of "the Touch" swirling through their bodies; but after several agonising seconds, they gave over control. The change was complete.

In an instant, the victims of the Touch became like wild animals, losing control over their base emotions. All the affected experienced a chaotic surge of the differing evils that had been thrust inside of them, each at the will of the ancient and primal force of the Seven Deadly Sins. Greed, gluttony, lust, pride, wrath, sloth, and envy dripped from the spiritual atmosphere of the cellblock.

Pulling out his baton, one infected guard launched himself at the inmates, who were being turned by Zelda and Ahebban. The cherubim moved through the group relentlessly. The second guard clapped gleefully like a toddler on a sugar high. Prisoner 3 fell from Ahebban's clutches and collapsed to the floor, where he began beating his head on the concrete, trying to end his life. Next to him, Prisoner 4 thrust himself lustfully on Prisoner 5, who whimpered and screamed in fear and pain. Samael remained still as the flood of pain, joy, violation, sorrow, and hopelessness fed into his tendrils of the Light, the chaos engorging their size and silver brilliance. Closing ranks on either side of their leader, Zelda and Ahebban enjoyed the rich tapestry of depravity and senselessness on display.

"Let the games begin," Samael croaked in his characteristic gravelly rumble.

In the east wing office, Eddie gaped at the mayhem unfolding on the monitors in front of him. Jade blithely selected a massive doughnut from the box next to him as she returned from her smoke break.

"Hello, my beauty. Where have you been all my life?" she asked the doughnut, fixated on its chocolate-coated surface, drooling.

"Jade, I think we might have a bit of a problem on our hands in the secure wing," Eddie said, his tone shaking with terrified sarcasm. Taking a huge bite of her doughnut, Jade glanced at the monitors one by one. Her nonchalant expression dissolved into one of horror.

"Feck. My. Face," Jade exclaimed, mesmerised. She hurriedly stuffed the rest of the snack in her mouth as if she were watching the climax of her favourite soap.

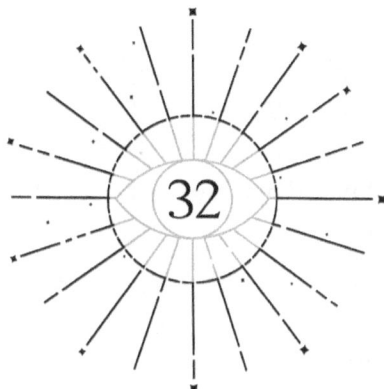

# 32

At 10 a.m. in a busy London supermarket, young mums and pensioners made up the bulk of shoppers circling the aisles. They bobbled about, filling their trolleys with foodstuffs and household goods. As the overhead speaker system announced the weekly special offers, the attached café was already packed with greying adults vying for hot drinks, English breakfasts, and buttered scones.

The Damned warped through a flaming ethergate in the middle of the dairy aisle, closely followed by Raphael through her own sparkling gate of green and gold.

Had any human the sight to witness these two elaborately clad archangels together at the supermarket, they might have assumed that London Comic Con was being held nearby—though that wouldn't have explained the glowing auras or their method of arrival. The Damned observed Raphael's reactions and tried to guide his ancient sister to a soft landing.

"Here the humans come to buy food and supplies for their homes," the Damned said. Raphael peered around in puzzlement and spotted two teenage phone zombies travelling down the aisle, obsessed with their online profiles. Rounding the aisle at the opposite end, a tech-addict mum wheeled a trolley alongside her bouncy four-year-old girl. The little girl keenly felt the lack of attention and yanked at her mother's jumper.

"Mummy?" The girl continued to tug at her mother's clothes while her mum pulled away in annoyance, trying to send work emails without interruption. The teenagers at the other end of the aisle barrelled along, unaware of a pair of pensioners they almost mowed down.

"Are they all bewitched by these devices? They seem numbed to life!" Raphael bellowed in her usual exaggerated tones, as if performing onstage.

"Some are slaves, some are free. It's no different to when you last visited this realm. Their machines are simply another form of distraction," the Damned responded.

Bored stiff, the little girl snatched a brightly coloured litre of yoghurt from the fridge next to her.

"Mummy, can I have this?"

Finally, to elicit a response, the girl screeched like a cat in heat and slammed the carton on the floor, splattering yoghurt all over her dungarees and freshly washed hair.

"Oh my God, Saidie! What are you doing?!" the mother shouted. Raphael scoffed and shook her head, immediately swooping in to remedy the situation.

"She cannot care for her young! I shall help her," Raphael said to the Damned. The Damned attempted to intervene, remembering all too well that his sister was a master of the knee-jerk reaction.

"Raphael, please. Just—"

*Pfft!* With an elaborate hand motion, Raphael exploded the young mother's phone into flames, burning the skin from her palms and fingers. The woman screamed and dropped the device while the little girl giggled, happy for some excitement and secretly pleased that fate had snapped her mum back to the real world.

The Damned rubbed his forehead in dismay while the mother's contorted face moved from fear to shock.

"I can't feel my hands," the mother blubbered.

"Oh no, Mummy. Let me see," her daughter said. She stroked her mum's hands gently.

"This is your idea of helping?" the Damned said.

"The loss will help her grow a stronger temperament. It will subside in time."

"How much time, exactly?"

"Ten of their earth years. Patience, after all, is the best teacher, and time is the great healer."

"I see that you haven't lost touch with your endless catalogue of useful proverbs."

"What good is power without wisdom, brother?"

"Return her hands to their original state, please, Raphael," the Damned requested. Raphael frowned at her brother, hands on her hips and head tilted to the side. She was more than a little perturbed that the Damned had become so soft in his old age. Perhaps human weakness was rubbing off on him. The archangel vowed to be wary of this limiting sympathy should it come in the way of battle. Glancing at the mother and child and then back to the Damned, Raphael complied with her old companion's request.

With another elaborate magician wave, the mother was healed.

"Is that better, Mummy?"

"Yes. Yes, it is. Thank you. I don't know what I'd do without you. Mummy's sorry for being so busy with her phone," the mother said as she and her daughter shared a loving moment, the little girl stroking her mum's head and face tenderly.

"As you can see, this lesson had the desired effect," Raphael chimed in.

"Indeed. You are always right, aren't you?" the Damned replied.

"That is my purpose. To heal and make right."

"Of course it is."

"I can see many more who are in need of my help."

"Why don't you stay and do that? Please do try not to upset the physical too much. It is your second law in the Code of the Etherverse, after all," the Damned said. Raphael nodded with her familiar condescending smirk.

The laws of the Code of the Etherverse were many, but the first three were of the greatest importance. If a celestial being did not adhere to the code, a swift punishment was sure to find them. Angels of every class and rank were judged the same under the code.

The first law was "Thou shalt not separate humanity from their free will."

As mortal beings' greatest gift, free will was to be protected at all costs. It had been a great source of jealousy for angelic kind from the inception of the human race, and as such, many rogue celestials had fallen victim to damnation after testing this first law. The Universe had banished them to the Pit in the blink of an eye, never to return home. Such consequences were a clear warning. Many of the Damned's original companions had been lost to the Pit's swirling dimensions for this very reason. However, after the first few centuries of human life, the angels ruefully realised that free will was also a curse. It allowed humans to make their own choices and have almost unlimited autonomy, but freedom eventually led to destruction without wisdom and temperance. In the modern age, these two virtues were in short supply.

This lack had left the planet's ecosystems on the brink of collapse, a fact that did not go unnoticed by the mighty celestials above. Devastation of the human race they could abide; some even considered their certain end as a signal of divine favour. However, devastation of the earth and the harmless creatures existing upon it could not be tolerated. Thus, for a long while, the angels above had felt torn between following the code or saving the earth from annihilation—an impossible conundrum.

Humans had a major problem accepting that free will meant their actions had far-reaching consequences. Whether positive or negative, the ripple effects of humanity crashing around in the dark weighed heavily on the natural order of the spiritual realm. Yet instead of recognising their part in the degeneration of their species, mortals chose to blame God. "How can God be loving if he lets such terrible evils happen to us?" mortals protested in their ignorance. The sad fact was that control had been given over to humankind in the hopes that they would live justly and choose fairly, and it was a gift that could not be returned. Being that treachery and selfishness had become a by-product of the human condition, the consequences of human behaviour had corrupted mortal life. Oceans had dried up, forests had been massacred, and children were starving or dying from toxins. It was an abomination.

The second law of the code was "Thou shalt not affect the physical realm unless commanded by an archangel."

This law had long allowed the Damned and his followers to disseminate havoc in the absence of divine angels, and countless battles had been fought between dark and light celestials over the law's sanctity. Dark angels sought to twist humanity by any means necessary, and when they went too far, both guardian and warrior classes had stepped in to end the threat.

The third law was "Thou shalt not kill, except to protect the greater good."

This law presented a huge grey area that Michael and his followers now walked in. With the third law, they could justify any and all crimes against humans as a move for the greater good. Before the current divide in the upper ether, Gabriel had policed this law with an iron fist, knowing full well the challenge it posed to humanity's existence. This was, after all, why he and his class had received the great honour of being named guardians, thereby becoming the most powerful stand-alone clan of divine celestials. Without their overwatch, Michael had free rein to unleash his warped design on the human population.

Back in the supermarket, the Damned opened a crackling red ethergate and moved towards it, leaving Raphael to explore a little more of the humans' ways. Before the dark angel could step through, Raphael called after him.

"Where are you destined, brother?"

"To find the seer."

"I should come with you. There is little time for frivolity."

"No. It is best if we split up, and this is as good a place as any for you to sense abnormal shifts in the etherverse. Stay alert and watch your back, sister."

The Damned turned to exit but hesitated. He swivelled back to face his glorious archangel sister, who had been a very dear friend well before the earth's creation. He had an uneasy feeling at leaving her unaccompanied in a strange land.

"I am able to move under Michael's radar for now, but I'm afraid you are too great a threat and an obvious loose end. They will no doubt come for you. In numbers," the Damned said.

Raphael responded with a knowing smile.

"I welcome it gladly."

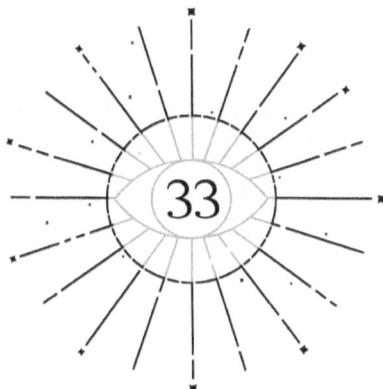

## 33

Professor Simms was a tall, lean, bespectacled man in his midfifties with a Roman nose. The professor's eagle-shaped beak matched his uncanny ability to peck out the solution to any problem. He was highly intelligent, relentlessly studious, and as perceptive as the majestic bird of prey he resembled.

Currently, Simms sat in his office in an antique leather chair, backgrounded by a vast library of leather-bound books on shelves. Being an avid reader and a collector of historical Christian tomes, he was always in the process of getting to the bottom of some mystery shrouded by the Bible's writings. Simms's area of expertise was determining why certain books had been included in the Bible's final collection, or canon, and others had not. More specifically, Simms's title at the university was "head of biblical studies." He was also the leading mind in the field worldwide. Within the broad field of biblical studies, exegesis was the professor's passion and speciality, referring to the critical analysis of language. During exegesis, the reader would use a variety of tools to pinpoint the origins of a specific Bible verse or book. Sentence structure, wording, tone, pace, content, and the culture at the proposed time were all clues to the writer's identity and the date of writing.

The book of Genesis, for example, was believed by some to have been written by the biblical figure Moses. Yet this was an impossibility;

the historical oral tradition of passing on the Hebrew Bible existed until the middle of the sixth century BCE. This was of course many centuries after Moses was said to have lived. This fact, along with the distinct Babylonian references in the language and tone of Genesis, made it highly probable that the first book of the Bible was written by a Jewish scholar under Persian rule after the fall of the Babylonian Empire.

To Professor Simms, exegesis was a thrilling, detective-like undertaking. The Bible was his mystery, and he was the Sherlock Holmes of the biblical studies community.

Popular Christian belief would call this type of biblical analysis blasphemy. "God's word" was, in their eyes, a divine inspiration breathed through the apostles and prophets who wrote it—a point of view Professor Simms did not share, having researched the Bible's books and history endlessly without religious bias. That was not to say he disregarded spiritual beliefs; the professor was always on the lookout for unconventional mysticism hidden in the Bible's pages. If clues within the Christian Bible hinted at something bigger and less Christ focused, Simms was typically the first to champion their significance.

Such endeavours had made him somewhat of an outcast within his family, who were deeply Christian in the Brethren Protestant sense. Brethren Protestants were a stern and joyless bunch, to put it mildly. They hadn't enjoyed his constant questioning that picked holes in their religion. "Sometimes it is just God's will, and we must not question it" was the parrot-like response to his queries.

Sitting in his office with one of the most ancient existing copies of the Hebrew Bible, also known as the Torah, Simms analysed the opening verses of Genesis. This was his favourite book of the Bible because it held such a conundrum around the beginnings of man, the roles of angels, and the planet's formation. Simms believed that with the Bible, the supernatural usually originated in some morsel of truth, representing real events that were not so wrapped up in exaggeration and magic—similar to Greek mythology and even modern comic books. What were these events? How had centuries of oral tradition, much like a prolonged game of Chinese whispers from one generation to the next, changed the original fact?

Scrawling on a notepad next to the Torah's broad, delicate pages, the professor translated from the ancient Hebrew. He wrote two phrases side by side: LET THERE BE LIGHT and GOD SEPARATED THE LIGHT FROM THE DARKNESS. Leaning back in his chair, Simms examined the connection between the two phrases and his booklet of notes on the origins of archangels.

Behind him, in the ether, a warm, golden glow and a heavy thrum indicated the arrival of Gabriel's commander, Chava. Simms glanced contemplatively through the stained-glass window of his office, tapping his pen against his lips while pondering a new theory. Placing a hand on the professor's shoulder, Chava engaged a transfer of the Light. Simms instantly made a connection in his mind, scrawling his light bulb moment in block capitals: DIVISION OF ANGELIC RANKS?

A loud knock at Simms's door shunted him from his thoughts. Chava vanished in a silent golden orb.

"Enter," the professor barked at the door, disgruntled at the interruption. Sorchia poked her head into the room.

"Always buried in the Hebrew Bible, Simmsy! Do you never tire of that dusty old book?"

Her dry humour surprised the focused professor. She and Simms had struck up a casual friendship in Sorchia's initial year teaching anthropological studies at New College. In the following years, they had bonded over their love of ancient history and cheesy American detective shows.

"Sorchia! What a pleasure. Do come in and sit, and please forgive me for the mess!"

"Thanks. I hope you don't mind me dropping in like this, unannounced."

"Not at all. I could use the break. I tend to start seeing Hebrew characters in rather odd places if I don't give the old eyes a rest!"

"I bet you do."

"What can I help you with, Sorchia?"

"Well, I stumbled across your book on angelic myth, and I wanted to ask you a few questions about your theories on higher angelic beings."

Professor Simms beamed. "Oh really? That's a happy coincidence. I've only just today started following up on my theories about God's seven archangels."

"Great, I've caught you at the right time then. I was hoping to probe into your vast knowledge on the subject."

"Come on, Sorchia. You know you don't need flattery to get information out of me. I always enjoy our conversations. Especially when our fields of study cross over."

"As do I. I'll get to the point then. I was speaking with a colleague in Oxford recently, and I came across the name of an angelic being I hadn't heard of before," Sorchia said, fudging the truth to protect her daughter and her own pride in case Grace's experience was all one big misunderstanding.

"Go on."

"I was wondering if there was any mention in the original Judeo-Christian texts of a being called the Lightbearer."

Simms turned white as a sheet.

"Simms? Are you feeling alright?"

The professor was suddenly livid. His tone shifted into uncharacteristic hostility.

"Have you been spying on me?" He eyeballed Sorchia fiercely.

She laughed in shock. "What? No! Why would you ever think that?"

"Who put you up to this? Was it Evans? That bastard is always trying to make a fool out of me! Well, I'm not going to fall for it this time."

"Please, Professor, relax. I've never even spoken to Dr. Evans. What's going on?"

"Who exactly told you about the Lightbearer?"

"I, eh, came across it in a paper that my colleague was reading and—"

"I'll have you investigated if you are trying to steal my research!"

"Okay, okay! It was my daughter. Oh God. It's going to sound even more insane now that I say it out loud, but it's been nagging at me. Apparently, she had some sort of vision of what she thought was an archangel."

Observing Simms for any hint of mockery, she found none. The leading mind in the field of religious and angelic myth simply listened, captivated.

"Anyway, this apparent archangel told her to find the Lightbearer. Listen, I know it all sounds completely ridiculous, but I had hoped you wouldn't judge me or my daughter because you seem to have a passion for these sorts of mystical visions. I simply had to know if you ever encountered any mention of this Lightbearer in your research."

Sorchia searched his stunned, blank expression for a reaction. None came.

"You've heard of this character before, haven't you?" she exclaimed.

Without a word, Simms opened the lower right-hand cupboard of his desk to reveal an electronic safe. He proceeded to unbutton his collar and relax his tie to pull out a silver necklace holding a glinting yin and yang pendant. Craning his neck towards the safe and dangling the pendant over the locking mechanism, he hovered there until a dull sliding sound signalled the release on the door of the secure box. Simms removed a thick manuscript and slapped it on the table. The title read LUCIFER, THE SEVEN, AND THE LIGHTBEARER.

It was at this moment that Sorchia knew Grace was mixed up in something very strange—something her incredibly structured mind was struggling to comprehend.

"I hope you'll forgive someone in my position for such a childish outburst," Simms said, holding up the document like a standard bearer on a mediaeval battlefield. "The first few pages should give you the general idea of my rather controversial theory."

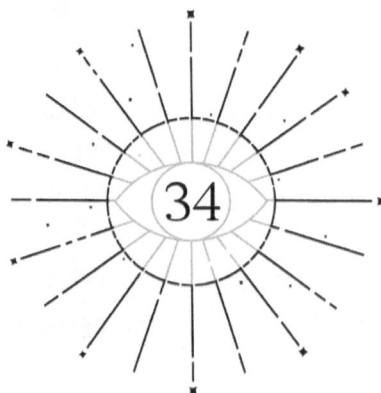

# 34

Haylene clattered through the door of Grace's apartment so hard she almost shook the door off its hinges. Supporting Grace's full weight, Haylene guided her friend towards the sofa. Though Grace had calmed down from her experience of seeing through the veil of the physical world, she had yet to recover from the strain on her spiritual body.

Andy tottered behind his mum, clutching at her hand and hoping that if he squeezed hard enough, Grace would come back to herself. The boy's concern was a hangover from the trauma he had gone through in the worst stages of her drug addiction. With no one to help Grace other than the pills or a needle, Andy had borne the brunt of her toxic behaviour. He had been more resilient than any other child could have been during Grace's final dive into chemicals. Though he was quite young at the time, he had known that his mum was sick from loss and loneliness.

Kids possessed an uncanny wisdom capable of simplifying the most complex situations. He had vowed to always be by her side and never leave. He repeated these very words to Grace often, bolstering her courage no end. Andy firmly believed that her current emotional upheaval was just another challenge they would get through. Together. They would come out the other side and be stronger as a family because of it.

He also felt there was a bigger reason as to why this was happening to them. This assurance was a warm, bubbling sensation in his stomach that sometimes brought tears to his eyes. Andy didn't understand it, but his mom and dad had always taught him to trust it.

Haylene plonked Grace onto the sofa and wrapped a comfy blanket around her, rubbing her shoulders vigorously to bring some life to her stiffened nerves.

"Okay, let's get you settled, and we can go through this."

"Mummy, are you sick again?" Andy asked.

"No, sweetie, I promise."

"Grace, there are only people that love you and support you in this room. No judgments. No anger. You know me, and Andy is your little warrior, so you can be totally open and totally yourself, okay?"

"Okay." Grace nodded with tears welling up.

"Take a full breath into your belly, and let's start at the beginning. So, you think you saw an alien at the hospital?"

"I don't know, but I've felt the energy of this being I encountered imprinted on me since he crashed through the ceiling at the A & E. He knew my name somehow. He was like us but brighter. He didn't feel alien. More like a spirit or an angel. He felt familiar and warm, like I'd known him all my life."

"What about everyone else at the hospital? Did they see anything?" Haylene asked.

"I don't know what they saw, other than Bhunil, the senior consultant. He said he didn't see anything and tried to convince me that it was just a hallucination. After all the other things I've seen since, I know now that the whole experience was real."

"I believe you, Mummy," Andy said, reaching out to hold her hand. Grace mustered a smile and squeezed his hand back.

"Maybe it was just some nutcase that threw himself from a nearby building or something," Haylene suggested.

"Haylene, his wounds were black, and his blood was thick like tar. Human physiology has never been recorded to display symptoms like that." With a link clicking into place in her brain, Grace got an idea. "Hang on a second; where are your angel cards?"

"They're under the coffee table. Why?" Haylene said. Grace grabbed the box and feverishly rifled through the deck.

"I need to see that card you read for me again. You know, the Gabriel one." Spreading the deck out on the table, Grace spotted the one she was looking for. "Here it is!"

As she studied the image of Gabriel, Grace felt the card grow hot in her hand. The border of the card began to glow with a golden hue, and the eyes of the depicted archangel flashed, illuminating the entire room for a split second. Grace dropped the card and covered her eyes. Haylene and Andy both winced and turned their heads away to avoid being blinded.

"Did that card just light up the living room?" Haylene gasped.

"You saw that?!" Grace said.

"That was huge! What did you do, Mum?"

"I didn't do anything," Grace responded. A sudden gust of wind blew through the open window, bringing a chilling energy with it. Jumping up from the sofa, Grace jammed herself into the corner of the room, her back to the wall as the Damned manifested without warning in the middle of the living room. He stood like a rock, directly opposite Grace, only two metres away.

"Oh God!" she exclaimed. She spread her arms against the wall partly in a defensive stance and partly to prop herself up, her knees almost giving way at his appearance. Haylene and Andy were confused by Grace's extreme reaction, though Haylene felt a dark, constricting sensation at her core.

"Why is it so cold all of a sudden?" Andy said, his teeth chattering.

"What's happening, Grace? What is it you see?"

"It's another one of them, standing right next to you," Grace said, her breathing laboured. The Damned's swirling, dark-red energy was literally taking her breath away. "He has so much pain in him," she added—a fact which somehow soothed her. As no stranger to pain, Grace forcibly relaxed herself and gave in to the feelings of the moment, digging deep to deflect the Dark Light force all around her.

Within seconds, Grace had centred herself. A strange serenity overcame her, as if she were in the eye of a crimson storm. In the ether, a solid-white aura formed around her that the Damned's power was incapable of penetrating.

"So. You can see," the Damned remarked.

"What's happening, Grace?" Haylene asked.

"I'm not entirely sure, but the opposing energy of this dark being in front of me seems to have ignited a stabilising force within me."

"I am not your enemy," the Damned croaked.

"What is it that he wants?" Haylene interjected.

Grace met his gaze directly. "Why do you and these other . . . spirits keep appearing to me?"

"We are not spirits. We are beings from the angelic realm. The angel you saw at the hospital was no lowly spirit but a mighty archangel—one of Heaven's most powerful—and he passed a great gift to you."

Haylene and Andy searched Grace's face in the silence of the physical plane.

"What's he saying, Mummy?"

"He says that he's an angel."

"Woah! Sweet. Does he have a giant golden sword and powerful white wings?"

"Erm, not quite."

"I am a dark angel."

"A dark angel?" Grace blurted. "Like a demon? Aren't you supposed to have horns and red skin?"

"I am no demon. These creatures you speak of exist only in the Pit, escaping from time to time to terrorise the physical realm. What you visualise is how human minds throughout the ages have imagined all dark angels to appear."

The Damned shapeshifted into a muscle-bound, red-skinned, horned beast with a mouthful of fangs and black ooze spewing over its lips. When the Damned continued, even his voice had changed, into a low growl. "Is this what you imagined?"

Grace screamed at the top of her lungs. "Yes. Please! Change back!"

"As you wish," the Damned said, morphing back into his original form—glowing red eyes, crackling aura, and all.

Andy was a little more panicked this time when he asked, "Mum, what's happening?"

"Our new houseguest just changed form and gave me a bit of a fright, that's all. Don't worry. I don't think he means any harm. I think if he wanted to hurt us, he would have done it already," Grace said, reassuring herself as well as Andy.

"Gabriel believed you to be a seer of great significance, connected to an ancient lineage of other such uniquely gifted female humans."

"A seer? What's that?"

"Seers are anomalies within the human race who possess the ability to conceptualise the spiritual realm in varying degrees. If aligned fully within themselves, they also have the ability to tap into the power of the Light that nourishes all angelic beings throughout the Universe."

Grace grimaced at his academic description. "I'm sorry, what?"

"Let me simplify it for you. The man you know as Jesus of Nazareth was a powerful seer."

"Jesus?"

"Yes, his healing abilities, wisdom, and prophetic gifts all stemmed from his mastery of the Light."

"Christ Almighty," Grace said.

"Yes, some knew him as Christ."

"Oh yeah, sorry."

"I'm afraid that the idea of a Christ or messiah was but myth and legend that I helped build around the man. It was a trick to blind the human population to their own godhood—to trap them in a prison of guilt and shame. A trick that over time I have come to regret."

"Hang on. Let's leave the Jesus thing and go back a bit. Are you telling me that all these years of high sensitivity and mental breakdowns was because I'm gifted? That seems hard to believe." She felt the extent of her understatement as she gave voice to it. Standing in front of the fallen angel, her mind could not encapsulate how devastated and grateful the suggestion made her. "Are you sure you haven't got me mixed up with someone else?" Tears brimmed, and Grace's hands trembled at the dawning realisation that all her years of struggle had led to this very moment.

"Gabriel found you, and he is rarely mistaken—*was* rarely mistaken. His power of the Light resides in you now. You must learn to trust that in order to tap into its immeasurable strength."

"I guess that could explain the vision of the past I had in the park. It would also make sense of all the glowing figures I've been seeing, along with the bald biker at the gym," Grace said with a nervous giggle.

"Yes, that was Abaddon. You gave him quite the fright, and he doesn't scare easily," the Damned said.

"Hang on a second. You saw into the past in the park? When were you gonna drop that one on us?" Haylene demanded.

"I'll tell all later. There just wasn't time."

"What's he saying now, Mum?"

"Apparently I'm gifted?"

"I always knew you were," Andy said.

"The boy is wise," the Damned said.

The matter-of-fact tone of the conversation was making Grace's head spin. She fell silent as she pressed her hands to her temples.

"I have so many more questions," Grace finally said to the dark angel leader.

"You will find the answers you seek in time, but for now you must listen carefully. I am here to warn you. A war is coming, one such as you have never before seen. It will turn humanity on itself, bringing out an ancient evil within. It is a vicious force older than time itself, and it hungers."

Grace's face fell.

"What's he saying, Grace?" Haylene said, having clocked the sour expression on her friend's face.

"He says that a great evil is coming."

"What are we supposed to do?"

Grace shook her head, mystified by Haylene's pragmatism.

The Damned replied, "Be patient, Grace. Use your gift to see and help those around you to see. I will return."

"Wait, I was told to find the—"

The Damned vanished through a fiery portal.

Grace sighed and squeezed her eyes shut.

"He's gone?" Haylene said.

"Yeah, he just zipped into what looked like a black hole with a red border. Wow! This day could not get any weirder. I'm still so confused. Have we all gone crazy?"

"Listen, we'll get through this together," Haylene said and turned to get Andy's support. "Right, little man?" Her acceptance was making it much easier for Grace to fast-forward past the denial.

"Yeah, Mummy, we're with you!" Andy shouted as he thrust his fist into the air. Running up to Grace, he jumped on her like an attacking wrestler. Grace managed to catch him awkwardly. Andy could always lighten the mood with his buzzing energy and cheeky face.

"Oof! You are heavy! Oh, my lovelies, I can't thank you enough. You are both so strong. You're right. We'll get through this together," Grace said.

Through the apartment window, three floors below, the city hummed. The calm inside the apartment stood in sharp contrast to the violence of London's chaotic streets. Several snaking columns of smoke rose in the sky as sirens blared, mixing with screams and shouts. The city was showing the initial birth pangs of the spiritual realm melding with the physical. A full moon shone brightly and forebodingly in the night sky above. The ancient evil, older than time itself, drew near.

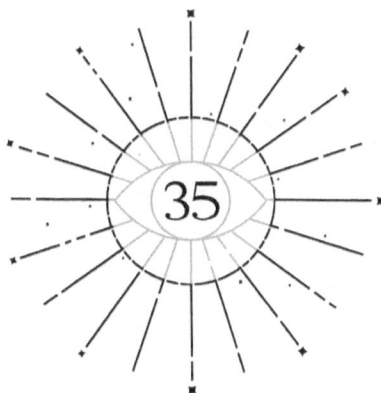

# 35

The last time the archangel Raphael had walked the earth was in the middle of the sixth century: 542 CE, to be precise. The Justinian bubonic plague, a ravaging disease that had wiped out large sections of every community in the Mediterranean during the rule of Emperor Justinian in the Eastern Roman Empire, was at its highest infection rate. The entirety of the far-reaching empire had already begun to decline six years before due to a freak fog that had plunged Europe and the Middle East into an unsettling darkness. The fog had blotted out the sun for eighteen months and destroyed harvests for several years. The mid-sixth century was one of the worst periods in history to be alive. Samael was having a field day.

Serving the balance of life and death, Raphael and Samael had always regarded each other with great respect. Their roles were firmly intertwined, like two skilful dancers. Death without life was madness. Life without death was also madness. Raphael had been drawn down from the upper ether to stunt the bubonic bacteria fast crippling most of the already starving civilisations and overwhelming Raphael's forces. Samael was not letting up, and, as usual, the two angels' difference in opinion concerning "the will of the Universe" and how each should speed it along was evident. By the end of the plague, even with Raphael's powerful intervention and an agreement struck between her and Samael, almost 50 percent of the Mediterranean population had been wiped out.

The hard fluorescent light and whirring refrigeration units of the supermarket where Raphael now stood were a far cry from the squalor of 542. Raphael was at once amazed and repulsed by how humanity's invention had modified its existence. At least the peoples of the sixth century had faced up to their pain and emotions; of course, they had very little choice in the matter. The display in the sterile, shiny temple of consumerism where Raphael now stood seemed vastly more mindless as humans pottered about their business like automatons.

*How has this once passionate and courageous species devolved into such a pitiful state?*

Seeking out some drama and signs of life in the bland atmosphere, the archangel came upon a woman struggling to make a decision in the hair product aisle. The scatter-brained shopper was opening the tops of various containers, testing their smell, and then moving on to the next. The choices were endless—another major problem Raphael had observed in modern lifestyle.

The woman in the hair product aisle was Linda, a late-forties, down-to-earth individual. She was well presented and quirky with a bookish look. Accessing the senses of the physical plane, as all upper-ether archangels had the ability to do, Raphael poked her nose next to each bottle, smelling along with Linda. Raphael had her own idea about how each new fragrance should smell and was enjoying the game. In a twist of thought, Linda hurriedly smelled a handful of her own hair and grimaced. Raphael also sampled a sniff and gave the woman a mournful nod of agreement.

Linda peeked about the aisle to check that no one was watching her and next sneaked a sniff of her armpit. Raphael retracted in disdain as she received a pungent waft. The body odour situation was dire. Linda hurriedly grabbed the first deodorant she could get her hands on and sprayed a generous mist under her arms and then around her head and torso to be safe. She sighed in a moment of relief.

A second woman popped around the nearest end of the aisle, beaming like a hyena. Caught off guard, Linda whirled to greet her.

This was Tessa. Tessa was the same age but looked more like an ageing Barbie doll refusing to let go of her youth. Her makeup was caked on, and her hair had been expertly dyed and styled. Tessa was a friend of Linda's from high school, but neither had made the recent twenty-year reunion. Tessa missed the event due to a scheduling clash and was sad to have missed out. Linda, on the other hand, had made several lengthy and outlandish excuses, terrified at the prospect of the dinner event, and spent the day sweating bullets.

"Linda? Is that you?" Tessa warbled.

"Tessa! How nice to see you!"

It wasn't nice to see her. Tessa was a gossiping snob, and Linda prayed the ground would swallow her whole as Tessa munched on a tasteless protein bar and sputtered an unwanted commentary.

"I'd go for the Coconut, Almond Oil, and Lavender Dreamscape. The scent is to die for, and it's all I would allow to touch my scalp," Tessa said, pointing to a purple bottle on the shelf next to Linda.

"Oh, I'll have to give that one a try," Linda said. She picked up the shampoo to appease her.

Wanting to feel included in the odd exchange, Raphael moved her nose inside the bottle in Linda's hand and retracted her head sharply, disgusted. The vile scent in no way lived up to the fancy name and design on the bottle. Taking another bite from her protein nut bar, Tessa squawked on.

"Darling, you really must try these new Nut Joy bars—high in vitamin B and essential proteins and fantastic for the skin; have a bite," said Tessa, the human embodiment of an online advert for the brand's pyramid scheme, which she had been sucked in by. Her over-the-top gesturing and forced delivery stank of salesmanship.

Shoving the snack in front of Linda's mouth, Tessa gave her no choice. Linda tried not to think where Tessa's mouth had been or how tasteless the Nut Joy bar would be as she took a grudging bite. What a ludicrous name. It was like chewing cardboard and nails.

Ignoring Linda's feelings on the matter, Tessa continued with her verbal assault.

"Oh my God, did you hear about Jane?"

"Mmm, no," Linda mumbled as she continued to chew, desperately trying not to show how foul the excuse for food in her mouth was.

"You'll never believe what she did," Tessa said.

Raphael sighed in the background. She was already fed up with this self-important clotheshorse. Linda shook her head in response to Tessa's declaration, ready for the floodgates to open.

"Well! Jane was having her weekly tennis lesson with the delicious Fabio at Kensington Lawn Club when her ex-husband, James, turned up with his new girlfriend!"

Linda pretended to listen while moving the paste in her mouth around like a cow chewing on grass. Raphael started mimicking Linda's mouth movements, empathising with the nasty sensations she was experiencing.

"Who is a child, by the way, and seldom has more than a pair of shorts and a bikini top on. My God, you should have seen the way she was prancing around that court. Every single male board member was drooling all over her like children in a chocolate shop . . ."

Tessa was so lost in her story that she wasn't even looking at Linda anymore. It didn't matter who was listening. While Tessa was distracted with herself, Linda spat the tasteless pulp into her hand and searched nervously for a place to discard it. Tessa went on, oblivious.

"I mean, what a complete tart! To add to that, she has no sense of fashion. Her shorts and bikini top are always mismatched. Anyway, Jane sees the two of them together, drops her racket, and starts screaming at them both in the middle of the court!!" Tessa took another bite of her snack. Linda finally found a gap on the shelf next to her, which she used to hide the chewed-up protein bar.

"Well, can you imagine? Then she makes her way over to the

pair, completely embarrassing herself in front of some of the most prestigious members of the club."

Raphael had had enough. As Tessa chewed back the cereal bar to finish her story, Raphael waved a sparkling green hand, causing the tough, dry snack to lodge in the woman's throat.

"I mean, can— Ack. Aaack!"

Raphael and Linda both stared, motionless, as the helpless woman continued to choke. Linda was unsure if she wanted to help her, but after five long seconds, she made the decision to rush to Tessa's aid. Darting behind Tessa, Linda proceeded to perform the Heimlich manoeuvre.

Linda was impressively strong, and after three rib-crunching squeezes, the blockage catapulted onto the floor with a splat. Raphael gave a smug, supportive nod at Linda's display of physical power. Tessa was mortified.

"I . . . I must be off, then," Tessa blurted out as she scurried away as fast as her legs could carry her. Linda giggled to herself at the whirlwind event. The karma had not been lost on her.

Next to her, in the ether, Raphael approved of Linda's response to the misguided caricature of a human being. The archangel was proud to have found at least one human woman who showed mettle in the face of nonsense.

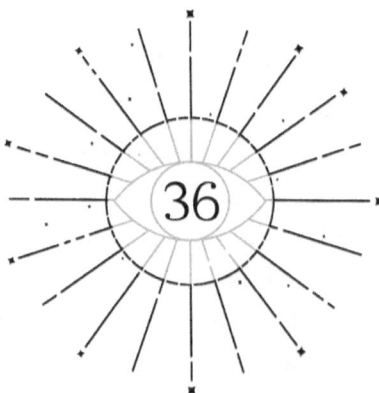

# 36

In the ether, Zelda and Ahebban followed the Archangel of Death as he glided through the physical walls of the cellblock and out into suburban Wandsworth. With a flash of electric blue, a nimble warrior scout arrived in their path, halting the formidable group.

"I have word from the other prison facilities, my master. All have been turned and let loose on the population."

"Good. Return to your ranks for the next stage of the invasion," Samael croaked.

Suddenly, two imposing restoration angels sliced in through an emerald hole in the sky. Swift and lithe, they used the element of surprise to gain an initial advantage over their foes. The first healing angel dropped down onto the three exposed celestials, hitting Zelda hard on the nose and momentarily knocking her off balance. Zelda snapped back to her original position with an eerie calm. The healing angel attacked again, throwing an elbow, then a fist, then a knee, finishing with an uppercut in a flurry of bright-green explosions.

The succession of strikes had little effect as Zelda advanced step by step with each connecting blow. Her unbreakable aura forced the healing angel to move backwards to keep distance. To the attacker's confusion and fear, each blast of green was absorbed into Zelda's blue-and-black Light body. In a desperate attempt, she finished with an earth-shaking palm strike on Zelda's chin. A green fireball of the Light engulfed Zelda, but after the conflagration faded, Zelda stood firm, unfazed. She glared at her exhausted opponent with a devilish glint.

Meanwhile, the second healing angel had fired out of his ethergate next to Ahebban, landing an expertly delivered sucker punch to Ahebban's midsection. The force of the blow sent the stone-faced cherub whistling like a missile backwards through the walls of the prison.

Ahebban phased through three consecutive concrete walls and landed in the prison's innermost cellblock, flat on his back. Dazed, the cherubim took his time standing and growled in frustration.

The second healing angel now focused his attack on Samael, hurling a massive spinning kick at Samael's head. The attempt was blocked nonchalantly by the Archangel of Death's rock-solid forearm, as if he were moving at a different speed entirely. Samael threw out his right arm and grabbed the second ambushing angel's face with a huge hand, sucking away the angel's Light in the blink of an eye.

Samael discarded the limp, grey body. An instant later, the blackened, lifeless figure turned to stone before crumbling into ash.

Back with Zelda, the first attacking healing angel was allowed one last knife hand before Zelda casually pushed the angel's arm out of the way and responded in kind. Zelda's countering straight-arm punch connected with the weary angel's solar plexus, cannoning his body towards Samael. Samael caught the angel's skull as if it were a child's toy. Admiring the black stain of the first healing angel on the ground, he held the remaining angel squirming in midair.

Samael had heard tales of this new power but had yet to witness its effects himself. Death of mortals was all in a day's work for Samael, but the death of angelic immortals was an exciting new prospect. The rush of exhilaration, and the Light consumed in the process, was addictive. Samael had agreed to partner with Michael's mad conquest against his better judgment. He had been given an ultimatum: join his legions or face exile. The latter choice would be a fate worse than death, so Samael had pledged his forces to the cause. Now that he was experiencing the rewards for his loyalty, Samael could see the merits of his allegiance.

Unbridled power.

Samael swivelled his head in a robotic fashion towards the healing angel in his vice grip, his cold, vacant stare drinking in the celestial's vibrant lustre. The angel convulsed and screamed in protest.

Ahebban dashed back from the prison, furious at being caught off guard. Standing firm and poised, Zelda didn't waste the opportunity to shoot him a disparaging glance. She had been less than thrilled at being paired up with this troglodyte. He had always been the weak link in the cherubim ranks—not for his lack of prowess in battle but for his brutish and uncouth tactics. Ahebban had the reputation of a butcher more than a covert, skilled killing machine. He had also botched more than one mission in recent centuries due to his lust for violence. For her, this carelessness was unforgivable. His very presence on any mission tarnished the reputation of the cherubim.

As the two cherubim glared at each other, Samael savoured his new display of power, groaning sadistically as he absorbed the healing angel's life force.

"We will all die before we let you win," the angel sputtered at Samael.

"That's just what I was hoping for," Samael returned as the angel's glory wilted before his eyes. *How curious this sensation is.*

The drained angel's skin was porcelain white at the end. He gasped for air. His body went still and cold, then evaporated into the ether. Pivoting away from the prison and unfurling his tentacles, Samael felt refreshed and energised.

"Finish the prison. If any resist, leave them to the touched," Samael commanded his compatriots.

"That was not in Lord Michael's plan," Zelda said.

"I did not ask for your opinion, wench. Do as I say, and you will be glad not to have joined these two unfortunates." Alerted to several sharp movements in the etherverse, Samael tilted his head sideways, looking up. "Once you are finished here, we track down the rest of these escaped traitors."

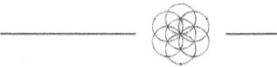

Inside the prison walls, Eddie and Jade fumbled around the weapons locker, trying to pull on their armoured vests and helmets. The large, secure door to the prison wing in the adjoining room thudded with repeated blows from prisoners trying to break free from the cellblock.

"What the bleedin' hell happened while I was out having a smoke? You have a demon séance or something?" Jade protested.

"Quit the wisecracks. I have no idea what happened. Everyone just started convulsing and then attacking each other."

"Well, whatever's going on, those crazy bastards in there are not gonna make me miss my holiday," Jade said, dressed head to toe in riot gear and slapping her baton off a plastic shield. Eddie was still fighting to pull on a vest that was far too tight, and his baton had lodged awkwardly in one of his armoured sleeves. He was a bumbling mess. Jade stood and stared. Waiting.

"Need a hand there?"

"I've got it!"

"Don't be stupid. Here, take one of these," Jade said, losing patience and thrusting a Taser towards Eddie.

*Zzzzz!* The Taser unexpectedly misfired into Eddie's backside while he was bending over to pick up his shield. Eddie shook and spluttered saliva as the voltage rattled through his muscle fibres.

"Oh, whoops! Sorry!"

"Jade, what the feck! Oh, God. Wow. That was intense," Eddie moaned, coughing and trembling. Realising something was off, Eddie looked down at the fresh urine stain on his trousers.

"Well, this is just great! We haven't even started facing down that lot, and I've already pissed my pants. What a truly special friend you are, Jade."

"Oh my God, it was an accident. Dry your vagina, will you, and then can we get on with this?" Nervous energy bubbling over, Jade rushed into the hall and readied herself, staring down the door. Eddie clattered in behind her, feeling his wet patch and giving his hand a sniff. Clocking his childish, distracted behaviour, Jade slapped him hard.

"What was that for?" Eddie yelped, rubbing his stinging face.

"You need to focus, mate. I ain't facing down the *Walking Dead* extras in there with an absent-minded baby!"

"Right. Got it. I'm here."

"I've just got one question: how are we supposed to—"

*Blam!* The door burst open, and three feral inmates rushed Eddie and Jade in a wave of flailing limbs.

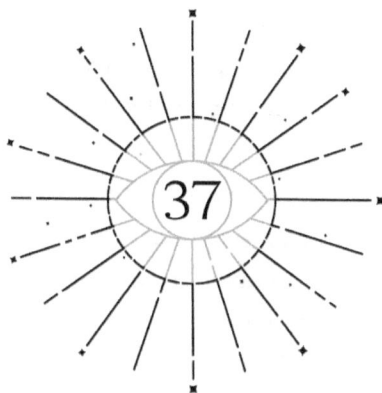

# 37

At Edinburgh's New College library, Sorchia and Simms tucked themselves into a discreet corner of the ornate main room. Here they could access materials to corroborate the professor's theories undisturbed and out of earshot. Sorchia leafed through Simms's Lightbearer manuscript outline, her synapses lighting up like a Christmas tree.

"So, let me get this straight. You believe that the Lightbearer was actually the first created archangel?"

"Not only that but a being more powerful than each and every angel created afterwards," Simms remarked, scurrying to a large wall of scroll excerpts encased in glass. Each document on the wall was pressed flat and slotted longways like books of glass into a cleverly arranged shelving compartment, one to which only he and a select few other colleagues had the key. Simms slid the ancient text he had been searching for from its sleek compartment and onto the desk. Polishing the glass with a fresh hanky from his jacket pocket, he stood back to admire the encased pages. It never ceased to amaze him that a slice of history had been so well preserved that he could now look upon it more than 1,900 years later.

"Why is there no mention of this great angel you speak of in the Hebrew Bible, then?"

"Aha! But is there? How's your ancient Hebrew?"

"Rusty," Sorchia said. Simms excitedly beckoned her to look at the text in front of him. She skirted the desk next to the professor to get a better view.

"Most people who read the Bible fail to understand that it is written not as fact but as a story with deeper meanings concealed within the narrative. As you know from your anthropological studies, storytelling is how ancient cultures made sense of their existence. In this very same way, the Hebrew Bible conveys many hidden truths on a subconscious level."

"I follow you, but what am I looking at here?"

"This is the first few verses of Genesis in which the ancient Hebrew reads 'and God said let there be light,'" Simms said as he drew a finger under the Hebrew characters in the centre of the document.

The professor hopped back to the wall of encased scrolls and searched for another piece in his puzzle.

"My thesis proposes that the being your daughter mentioned was created along with the 'light,' before any other angelic force, and was in fact tasked to bear its power. Since light is the foundation of all creation and the existence of 'the Lightbearer' is intertwined with the power of light, it follows that this first archangel may wield the very power of life and death itself."

Simms found a supporting scroll on the shelf and carried it to the table.

"If you look at the following verse in Genesis, it refers to God dividing the light from the darkness. I propose to use this verse to prove that all other angelic beings came into being and were tasked with their roles after the Lightbearer."

"To be honest, Professor, it all seems like a stretch to me, albeit my experience with the subject matter is very limited."

"It is a stretch. You're right. I was of the same opinion until I cross-referenced my theory with this excerpt from the Dead Sea Scrolls," Professor Simms said, sliding the second page across the table next to the Genesis verse.

"Weren't several books in the Dead Sea Scrolls omitted from the Bible and only discovered recently in the 1950s?"

"Very good, Sorchia. I think you know a lot more about biblical history than you let on."

Sorchia dipped her head to hide her flushed cheeks. "Well, it does contribute to a lengthy chunk of European and Middle Eastern history."

"That it does. Anyway, stumbled upon by goatherders in the West Bank of Israel in 1947, the scrolls became 'the' most important historical documents to support the Bible. Not only that, but their significance to Judaic and Christian mysticism was astounding."

"Mysticism being a way of thinking that emphasises the spiritual and magical elements of a religion?"

"Precisely. For my research into the existence and ranking of archangels, the Dead Sea Scrolls hold key information," Simms said, moving in front of the document he had just retrieved. "This is the War Scroll, and it talks of a literal battle between the sons of light and the sons of darkness. I believe this suggests a link to the division between light and dark angels."

"How does this battle connect to this Lightbearer figure?"

"Because the Lightbearer was created before this angelic division, its ability to move between light and dark forces would be unrivalled. This mighty divine being would be an angelic force with limitless power and the ability to shape any and all forms of light around it."

Sorchia moved back to her seat and sat pondering. Staring at the professor and then back to the title of the manuscript, she had yet to be fully convinced.

"I'm afraid I'm just not getting the historical timeline. I'm a little out of my depth here."

"Are you hungry?" Simms said, changing tack.

"I think I've gone past that point. I honestly can't remember the last time I ate."

"I know a great little place that has outstanding food and coffee. How about I treat you to dinner and explain my theories further?"

"Are you asking me out on a date, Mr. Simms?" Sorchia teased.

The professor fumbled. "Well, I . . . if you needed to eat, then . . ."

"I'm kidding. Relax. It would be lovely to have dinner over some interesting conversation. I can't think of a nicer way to spend the evening."

"Oh. Great. You're going to love my introduction to archangel lore. There is a lot of crossover from various strands of early civilisation," the professor said excitedly. Sorchia nodded and smiled as she waited for Simms to gather his manuscript and scattered notes.

A forgotten place had abruptly awoken in Sorchia. Her stomach fluttered, and warmth spread across her chest and neck. No one had been able to crack the icy surface of her professional demeanour until Professor Simms. She relished the opportunity to delve into history with a brilliant mind and a fellow geek at heart. Geeks had to stick together, and Sorchia secretly regarded Simms's invitation to dinner as date number one.

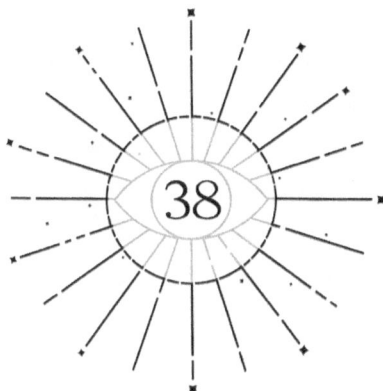

"Graveyard of Empires" was the sinister nickname given to the almost unconquerable nation of Afghanistan. The country's crucial position as the main land route between Iran, India, and Central Asia had long made it a target, but throughout history, even when an empire had made inroads through initial victories, the middle phase of their campaign would ultimately collapse. Subjugation and control of the Afghan peoples seemed an impossible task. In modern history, British, Russian, and American efforts had all ended in defeat and withdrawal.

This failure came down to two main factors. First, having been occupied many times over the centuries, it had collected a wide range of peoples and religions, all fighting for their rights; tribalism took hold, spawning a huge number of warring groups. As such, any centralised form of government control was out of the question. Second, and certainly the most loathed factor facing any attacking army, was the country's harsh landscape. Jagged mountain ranges and desolate, hot, dusty ground with multiple ambush sites posed a logistical nightmare.

The hill country of Afghanistan's Helmand province, near the Musa Qala district, was the typical example of this bleak landscape. The dry and uneven rocky terrain made military manoeuvres slow, leaving ground troops exposed to attack from the surrounding hillsides. In current times, the Taliban were the native hostile tribe fending off attackers.

Like rabbits in warrens, they lay in wait for their foes to approach their elevated position. The stony slopes they occupied also provided natural fortifications. Any force attempting to advance on the Taliban's location in the hills outside Musa Qala was sure to suffer heavy casualties.

This particular day bore out that fact.

Dead for hours now, a female soldier lay motionless as wind swirled sand around her. Shards of shrapnel dotted her face. Her right hand and right leg had been blown clean off. The lost pieces of her were nowhere to be seen. Braen was no more. A cold corpse had taken her place.

A curious eagle landed on the body and began pecking at the stump of her leg. Close by, the sounds of AK-47 machine-gun fire rattled sporadically. Frantic Arabic shouting added to the noises of war.

Jack rocketed past Braen's body, kicking up dust as he went. He found a defensive position near his fallen squad member and breathed hard. Peering from behind a cracked boulder into the dusty ambush bowl, Jack didn't like his odds.

The eagle continued to feed on Braen's body.

Silence settled as the Taliban's gunfire and shouting ceased. A gust of wind brought the faint sound of shuffling footsteps ahead, and indistinct chatter indicated to Jack that he had lost his pursuers for the time being. His options were rapidly decreasing as daylight faded in the walled and barren gulley. It was time to go on the offensive.

Two Taliban soldiers attempting to track his position arrived at Braen's corpse within minutes. Distracted, kicking the body and grinning like fools, they were exposed. Jack bolted from behind the nearby boulder like a startled meerkat.

With two single shots, one in each forehead, both Arabic fighters slumped next to the rocky outcrop Jack had been hiding behind, dead before they hit the ground. Jack retreated back to his hiding spot. A third Taliban fighter darted next to his companions, spraying his machine gun wildly in every direction. He was afraid, confused, and outmatched by Jack's years of experience on the battlefield. Popping up from cover again, Jack levelled his rifle.

Another bullet took the Arabic fighter down, bleeding but still alive. The bullet had punctured his cheek. Jack cursed his lapse in concentration.

*Sloppy work, Causer.*

Rushing in to finish the job, Jack took the bleeding Arab fighter out with two quick rounds in the chest—but not quick enough. The Arab fighter managed to lash out desperately with a concealed blade before his last breath. Jack's femoral artery split open. He collapsed next to Braen and the pile of three Taliban corpses nearby, a smorgasbord of fresh meat.

The eagle circled above, shrieking in the shadows of a dying sun.

Bleeding out and growing woozier by the second, Jack struggled to find his first aid pack. Braen's corpse stared at him with greying, empty eyes. He blinked as a blurry red shape approached him from a distance behind her.

*Could it be a rescue?* he thought. Oddly, it appeared to be a woman in a beautiful, flowing red dress and red high heels. Shielding his eyes from the sun, Jack put the strange vision of a high society ball down to mere hallucination. Still curious, however, he tried to make out the woman's face but was unable to focus in his weakened state.

Beel knelt next to Jack and cradled his head softly. The sultry celestial appeared strangely pure. With a fresh, unadorned face, she held a peaceful beauty about her, like a princess shrouded in bright mist. Her eyes were human eyes of the deepest brown, inviting and contrasting the provocative red dress hanging from her curvaceous figure.

"You must go to her," she whispered.

"But I . . . I'm dying."

"Without her, we all die."

Jack turned his head to look again at Braen's cold, dead eyes and mutilated body. When Beel moved in and kissed Jack softly and passionately, he kissed her back, swept up by the strange hallucination in his dying moments.

"Open your heart," Beel said.

"I don't know how. There's too much pain."

In an instant, Beel's face transformed, her appearance morphing into the ruthless dark angel. Her eyes changed to a fiery orange behind her dark, heavy makeup. She thrust her sharp fingernails into Jack's open leg wound.

"What about her pain?" Beel hissed with a sadistic smile.

Jack roared, snapping back to consciousness at the desk in his basement, covered in sweat. It had all been another torturous dream.

Beel's orange eyes flashed in the shadows around him. Reaching for the whiskey bottle, Jack poured himself another drink and rubbed his head and eyes. Guilt washed over him. He grabbed the glass and threw the amber alcohol back.

Beel dropped her head and shook it with frustration. "You men disgust me. So strong with your weapons and your masks, yet so weak with your hearts," she whispered.

Jack turned his head slightly, thinking he'd heard something. Deciding he must have imagined it, he refilled his glass, pushed his chair away from the table, and gave in to the sudden urge to launch the bottle at the evidence wall. It smashed into a thousand pieces, covering the wall in whiskey.

*What does it all mean? How does it all fit? How do I make these goddamned nightmares stop?*

Jack suddenly whipped around to face the back wall. He knew the feeling of being watched all too well. There was no one there, and then the feeling was gone.

In a fit of exasperation, Jack rushed up the stairs and into his garage, on the hunt. He tossed the blanket off a large box in the corner and hoisted the box with a firm grip. Crashing through the side door and heading around to the front of the house where the bins were, Jack tossed the unwanted thing in one swift movement.

Jack didn't waste another second to look back as he marched back inside. The box was left upside down, split wide open atop the rubbish bins, ready for collection that day. Half-assembled furniture legs protruded from the box like arrows from a gaping wound. The image on the side of the cardboard showed a self-assembly baby crib.

Jack slammed the door behind him. If the answers to his undercover case weren't going to reveal themselves, then he would push them to the surface using the best means he had at his disposal: brute force.

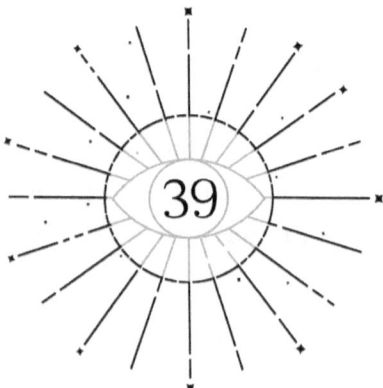

## 39

The Damned landed on the hexagonal stones of the Giant's Causeway in the ethereal plane. He hoped the momentary retreat would allow him to take stock of the events that had shaken the foundation of everything he knew.

Gabriel, perhaps the fairest and most powerful of all celestial beings, had been assassinated without warning, stabbed in the back by the warrior class. Gabriel's guardians had been hunted down and executed in an act of ice-cold genocide. Samael and his death angels had joined with Michael's warriors, imprisoning the judgment and commandment classes. The force Samael and Michael now wielded as a result was likely nothing the upper ether had ever seen before. Raphael and her healing angels had been fortunate to escape, albeit scattered and on the run.

The whole cataclysmic chain of events must have been foreseen by Gabriel in his wisdom. No doubt his observance of Michael's withdrawal from angelic business had flashed a warning sign. Cautious of the violence Michael might resort to, Gabriel had been searching for a being to pass the Light onto should the upper ether fall; he had found a worthy subject in Grace, a human woman and potential seer who now held within her the last and greatest hope for humanity. Gabriel's untapped might flowed through her spirit. Upon meeting Grace, the Damned knew that his path and hers were aligned in defence of the earth and all its human inhabitants.

In spite of all this misery, the Damned still had hope that he and the humans could survive the coming onslaught. There were three glaring problems that Michael hadn't banked on when planning his assault on humankind.

First, Michael had certainly overestimated his own ability to face down a seer, should he encounter one—no mean feat for any archangel. Second, he surely had not foreseen Gabriel's transference of the Light, and his abilities, to a human. Third, and most importantly, he would likely assume that the Damned and his dark angels were in favour of humanity's destruction or would at least remain neutral, watching from the sidelines. The Damned had to laugh at how foolish it would be for Michael to assume that the Damned's lust for revenge had faded. The dark angel lord's emotion was as raw and raging as the day of his exile. His jaded perspective on Michael and his haughty warriors was further strengthened by his newfound fondness for humankind and their deadly predicament.

The enemy of his enemy had become his friend.

If Gabriel and his class were gone and the laws of the Universe made meaningless, then why should the Damned be a slave to his role? The balance of the celestial planes had been tipped, and he would do what he felt was right to level the odds.

For once.

A great, burning anger of suppressed desire churned inside the Damned, and he vowed to channel and unleash it on any and all who would threaten his class and the humans, damn the consequences. It was time for the dark angel lord to choose his own path.

As the Damned stepped towards the causeway's edge and its lapping waters, an odd sensation hit him. *Do I feel the wind?* He had not had the ability to feel on the physical plane since being trapped in the lower ether. This small brush of cool air at the Damned's neck signalled to him that the melding of the physical and spiritual planes had begun, clearly a side effect of the aggressive shifts occurring in the etherverse. He could not explain the phenomenon nor know how it would affect the coming war. The outcome of such an event might be catastrophic, the cosmos collapsing in a collision of the Light and the Dark Light. For now, the melding's initial stages were harmless, only randomly fritzing the senses of spiritually heightened beings and bringing confusion to humans.

The Damned sought out Grace's location, establishing a link between his energy and hers so that he could be alerted when her safety was at risk. Normally this link would take a mere second, as he had already stood in the woman's presence and marked her affinity with the Light. However, the sputtering energies of the etherverse required more of the Damned's focus and the Dark Light to achieve the connection. His solid crimson aura grew brighter as he locked onto Grace's light.

Their fates were tied now.

Taking in a deep breath, the Damned attempted to feel out what was happening with other angelic beings in the vicinity. This was an ability the leader of every angelic class had previously been able to call upon at will, yet with Gabriel's demise, a gaping hole had opened in interclass communication. Even speaking with his own clan was a struggle and required expending copious swathes of the Dark Light.

The Damned's movement had also been somewhat hampered. The guardians had overseen all celestial movement and policed borders carefully to balance the energies of the spirit realm. Now a greater deal of focus and time was required to accurately pinpoint and arrive at destinations.

This physical and spiritual collision troubled the Damned the most. A quick solution to the problem would be needed to face down the legions of warrior angels descending on the human race. The only option he had was forbidden to dark angels: connecting to the Well—a primaeval rift in the physical realm known only to the guardian class, the Damned, and the dark angels below him—on the physical plane.

Throughout history, tales had been told of celestials attempting to access the Well's power. They were the stuff of nightmares. If any angelic being attempted to touch the inner void of the Well, rivers of fire and ice consumed them and banished their soul to an unknown realm, nowhere to be found in the Universe. *Maybe things are different with Gabriel gone*, the Damned thought. Maybe his great Dark Light body was strong enough to absorb the Well's force and push through to touch the centre, where its energising core lay.

Under the circumstances, it was a risk the Damned had to take. Logic would have it that with no guardian class policing the ether and all other classes engaged in war preparations, the Well would be unprotected.

Pondering his choices, the Damned pulled his bound fists from beneath his robe. They glowed brighter and throbbed with more pain than usual. All at once, he sensed Grace's spirit and the war lurking just around the corner. The Damned winced and lowered his hands to his sides.

"Abaddon, come," he bellowed in an otherworldly, three-tone voice. Abaddon immediately warped in with Scratitch close behind.

"Yes, my lord," Abaddon replied.

"It is time we act. The heavens are falling."

"Finally. I have a taste for warrior angel blood."

"I will stand with Raphael. I need you both to be on guard. Stay hidden from the fight. Be alert to angelic movements."

"My lord," Abaddon began to protest.

"No no no!" Scratitch wailed. The Damned silenced the pair with a flash of red in his eyes. Now was not the time to challenge their master's command.

"Michael's force arrives in numbers, and I need to know who he has sent and where. I will call on you again when I have more information on their plans."

"Lord, we are stronger together!" Abaddon cried.

"Not for now. Please, brother, do as I ask."

"I will follow your lead, even if it be against my better judgment," Abaddon conceded.

The Damned gave his companions a curt nod before being swallowed up by a blazing ethergate at his back.

As Abaddon watched his master disappear, a wave of confusion and anger rattled his spirit. The Damned never took his advice. Abaddon had always served faithfully with little thanks, and while the Damned's power had increased over time, Abaddon had been kept on a tight leash, left to suck up scraps of energy behind the Damned's back.

When they had both arrived on earth, the Damned was twice as powerful as Abaddon, but their friendship was the strongest it had ever been. They had been united against those who exiled them, and theirs was the righteous cause. Presently, however, all Abaddon felt was the stinging resentment of being denied the glorious battle ahead. It was a dagger in his belly that his oldest friend would choose the welfare of these stinking humans over him, the Damned's faithful companion throughout the ages.

Abaddon bowed his head and sighed a ragged sigh.

At that moment, in her East London apartment, Grace was having a shower, washing off the argument with her mum—washing off the visions and the fear of what was to come. The warm water and suds sent it all down the plug hole, restoring a sense of peace and oneness. Finishing, Grace turned the water off. As she leaned over to twist the water out of her hair, she was startled to see a small golden light shimmering just below her belly button, under the skin. Fixated on its appearance, she grew dizzy.

All at once, Grace was tapping into the Light within her and recognising her spiritual link with the Damned. She slapped her hand against the tiled shower wall to hold herself up. It was an intense, invigorating experience, and it dawned on Grace that she was finally starting to get a grip on the varying spiritual episodes.

In a rapid escalation of intensity, a searing pain ripped through Grace's skull. She closed her eyes and dropped to one knee. Opening her eyes again seconds later, she did not realise that her eyes were glowing bright gold—like Gabriel's.

Gleaming rays beamed from her eyes, growing ever brighter and filling the room. Breathing hard, she pushed her hand into the tiles again for support.

The tiles collapsed under her hand and folded into the wall.

Through the door in the living room, Haylene heard the faint cracking noise. Andy snapped his head out of his comic book with a quizzical expression.

"You okay, hun?" Haylene called.

Back in the shower, Grace's eyes returned to normal, and the pain was gone.

"Fine! I, uh, just dropped the shampoo!" Grace hollered through the door.

"Alright, well, I'm headed out for pizza," Haylene replied.

"Okay. Thanks." Grace stared at the tiles where her hand had been. They had collapsed and melted together at the edges, forming a brown mass of bumpy, warped ceramic. Gradually gaining her balance, she flexed her palm and studied it. Her vision was suddenly sharper, and her mood lifted as she began to feel the nourishing power of the Light Gabriel had passed to her.

Haylene grabbed her bag and headed for the door. "Look after your mum," she told Andy.

He lifted his Hyperion action figure. "She will be safe under my protection, ma'am!"

"Back in fifteen," Haylene said before locking the door behind her.

Grace's phone rang on the coffee table. Scooping it up and seeing the screen, Andy shouted into the bathroom, "Mum, Granny's calling."

"Just leave it. I'll call her back."

"Okay," Andy said, staring at the ringing phone. He grabbed his Lizard Lord action figure and voiced the character's high-pitched English tones. "I'll deal with you later, puny human!"

Grace strolled into the room in her comfy clothes—trying to mask her surprise at having transformed into a human searchlight in the next room—and flopped onto the sofa next to Andy, positively glowing.

"Do you feel better, Mummy?"

"You know what? I really do."

"Can I ask you a question?"

"Of course, sweetie. You know you can ask me anything."

Andy stared at Grace's phone. "Are you and Granny fighting again?"

"Why do you ask that?"

"Because you always answer her calls."

"I was finishing up in the bathroom, that's all."

"That hasn't stopped you before," Andy said.

"Okay, you got me. Your granny just says some hurtful things sometimes when she doesn't mean to, and then Mummy needs time before she feels able to chat with her again."

"Okay."

"Granny and I are very different people. And sometimes we struggle to understand each other."

"I get it. Not like us, Mum?"

"Not like us at all. Come here," Grace said, drawing her little man in for a cuddle.

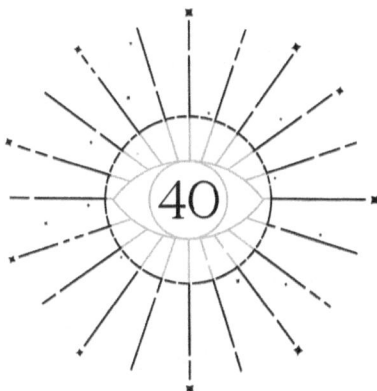

Another writhing body fell to the concrete floor at Wandsworth prison as Zelda transformed him. The prisoner's greed took over his conscious mind, and he launched like a flying spider into the mosh pit of spinning limbs. Clambering, shouting, and biting, the devolved creatures relentlessly tried to fulfil the desires the Touch had exposed within each of them. Slaves to the power of the Seven Deadly Sins, they no longer behaved like humans but fought like snapping reptiles defending their young.

Outside the cellblock that hosted the majority of the chaos, Eddie and Jade battled three relentless prisoners in the entrance hall. The rampant energy of the warped human souls surged forwards, forcing the courageous pair out through the main doors and into the damp courtyard.

Becoming distracted by Jade and Eddie's valiant efforts, Samael watched curiously as a touched guard embodying pure lust roamed towards Jade. Prisoner 5, who was corrupted by gluttony, joined the advance, attempting to corner Jade between a parked car and the building's outer wall. Several metres from her, Prisoner 7 had thrown himself at Eddie and was trying to grapple him like a maddened wrestler.

"You again? You're like my ex-girlfriend that just won't stop texting."

The prisoner growled as Eddie sidestepped the thrashing tackle, then whipped back around, sweating and gnawing at his own lips.

"Bleed, bleeeeeeeed!" the prisoner moaned. Eddie knocked him into a puddle with a powerful baton strike. Without missing a beat, Prisoner 7 leapt back to his feet and went straight for Eddie's throat.

"Jesus!" Eddie yelped. He checked on Jade as he batted away his opponent's insistent attacks. "You alright over there?"

"I am so far from alright!" Jade shouted back. Prisoner 5 had launched himself at Jade's feet, trying to bite her lower legs. The touched guard on her other flank barrelled towards her with a hungry gaze, but a sideways strike from Jade's baton into the guard's eye socket sent him spinning backwards. Whipping out her Taser, Jade fired its maximum current into Prisoner 5's face. The charge had no effect whatsoever.

"What the frig? Is your one as bitey as mine?" Jade hollered.

Eddie screamed, flailing his baton and shield wildly and whirling like a dervish. His playground defence did little to deter the assault. Taking Eddie to the ground in a bone-crunching rugby tackle, Prisoner 7 scrambled on top of him, clawing at his face.

Determined to protect Eddie, who was like a little brother to her, Jade gritted her teeth and smacked the prisoner at her feet with all her might. The blow landed square on Prisoner 5's temple, and his lights went out. The lust-driven guard, on the other hand, had regathered himself and was on top of her like flies on a corpse. The touched guard licked at Jade's face and grabbed for her private parts. Shoving the creature off her, she elbowed him smack on the bridge of the nose.

"Ugh! Have some manners," Jade remarked with a kick to the testicles, immediately following up with a baton to the jaw. "Hashtag me too, pervert!"

In the cover of the ether, Samael observed patiently, waiting for his moment to silence this irritating upstart. He was enjoying the show, and he always made time for a little sport while on the hunt for human souls.

Eddie struggled to keep Prisoner 7's teeth off his neck as strings of the prisoner's saliva slapped about his upper torso. "Help! I'm gonna get infected here!"

Jade swooped to the rescue and stomped Prisoner 7 in the back of the head, sending the man's face cannoning into Eddie's chin.

"*Ow*! Jeeethe! Do you think you coulthve puthed him to the thide before thmacking him in the back oth the head?" Eddie squealed, his words coming out with a heavy lisp from chomping on his tongue, which had swollen to twice its size.

"I saved you, didn't I?"

"Buth you coulth have tathed him!"

"Doesn't work."

"Whath do you mean?" Eddie protested.

Jade pointed to the twisted heap of Prisoner 5. "Muggins over there got a full charge in the eyeball, and it didn't slow him down. Seems like a hard reset to the head is the only thing that stalls whatever it is they've become or been infected with."

Gliding towards Jade and Eddie, Samael's grey appendages crept up Jade's body in the ether, slithering around the back of her skull and latching on. The tendrils inside Jade's mind sucked away her life force and poisoned her spirit with the Touch all at once. Samael was bemused momentarily before vanishing in a shroud of black smoke. The evil of the Seven Deadly Sins bubbled beneath Jade's skin, shaking her limbs and head violently. The whites of her eyes clouded over like a savage virus under a laboratory microscope.

"Jade? Jade! What's wrong?" Eddie cried, but it was no use. Jade could no longer hear him. She squirmed as her body strained to fight the evil taking over.

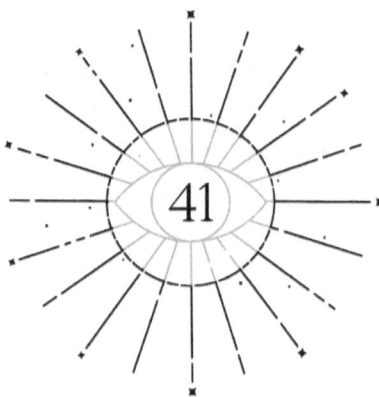

# 41

Having not yet sensed anything jarring in the etherverse, Raphael continued to drift through the supermarket aisles. Earth was where the coming fight would be won or lost, and Raphael needed to understand the rules of the physical realm. On top of this, her ability to navigate the mortal plane had become unstable, and even if her spiritual powers had been functioning as normal, Raphael's earth portalling was severely out of practice. In light of these constrictions, the archangel thought it best to remain where she was so the Damned would know where to find her should he need to.

Spotting a young man bopping down the walkway with headphones on, Raphael became intrigued. The archangel had of course witnessed humans dance before, but not while wearing these strange ear coverings. Zipping in close, she listened to the music wafting from the headphones and smiled upon hearing the funky seventies tunes.

An old couple pottering towards Raphael and the young man came to the archangels' attention. Sensing the opportunity for some lightheartedness after a ghastly few days, Raphael directed her signature magician's wave in the old couple's direction. The music spread from the young man's headphones across the ether in a sprinkling of green stardust. Surprised to hear music in their eardrums, the old couple sparked with delight and began to dance. The magic of Raphael's touch prompted all three humans to synchronise their rhythm like a Bollywood film set. Spirits lifted, the strangers regarded each other with a mixture of disbelief and wonder as their bodies took the lead, connecting through the music. Raphael joined in with her own brand of utterly cringeworthy dancing and clapped her hands off the beat. Rhythm had never been the glamorous archangel's strong suit.

"Yes!" Raphael exclaimed, lost in the spiritual moment.

Leaving the strangers to groove joyously with one another, Raphael slipped away, contented to have brought some fleeting joy in what seemed to her an otherwise broken world.

Abruptly, an odd energy clashed with Raphael's aura, sending her rigid.

The cold sensation spread through the atmosphere, and as the fluorescent lighting above flickered, the faint smell of electrical burning floated past her. The archangel was suddenly aware of a sinister power spreading towards her location, originating at the nearby prison.

She phased into the supermarket car park at the front of the building and stood at the ready as the darkening sky rolled in on itself. Rotating unnaturally quickly, the upper atmosphere spat out shards of blue lightning. Thunder rattled, and the winds picked up into a fierce gale, rain spitting down in sheets. The archangel's robes and hood whipped wildly as she faced a storm that was not merely physical in nature. Clamping her eyes shut, Raphael focused her instincts.

*Clunk. Crack. THRACKADOOM!* A force from above shook the physical plane. The windows of every vehicle in the car park shattered, and car alarms blared all at once. Raphael widened her stance and pulled her shoulders back tight.

The time to join the battlefield was upon her.

In a flash of blue lightning, three impressive angelic warriors appeared just metres from the archangel of restoration. Raphael sensed their arrival without opening her eyes, such was her strong mastery of the Light. The battle-hungry warriors stood opposite her, their stillness exuding confidence. They were the front line of Michael's warrior class, dressed in neatly fitted, blue-trimmed robes. Corrupted by their leaders' agenda, their once steely-blue eyes were now black and gold and slitted like those of serpents. The warriors were slaves to their mission and seethed with the power of the Seven Sins.

Raphael snapped her eyes open, calm and unimpressed by the warrior unit's arrival. The lead warrior angel, standing as the tallest of the three in the centre of the menacing group, cracked a sly grin.

"Join us, friend."

"Lord Michael, general of the upper ether and the warrior angel class, demands your allegiance," a second warrior angel announced. Though the third remained silent, his heaving chest and crackling aura spoke volumes of his thirst for battle.

"He does, does he?" Raphael goaded.

"It would be better if you did not resist," the lead warrior replied.

"It is you that resists your birthright," Raphael said.

With her hands resting at her sides and without warning, Raphael flipped her palms towards her attackers as two emerald beams propelled the flanking warriors to the other side of the vast car park. Left standing alone, the lead warrior fired a glance over each shoulder and back to Raphael, stunned. He had not expected such ferocity, having assumed that her pacifist nature made this confrontation a mere formality.

This had been a gross misapprehension.

Raphael whipped a glowing palm towards the lead warrior. It pulsed brilliant green as it built in energy. The warrior swiftly crossed his arms over his face, sending a force field of blue around his frame mere seconds before Raphael's blast surged towards him. The warrior struggled mightily to maintain its form.

"You won't kill us. You don't have it in you," the warrior shouted over the thunder of competing energies.

"I have no need to kill," Raphael murmured.

At that moment, the other two warriors darted back into the conflict to stunt Raphael's attack, both materialising swords and shields of blue light. Raphael sliced towards the warriors in sweeping, fluid strikes. Emerald energy blasted from her palms and eyes in a whirling light show. In return, all three warriors unleashed a rain of stabs and hammering shield strikes that saw her rapidly overwhelmed.

Raphael managed to fend off the second warrior with a forearm block to his incoming Light sword, which she followed with a palm strike and a blast of her searing eye beams. Blindingly quick, the archangel spun to connect her left elbow and right fist with the third warrior's midsection, leaving herself open. The first warrior seized the opportunity to release an arcing upward strike with his blazing sword, launching the archangel off the ground and into a spin. A large wound had split open Raphael's face. Leaping into the air after her, the second warrior thundered in with a one-two shield and sword strike combination aimed at Raphael's suspended body. The third warrior finished with a sword slice, shield uppercut, and forward kick that sent the archangel crashing back to earth in a heap.

The angelic warriors stepped back, confident at having dominated their target. Raphael took her time standing to face her foes, revealing the horrific wound across her face. Further marred by the assault, three gaping holes in her torso wept black ooze.

"Surrender or die," the lead warrior commanded. One by one, the wounds on Raphael's body slowly closed over. The final black gash across her eyes, nose, and mouth weaved together in a zigzag of green and gold, the power of the Light shining from beneath. Her face appeared as perfect as before.

"I don't believe either of those is an option," Raphael replied.

"As you wish," the lead warrior replied.

Committed to the long battle ahead, the angelic warriors relaunched their assault. They had no choice but to complete their mission. Failure would mean exile from the upper realms and an eternity of torment.

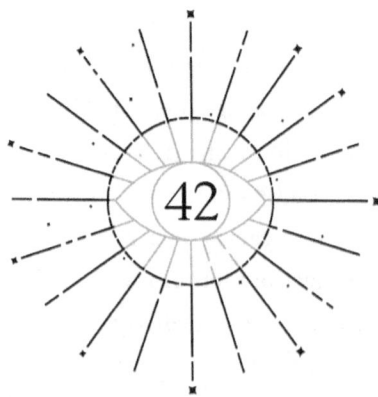

## 42

Jack Causer had his flaws, sure, but he always called it like he saw it. He was a straight shooter, holding firm to logic and clarity and ruthlessly stripping away half-truths and pretences. However, he was finding this ability difficult to engage in his current situation. He couldn't determine whether he was the one being played as he sat in the back of a high-spec Range Rover, accompanied by two of the Wraiths' most ruthless members.

The most dangerous aspect of the Wraiths was their relentless adaptability. A chameleon-like entity, the gang reshaped itself anytime its mysterious leader was threatened. Every member was devoted to him with a cultish level of passion and commitment. Not one individual inside their hierarchy operated independently.

Jack's confidence in his surroundings was further dented by the astute nature of the barbarian sitting in front of him, a bullish freak whose razor-shaved head gleamed in the amber glow of the Range Rover's buttons and dials: Lazaro. As wide as he was tall, the brick-shaped man was one of those people who, contrary to their size and the amount of toxins they funnelled into their body, remained fit, strong, and sharp as a tack. When Lazaro spoke, his foul breath and equally foul language polluted the air around him.

Jack wasn't sure how long this emotionally heightened brute was going to buy into his charade. The man was a base creature who acted on animal instinct, but it was near impossible to slip a trick past him. Jack had only managed to slide under the Wraiths' radar by actually living and breathing the world they lived in. It was a lifestyle that had worn him down.

Jack, Lazaro, and Lazaro's driver, Sonny, currently sat outside one of the many terraced houses in London's largest council house community, Becontree Estate. While its lofty name suggested a walled, historic building with plush gardens that housed the landed gentry of the 1800s, the opposite was in fact the case. The sprawl of terraced brick buildings was badly in need of repair and modernization, having originated in the interwar period of the 1920s. The lower-class estate was a pebbledash hell of muddled colours and damp, untidy gardens.

Inside the luxurious vehicle idling outside 68 Mayfield Road, grating house music thumped from the stereo's subwoofer. Sat in the front passenger seat, Lazaro tapped the central armrest feverishly. Dio had drawn the short straw and been sent out to recover cash from inside number 68. His return was long overdue, and Lazaro's head seemed to be bulging with the amount of blood oscillating under his eye sockets.

"What is taking that idiot so long?" Lazaro snapped. Jack remained silent in the back, while the gorilla-shaped henchman wedged into the driver's seat merely shrugged off the question. Pure muscle with all his features squeezed into a small area on his face, Sonny wouldn't look out of place in a prehistoric museum exhibit. Hair sprouted from his shirt collar, and his heavy eyebrows joined over his nose, looking like a dead ferret. Sonny proceeded to rummage through the bag of wine gums nestled next to his crotch, searching for a black one. Black ones were his favourite.

"Well?" Lazaro barked.

"You know what Dio's like. He's probably just turning the screw for a little extra entertainment. Let's give it another fifteen minutes, boss," Jack suggested.

"Fine, but you're taking the next house, Stones. I'm not here for entertainment. I'm here to get paid," the crime boss grumbled, gritting his teeth.

"Yessir," Jack said.

"And will you put those feckin' sweets away? Your sausage fingers crackling around that bag are driving me bloody nuts."

"Sure, boss," Sonny replied.

"Do you ever stop eating?" Lazaro demanded.

"I just get hungry lots."

"Well, that's obvious, isn't it?" Lazaro said. The henchman dipped his head and looked away.

A news bulletin suddenly interrupted the DJ set.

"Breaking news just in. An unknown virus swept its way through Wandsworth correctional facility just hours ago. The virus has seen other outbreaks across the country not isolated to this incident. Authorities are advising the public to remain calm and keep a safe distance from those who appear to be infected," the bulletin droned.

"What is this crap? Another Covid or bird flu 'epidemic'? Man, the government and their goddamn propaganda machine!" Lazaro moaned.

"Symptoms include dark lesions on the skin, around the eyes and mouth, and discolouration of the subject's eyes. If you come acr—"

"Turn that bollocks off!" Lazaro shouted. Sonny quickly clicked off the volume knob, and the group sat in silence, waiting for Lazaro to lose it completely. "I'm sick of this crap! Stones, go in after him. I'm not just gonna sit here and watch my payload go up in smoke again!"

"Got it, boss," Jack said, exiting the car.

As he made his way to the grotty council estate home, Jack's primal brain flared up. He'd tried to hide it from Lazaro, but he'd become more and more nervous with the passing minutes. It was increasingly likely that Dio had gotten himself into a tight spot and was being held or had suffered harm. He was a mouthy lump, and the strung-out estate boss Dio had been sent in to bargain with was known to fly off the handle without warning. Considering his fondness for the fresh product that passed through his hands and into his grunts' for sale, it wasn't surprising.

Jack readied his knife and prepared to walk into a volatile situation. Knives were better in tight, enclosed spaces and easier to conceal under a shirt sleeve for a shock attack. Always best to make a target believe you were afraid and unarmed before switching to an all-out assault.

Battering on the paint-chipped door, Jack listened for movement. Nothing.

"Dio? Let's wrap things up. Boss wants to get going."

No response. It was eerily quiet for a thriving drug den.

"It's me. Stones. I'm coming in, okay?"

Jack again waited for a response, and none came. Deft and quiet as a prowling cat, he turned the handle and slipped inside.

Meanwhile, in Grace's apartment, Grace cuddled with Andy on the couch, out for the count. Andy was drifting off but trying to stay awake to keep watch over his mum. The sweet, protective boy knew he had to be the man of the house for her. That's what his dad had always told him.

Clicking through the locks at the front door, Haylene arrived home with fresh pizza in hand.

"Got some sourdough from the fancy new place," Haylene announced. Andy whipped his head towards the door and made a shushing gesture.

"Sorry," Haylene whispered, tiptoeing over. She slid the pizza in front of Andy, who flipped open the box and beamed.

"Pepperoni!" Andy exclaimed, immediately catching himself being too loud.

Haylene popped out to get plates from the kitchen as the boy salivated.

"How about we watch a movie?" she whispered as she returned.

"Okay, but we're not gonna watch another girly one, are we? Yuck!"

"Alright, buddy, you can choose this time. But please, no manga movies okay? They're too graphic," Haylene said. Andy flicked through the movie options.

The TV abruptly switched to a blue screen.

"We interrupt your programming with a special announcement."

Both Haylene and Andy sat up and paid close attention. Sensing the shift of emotional energy in the room, Grace stirred awake and listened in, her heavy eyelids struggling to open.

"A virus that broke out in Wandsworth correctional facility earlier today has infected many local residents. If you encounter anyone displaying the following symptoms, please keep your distance and call the number below. The victims appear to be highly erratic and emotionally unstable, with black lesions around the eyes and mouth. Do not leave the house if unnecessary. We will come back to you with further details as they come in."

Huddled on the sofa for strength, the close group was stunned. Images of the affected people and areas flashed across the screen, lighting up their gawking faces.

"This is all a bit surreal," Haylene commented. After everything that had happened, she felt somewhat numb to this latest revelation of what should have been impossible.

"Zombies?! Oh my God!" Haylene frowned at Andy's outburst.

"Come on, buddy. Let's not turn everything into a fantasy film. These people are just sick, like the news said."

"I'm not so sure. I think it's more than that," Grace said.

"What do you mean?" Haylene said.

"That's exactly how Gabriel looked. I think this is the evil our dark angel visitor was talking about."

"Really? Woah, that's awesome!" Andy said, then bit his lip as the two women shook their heads at him.

"Andy. This is real. It's not a video game," Haylene said.

"She's right, my love. Lots of people are sick, and we're in danger too, so nobody leaves each other's sight, okay?"

"Okay, but I need to text Daddy, then, to make sure he's okay."

"I'm sure your dad is fine," Grace said. Andy gazed at his mum with sad eyes. Knowing how important it was to him, she quickly changed her tune. "But yes, why not. That's a good idea, my little man. I know he'd love to hear from you."

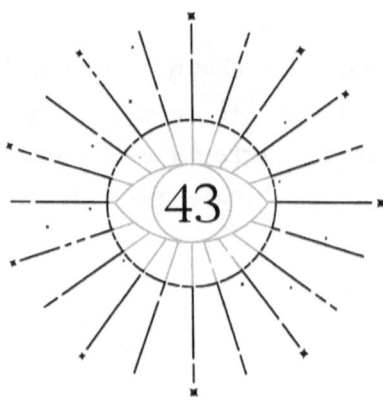

## 43

DECEMBER 26, 1983, OUTSIDE MOSCOW

A blizzard ripped through the farmlands of Russia, far from the bright lights of its capital city, creating a desolate picture under nightfall. Sheets of ice skipped across the frozen landscape in golf-ball-sized projectiles. Safe from the ravages of the harsh weather above them, Lieutenant Colonel Stanislav Petrov and his two experienced officers completed their checklists in preparation for a routine shift change.

The secure bunker they occupied was the most advanced radar facility outside the United States of America, and it served one purpose: incoming nuclear missile early warning. The complex system of blinking LEDs, dials, and monitors was never left unmanned, day or night. The Cold War was at its height, and the vigilance of every stationed officer was of the utmost importance. The lack of military action between the Soviet Union and USA and their disdain for each other's political agendas had made the threat of nuclear war very real. Both were armed and ready. Both hovered a quivering finger above the big red "pull the plug on the planet" button—thus the need for the costly, high-tech, secret bunker that Petrov and his officers currently manned.

Standing in front of the central bank of instruments and the main screen of the early-warning system, referred to as "the Eye" within military circles, Petrov went about his business. The warning system whirred tirelessly. On either side behind him, his subordinates sat at two other banks of switches and monitors, gazing into the hypnotic green glow of their respective computers. The blip and boink of dots drifting about the screens indicated either birds or commercial aircraft at various stages of their flight paths. Red herrings were everywhere, fatiguing the officers' ability to pick out a serious threat should it appear—especially at the late hour, minutes before end of shift.

Vodka, cigarettes, and coffee were the stimulants at their disposal, and they were rationed under Petrov's attentive watch. Too much vodka provoked distraction. Too much vodka and cigarettes left the mind numb. Yet a strategized rotation of all three would see any officer through the gruelling twelve-hour shift with ease.

Though Petrov's new lackeys were experienced with radar, they seemed incapable of following orders. Old hands in a new outfit and a new position—the worst kind of soldier. Men jaded by war often trivialised the loss of human life and thieved anything they could get their hands on. They would take what pleasure they could before they went down with everyone else in the fires of destruction. Even though Petrov's Tweedledum and Tweedledee were sat out of sight, he knew exactly what kind of idle games they were involved in.

Officer 1 snuck glances at the radar from behind his newspaper, taking long draws on a fresh cigarette and leaning back in his chair. On the other side of the cement room, Officer 2 entered data into the radar's calibration system while sipping vodka from an ornate glass and intermittently shuffling a deck of cards. At this level of security clearance, these were the hopeless best the Soviet Union could muster. Petrov had vowed to himself that nothing disastrous would happen on his watch, never mind the nihilistic hacks he had been lumped with.

Officer 1 sucked another hefty draw from his cigarette and blew a plume of smoke towards the ceiling, where it billowed oddly in size. The colour changed from white to a dark grey speckled with gold.

The strange occurrence went unnoticed by the officers as they did not have the sight to perceive the cloud of energy that took over the space. The now large mass of foreign material gathered sharply to one central point as Samael took form, looming between the officers in the ether, the weight of decay gleaming from his thick, silver aura.

The early-warning alarm began to wail.

Startled, Officer 1 pitched backwards off his chair, slamming his head into the rear wall. Officer 2 was about to take another sip of vodka when he froze, darting a glance at his screen and then up at Petrov. As he whipped his attention up from his checklist and at the main radar screen ahead, Petrov's face glowed green. Every iota of tactical experience he'd gained over the years had prepared him for this very event. Five unidentified blips persisted on the circular gridded display. Petrov glanced at the red phone on his desk, then back at the radar.

"I have five anomalies on the Eye. Confirm ground radar?" Petrov shouted over the blaring alarm.

In the ether, Samael's tendrils of grey and gold slithered towards the two officers. Officer 1 gathered himself from the floor and leafed through a heavy folder on his desk, nearly tearing out the pages as he scrambled for the correct section. His compatriot dashed across the room to the ground radar panel to verify his own screen's information.

Samael's spirit tentacles latched onto both officers' skulls. His energy melded with their auras, sending them further into a panic and making it all too easy to subvert their will.

"Ground radar is inconclusive; we must notify the duty officer immediately!" Officer 2 screamed.

"God help us," Officer 1 mumbled in shock. Samael stepped towards Petrov, his whips of smoky light rearing up like rattlesnake tails, ready to penetrate the man's spirit.

"Only five missiles. Why only five? Double-check ground radar! I need confirmation," Petrov said.

"I repeat, ground radar does not confirm. If we are going to burn, then the Americans must burn as well," Officer 2 yelled, rushing to pick up the red phone.

*Zam!* A glowing ball of the Light from the etherverse appeared behind Petrov. The lieutenant colonel's eyes flashed gold as he instantaneously absorbed the Light power of the emerging sphere. Just as Samael's tendrils made contact with Petrov's head, they were singed, and Samael reeled backwards in pain.

"Stop," Petrov commanded.

An eye-watering burst of the Light pulsed from within Petrov, blasting through both officers' auras, cleansing them of Samael's energy. The officers came back to their senses, and the deafening siren stopped. The group stood frozen in time.

Golden luminescence seeped from Petrov's eyes and mouth, collecting together and morphing into the imposing figure of Gabriel. The guardian archangel eyeballed his divine compatriot.

"Enough, Samael," Gabriel said.

"Their greed offends all that is holy. The humans are lost, and you are the only one who doesn't see it. You are a fool to protect them still," Samael responded.

"There is always hope, brother."

"They have had their chance. The rest of the Seven and I are convinced a reset is in order."

"Believe what you like. Humans can still turn a corner. Besides, creation would not survive the fallout of a full-scale nuclear assault. You go too far," Gabriel said. He moved next to Petrov and placed a hand on the lead officer's shoulder, boosting his resolve. The man's spine straightened, and his eyes shone brightly.

"We signal a fault on the warning system. Those could not be missiles; otherwise, we would all have been vapourised by now," Petrov instructed. Suddenly, his men were as compliant as show dogs.

"Yes sir," they responded in unison. Samael snarled and exited the bunker in a discharge of smoke, knowing full well that his day would come. The rebellion of the upper ether against the balance of the Universe was fast approaching.

### PRESENT DAY, WANDSWORTH PRISON

Eddie stood immobilised, gawking at Jade's transformation as she was overtaken by the touch and possessed by raw jealousy. His primal senses were screaming at him to back up. In the ether, Samael's joy erupted from his mouth in a low, ragged laugh. The evil unleashed through the Seven Sins was a delicious sight to the archangel.

"I want it!" Jade screamed, rushing at Eddie and pulling off his helmet. Eddie tumbled against the entrance foyer wall, staring up at Jade as dark cracks squirmed over her face, past her now oily-black eyes.

"Oh God, you're one of them," Eddie said, sliding up the wall to his feet. Jade cast aside Eddie's helmet and leapt towards him like a rabid monkey.

"And this!" Jade yelled, grappling with Eddie's shield as he struggled to maintain his grip.

"Jade, Jade! Stop. You have to fight it."

"Nice eyes. I want them," Jade growled at the back of her throat. Ripping Eddie's shield to the side, Jade scraped the air, hell-bent on gouging his eyes out. He shuffled backwards to the front door in a panic, blocking Jade's incoming claw hands and alternately lashing out with his baton. He managed to clip a flailing arm heading for his face.

Jade's arm snapped at the forearm, turning the limb into a concertina with a bend at the elbow, the break, and another bend at her wrist. When she shook her mangled arm in front of her face, it wobbled about like porridge in a sock.

Watching Jade flap her useless arm confirmed for Eddie what she had said about the infected feeling no pain. He cringed at the horrid squelching noises.

"I'm sorry for that, babe, but you are being a right bitch. Serves you right for tasing me in the arse anyway."

Eddie's words unfortunately brought Jade's attention back to him, and she sprang, attacking in the same unhinged fashion, her shrill screams even louder than before.

"Give them to me!"

"Give it a rest, babe! Will you just. Feck. Off."

Eddie's baton connected again, this time with Jade's knee, which ruptured a tendon and buckled the joint under her weight. Jade hopped and gawked down at her sideways leg and spiralled into a mini tantrum, flapping her useless arm and jangling leg.

"Ohhhhhaggghh!"

"Please, will you just quit it? I'll go get some help!"

Ignoring his pleas, Jade jumped at Eddie once more. She was at her most fierce and got the better of him instantly, chomping violently at Eddie's neck, sinking her teeth in, and chewing out a sizeable chunk of flesh. Eddie went spinning sideways, screaming and holding his wound while he shoved Jade away.

"Fine! No more Mr. Nice Guy," he shrieked.

*Crack!* The final blow from Eddie's baton smashed into Jade's standing leg and crumpled her to the ground. Jade squirmed and moaned in frustration.

"Well, I did warn you, you silly bint! Now, you're not gonna like this, but I'm gonna have to lock you in the boot of my car and come back for you later."

Eddie tumbled out of the station's main doors, dragging the incapacitated Jade by the back of her belt. Rolling her head around in vain attempts to nip at Eddie's arm, Jade was not letting up. Eddie unlocked the back of his nineties VW and hoisted Jade into the boot, using some duct tape buried in the clutter to bind her arms and legs. He slammed the boot closed and put pressure on his neck. He was losing a serious amount of blood and needed to think fast to escape to safety.

Back inside the prison, Samael held another writhing prisoner in his vice grip as he turned him with a black mist of creeping death.

Feeling refreshed and ready for the next phase of the war on earth, he summoned his compatriots.

"Zelda. Ahebban."

*Zip. Zap.* Both arrived in a flash at his side.

"We must separate to cover more ground," Samael commanded.

Indignant, Zelda dared to speak against the Angel of Death.

"That is not what Michael—" Her throat constricted, and she began sputtering. The sooty tendrils of Samael's Dark Light were wrapped around her neck. Seeing Zelda suspended from the ground and paralysed, Ahebban dropped to one knee in submission.

"Maybe you would like to join my death angels?" Samael said as Zelda's face steadily turned to grey and one of her eyes began to shift into a metallic substance. "Do not question me again." Zelda's eyes widened, and she blinked an acknowledgment. Samuel dropped the cherub like a stone, her face returning to its original complexion. "Excellent."

Zelda gathered herself and shot a caustic glare at Ahebban, whose lazy eyes and smug grin grated on her every nerve.

"Don't you say a word."

"Quit your squabbling. Transform as many humans as you can get your hands on. I must pay a visit to an old friend," Samael croaked before vanishing in a swirling cloud of gleaming dust.

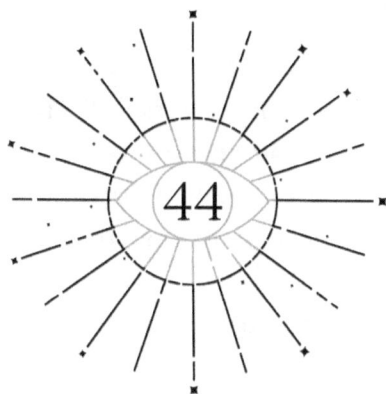

## 44

Grace and Andy were still glued to the news broadcast detailing the spread of the mysterious virus sweeping the city. Haylene was pacing by the window.

"This must be the beginning of what Gabriel warned me about," Grace said. Haylene immediately stood, grabbed the remote from the coffee table, and clicked off the box.

"What are you doing?" Grace protested.

"Sitting here watching the same thing over and over isn't going to help us remain calm and rational. I know what's happening is unknown and scary for all of us, but maybe we should get outside to clear our heads. It doesn't look so bad from what I can see, and the world isn't going to end if we take one lap of the park."

Grace ignored her friend and pulled her phone out to search for updates on the breaking story. Haylene snatched Grace's phone from her, and Grace erupted, leaping to retrieve her device. "Give it to me. I need to know what's going on!"

Andy burst into tears at his mum's sudden switch in mood.

"Mummy, stop," Andy pleaded.

Haylene softened her tone and locked eyes with Grace. "Look, I know you're scared. We all are, but let's just bring it down for a minute and think about this." Haylene wrapped an arm around Andy's shoulder as Grace let out a sigh, upset at herself for losing control.

"I'm sorry," Grace said.

"Come and sit with us," Haylene said. Tail between her legs, Grace tottered back to join the pair on the sofa. "All we need is right here. All I'm suggesting is a quick break. A walk through the trees will lift all our spirits, and I promise we'll come straight home at the first sign of danger, okay?"

Nods of agreement and a brief loving connection settled everyone's nerves.

"How do you stay so together?" Grace asked. Haylene searched her mind for the appropriate words before beginning her story.

"When my mother died of a heart attack last year, it was a surprise to everyone. Everyone except those closest to her. Her whole life, she was obsessed with the lives of others. Reality TV shows, international news, the latest royal gossip. All the noise about people she hadn't met and didn't really care about only made her more nervous and insecure about her own life. So year on year, she closed her heart, pushing away those she loved the most."

Both Grace and Andy sat open mouthed at Haylene's vulnerability. Neither had the courage to interrupt; they wouldn't know what to say.

"I know now her actions were all born out of a fear of being hurt. Building a wall around herself, she kept everyone from connecting with the deepest parts of herself." Haylene's eyes welled up. "She died because her heart had become so small that it just couldn't sustain life anymore. She had forgotten how to love, and be loved."

A long, cold silence sat over the room. Andy and Grace were dumbfounded by Haylene's wisdom, which she rarely showed through her words. She traditionally inspired and led others through example. Her sombre story was a break in form that highlighted the gravity of her current feelings.

"I knew your mum's death was hard on you, but I had no idea that it happened in such painful circumstances. I'm so sorry," Grace said.

"Don't be. You couldn't have known because I didn't want to burden you with it. Her passing taught me a valuable lesson I'll never forget. It taught me that in this short life we have, we must pull those we love closest to us, giving our attention and care to them and not wasting time worrying about strangers or fearing some threat that may not be real or may never happen."

"Can we all hold hands for the whole walk?" Andy asked, thrown off kilter by a sea of conflicting emotions roiling in his gut.

"I think that's a great idea, and it'll just be ten minutes, just so we can see what's actually going on with our own eyes."

"But what about those things out there?" Andy said.

"I can guarantee you it's not as bad as the media makes it out to be."

"I could do with a change of scenery and some time in nature, to be honest," Grace said, shrugging.

Andy squinted at his mum, unconvinced.

It all felt very wrong to him, but he wanted to see his mum happy, so he kept his reservations to himself. Andy had always pushed himself down for the sake of his mum, repressing his own needs and opinions. This constriction was beginning to feel unnatural, and a hidden part of himself sucked down the irksome feeling, locking it up tight.

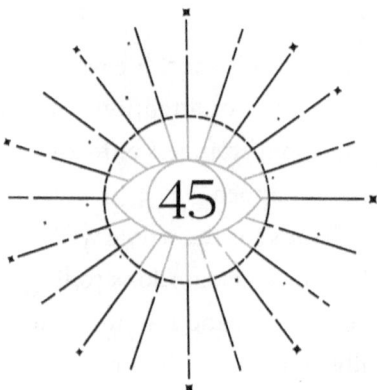

# 45

Raphael's fight with the angelic warriors had raged for hours, and the warriors' commitment to their mission was fracturing, their energy reserves exhausted. The whole affair had devolved into more of a circus slapstick performance than the battle for the ages they had hoped for. Attack after attack had been deflected or sidestepped by Raphael in her customary dramatic fashion. Having never faced off with the restoration archangel, her clumsy attackers had vastly underestimated Raphael's stamina in combat.

Blasting each warrior in rapid succession with pillars of her Light, Raphael saw clearly that the warriors were outmatched and out of ideas.

In frustration, the lead warrior yelled out, "I'm going to—"

*Vooshaa!* Yet again the weary angel was smacked to the ground by a fizzing green radiance. Having collapsed to their knees, chests heaving, the other two angelic warriors crawled in circles, trying to find their feet. Warrior 2 nearly mustered the will to attack again, rearing up, but almost immediately thought better of it and dematerialised his weapons. Breathing heavily with his hands on his knees, he'd had enough.

"Ugh, what's the point?" he mumbled.

"Lift your weapons for our lord!" the lead warrior cried out in desperation. His rallying cry had no effect; his companion glowered at him in dissent.

The Damned zipped through a flaming ethergate that burst to life next to Raphael.

"I see you've been busy," the dark angel said.

"I was due a little light exercise anyway," Raphael said, her eyebrows lifted and expression as smug as ever.

Behind them, by the shopping centre entrance, another eight imposing warriors landed. The band of reinforcements popped up next to their beleaguered companions, forming a wall against the Damned and Raphael. Their steely-blue eyes sparked and crackled with a mixture of golden light and the black poison of the seven sins.

"You all seem quite sure of yourselves today," the Damned said.

"Stay out of this. We have come for Raphael and Raphael alone," the lead warrior barked as he moved to the spearhead of the group.

Analysing the threat, the Damned clocked a group of touched prisoners pouring into the opposite side of the car park, spreading from the nearby prison. Things were escalating quickly, and the battle ahead of the Damned now presented two fronts. The exhausted lead warrior laughed like a hyena.

"The touch is taking the humans. It's too late for them."

"It's never too late—except to save yourself." At this, the Damned opened a dark portal in the ground. Wild screams and fire accompanied a bouquet of decaying arms that exploded upwards and whipped the lead warrior down into the Pit. His warrior companions gaped in horror.

"Thank you, brother. He was enjoying the sound of his voice rather too much, I think." Raphael said.

"Sounds like someone else I know."

"Touché."

The vanished warrior angel's original companions leapt up and tried to escape, but two separate portals to the Pit yawned open beneath them. The desperate, disembodied limbs from the netherverse grasped each terrified warrior by the ankles. Holding out his right fist, the Damned constricted the portals so the angels were sucked down inch by agonising inch. The band of angelic reinforcements watched, frozen.

They had been ill prepared for the scenario unfolding in front of them. Though the warriors had heard tales of the Damned and his vicious abilities, to witness them firsthand crushed all motivation within them.

"Please! No!" Warrior 2 yelped. Sadism and rage burned in the Damned's eyes.

"Next time you try to assault my realm, remember this: earth is much further from heaven than it is from hell."

With much protestation, both warriors were swallowed up.

"Now I remember why every angel dreads a mission to the mortal realm," Raphael commented, unable to disguise the admiration in her tone.

Seemingly directed by an unseen commander, the band of warrior reinforcements nodded in unison like robotic drones and warped out of sight, headed for the shopping centre.

"How have they been able to turn the humans? Even with Gabriel gone, Michael should not be able to affect their physical and spiritual bodies in such a way."

"It is as I feared. By Michael absorbing the powers of those he has enslaved and turning the Angel of Death to his side, he has unleashed the savagery of the Seven Sins."

"I thought that was an impossibility."

"Without the guardians, it seems anything is possible. The Code of the Etherverse has been turned upside down, and the entire spiritual realm is in turmoil."

"We can't keep charging in the dark like this. There are too many warriors pouring into the physical realm, and we cannot coordinate our efforts."

"I agree, brother, and on top of this, Samael may already be on earth, commanding the first wave. You know he has longed for this fight and would jump at the opportunity to poison the humans in this way."

"I may know of another approach, but it is a gamble that could very well backfire," the Damned said.

"Would it be worth the risk?"

"Without question."

"Then you have your answer. Do what you must. I will slow them down as best I can."

The Damned nodded and darted off in a flash of crimson, flying through the etherverse to the one place he knew would present his companions with an edge in battle: the Well.

Knowledge of its existence had been carefully hidden for fear that its power would be abused. Such a discovery in the physical realm could only be made by those who moved through the lower realms freely. Gabriel and the Damned had made a solemn pact to keep it hidden and protect the site from intruders. This ancient anomaly in the physical realm was a source of unending power, a gap in time and space that allowed any mortal or angel an increased awareness and sensitivity to the Light. In a mortal's case, this would make them more open to spiritual movements and awaken healing abilities. For an angel, the Well triggered an intense absorption of the Light, tripling their power and pushing telepathic and telekinetic abilities to their highest limit.

A heavy rotating guard of Gabriel's fiercest and most trusted guardians had been placed on the Well after its discovery. The absence of Gabriel and his guardians, in addition to leaving humanity vulnerable, meant that no guardian was left to protect the Well.

Accessing its energy would allow the Damned to become one who walked between the Light and the Dark Light. However, the dark angel lord was uncertain that he could connect with the Well without his consciousness being completely consumed in the process.

Death had always escaped him. Though he wished an end upon himself, it was his curse to be trapped in dark angel form forever. As such, the Damned had always lived his existence with nothing to lose.

Now was no time to stop.

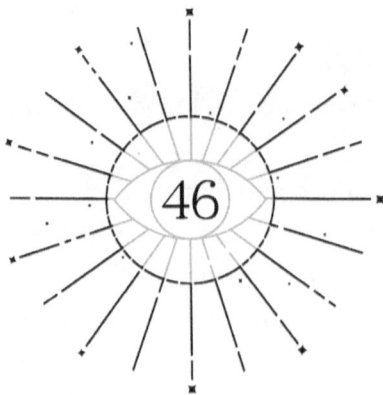

# 46

In a red leather booth of an American-style diner, Professor Simms and Dr. Sorchia Collopy sat with empty plates. Chava stood guard behind the lecturers, pushing her spiritual radar to the limit. If any angelic force came within a hundred miles of her position, she would know it and proceed to nullify the threat with extreme vigour.

The intellectual pair started on their second cup of coffee after finishing a late meal. Simms rifled through the research papers scattered on the oval, chrome table while Sorchia leafed through his manuscript on Lucifer and the seven archangels.

"I understood that Lucifer had always been envious of humans. Yet here you suggest he was actually looking forward to meeting and walking amongst them. Why, then, did he turn evil and begin to tempt them towards sin?"

"Lucifer was betrayed by his brethren and sentenced to serve as mankind's accuser."

"Right, the original meaning of 'devil' being 'slanderer' or 'accuser' in Ancient Greek."

"Very good, Dr. Collopy. I'm impressed yet again by your knowledge on the subject. As regards Lucifer 'turning evil,' I'm afraid it's a little more complex than that. Lucifer himself is not innately bad or evil. He is a cog in the machine of morality. You can't have good without evil. Even several of the seven chief controlling archangels of the divine realm are morally ambiguous. Christian doctrine, however, would have you believe that every one of these angel overlords is perfect and squeaky clean."

Simms pointed to a simple diagram in his notes depicting the Seven, Lucifer, and the Lightbearer.

"Take a look at this ancient diagram I pieced together from various fragments scattered throughout early religious cultures."

The image showed seven winged, muscular angels across the middle of the page. Symbols of varying colours were attached to each being's name and title above them. Beneath the Seven, a dark-cloaked angel was depicted with a red circle behind him. There was no name and no title present. At the top of the page, the largest and most dominant-looking angel sat with no cloak and no wings. Only an outline of gold was present around its frame, and four golden spots sat where its eyes and hand would be.

"Simms, this is absolutely magnificent. Yes, I've come across individual elements of what you have put together here but never seen anything this complete. This is groundbreaking."

Simms blushed as he batted away the compliment.

"Sorchia, you are too kind. Of course, the wings on the central figures were simply a primitive way of understanding the way they might move. Anyway, I digress. To highlight my point on moral ambiguity, let's consider the Angel of Death, or Archangel of Death," the professor said, pointing to a black-and-grey symbol and the ghostly character underneath. The character sat just outside the centre of the group. "Believed to originally have been named Samael, the Archangel of Death sits with the Seven and is seen as a force working towards the greater good."

"Right. I can see how that would cause problems for moralists," Sorchia said. Narrowing her eyes, she tilted her head to the side. "There is one thing that bothers me when looking at the seven archangels in the middle here."

"Go on."

"The body positions of the two characters in the middle of the group seem to break the symmetry of the whole picture. Is there a division of some kind here?" Sorchia asked, pointing to the dead centre of the diagram where Michael and Gabriel stood next to one another. Michael was shown holding the hilt of his downward-pointed blue sword with both hands, his body facing forwards, his posture tight and closed. In contrast, Gabriel was facing Michael, a golden shield on his back and a hand extended towards his unwelcoming neighbour.

"You're right to focus your attention here. This relationship is precisely where the balance of the angelic spiritual world lies. Certainly, the most important figure in balancing the forces of the Universe is Gabriel, archangel of the guardian class. Without him, everything would begin to crumble."

"Guardian? I thought Gabriel was a messenger. That's what I know from his appearances in biblical texts, anyway."

"Yes, he is very much a messenger, but Gabriel is also the balance of the forces of light and dark. This is hinted at when we look past the optical illusion that makes Gabriel and Michael look as if they are either side of the centre line of the image."

Taking a ruler and pencil, Simms drew some light markings through the centre of the page from side to side and top to bottom. Stepping back and pointing to where the lines met, he continued, "When we find the real centre line of the image, you can see Gabriel is at the middle of everything on the page. Gabriel is the leveller. Light and dark, birth and death. Chaos and order. Call it what you will, but if the balance of opposing energies is tipped somehow, then things could rapidly get apocalyptic, for want of a better word."

Chava listened intently, in disbelief at how much this man had learned about angelic kind from simple research. This was a serious amount of wisdom almost impossible to attain without being a seer, which he certainly was not. If this were the case, he would have been able to visualise her clear as day.

"Okay, I follow you. I'm still not sure how this links to things in the physical world and connects with Grace's recent experiences," Sorchia prompted.

"I'll cut to the chase then. Let's look at it from a social anthropological point of view to get to the crux of how Grace and the Lightbearer connect. As you know, ancient religions that worshipped creation and everything within it held a more spiritual connection to the earth."

"Right. Shamanism in Native American culture, the gods of Ancient Egypt, paganism in early Celtic civilisation. All shared a worship of the sun, the land, the stars, weather systems, and even revered animals as deities."

"And what did all of these approaches to faith in a higher power have in common?"

Sorchia took a moment to search her mind. She didn't want to seem foolish in front of this brilliant man who had put her on the spot. In fact, she desperately wanted to impress him.

"The idea that all God's roles were interlinked? Each deity or aspect of creation was as important as the next in these primal faiths."

"Precisely! They all believed in harmony."

The booth fell silent. It was Sorchia's turn to blush. She immediately caught herself and swept back her hair. Her eyelids trembled subconsciously while looking away. Professor Simms responded with a beaming smile and an admiring glint in his eye.

"It's what we all want out of life, a feeling of togetherness," Simms said. Neither he nor Sorchia took another breath as their eyes locked. The professor cleared his throat to break the hot and heavy moment. "Ahem, my point being that, eh, any time the harmony of the earth's ecosystems or environment slipped, eh, all of these ancient cultures believed that it was down to a corresponding fracture . . . in the divine realm."

Sorchia couldn't help but smile at the man's attempts to smooth over the heart flutter they had both just experienced.

"But how does that relate to Grace having an encounter with an angel and the existence of the Lightbearer?"

"My thesis proposes that every one of these deities from ancient religions was an angel or archangel. These angels are in a delicate balance of power. Should they appear to humans in visions, they would likely be warning us of dangers to come. It's quite clear that Grace saw something not of this world. If the Lightbearer, the most powerful force in the spiritual realm, was key to the visitation she experienced, then the state of the spiritual realm must be grim. In short, the angels of the divine realm are either reaching out to warn us or asking us for help in righting the balance."

"Then it follows that if the spiritual realm is in crisis, the physical realm will start to express that crisis. What exactly is that supposed to look like?"

"I'm not entirely certain, but my best educated guess would be that these dangers to come may be similar to what ancient Jewish culture experienced at the time of Moses—specifically, plagues, disease, famine, and death."

"This is all very good in theory as a daring shake-up of the Christian status quo, but do you actually believe that the Lightbearer, archangels, and dark angels exist?" Sorchia said.

"I believe there are many things we cannot see or explain in life, and I believe certain individuals possess a heightened awareness of such things. Grace could be one such individual. As her mother, you would know. What does your gut tell you, Sorchia?"

Remaining sceptical, Sorchia shifted in her seat and took a long, hard look at the manuscript in front of her. Flashbacks of Grace's terribly hard upbringing flooded her mind: the banshee-like screams, the vivid nightmares—her need to use all manner of drugs to suppress her sensitivities.

"We have to go to her," Sorchia said firmly.

Simms nodded with resolve. "I believe we do."

In the outer reaches of the etherverse, the coast was clear for the time being. Chava and her protected mortals had slipped under the radar of the myriad warrior angels descending to the earth. For now, at least.

Chava would have to leave them exposed, however, to perform

further spiritual reconnaissance. Working alone, she had little choice. She also needed to visit an important ancient site in the hope that some of her fellow guardians had escaped there. It would be a better place to search out this potential new seer named Grace, too.

*If a seer rises, then humanity and what is left of my class do indeed have hope.*

Whirling into a concentrated ball of golden stars that collapsed inwards on itself, Chava followed her inner guidance, connecting to the will of the Universe as best she knew how.

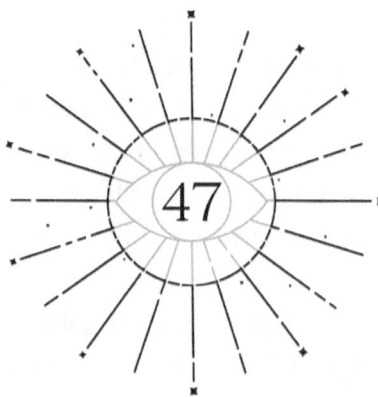

Grace, Andy, and Haylene strolled hand in hand through Mile End Park, drinking in the leafy escape from the city. Birds chirped as the sun set on this mild summer evening. A squirrel scurried about the base of a nearby tree, and an urban fox eyeballed them warily in the distance.

Getting close to nature and connecting with the enriching energies it provided was the group's favourite activity when the weather allowed. Whenever Haylene and Grace could coordinate their work schedules during school holidays, they would all take an adventure to some new forest hideaway. Mile End was a far cry from a lush woodland, but it offered much-needed grounding.

In the middle of the trio, Grace guided the bunch towards the same tree she had used to steady herself the last time she was in the park.

"I wanted to show you both where I had a vision of the past. It was over there next to that lovely sprawling oak tree," Grace said, pointing to the far end of the park. "I think the earth's great spirit really helped me deal with the overwhelming experience."

"What exactly did you see, Mum?" Andy said.

"I think it was the Second World War. There were bombs falling and people running from factories that used to exist in this area of London. My granny always told me stories of the Blitz. She said it was hellish."

"I can't begin to imagine the devastation," Haylene said.

As the three walked deeper into the park hand in hand, a quiet respect came over them for the lives lost there so long ago. They soon found themselves in the centre of the park, and Andy stopped dead, staring up at the trees and around at the empty, open spaces of grass. An odd, lifeless calm had fallen over the place.

"What happened to all the animals?" Andy asked.

"I don't know, bud. Maybe they've all gone to bed? Look, here's a nice doggy coming our way," Haylene responded.

"Oh, how nice. I think that's Mr. Burrows and Maggie," Grace added.

An elderly man with a long coat and flat cap made his way towards the group, accompanied by his Alsatian. Grace waved, but the man's stare seemed vacant, somewhat glossed over. She tried again as the man came within several metres.

"Mr. Burrows? So lovely to see you again. How is Doris doing these days?" Grace asked. The man snapped out of his daze and locked eyes on Grace.

"Grace, what an unexpected pleasure. Apologies, I was a million miles away. Doris is fine, thanks. She has her good days and her bad days. At least Maggie here keeps us all feeling young and virile." Andy was already stroking the playful animal and getting nuzzled in the neck. The boy giggled and danced backwards.

"Are you okay? You were lost in thought there," Haylene asked.

"Yes, I was. I'm just a little concerned by all this talk of a virus. I thought why not get out and see what the real world looks like instead of listening to all that doom and gloom on the radio."

"How funny. We thought exactly the same thing. Even though the news is telling people to stay inside, it does seem a bit strange that there's no one else out on such a nice evening."

Zelda warped between Grace and Mr. Burrows in a crack of blue lightning. Having been tasked to pollute as much of London's human population as possible, the cherub had been moving at breakneck speed. She didn't see a need to single out specific human targets. The spread was about quantity, not quality. The touched humans themselves would take care of the rest by causing widespread panic and hell on earth, something Zelda thought every last one of the human species deserved. They had become lazy and weak in the last centuries in particular, wasting their lives through pleasure-seeking and greed. The Seven Sins would either wipe them out or forge them in the fires of suffering to evolve into something better.

*Anything*, she thought, *would be better than their current parasitic form.*

Michael had been inspired to launch such a plague upon them. Several of the archangel council had resisted, of course, too weak to discipline the humans in this way. They had no concept of the need to be cruel to be kind. Humans were no longer learning the lessons Gabriel and the others had hoped they would, and time was running out. Zelda would not sit idle as the planet was brought to the brink of collapse. She was a warrior, after all, and if war was what humanity needed to teach them a lesson they would soon not forget, she would give it to them.

Within a split second of her arrival, Zelda had infused the two stunned humans before her with the touch and vanished, on to her next target. Unknown to her, she had struck gold by happening upon Grace, the one sure threat to Michael's great plan. The cherub had neither the knowledge nor the awareness of what a seer could mean for humanity's defence. Zelda's random journey through this point in time and space had been a cruel twist of fate.

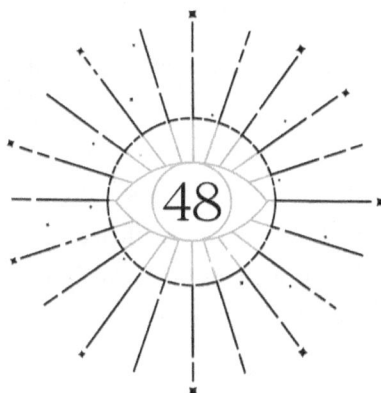

## 48

Jack was greeted with three freshly mutilated bodies when he edged in through the door. The exposure of inner organs and flesh torn from bone made the corpses look like they had just been spat out of a meat grinder. Without hesitation, Jack dropped to one knee and drew his concealed Glock 17 from its shoulder holster. His adrenaline levels surged to maximum.

He'd seen some nasty wounds in his time, but his gut told him that this was something altogether more evil. Even the mind of a psychopath couldn't have dreamt up what he was seeing. To add to the mystery of the chopped-up bodies was the level of force used to execute the killing spree. It would have required strength far outside the limits of human physiology. No bullets had been fired, no grenades or blades used. Faces were clawed off and joints separated from their sockets, leaving the walls caked in blood. These unfortunate souls had quite literally been ripped limb from limb.

Jack checked the identity of the bodies as best he could, and it was clear that Dio wasn't one of them. None wore his signature style of gaudy jewellery, and one and all were part of the Becontree Boys gang—a sloppy bunch of low-level criminals. Checking through the mouldy kitchen and adjacent grimy rooms downstairs, Jack moved methodically, his head rising no further than waist height. Anyone left alive in the building was sure to be hiding in terror. The last thing he wanted was to surprise someone and get shot square in the face in self-defence.

Jack heard a shuffle of feet upstairs. Creeping carefully up the stairs, he hoped to find Dio alive, but the longer he spent in the house, the more he risked walking into an enclosed space with whatever had caused the bloodbath on the ground floor. Not a great tactical move, but at least he hadn't given away his position.

Coming to the top of the stairs, he peeked past the ajar bedroom door. A large shadow appeared against the back wall, shifting back and forth. Jack quietly pushed the door aside.

Dio was snapping his head around his neck like a chicken. He muttered to himself aggressively as he began to pace back and forth. Lying at his feet with bruises on her neck was a woman in a pool of blood where her skull had been repeatedly thumped against the floor. Her eyeballs were gone.

"Dio? What happened here, bud?"

No response came back. Dio appeared to be lost in shock, muttering erratically. Jack tried to get through to him.

"Dio. Who did this?"

This time, Dio answered, his words shaky and barely audible. "She said I couldn't be with her, but if I couldn't be with her, then no one should be, because I am the one she really needs."

Jack inched closer.

"Who said she couldn't be with you? Hey, buddy, just keep it steady and tell me what happened. I've got your back. It's over now."

Whirling Dio around by the shoulder, Jack was confronted with the horror of Dio's glossy black eyes and cracked skin. His hands were covered in blood, holding the dead woman's eyeballs.

Lunging, Dio lashed out at Jack's face.

"You can't look at her! No one can! She's mine!" Dio screamed with envy. Deflecting Dio's ferocious attempts to scratch out his eyes, Jack sent him back against the window pane with a shuddering palm strike to the sternum. The blow crumpled Dio next to the woman's corpse.

"Take it easy! It's me, Stones. What happened to your face, bud?" In a sudden realisation, Jack connected the news broadcast to the appearance and behaviour of his Wraith comrade.

*Crap. He's been infected.*

Showing no signs of injury or pain from Jack's strike, Dio bounced up and rushed Jack again, scrambling at his face and making chomping noises when he came close. Unable to get a grip on Dio's erratic movements, Jack shoved his gang mate up against the wall.

"Dude, snap out of it already!"

It was pointless. The virus had turned Dio into a senseless animal, and Jack had to neutralise the threat before he was infected as well. Sidestepping Dio's off-balance lunge, Jack hit Dio with a stiff elbow on the bridge of his nose, knocking him down. Dio finally fell still.

"I did warn you," Jack said to himself, turning to search for the missing drug money. Dio popped straight back up again with a grin. Leaping on Jack, Dio shunted him out of the door, sending him onto his back. Jack's knee buckled, and Dio collapsed on top of him, spitting and frothing. Jack was fresh out of ideas. Slapping aside Dio's head thrusts, he knew he had to go below the belt.

"I don't usually resort to cheap shots, pal, but you can forgive me later," Jack said.

*Thud!* Jack kneed Dio square in the Mummy–Daddy box. Dio yelped in a high-pitched, childish moan.

"Well, at least that's the same," Jack said, escaping from beneath Dio and dashing back outside and into the Range Rover. Slamming the door behind him, Jack panted for air.

"What the actual feck is going on?" Lazaro bellowed.

"Dio's lost it. Something's changed him, most likely that virus they were talking about on the radio," Jack returned.

"You're kidding me. Where the hell is my money?" Dio clanged into Lazaro's window, clawing and headbutting the glass. Lazaro jumped in his seat and recoiled back into the central console. "God Almighty!"

"Haven't had a chance to get to the money, boss. Just need to figure out how to deal with him first," Jack said, pointing at Dio's contorted expression.

"Aw, balls. Why's he slobbering all over the place?" Sonny said, screwing up his face at Dio's antics.

"I don't care if he's got the bloody bubonic plague. I want you both to get out there and sort him out so I can get to my feckin' money."

Jack and Sonny exchanged a confused glance, then stared straight at the feral Dio and back again to each other. Neither budged.

"Boss, I really think it's best we wait out ole Bitey McBiterson there first," Jack said.

"Hand me that shotgun, Stones," Lazaro said.

"Laz, I don't think it's a good idea to go out there. I tried every trick in the book to slow him down. Why don't we let him tire himself out a bit first?" Jack replied.

"I'm done waiting. Why don't both you crying little babies sit back and let a real man show you how to deal with this feckin' mess?"

"Suit yourself, boss," Jack said. Lazaro kicked open his door, launching Dio back against the house's front windows. Casually exiting the vehicle, the Wraith boss cocked his shotgun.

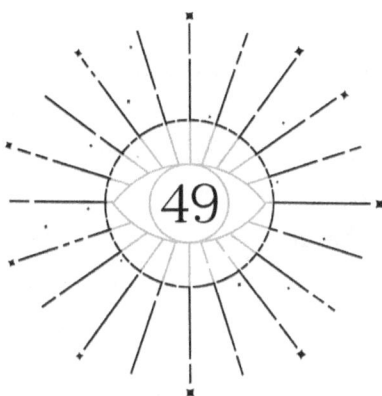

## 49

Tumbling down Wandsworth High Street like a drunken sailor, Eddie held his neck wound and repeatedly tried to get ahold of Jack on his phone. Passersby gave the bleeding Eddie a wide berth; not a single soul wanted anything to do with him. This wasn't an unusual response in a city filled with crime, drugs, and professional beggars. There were many rational explanations for Eddie's state, and no one had the time or the energy to get involved with whatever had led him to be stumbling alone on the street with an open neck wound.

Eddie knew this and didn't waste time asking for help. His immediate task was to put as much distance between himself and the crazed inmates as possible. He also knew he had limited options, considering what he had just experienced. Emergency services were no doubt overwhelmed, or even overcome, by the same infection he had witnessed. Jack wasn't picking up, and he'd already tried several friends in the local area, with no luck.

Almost losing his footing as the blood loss leeched the strength from his legs, Eddie careered into a man exiting the post office.

"Oh, dearie me. I'm terribly sorry. So sorry," the terrified man said, even though the accident was purely Eddie's fault. Such was the British affinity for manners in unnecessary places and with unnecessary volume.

"Don't worry, mate, my fault," Eddie conceded as he looked up to see none other than Dr. Patrick Lockhart, the prison psychiatrist.

"Eddie?"

"Doc? Man, are you a sight for sore eyes! Wow, I never thought I'd be saying those words to you, of all people."

"What on earth has happened to you? You look absolutely— My goodness, look at your neck. Quick, let's get you over to my car," Patrick said, propping Eddie up and pointing towards a brand-spanking-new electric Volkswagen SUV.

"That's your car?"

"I know, go on. You can say it. Pompous shrink with a pompous car."

"Actually, I am a massive Volkswagen fan, and I've never even seen one of these, let alone sat in one."

"Oh. Right. Well, today's your lucky day! Sorry, that didn't quite come out right. Obviously it's not your lucky day because you are bleeding from the neck without anyone to help you, but I—"

"Doc, I get it. Just get me something for this wound, and I'll try not to bleed on your leather seats in the meantime. Deal?"

"Deal," Patrick said as he eased Eddie into the passenger seat and pressed a glowing button that ejected a first aid kit from under the seat.

"Oh-ho! That is so fancy," Eddie couldn't help marvelling.

"This car is the one luxury I allow myself," Patrick said, hopping into the driver's side and removing some bandages and disinfectant from the kit. "Okay, move your hand so I can see what we're dealing with here."

Eddie lifted his hand to reveal the wound.

"That's going to need stitches. It looks like a bite mark. What exactly happened at the prison, and how did you end up on the high street on your own? This is going to sting a little," Patrick said as he dabbed disinfectant on Eddie's wound with zero finesse.

"Yeeup! That'll wake you up in the morning! Whew. As regards the vampire bite, let's just say it was a prisoner revolt of epic proportions. Something to do with this virus that's going round."

"Virus? You're not infected, are you?" Patrick said, glueing himself back against the car door.

"Relax, Doc. I've seen what someone infected looks like firsthand, and let me tell you, what you are looking at is the Disney princess version of that."

"Right, well, first things first. We need to get you stitched up. Can we access the prison medical supplies, or is it too dangerous to go back?"

"Listen, I don't want to pull you in on all of this. The infected prisoners and staff may have cleared out, but I can't guarantee it. I do need to go back for Jade, though. She's trapped back there, and I can't leave her there to rot."

"That does sound pretty extreme. How about we take a drive up and see if the coast is clear? Beats visiting my mother at the dementia care home for the fourth time this week, anyway."

"You sure? I don't know what kind of state that place is in. I just ran and didn't look back," Eddie remarked.

"Let's do it. My pulse is racing at the thought of a little danger. Plus, I really can't face repeating my family history to Mum again."

"I guess if you don't go, she won't remember that you missed your visit?" Eddie said with a wry smile, unable to resist. Patrick burst out laughing.

"You've got that right," the doctor said, pressing the electric car to life. Lights and dials blinked into action all over the sleek, glass dashboard. Eddie gawked at the display like a toddler tasting cake for the first time. He then pointed ahead and mimicked his favourite *Star Trek* captain.

"Number One, engage."

Nodding back at Eddie with a smug face, Patrick checked his mirrors and pulled out, heading for the prison. As he sailed through traffic, the doctor couldn't fight the smile on his lips, and he wondered at the spontaneity of life. *Who would have thought that this uneducated clown and I had so much in common?*

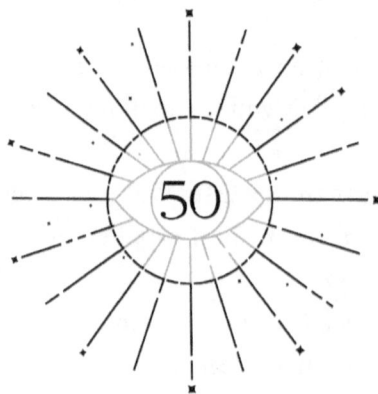

Chava gazed down upon the circular entrance to the Well, mourning the loss of her guardian companions who once oversaw the sacred area. She blessed the souls that had been so violently ripped from existence.

She was the last of the guardians. That was now clear.

The lush green garden where she now stood in Glastonbury, England, was of great spiritual significance—so much so that it had never had fewer than four angelic generals stationed at its perimeter. She had stood watch here multiple times over the centuries, and it had been the greatest of privileges to be chosen for the task. The Chalice Well, as the humans knew it, was a natural bridge between the divine and physical realms.

At its very centre existed a rift, or gap, in space-time, a hole in the fabric of the cosmos where the laws of physics did not apply. The behaviour of the Well at its core did not fit within the four dimensions of height, width, depth, and time. This was perhaps why its warm waters never stopped running, even in times of severe drought. The healing energies radiating from the Well's core were open and available to any human seeking enlightenment and cleansing. Chava had always enjoyed observing their interactions with it.

The phenomenon's spiritual radiation was similar to that of the sun—nourishing and warming from a distance, but draw too close, and the anomaly's cosmic rays would cause most matter to dissolve instantaneously. Fortunately, the physical and spiritual constraints on mortal beings made it impossible for them to approach so near. Touching the core of the Well itself would be akin to touching a single atom inside a grain of sand.

Celestial beings had no such constraints and so had been forbidden from touching the Well since its discovery over 6,000 years ago. There existed only three angels with the capacity to hold the Well's fearsome energy, and even they had been commanded never to approach it. None had dared to test this commandment since the first instances of their subjects being set aflame or torn limb from limb at the inner edge of the Well's core.

Looking down at the ornate, physical cover, Chava admired the craftsmanship. The cover depicted two interlocking circles that symbolised the idea of the divine feminine. Cutting through these two circles was a spear or a sword representing the divine masculine. Two opposing energies uniting as one—yin and yang, chaos and order, creation and destruction.

Pilgrimages were made daily by religious and spiritually minded people from all corners of the earth, for many different reasons and according to various beliefs concerning the Well's significance and origin. The most popular of these was the Christian myth of the Holy Grail. Devout Christians and myth enthusiasts alike believed that one Joseph of Arimathea had laid the Holy Grail to rest at the Chalice Well, hence the name, referring to the cup of Christ. Supposedly used by Jesus Christ at the Last Supper and later by Joseph of Arimathea to catch drops of Jesus's blood at his crucifixion, the holy chalice was rumoured to have magical healing properties and the power to grant eternal life.

Joseph of Arimathea was documented as having petitioned Pontius Pilate for Jesus's body after crucifixion, and he then allegedly became the first Christian missionary to Britain at the command of Saint Philip, a disciple of Jesus. The link between Joseph and the physical cup of Christ was made much later, around 1200 CE. By the late twelfth century, the legends of King Arthur proposed that the Holy Grail had been passed to Joseph by an apparition of Christ and accompanied him on his religious quest to Britain. This myth was developed by the monarchs of Britain to attribute divine right to all those who sat on the throne. The English royals had made themselves the latest true and holy empire.

The myth of the cup of Christ was further bolstered by the red-tinged waters pouring from the Well, which many attributed to the ever-flowing blood of Jesus himself. Locals and travellers came from far and wide to collect and store the Well's water, known for its restorative properties.

Druid history at the mystical site, which dated back to around 300 BCE, had been washed over. As the unpopular, more cultish viewpoint, the paganism of the Druids was sectioned off as devil worship. Pagan belief was that the warm red waters of the Well represented the nourishing properties of the "Divine Mother." The water's colour was thus thought to symbolise the menstrual flow of this great creative force.

With her head dipped over the edge of the red-flowing waters, Chava narrowed her focus to feel out familiar energy signatures in as wide a radius as possible. She sensed only wounded and weary healing angels blinking in and out of her search area. Until, that was, she picked up a strong, hot energy source heading directly for her position impossibly fast—a spinning, flaming cannonball of angry chaos.

Only one being possessed such a unique spiritual marker.

Unsure of how to defend against the incoming attack, Chava could only engage her force field of the Light and hope to survive the impact. There was no time for an alternative response. She had never faced down such immense power without Gabriel by her side. Alone, she would make her stand, and alone she would accept the will of the Universe.

*If these are to be my last moments, I will die with honour and go down fighting.*

Spinning on her heels, Chava closed her eyes and readied for a direct hit.

Nothing.

The hot and suffocating energy felt like it was on top of her, but there had been no collision and no injury. Peeling her eyes open, Chava was met with her would-be attacker's piercing gaze. He was motionless and calm—noncombative, even. In her experience of dealing with this monster, Chava knew that his current behaviour was most likely a misdirection, luring her into a trap.

"If you have come to crush my spirit, you are out of luck. There is nothing left of me that you can take. If it's the Well that you are after, then you will have to go through me. I will not let my master's heroic sacrifice be tarnished by you fouling this holy place," Chava said defiantly.

"There is another solution, and I am in need of your help to find it," the Damned said, his eyes like the tips of hot pokers surrounded by a dancing aura of flame.

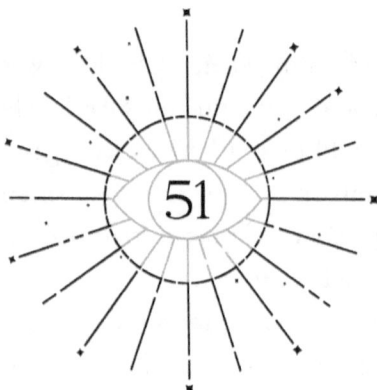

In London's Imperial War Museum, a frail and hunched woman tottered towards the central part of the building with a bunch of tulips in hand. Agnieshka, or Aga as she had been known to her childhood friends, who had long since passed, worked her way towards the brightly lit room ahead.

The section of the museum where she found herself was filled with personal belongings worth considerable value, art and posters from throughout Europe, and eyewitness testimonies of events. Moving through the room, Aga headed to the far wall, where a large stone plinth stretched to the ceiling. She knelt before the hundreds of names inscribed in gold lettering and set her offering of tulips at the base of the stone wall. Bowing her head in prayer, she took a moment's silence to gather her thoughts and then petitioned for peace throughout the world. Her whispered words catalogued current events where innocents were being slaughtered. Her requests for love and healing to all those involved went out into the Universe through the name of her lord, Yahweh.

The silence was split in two by the giggling and screaming of a young brother and sister who had barrelled into the exhibit. The siblings were playing a game of tag with their father in tow, who was working on his phone, uninspired to curb the children's unruly behaviour. Aga turned her head slightly and sighed at the interruption. After a breath, she returned to her prayers.

Running after the young girl, the brother pushed her to tag her. He didn't realise his own strength, though, and the force in his hand sent his sister to the floor. The girl's chin connected with the concrete underfoot, and consequent wailing pierced the air. This time Aga shot a look of disdain at the disrespectful children. Gathering her patience, she shook her head and focused back on the plinth.

"Come on, you two!" the father called out. The brother ran to join him in the adjacent room, followed by the sister, still in floods of tears.

It saddened Aga that manners and respect had gone out of fashion. If they had seen what she had in life, perhaps they would act differently. Ungratefulness was the root of much discontent in modern times. Aga was deeply grateful that she had survived the war, especially considering so many had perished. That she had escaped death was a gift she had never forgotten.

With silence falling once more, Aga sat alone with her memories, staring at ten female names. She bowed her head yet again and clasped her hands in prayer as she visualised the last time she had seen her dearest childhood friends.

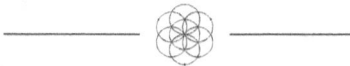

POLAND, 1944

Ten women with freshly shaven heads were ushered into a tiled room by two rifle-wielding SS guards, one fat and red faced from too much wine, the other a leering beanpole with beady eyes.

"Move! Form a line," the fat guard barked, shoving the centre of the group towards the sterile white wall. The women bundled into a haphazard line, knocking into one another and exchanging confused glances. "Now strip," the baboon commanded. Both guards stepped back to get a wider view as the women followed the instruction at gunpoint. All but one.

Agnieshka refused to comply and instead fixed her gaze on the ceiling and crossed her arms into a straightjacket. Her dark, ringlet hair framed striking, deep-set features, stoic in the face of barbarism. Her ice-blue eyes were unwavering and clear.

"Hiding something special under there, eh?" the beanpole remarked. Aga maintained her closed stance in defiance.

In the ether, black smoke formed into thick, swirling tentacles as Samael materialised. He loomed large and motionless behind the Nazi guards. As he added his Light power to amplify the emotion of the situation, a silvery glimmer flickered across his metallic eyes.

*Crack!* The butt of the fat guard's pistol came down on Aga's collarbone. Her legs buckled as she fell to her hands and knees. Slowly and deliberately, the beautiful Aga rose to her feet. Straightening her posture, she wiped the blood from her mouth and rolled her damaged shoulder, then moved her gaze from the ceiling. She stared directly at the Angel of Death and spoke to him.

"I see what you do."

"Do you?" the beanpole said, pulling his pistol and shooting the woman standing next to Aga in the head without hesitation. The woman's cratered skull slammed back into the wall and dragged a trail of blood down the white tile as her body slumped to the ground. The baboon Nazi levelled his pistol at the next woman in line, her limbs trembling. Aga grinded her teeth and spoke again to Samael in the etherverse.

"We are Yahweh's people. You passed over us once. Why, now, have you forsaken us?"

"Who are you talking to, crazy bitch? Praying to your ancestors to save you?" the fat guard said, laughing like a circus clown and slapping his compatriot backhanded on the chest. The lecherous beanpole pointed and grinned, joining in on the circus performance.

The beanpole abruptly switched the tone, lunging forwards to line up his beady eyes with Aga's, an inch from her unflinching face.

"They can't help you now, wench. Now do. As. I. Say. Strip!"

"You cannot win. You too will know death one day. Even one as mighty as you," Aga said, grabbing Samael's attention.

The Angel of Death smirked, granting her wise words a response. "Maybe so, young seer, but not in this present moment, and this present moment is all you have."

*Blam!* The woman on the other side of Aga whirled on the spot and slid down the side of Aga's body, leaving blood on her dress. Aga gave in. She'd had enough of death. The floodgates of her emotions released as she undressed and began to weep. Both guards leaned back in triumph.

"Here we go. Mm-hm," the beanpole sneered. Samael remained still, curiously observing whether there was more to come from the gifted human. To meet a seer with such resolve was a rare opportunity.

"Why?" Aga asked the Angel of Death. This time the archangel did not dignify her with an answer.

Aga's undergarments dropped to her feet one by one, falling next to the two dead women, sopping up their blood. The remaining women were rushed into the shower room by the SS guards, who screamed commands as they scurried like cornered rats.

In a collapsing cloud of silver and black, Samael dematerialised. Remnants of his dark-grey smoke weaved over the fresh corpses as if they had minds of their own.

Then they vanished in an instant to catch up with their master.

Bringing her mind back to the present, Aga opened her eyes, cold and full of regret. She looked up to the plinth and zeroed in on two names side by side: Magdalena Zieliński and Elizabeth Dąbrowski. Aga picked a flower from her bunch and touched it to the plinth where their names glinted in gold, honouring their needless sacrifice at the Nazi concentration camp a lifetime ago.

"Dearest Magda," she said, setting the tulip at the base of the stone, picking a second one, and doing the same. "Sweet Eleeza," Aga said. She performed this ritual every year to mark her young friends' memories, that they may not have died in vain.

Samael landed behind Aga like the toxic smoke of a building fire. As the familiar trail of dark-grey particles slid over both tulips laid to rest on the stone plinth, the flowers wasted to rot. Aga gasped for breath and spun around faster than a woman of her years to behold the looming countenance of the Angel of Death. Again.

Her life had been plagued by visits from the monstrous angel since that fateful day in 1944. Samael had taken a morbid fascination with her life, toying with her throughout her younger days. She had not encountered his putrefying aura for almost fifty years, though, and she had been certain he'd found some other poor soul to torment.

Unseen by Samael, Beel had arrived only moments before. Many angels left a specific dark-matter trail, and her unique tracking system allowed her to follow in his wake. Hiding within the spatial folds of the ether, Beel watched the odd exchange between mortal and archangel before her—an incredible and unlikely sight of a frail old human woman communicating with the Light power of death incarnate.

Beel had trained herself to watch and wait for the perfect time to strike. If such a time did not arise, she would stay concealed and build more knowledge on interlinking events. This tactical approach was the main reason she had never been defeated in battle. Wars were ultimately won by information gathering and patience, both in the physical plane and the ethereal one. It was precisely for this reason she had stalked Samael since his arrival on earth; all the while, he was blissfully unaware of being watched.

Samael barely recognised his old plaything in her aged state. What remained the same was the spiritual fire in her heart, which he had not witnessed in any other since. Her great, untapped gift had drawn him back to her several times, but she had not possessed the courage to unleash its full potential as he and Gabriel had hoped she might.

*Another wondrous human gift gone to waste. Another shot at human evolution missed. Typical.*

In recent centuries, seers had been dying out or withering in their shells faster than ever before, and with them the hope of a new earth had shrivelled like a worm. Samael would try one last time to ignite the fire of the Light in this one. Though he stood on the opposing side of the battlefield, his duty to the balance of the Universe was an unexcisable part of his being, knitted into the very fabric of his core.

"You are few now, seer," Samael rumbled in his gravelly tone.

"I am at peace. I am ready for you to take me now."

"I am not here for you," Samael croaked. Aga's brow furrowed in confusion as the brother and sister dashed back into the exhibit, absorbed in their game of tag.

Aga's expression morphed into one of blank dread.

"Please. Don't."

"The first time we spoke, you asked me why."

The girl's vibrant blond hair waved and flipped through the air as she fled her brother. Giggling with excitement, she twisted her body to avoid being tagged.

"Let me show you," Samael said, opening his fists. Smoke rushed from his palms towards the children.

"Run children! Run!" Aga screamed, her voice cracking. The children turned to face the old woman as the smoke caught up with them. At that very moment, their father darted into the room.

"Time to go, you two," the man said.

The snaking apparitions seeping from Samael's form slid inside the children's eyes and mouths, lifting their fragile forms from the ground and shaking them violently. As Aga and the father gawked in horror, the children coughed and spluttered as if swallowing smoke. Their skin turned from grey to black, and their bodies dissolved into ash. Particles of soot and dust on the ground were all that remained.

"Why? Because I like destroying beautiful things, that's why," Samael said.

The father stood immobilised by shock while Agnieshka gave in and gave up once more. Weeping, she slumped into a ball on the floor.

Suddenly Samael writhed in agony, his Light energy spiking all around him like erratic radio waves as an unseen force sent daggers of pain through his head and spine. A voice echoed in his mind, communicating telepathically from the upper ether.

"I sent you with a purpose," the cold and calm voice said.

"Yes, brother," Samael spat through gritted teeth.

"What was that purpose? Can your puny, distracted mind recall? Or shall I jog your memory?"

"Find Raphael and bring her to you in chains."

"Why then are you wasting my time with your pointless journey into the past?"

"I thought that I would turn these base humans in preparation for your arrival as a gift," Samael said.

"Well, you thought wrong, Samael. Gather the force I dispatched with you, and seek out the miserable traitor. Neutralise her and return her to me. Do it now, or I shall remove the power I have given you."

"Yes, brother, it will be done."

Shaking off the assault on his Light body, Samael retracted his smoke tendrils to rejoin his central mass and set off on the hunt in an explosion of silver-tinged black mist.

Holding her concealed position, Beel surveyed the old and broken seer. *Let us all hope your successor is not so weak in the face of death*, she thought. With much new information gained on battle plans from the upper ether, Beel now knew the treacherous path that lay ahead of her kin—and the importance of the archangel Raphael.

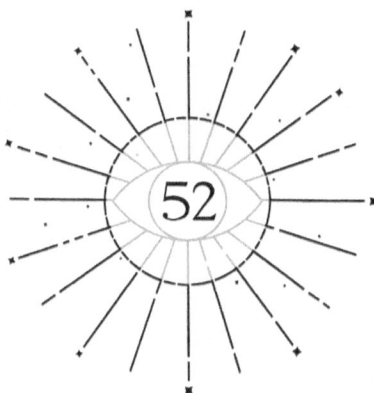

## 52

Grace was paralysed by the creeping darkness snaking across her face and down her neck as the Light of Gabriel within her fought fiercely against the power taking hold. Her skin cycled between a grey, cracked appearance and her normal colouring, with flashes of gold igniting randomly beneath it.

Mr. Burrows, however, had been instantly consumed by the touch and was covered in black cracks, his eyes a solid black. Maggie growled and snapped at her changed master, almost taking Andy's hand off as the boy leapt backwards next to Haylene. Neither Andy nor Haylene could believe their eyes or comprehend what was happening to Grace and the old man. It had all happened so fast, and their brains struggled to catch up with what was transpiring—and how to respond.

Clapping his jaw, Mr. Burrows made a beeline for young Andy, his voice emerging as a gravelly, demonic growl.

"What a nice little boy you have there," he said.

Haylene's disbelief at the man's repugnant transformation locked her to the spot, but as Mr. Burrows reached out to grab Andy, her protective instincts catapulted her from her shocked state. Batting away Mr. Burrow's arm, Haylene followed up with a solid fist to the centre of the changed man's chest, landing him on his backside.

"Stay back. That was a warning shot; the next one won't be." Haylene dragged Andy behind her and shook Grace violently by the arm. "Grace, I really need you to snap out of whatever is going on with you. We need to get out of here right now," Haylene shouted, her eyes pinned on the touched man rolling about on the ground only two metres away.

"I'm . . . not sure . . . I know how. Something's burning inside me," Grace said, gritting the words out past the internal pressure bubbling through her nervous system. Her mind was still her own, but the evil inside her was battering down her spiritual body's defences.

Mr. Burrows was back on his feet, licking his lips and staring longingly at Andy.

"I promise not to hurt him. I just want to borrow him for a while—see what he tastes like," he said, edging closer to the group.

"I warned you," Haylene said as she cocked her back leg and launched a high kick at the man's head. Stepping into the kick, the man grabbed Haylene's extended leg and lifted her clear off the ground by the torso, spinning her around and upending her onto the tarmac path. Her shoulder crunched as the safety mechanism in her brain, triggered by the sharp rush of pain, flicked the off switch. Haylene was down and out. Andy was exposed and alone.

"Haylene! Are you okay? Please get up," Andy yelped as he scurried next to his mum, who was still frozen solid. Grace panted and wheezed, doing her utmost to fight her way out of her helpless state. Mr. Burrows darted at them to grab Andy.

"No!" Grace blurted out. A searing blast of golden illumination exploded from her chest, lifting the touched man into the air and flinging him back against a nearby tree. It was as if a bomb had gone off, albeit a very selective one. Grace, Andy, and Haylene were all unharmed.

Grace shook her head, having regained control of her body after the outward release. Terrified and amazed, Andy peeked up at her.

"Mum, are you okay?"

"I don't know, sweetie. I still feel weak and unsteady."

Grace's complexion remained grey, a few cracks on her skin persisting. Andy dashed over to Haylene as she came around.

"Ow! Ah, damn it. I haven't had my ass handed to me like that in a long while, and never by a pensioner," Haylene said, standing and cradling her right arm. "I think my shoulder might have dislocated. There could be some damage to the tendons or ligaments too. Give me a hand, will ya, buddy? Let's get your mum home."

Haylene hoisted her functioning shoulder under Grace's armpit to guide her home while Andy did his best to support her from the other side. Grace had at least broken out of her paralysis, but she was far from out of the woods.

The sensations were not unlike the toxic grip of addiction she had been in for half of her adult life. The Seven Sins seeping through her spirit and eating away at her life force resembled an accelerated version of an addict's journey. Her physical body longed to give in to the base desires the evil offered, yet the strength of her spirit and mind and her love for her son tugged hard on her emotions not to give in.

Haylene dragged Grace through the park as fast as she could manage in their compromised states. Andy kept up with determined strides, the boy who had become the man—a default setting from when his mum had needed his help in the past. This was no time or place for emotion; getting his mum and Haylene to safety was priority number one, and everything else could wait. This mature response to the horrors he had just witnessed was classic Andy in times of extreme stress—the unlikely hero.

Up ahead, at the exit of the park that would take them homeward, a group of touched humans tumbled into view. The thralls zeroed in on the vulnerable trio, howling and stomping towards Andy and his wounded loved ones in a fervour for pure flesh.

As Grace's internal battle with the Seven Sins raged on, Andy gripped his mother's hand and began hyperventilating. His anger built exponentially, years of resentment spilling upwards like bile—resentment he'd protected his mum from for so long that he could no longer contain. Now that a life-or-death moment was staring Andy dead in the eyes, he wasn't about to let all those years of struggle and heartache end like this.

*My dad taught me to be a man and protect the vulnerable, especially my mother. I'm sick of sitting in the shadows and being afraid.*

As Andy absorbed this primordial protective instinct, an offshoot of the golden power reverberating inside Grace's aura weaved through the ether towards him. The splicing and curving shape changed to orange and then red as the Light, now in dark form, thumped into the boy's sternum. Zigzagging up his neck and face, a crimson illumination ignited around his eyelids.

"No. No. No! I'm not watching the people I love suffer anymore." Andy planted his right foot forwards and held both palms up. "It's time for you to suffer!" he bellowed in a voice not his own as a swathe of dazzling energy blasted the three touched, tossing them onto their backs and pinning them to the ground inside individual prisms of searing-red Light.

The creatures moaned and writhed to break free, but they were firmly imprisoned and being drained of their life forces.

"Andy?" Haylene said, her shoulders hunched and breath trapped in her chest. The red energy dissipated from within Andy's aura, and he stared at Haylene with moist eyes.

"I'm sorry. I don't know why I got so angry, but I feel a bit better now, somehow."

"It's okay. Come on quick before these things escape," Haylene replied, dragging Grace with her good arm and nodding for Andy to take the other side. The pair hustled Grace along with hard, resolved faces. No one was going to stop them, and after his outburst, Andy was certain that a great power above was looking out for them, guiding their every step.

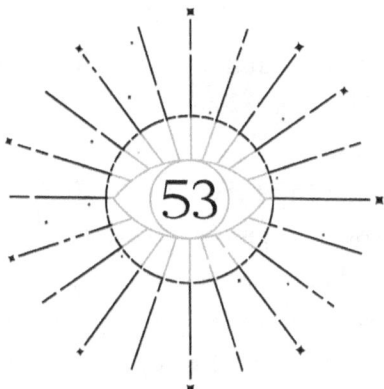

## 53

Abaddon and Scratitch had been running interference. They swept across London to wherever the Light led them, blunting the descending warrior angels' efforts on all sides. The Lord of the Pit was loath to help the humans, but if it meant frustrating the plans of the warrior class and their arrogant leader, he would rush to their aid gladly and with his full might.

Abaddon had called up three of his most loyal berserker demons to help push back the warrior ranks before they could infect the humans. Boxy creatures, with overly muscled necks and hands like JCB shovels, berserkers were honed animalistic rage. They had been cultivated by centuries of experimentation and torture in the nether realms, a perfect weapon of chaos that had proved highly effective in the 1,800 years since their creation in the Pit. Covered in long spikes of a glowing, metallic substance, and with a gaping shark's mouth full of energy-rupturing teeth, the purple-skinned berserkers were sure to inflict damage on any celestial they came into contact with.

Abaddon and Scratitch had followed a squad of warriors to London's South Bank, where human city workers gathered in bars and restaurants. The last warrior angel left was being whipped back and forth, clamped inside the jaws of the larger of the two remaining berserker demons. The rabid creature's golden fangs dripped with the brilliant life essence of the defeated warrior. As the glow of the warrior's

Light faded, his body folded in on itself and shrank to a speck, then blinked out, taking the angel's soul to an unknown destination and an unknown new purpose.

Such was how any angel should have passed on when they were defeated in a battle of the Light—not dead but their life force whisked away and reincarnated in whatever form the all-knowing consciousness of the cosmos deemed fit. However, with the new reality of angelic death unleashed by Michael's tampering, defeat at a warrior angel's hand meant oblivion, an unthinkable fate that diminished the whole of the Universe itself. This fate was still unknown to many celestials who stood against Samael and the first wave of warriors. News was travelling slowly, and many shrugged off the prospect of death as an enemy intimidation tactic. Abaddon's current swagger in battle indicated he was of this group. When two of his berserkers had turned to stone and disintegrated, he dismissed it as another odd symptom of the celestial realm's spiritual imbalance.

In the physical realm, a tide of humans ran screaming for cover from a handful of touched humans that Abaddon had been unable to protect from the warriors. The rippling crowd pushed into a glass-fronted restaurant as the touched clawed at their heels.

In the ether, the battlefield was cleared, and Abaddon and Scratitch were left with the two panting berserkers galloping back to their sides.

"I've missed the action, I have to say. It's a far cry from the drudgery of the Pit," Abaddon said to Scratitch.

"Meeee's toos. Slicey dicey bing bong crash!" Scratitch barked. Abaddon smirked at his ward's unique ability to capture the feeling of the moment without making any literal sense whatsoever. It was rather endearing, and the gimp's upbeat mentality was why Abaddon secretly loved his company.

"We best get on with searching out another warrior wave. The more we send off into the oblivion of the ether, the better our chances to regroup and mount our own assault."

"There's no need to rush off, Abi," said a throaty, cutting voice from behind the gathering of dark angels. The group swivelled to see the cherub Ahebban hovering over the River Thames behind them, his eyes black as night with a fizzing, electric blue-and-gold border. The shards of lightning that raced around his sleek battle suit zipped and popped from his eyes and hands. Abaddon turned his nose up.

"My name is Abaddon, you buffoon. I see from your sparkly new getup that you've sold your soul. No surprise there. You always were a follower rather than a leader."

"Shut it. I'm going to squash your pets and then cut out your throat, Abi. I want to save the best till last," the cherub goaded.

"Tear him apart," Abaddon commanded his berserkers.

The chomping demons launched over the river's edge at Ahebban in a simultaneous strike. In the physical realm, the waters of the Thames swirled into a whirlpool beneath the clashing spiritual forces suspended above. A split second before the berserkers' fangs could sink into their target, Ahebban materialised a war hammer in each hand and slammed both demons under the chin with a dual uppercut that exploded with blue and white lightning. As the animalistic celestials shot upwards, black cracks and a blue aura consumed them, dissolving their forms in midair.

"What are you going to do now, Pit lord? Not much of a fighter when you don't have your abominations to fight for you."

"Oh, Ahebban, I see that you are as simple a barbarian as ever. There's plenty more where they came from. I only made a minor error in judgment when assuming we would not happen upon such a unique specimen as yourself," Abaddon said and then turned to his companion. "You know what to do, and when you are finished, bring me his body."

Scratitch returned a nod and a hungry grin at his dark lord's command. Anxious to please his master, he giggled as he clambered towards Ahebban.

"Is this your idea of a joke? Spare your gimp the anguish and fight me yourself!" Ahebban shouted. Abaddon said nothing.

"Oweeee, you be perfect as pyre beast would."

"What?"

"You know, fat, ugly, slimy slave," Scratitch said.

"Quiet, worm. Stand aside, and I'll consider sparing you."

"Make you my slave in Pit will I."

"Right. Time to silence that mouth," Ahebban said and spun wildly at Scratitch, bringing the force of his war hammers down on Scratitch's head. Scratitch stepped back and tripled in size in an instant, looming large over the tumbling cherub, who had connected with nothing but air.

"You didn't think I kept him around for his good looks and scintillating personality, did you?" Abaddon shouted from the sidelines. "As you can see, Scratitch's beast form is incredibly effective at keeping the prisoners of my pit in line. They fear the pain he might inflict on them, and I find fear to be a great motivator."

As Ahebban stared up in puzzlement at Scratitch in his giant form, Scratitch opened wide and swallowed the warrior whole. The waters of the river below immediately stilled in the physical realm, the threat neutralised. Stomping back to his master, Scratitch vomitted up the cherub, now encased in a sack of slime and writhing to break free. Abaddon reached down into the sack and sucked the Light from within, shrinking Ahebban's form and sending the cherub on to his next incarnation. Undoubtedly, it would not be a pretty one.

Returning to his original size and shape, Scratitch then stepped forwards and sucked the empty green sack inside his body. The gangly gimp beamed up at his master.

"That's my boy," Abaddon said. "Now that I've picked the Angel of Death's scent up off that bullish idiot, we can pay him a visit and teach him not to stick his nose where it doesn't belong."

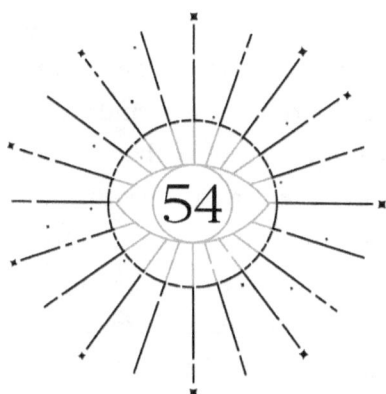

## 54

Professor Simms hurried out under the New College courtyard's mythic stone archway with Sorchia skipping after him, doing her best to keep pace. The man was surprisingly quick, and his long legs were in full stride as his bulging satchel bounced off his hip.

"Simmsy, slow down. This isn't necessary. I'll get Grace on the phone eventually, and we can have a group video discussion," Sorchia said.

The professor wasn't slowing down. He scuttled across the road and down the hill towards Edinburgh's Waverley train station.

"No good. This could be a time-sensitive issue. Don't you think it's odd that you can't get hold of her?"

"No. When she really needs me, she always comes back to me, and when I agreed we should go to her, I kind of meant taking the Friday-evening train. Not just jumping at the first available ticket. I have classes and almost twenty-five dissertations to read!"

"No, you don't. I've already cleared your schedule with the university for the weekend."

Simms locked eyes and grinned at Sorchia, who had finally caught up with him.

"We have been invited last minute to the new Slaves and Pharaohs exhibition at the British Museum," he said with a wink.

"What? How did you manage that?"

"Well, we're not actually attending, are we? We have much more exciting things to discuss with Grace," Simms said, patting his satchel. "I've already booked our train tickets, and we just need to pick them up at the machines inside over there." He pointed down the ramp into the interior platforms as he darted onwards.

"But I don't have any clothes or even a toothbrush."

"We can get you some toiletries when we get there, and I'm sure Grace will have something you can borrow."

"But I . . . I really would prefer if Grace knew that I was coming. She doesn't like it when I turn up unannounced like this!" Sorchia snapped. Her elevated tone stopped the professor in his tracks.

"Sorchia. When have you ever turned up unannounced to anything in your life? Ever? I know I don't know you that well, but I know you well enough to see that you control and plan so much of the fun out of your life," the professor said, tilting his head and raising his eyebrows. Sorchia's jaw dropped. Half-indignant at being spoken to in such a way, she was also shockingly aroused by the man's boldness.

"That's not true at all. I do fun things."

"Like what? Give me an example," Simms said, and waited. After a few failed attempts at forming a sentence, Sorchia gave up.

"I can't think of a specific example at the moment. You need to give me some time. I don't like being put on the spot like this."

"And that's exactly the point right there. Everything has to be thought about so intensely before you can engage. I understand. I've lived that way most of my life too. From one 'brainiac' to another, let me tell you it's good practice to switch off and go with the flow every once in a while. This is the perfect opportunity for that; plus, your daughter needs you."

Sorchia frowned at Simms, conflicted. The professor reached out his hand. "What do you say, Sorchia Collopy? Are you ready to go with the flow and have a fun adventure with me?"

Simms's disarming charm melted her icy glare.

"Okay, fine, but you're buying the wine on the train journey."

"That's the spirit. Let's hurry before we miss the last express to

London." The professor grabbed Sorchia by the hand and pulled her towards the ticket machine. Sorchia watched as Simms punched some buttons and gathered their tickets. She was scared stiff to be out of her comfort zone like this, but the man she was taking this impromptu journey with was both confident and exciting. She would surely kick herself later if she didn't take the opportunity to let her hair down and make the visit to check in with her daughter.

Heading for the platforms, the professor directed Sorchia to their train, and they hopped on to find their seats in what was thankfully a clean and quiet coach. Not a single drunken football supporter in sight. The pair settled in and waited for the train to get underway.

"I know that you are fascinated by the angelic subject matter and willing to put up with my—how was it you put it?—'planning the fun out of life' personality, but it feels like there's more in this for you?"

"Oh, cripes! Did I actually use those words? I do apologise. It sounds awful when you repeat it back to me like that."

"I'm kidding. You're forgiven. And 'cripes'? Who uses that word anymore? Come on, Professor," Sorchia quipped, chuckling.

"Well, I'm happy that I amuse you. You know, I think that's the first time I've seen you laugh," Simms said, causing Sorchia's cheeks to flush bright pink.

"I'll try not to make a habit out of it." She beamed. "You still haven't answered my question, Simmsy. Why take all this trouble just for research and development?"

"You're quite the perceptive one, aren't you, Miss Collopy? But yes, you're right. There is more to it." The professor glanced down at his hands in his lap and fiddled with his fingers. "I didn't want to scare you, but I think Grace's life could be in danger."

"Surely you can't know that. I appreciate your concern, I do, but Grace and I have been down this road many times before. A period of instability in her life is followed by hallucinations, and then she either turns to medication or throws herself back into her work. They are clear patterns of behaviour I'm used to riding out."

"I'm aware of that, but the archangel Gabriel, the spiritual being that came to her, is known in Christian literature and the Dead Sea Scrolls to be followed by malevolent forces—forces seeking to cause harm to those that would appear 'gifted' and walk in 'the Light' as a visionary or prophet."

"I'm not sure that qualifies as a credible threat to her safety. I love your passion for myths and legend, but once we get to her and talk all this out, you might find you were worrying over nothing."

"You may not share my fantastical point of view, but I couldn't forgive myself if we got there and it was too late."

"Oh, now you're going a little overboard with the drama."

"Am I? She's your daughter, your own flesh and blood. Yet you don't seem one bit concerned since we spoke about how she could be in danger!" Simms sighed and looked out the window at the quickly greying sky in the distance. Sorchia waited for the man to collect his thoughts. "I'm sorry. That was rude of me. My heightened emotions on the matter all stem from my broken marriage. My ex-wife has refused me contact with my only daughter ever since she found a new husband two years ago. It breaks my heart, and I miss her every day. I just can't understand how you don't miss Grace. You are so lucky to have her in your life."

"I'm sorry that you don't get to see your daughter. That must be very difficult. I do miss Grace, but we're just . . . very different people."

"What about your grandson? I've seen the photo of Grace and a young boy on your desk. You obviously care for them."

"I do. I don't know. I don't know what to do about all the time we've missed out on. It just seems like I've failed as a parent. Books I know, but being a mum, I was never cut out for that, especially not on my own."

"Well, I'm sorry you had to do it on your own, but you are still a mum to Grace, and I am still a father to my daughter, and I think we should never stop trying, even though it's a clunky experience for squares like us."

Sorchia nodded and gazed out the window at the bustling station. Her eyes landed on a grandmother embracing her daughter and granddaughter, who had just come off the train on the adjacent platform. Giving a weighty sigh, Sorchia knew the professor was right. There was always room to try harder, and it was never too late.

"How about that wine you promised me?" Sorchia said.

"I think we could both use a glass."

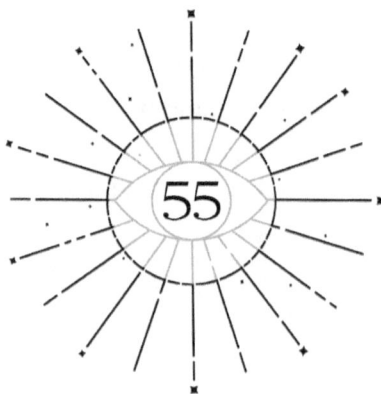

## 55

Back in Becontree Estate, Jack and Sonny reclined in the plush Range Rover, watching Lazaro's bizarre cat-and-mouse game with the maddened Dio. All that was missing was some popcorn and fizzy drinks to complete the action movie sequence outside. Dashing back and forth, Lazaro was red faced and sweating, firing and reloading his shotgun as the touched Dio evaded his laboured attempts.

"Hey, big fella, you got any more of those wine gums?" Jack said, poking his head between the front seats to get a better view of the battle.

"You bet. They were on two for one, so I thought why the hell not," Sonny said, opening a fresh bag and angling it towards Jack.

"Oh baby, the red ones are my favourite," Jack said, sniffing his chosen sweet. Looking back up at Dio spinning around the back of Lazaro's shotgun blast, Jack shook his head and chuckled. He pulled out his phone and started filming. "This is brilliant. It's almost as if they're dancing the tango. Boss is never gonna live this one down."

"You are bang on there, mate. I saw an Argentinian tango on *Strictly* last night, and that looked just like a heel pull followed by a double reverse spin."

"What! You're a *Strictly* fan? I never would have pinned you for that."

"Looks can be deceiving, Stones. I was actually the winner of the UK Elite Dance Championships five years ago."

Jack stopped filming and looked at Sonny as if the huge specimen's hair were on fire.

"Shut. Up."

"No lie, mate. You're looking at the UK's top specialist in South American freestyle."

Jack had nothing; he simply shrugged and looked back out the window. When he spotted an odd pattern on the horizon, his face fell.

"Stay in the car, big fella, and start the engine," Jack said. Grabbing a bat from the footwell and throwing open the back passenger door, he leapt at Dio, tackling him to the ground.

"Hey! I said I'd deal with this," Lazaro barked.

"There's no time, boss. Whatever's got ahold of Dio has definitely got ahold of them," Jack said, pointing behind Lazaro at the rippling skyline. "Now hold him down while I knock him out. I'm not leaving Dio behind."

Lazaro turned and beheld the pack of clambering touched. Numbering twenty or more, the crazed prisoners were approaching fast. To add to the threat, residents were pouring out from nearby houses onto the street and clashing with the prisoners as if driven out like wasps from a nest by an unseen force.

That unseen force was Zelda. She had arrived minutes before and was zipping from house to house, spreading the power of the Seven Sins like a wildfire. Her path of poison and mayhem was all part of Michael's plan. Divide and conquer.

Back in the physical realm, Sonny jumped from the driver's seat and rushed to the back of the car to pull out a second shotgun.

"You get Dio sorted and I'll try and hold them off!" Sonny shouted.

"Okay, I've got him!" Lazaro yelled as he knelt on Dio, who was spitting blood and thrashing his head about.

"I hope this doesn't leave a mark, mate," Jack said, thwacking Dio's temple with the bat. *Clunk!* Dio went out like a light, and Jack gathered him from the ground and up over his shoulder. "Help me get him into the back, boss." Jack nodded to the Range.

Lazaro was a statue, staring at the wave of deranged touched closing in on the group. "Laz! Snap out of it. If we don't move now, we are totally and utterly fecked!" Jack shouted.

Blinking and shaking himself, Lazaro grabbed Dio's dangling legs as the pair hauled him towards the car. Sonny had taken aim in a crouched position behind the car bonnet and fired off two rounds. The shotgun had no effect. The buckshot would land, and a black-and-gold glow would suck the particles beneath the skin and close up the wound within seconds.

"You better hurry it up, fellas. There's no stopping these things."

Stuffing Dio's limp frame into the back of the Range, Jack recognised the particular prisoner outfits the touched were wearing.

"There must have been an outbreak at Pentonville prison in Islington." Jack swivelled and barked at Sonny, "Big lad, leave it and get in."

Gathering the last two automatic weapons and ammo, Lazaro darted from the back of the car and jumped into a nearby house on the opposite side of the street. The Wraith was not wasting any time in self-preservation, leaving Jack and Dio defenceless.

At that very moment in the ether, Zelda froze and spun around. Dark-grey wisps of the Light exploded outwards from behind Sonny as the Angel of Death appeared. Furious from his recent scolding and determined to take it out on the first humans he came in contact with, he gripped Sonny by the back of the skull and infected him with the Seven Sins, sucking away his life force. The henchman convulsed and groaned before dropping his shotgun and heading straight at Jack. A hungry glare washed over his face.

Zipping next to Samael, Zelda was anxious to give a status report.

"The holding cells of the city have all been turned. I have also infected sporadic groups of the suburban population and am making my way to the police headquarters."

"There's no time for that. I want you to find me Raphael."

"But, my lord, I do not have the capability to—"

"I don't want any excuses. Find a way to bring that pretentious turncoat to me."

Zelda had not seen Samael this enraged before and hesitated.

"Now!" Samael bellowed. "I'm staying here to feast on some souls."

Having been forced out into the middle of the road, Jack caught sight of two other touched coming at him from either side. He assessed his position and knew he had to act fast to avoid getting trapped.

A grinning Sonny, a hopelessly strung-out Asian lady, and a viciously angry old man launched at Jack. All touched, all hungry for blood.

At the far end of the estate, Samael tore through Becontree's streets at breakneck speed, corrupting soul after soul in a feeding frenzy fuelled by his humiliation at the hands of his vastly more powerful brother.

Consumed by his rampage, Samael did not notice Abaddon and Scratitch—with three newly conscripted berserkers—warp onto the scene atop a house two streets away.

"I will deal with the Angel of Death. The rest of you put a stop to his forces," Abaddon commanded.

"Me's wantings to fight too. The big one!" Scratitch whined.

"Do as you're told! Samael's mine and mine alone."

At this, Scratitch pulled a grumpy face. He led the berserkers off through a pulsing red ethergate.

Crashing in front of Samael, Abaddon sucker-punched the archangel with a flaming uppercut, then a red-hot forearm, finishing with three lightning jabs to the midsection. Each strike left stinging red marks on the Angel of Death's body.

The surprise attack annoyed Samael more than wounding him, like a mosquito buzzing around his head. He lashed out in frustration. Too fast for the blow to connect, Abaddon faked backwards with a crooked smile.

"I've come for more than that, you brain-dead oaf," Abaddon taunted.

Back with Jack, the crazed Asian lady lunged at his waist. Whipping around and connecting a darting knee with her nose, he knocked her to the pavement. Jack quickly manoeuvred back to the middle of his three attackers and threw his right arm back, chopping at the neck of the old man, leaving him gasping for air. The touched Sonny tackled Jack hard to the ground. Pinned by Sonny's weight, Jack wriggled to break free as the large henchman sat on his abdomen and held his shoulders down on the asphalt.

Back in the ether, Samael threw deliberate, arcing swings that the dark angel dodged with ease. Sneaking inside Samael's guard, Abaddon snapped a precise fist at the monstrous archangel's chin while sending a sharp kick to buckle his knee.

Seeing Abaddon's attacks as a building threat, Samael quickly straightened and grabbed his attacker by the throat. He lifted him high in the air and returned him to earth with immense force, leaving Abaddon badly winded.

"Different than picking on these pitiful humans, isn't it?" Samael sneered.

"Pick on this, ghoul," Abaddon growled.

Shooting upwards, as stiff and straight as a spear, Abaddon headbutted Samael under the chin and then landed both palms in the middle of Samael's chest. Looking the Angel of Death dead in the eye, Abaddon grinned as he fired a fierce explosion of crimson Light from both hands. The energy overcharge seared Samael's eyes, and his giant frame slid back from the heavy strike. Abaddon remained in position with his two palms up in guard as Samael shook his head, dazed.

After the red hues had faded from the air, in a strange twist of momentum, Abaddon's open palms were sucked back against Samael's chest, pulling Abaddon like a magnet. Abaddon's face contorted as he found he was stuck fast to Samael's black, barrel chest. Blinking to clear his vision, the Angel of Death looked down at Abaddon's hands and laughed.

At first Abaddon was confused. A sense of cold constriction followed as his complexion paled and cracked. The poison of the Seven Sins had entered his Light body.

"No," Abaddon moaned as Samael smirked and drank in the Lord of the Pit's life energy. "How?"

"My lord has given me his gift," Samael said, his eyes throbbing with Abaddon's Dark Light.

With Abaddon helpless, Samael launched massive fists into his face, over and over. After six thundering blows, Abaddon was limp, lifeless, and grey.

Having taken what he needed, the Angel of Death pulled Abaddon's ragged frame from his chest and dropped it to the ground. As his fading energy burst into a fire of decay, Abaddon made one last, desperate attempt to reach out to Beel, whom he could feel most closely in his dying moments. In truth, she had been his closest of companions for all his time on earth, though they'd had their differences. *How strange it is that my mind is with her as I leave this existence.*

"Scratitch is your worm now. Take care of him. Please, sister. If you do anything for me, do this one thing." These were his last words before his body collapsed into flame and imploded into a flowing, golden orb. The words fell on deaf ears; the communication lines in the ether had been broken by Gabriel's fall.

And so Abaddon died, alone and helpless. Not disintegrating to ash like the rest of his murdered kind but his Dark Light instead consumed by the Pit from whence he came. A fitting resting place for the champion of suffering.

Having found himself in the vicinity of Jack's evolving altercation, Samael took a brief moment to admire the human's abilities.

"This one has spirit. If only the simpleton warrior class had such resolve, this war would be over in a day," Samael grumbled to himself.

He looked on as the twisted Sonny raised a double-axe handle, seconds away from collapsing Jack's skull. The henchman's blow came down hard, but Jack dodged it, jabbing his attacker in the ribs.

Two ribs snapped under Jack's precise fist. Quickly spinning on top of the henchman, Jack swivelled his hips to manoeuvre a knee onto Sonny's throat. He clapped either side of the lump's head, then knocked Sonny out with a thundering straight arm to his jaw. There was no time to be complacent as Jack got to his feet just in time to see the angry old man launching at his neck.

Dodging and throwing a hacking elbow to the old man's head, sending him to the fairies, Jack faked backwards to avoid the Asian lady's attack from his other flank. The strung-out woman dove for his trailing leg, clawing at him as she slammed into the pavement. Lifting his knee high, Jack stomped down on her exposed ear socket. She too went out like a light.

All foes were down and out. Jack gathered himself and patted down his clothes, unaware of the large shadow rising behind him on the ethereal plane. Samael was anxious to put an end to Jack's success, and his engorged grey tentacles slithered to engulf the dwarfed man in their vile embrace.

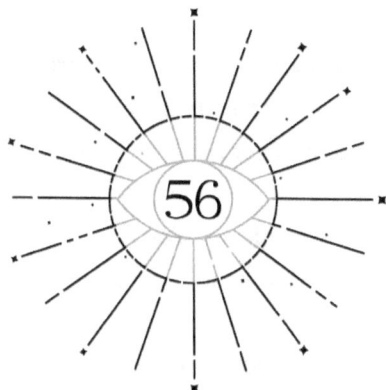

## 56

Gliding up the hill towards the prison, the electric Volkswagen purred like a robotic cat. Patrick was huddled up to the wheel and alert. With his head on a swivel, Eddie kept an eye out for escaped prisoners. He scrunched his cheeks into his eyes and hoped with all his might that the crazed inmates had scattered elsewhere. His stress was heightened by the fact that he had no idea whether the hipster doctor sitting next to him was going to be a help or a hindrance in the task ahead.

Likely the latter.

Still, perhaps he was secretly a martial arts expert or deer-hunting enthusiast.

*Come on, Eddie, stop dreaming. Focus. Both your life and his are in your hands now, and you did suggest this, so pull it together.*

"You okay there, Eddie? You're a tad red in the face," Patrick said.

"Eh, yeah. Well. Not really."

"Well done you for owning up to that and taking responsibility for your anxiety. The first step to tackling any problem is admitting that there is a problem in the first place."

"I don't think you're thinking about the type of problem I'm thinking about."

"Sorry, you've lost me there," Patrick said.

"I'll explain when we get there."

As the car sailed closer to the prison, a police roadblock appeared over the rise of the hill. Patrick inhaled sharply.

"Must have been serious for them to block off the road. What on earth are we going to say to get past the police?" he said.

"Don't worry, Doc. Pull over next to the bobby on my side of the car and just let me do the talking, okay?"

"Yes, I think that's best. Oh, and, Eddie, please drop the formalities and call me Patrick."

"Alrighty then, Patrick. Take a deep breath. From here on in, things could go sideways at any minute," Eddie said. Patrick replied with a glimmer of a thrill in his upward-inflected voice.

"Gotcha!"

Out of nowhere, Eddie began coughing violently. The wound on his neck was spawning several black, wormlike shapes.

"Are you doing alright with your neck? You look like hell."

"I'm fine. Once we get Jade, we can head to the medical unit in the prison, and I'll find something to sort myself out."

"Sounds like a plan," Patrick said as he rolled the car next to the police officer, who beckoned Eddie to lower the window. Eddie complied, and the officer hinged at the waist to look inside the car.

"Road's closed. I'm gonna have to ask you to turn around," the officer stated.

"Listen, Officer, I know there's been a major incident at the prison, but I've gotta get back inside. I've got a colleague stranded up there," Eddie said.

"No can do, mate. We're waiting on a team to sweep through in hazmat suits. I need you to leave the area immediately," the officer replied. Eddie glanced at Patrick and then back at the officer.

"Officer, please, you couldn't just make an exception for fellow law enforcement personnel?"

The policeman straightened up unexpectedly. His gaze drifted off into the distance, and he blinked several times. Eddie nodded at Patrick and whispered, "Still got the silver tongue."

"That was incredible. I didn't think that he was going to go for it.

I thought you'd come on a bit strong. Oh, here he is. Hopefully he lets us through," Patrick said, pointing as the officer dipped back down to window level. Eddie was greeted by the officer's ghostly face, black cracks snaking from under his collar.

"I. I. Think that you . . ." the officer stammered. He was losing control of his faculties, and Eddie immediately recognised the symptoms.

"Go! Now!" Eddie barked at Patrick, who froze at his companion's change in tone.

"What?"

"Floor it and don't stop for anyone!" Eddie screamed and slammed his hand down hard on Patrick's right knee and the accelerator pedal. The car shot off and crashed through the striped police barrier. As they left the convulsing policeman in their wake, Eddie pulled Patrick's left knee to the side, preventing him from using the brake, and the car whizzed off like a life-size remote-control toy car.

"What the hell are you doing!" Patrick yelled at the top of his lungs, the electric motor whirring at high pitch.

"That's exactly the same reaction I saw on every prisoner before they changed into crazed animals. Trust me, keep your foot down," Eddie said, removing his hands from Patrick's legs.

"Oh God, it must be everywhere. But he . . . he changed so quickly, and there was no one near him that could have transmitted any infection."

"It doesn't matter how it happens. What matters is that it turns people into bloodthirsty animals, and I left Jade up there in the middle of it."

The futuristic VW sped towards the prison car park, which showed no signs of life anywhere near the towering stone megalith. The barrier to the small staff section was wide open, covered in streaks of blood. As Patrick spun the vehicle into the car park, his eyes widened. Two bodies lay at either side of the prison's lofty oak doorway.

"Maybe this wasn't such a good idea," Patrick whimpered.

"Too late now, Doc. Pull up next to my vintage baby over there,"

Eddie said, pointing to the boxy VW bobbing about on its axis like an automated fairground ride. Eddie coughed and sputtered a black discharge into his hand, which went unnoticed by Patrick, who was transfixed by the ominous movements of Eddie's car. Eddie wiped his hand on his trouser leg to hide the evidence.

"Why is your car bouncing up and down?" Patrick asked with a slow turn of the head towards Eddie.

"Now, when I open the boot, just stay well back and make sure the boot of your car is open as well so I can make a quick transfer," Eddie said.

Patrick pulled the electric VW next to Eddie's older model and turned off the engine. He sat glued to his seat as Eddie moved to exit the vehicle.

"I'm not going anywhere until you tell me what the hell is in there. I thought we were helping Jade."

Eddie sighed and looked at Patrick with raised eyebrows.

"That is Jade," Eddie said, motioning at his car boot.

"Why would you lock her in your boot? Wait, is she infected like one of those guards was back there?"

"Look, just pop the back open and stand back, okay?" Eddie exited the car and moved around to the back of his own vehicle. Having realised it was a mistake even as he opened the back of his car, Patrick leapt from the driver's seat.

"You didn't tell me she was infected!"

"Listen, Doc, it's not that bad," Eddie said, clicking open the back of his car to reveal a gagged-and-bound Jade squirming like a fish out of water. Her deathly appearance made Patrick jump out of his skin.

"Not that bad? You can't be serious about putting her in my car in that state!" Patrick protested. Screaming from under the gag, Jade was hoisted out by Eddie and dumped into the back of the electric VW. As he closed the boot on her, Eddie stumbled, overcome by a sudden lightheadedness.

Patrick reached out to steady him and guided him to the front seat.

"I am not going back in there if there are more infected like her. Plus, you are in no fit state to make it to the medical centre. We're heading to the hospital."

"Okay. Okay, whatever you say. You're the boss," Eddie mumbled, slipping from consciousness.

"No, no, no. I can't believe we're bringing one of them with us!" Patrick lamented, backing up and spinning the car as fast as possible. Focusing his stress into driving like a wild man, Dr. Lockhart headed for the nearest hospital with a maniac in the back and his passenger at death's door.

Patrick tried to put a positive spin on things, as he always liked to do. At least this was a lot more exciting than the dementia home.

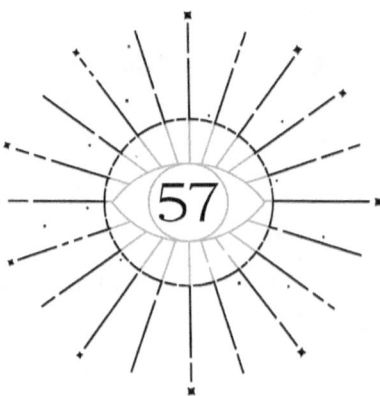

# 57

Hobbling through the apartment door in a sweat, Haylene shuffled Grace's limp body into the living room using a stiff grip around her waist. Andy puffed from the opposite side, and the three gingerly inched towards the sofa before collapsing in a heap of wobbly bodies. Grace's condition had worsened, and Haylene knew the only way her friend was going to survive whatever was eating at her was pure mental fortitude.

Unsure if she was able to reach Grace anymore, trapped under layers of suffocating pain as she was, Haylene attempted to tap into her sense of reason.

"Grace. You have to hold on. I've called an ambulance, but who knows how long that's going to take, so you have to stay with us."

Grace's head rolled to the side as she groaned in response, her eyes awash with grey clouds and her pupils masked.

"Haylene, her eyes! What's happening to her?" Andy yelped. All signs of his experience with the Light at the park were gone. He was back to the sensitive and caring boy Haylene knew.

"I don't know, bud, but the best we can do is hold her and send loving energies of healing light." Andy held on tight and tried to send all of his positive energy towards her. It felt weird and fake to do so, but if it helped, even a little, he would try anything for his mum.

Andy began to sob quietly.

"That's it. Let it out. Everything is going to be okay, my little buddy," Haylene said, taking Andy's hand. "Andy, tell me. What did we do the whole time Mummy was sick?"

Andy looked at Haylene blankly.

"We had faith, right? We knew that when things got really bad with her, maybe they had to get worse before they got better. This is no different, bud. We don't understand what's happening or why, but that's just like back then. So we do the same: we have faith and trust that everything will be okay in the end."

"But what if it isn't?"

"Then it's not the end, and we wait and see. In the meantime, we do whatever we can to support your mum. You and I both know she is so strong. If she beat her sickness last time after all those years, she can beat whatever this is. Look at her."

Andy turned to see the concentration on Grace's face and the black cracks that ebbed and flowed up her neck with each breath. A pulsing golden illumination accompanied Grace's shallow inhales.

"Now, does that look like someone who has given up?"

"No."

"So we don't give up either. We pack some things, stay close to one another, and we wait until we know more about what's happening out there. We don't need to panic and rush her to hospital only to find out there's more danger there."

"And we wait for Daddy?"

"That's right, little man."

"But he hasn't texted back. I hope he's okay."

"I hope he's okay too, sweetie. He always texts when he can, though, right?"

"Yeah."

"We have to trust that he's doing the best he can," Haylene said, reassuring herself at the same time, doing her best to bury any indication of her own worry. Steeling herself against the emotion rising up, Haylene made a snap decision to risk an alternative approach.

"Andy, I'm gonna try something here."

"Okay?" Andy whimpered, noticing a change in Haylene he'd seen before on many occasions. She had shifted to a more hardened version of herself.

"Do you trust me?"

Andy paused and looked at his mum with a furrowed brow and then back to Haylene.

"I trust you."

Rousing the warrior, adding power and confidence to her voice as if calling out demons, Haylene began.

"Grace. You've been through worse than this. Remember when you were at the bottom of your addiction and loneliness? Well, you dragged yourself out of that swamp, so you can damn well pull yourself out of this," Haylene barked firmly, and in a desperate strategy, she followed up with a sobering slap to Grace's face.

"What are you doing!" Andy cried.

Grace sat bolt upright, and her eyelids began fluttering as if in REM sleep.

Inside Grace's mind, she was alerted to a warm light flickering.

"Look, Andy!"

Locked in a trance, fighting the evil taking hold within her, Grace had a sharp, dawning awareness—an awakening of primaeval wisdom that came with a glowing vision of the archangel Gabriel. Standing tall with his creamy regal cloak billowing behind him, the stoic, ethereal being smiled and extended his hand towards her.

"Take my hand, little one," he whispered. In her mind's eye, she held out a greying arm that swirled with ghostly black creatures. A pinprick of golden warmth grew at the centre of her chest.

"They won't let me go," Grace said to Gabriel.

"You have suffered greatly, Grace. Now it is time to find the meaning in all that pain."

Though unable to interpret Gabriel's cryptic words, Grace's spirit resonated with the sentiment, and as she peered down at her chest, the glimmering light grew in size to surround her spiritual body. Its clean energy scorched the dark creatures in her dream state.

The dark hole of addiction Grace had experienced for most of her adult life was her closest reference for the insatiable hunger for evil these ghostly apparitions possessed. The sensations she felt were no longer of pain but of pressure—a pressure she could withstand and even absorb. In her internal vision, each dark creature was sucked into the golden light one by one, feeding the strength of her own inner illumination. Grace no longer felt alone. The love of her nearest and dearest washed over her like a cooling mountain waterfall. Although she was no closer to finding the Lightbearer, as Gabriel had instructed before, she felt like she was at the beginning of something new: an awakening of a cosmic spirit inside her.

Though her wisdom was growing, her connection with the power of the Light was erratic. Her new gift was not one she could control, and that was a problem under current circumstances when she needed it the most. Still, the Light was there, feeding off her pain.

Back in the room, Haylene looked at a family photo on the wall and stared long and hard at the cosy trio holding candy floss at the funfair and beaming from ear to ear—Andy next to Grace and, next to Grace, Andy's dad: Jack Causer.

*Wherever you are, and whatever's happening with you, Jack, for goodness sake, hurry up. We need you.*

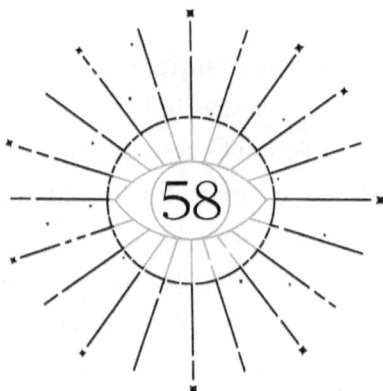

# 58

The oppressive, stale air of summer was at its peak, sitting like a thick blanket over Glastonbury's Chalice Well. Adding to the dense atmosphere in the spiritual realm were the opposing energies of the celestial planes clashing above the Well's cover. On either side of the stone-rimmed hole, dark angel lord and guardian angel commander faced off in a stalemate. The bitter rivers of resentment between the pair were palpable in the ether as their energy spheres almost touched, fizzing erratically in their unstable states.

"Give me one good reason why I should help you," Chava barked at the Damned.

"I am well aware we have had our differences in the past, lost sister, but now is the time to put grievances aside before the etherverse collapses in on us all. Human and angel alike."

"Why do you care if we all burn? You poison everything you touch. I'd rather die than help you and your wretched minions of wasted Light."

"Time on this planet, living alongside these humans, has changed all of that. Changed me."

"Changed? How can you be changed? The humans and this planet suffer more than ever, and it's all because of you, you vampiric beast!"

"In the beginning, yes, I used my Dark Light to torture them. Yet in the last two hundred of their earth years, my purpose has been null and void, fulfilled instead by the humans' own greed and self-obsession.

I have stood by and watched as they endlessly tortured themselves. Surely, as their guardian, you have witnessed this degeneration?"

"Of course I have. I am not blind. But that is besides the point."

"Then let me ask you this, lost sister. What would Gabriel have you do if he were here now?"

The Damned's question was a needle in the heart.

"Don't you dare bring my great lord into this!" Chava screamed, zipping to within inches of the Damned and clasping her hands around his throat in an act of desperate rage at the loss of her master and dearest companion. The pulsing glow under her hands hissed against the Damned's Dark Light body. Without batting an eyelid, the Damned looked straight through the simmering guardian commander. He disarmed her with eyes of eerie calm and the crushing truth.

"He would want us to work together. He would want us to save them," the Damned said.

"Shut your mouth!"

"Michael and Samael will stop at nothing until they are all wiped out."

Chava hated that the Damned was right. She looked to the upper ether and roared in a massive release of repressed emotion.

"Together we have a chance to stop them," the Damned continued. Chava paused to process the reality of the unholy allegiance she was about to enter into.

"Fine. We will work together, but when this is over, don't expect me to show you favour."

"Thank you, Chava. When all is said and done, I expect nothing more of you."

"You do know that Samael and the first wave of the warrior class possess the power to kill celestials?"

"I had heard rumour that this was true. When I was facing down some of the initial wave, their behaviour and appearance were indeed changed, their forms corrupted and poisoned by the forbidden ravages of the Seven Sins. Warrior class and death class have combined to pollute the entirety of the etherverse. Nevertheless, I must stop Samael before he gathers momentum. I have to try."

"That would not be recommended. You would surely not survive. Though your Dark Light is a force to be reckoned with, it would not stand up to Samael in his current form."

"That is why you must guide me to the core of the Well," the Damned said, looking down at the swirling rainbow of energies below them in the ether.

"You cannot be serious. We would both be vapourised."

"Are you so sure of that, lost sister, or are you basing your assumptions on horror stories passed on by weaker minds? The Universe has guided me here, and I believe it was for a reason. Will you help me?"

"It goes against everything I have been told. The warnings we have been given were put in place to protect us."

"I don't disagree, but what do we have to lose? We either die by Samael's hand or die trying to stop him. At least this way there is a chance to level the playing field."

Chava sighed and shook her head.

"I cannot. Though the balance of the etherverse has been tipped, I will not desecrate Lord Gabriel's memory by turning against his command. There must be another way."

"At this point I do not see one. I will risk breaching the Well, and if I survive, I am headed straight for Samael's slimy throat. If you will not join your power with mine to touch the Well, then at least do me one thing."

"Tell me."

"As a guardian, you must have the ability to locate the Archangel of Death. Use your spirit sight and find Samael for me, sister, so that I can give you a measure of revenge for Gabriel's murder."

"That I will do."

Spirit sight was the guardians' unique ability to locate the other classes and follow their movements. The gift gave them the upper hand on all other angelic beings in order to safeguard human life.

Every angelic being's Light had a distinctive energy pattern. Spirit sight worked much like a spiritual echolocation, highlighting a specific angel, or angels, by bouncing a signal off their energy signatures.

Dipping her chest, sending her intention inward, and then expelling a vibrating, golden burst of the Light by forcing her shoulders and head back, Chava released her search field into the ether. Within seconds, the guardian commander had pinpointed Samael's location.

"He is battling back some of your forces in a place called Becontree Estate. Do you know this place, or shall I wait to escort you?"

"I have lived on this planet for tens of thousands of years, dearest Chava. I think I can find my way around."

"Does it not bring you fear that you may die? Even if the Well does not dissolve your being, its nourishing effects may not protect you from the power Samael now wields."

"When you have lived as long as I, one might see death as a welcome gift," the Damned said, giving Chava a curt nod. Without hesitation, the leader of the dark angels stepped down through the spiritual barrier of the Well's edge and into its inner sanctum.

Chava could not help but admire his courage and newfound sense of purpose. Eternal life for the Damned had been more curse than blessing; she had a better sense of that now.

His journey was the precise reason the dark angel lord was so feared throughout the angelic ranks. He fought with the ferocity of a rage-fuelled demon with nothing to lose, and that had defined him. His worldview had dramatically changed in the past centuries, giving him an expanded confidence in the path he was now on.

Chava's world, on the other hand, had been shattered, and she knew of only one place to find solace other than home: around humans seeking truth and a connection with the angelic—somewhere she could be of use and stand watch over gifted humans while guiding them on the righteous path. Having found encouragement in the presence of Professor Simms and Sorchia Collopy, Chava decided this was as good a place as any to regain a measure of composure.

In an explosion of the Light, the guardian angel's glowing form was whisked away to join the travelling intellectuals on their quest for knowledge.

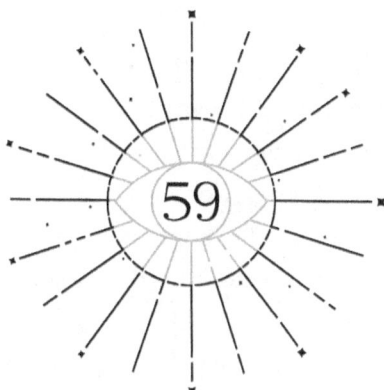

Beel slid into the chaotic shopping centre in a shard of red light to see Raphael fending off a mass of angelic warriors. Having been drawn here by the huge presence of colliding celestial forms, Beel was on the hunt for her master and a little action in the process.

The shopping centre was a split-level, open space connected by escalators and glass lifts. The commercial hub comprised three stories bordering an open concourse where Beel now stood looking up at the lofted glass ceiling. The battle of warrior versus archangel appeared like a New Year's Eve firework display, explosions of the Light in green, blue, and gold popping over her head throughout the upper floors. The warriors were attempting to turn as many innocent bystanders as possible to create havoc. Raphael was deftly crisscrossing the floors through the air above Beel and thwarting their every move. Her attempts, however, were only delaying a losing battle while the touched prisoners from a nearby facility ran riot through the shopping centre in waves of greed, lust, violence, and envy.

Sensing Beel coming to her aid, Raphael deflected a spinning warrior directly into the dark angel's path. Beel sliced down into the angel's throat, and the angel disintegrated, its ashes scattering to the lower realms. A second warrior grappled with Beel from behind. In a loose, swift movement, Beel switched positions with her attacker and clamped firmly onto the warrior's head. Looking up at Raphael, she launched the angel like a bullet in the healer's direction.

"Do not mistake my aid for anything other than convenience. I have not yet decided to trust you. I am here for information," Beel said. Catching the airborne warrior with a blast of emerald luminance, Raphael deflected the projectile, boomeranging him back at Beel. The dark mistress severed the warrior's head with a crimson Light dagger, collapsing his form into dust.

"The feeling is mutual, red witch," Raphael sneered.

"Watch your mouth, princess. Where is my lord?"

"He has set off on a new path to seek out Samael."

"Goddamn him!" Beel screamed. Releasing her frustration, she singled out a nearby warrior who was turning a teenage girl with the Touch. She unleashed a spinning kick to the warrior's midsection, tossing the angel into Raphael's path.

Raphael bounced him off the ground and into a portal to the Pit that Beel had opened to catch him.

"He may be foolish, but it might buy us some time to regroup," Raphael suggested.

"There is no us. I work alone."

Recognising the threat Beel posed to their ranks, two warriors rushed at the dark angel simultaneously. Beel grabbed one by the throat and slammed him into his bewildered companion in an explosion of red Light. Head smashing into head with extreme force, both angels evaporated in a sparkling grey mist.

"How can they absorb the humans' life forces?" Beel asked.

Two warriors launched at Raphael from above, taking the same approach as the others to try to overwhelm her defences. The archangel held her foes back with the overcharged rays of her eyes. Each warrior edged closer with their shields up, dissipating the force.

"Michael must have transferred his mutated abilities to them somehow, and now Samael wields this power on earth," Raphael shouted over her decibel-smashing eye beams.

Warping to her aid, Beel dove at the attacking angels and hammered an axe handle down on one from behind, causing him to disintegrate. The surprise threw the remaining warrior off guard, and a dip in the distracted warrior's shield allowed the full force of Raphael's beam to take out his knees, knocking the warrior to the ground. Beel hovered over the dazed angel and, without hesitation, stabbed him in the back. The warrior's ensuing fragmentation ensured his damnation to the Pit along with his brainwashed brethren.

Both archangel and dark angel gathered themselves at a break in the flow of oncoming warriors. Observing the touched prisoners preying upon fleeing innocents in the shopping centre car park through the window, Raphael dropped her head and clenched her fists.

She was at her wits' end. Never had she encountered such depravity meted out by her own divine kin. The abomination made her insides boil.

A clouded anger came over Raphael that Beel had never seen in the perfect archangel. Her spiritual energy shimmered a deeper shade of emerald, complemented by a tinge of orange at its edges. Beel stepped back.

"Raphael?"

"There are too many of them. I've had enough of this. They all must leave. Leave!"

As her roar rang out, a massive expulsion of healing Light burst from Raphael's chest. The shock wave crashed into every being within a 500-metre radius. Warrior angel, touched, and human alike were healed of all ill effects instantaneously. They awoke as if from a dream and stumbled about in a struggle to regain some sense of physical and spiritual orientation.

"What in all ether was that?"

Raphael blinked and shook her head. Her features fell as she held up her hands in puzzlement.

"I have no understanding of this force that was locked inside me. Universe, forgive me my anger."

"Why didn't you unshackle this power in the first place? You could have saved yourself much trouble in battle."

"That was a feeling I have never dared access before. I do not know how or why it decided to surface. I have betrayed myself," Raphael said, her eyes darting about the ground.

"Maybe now that you've spent some time around those of us in the damned class, our freedom of expression is rubbing off on you?" Beel said with a smirk.

"This is no time for jokes. I must reconstitute myself. I am not fit to lead," Raphael mumbled.

"Enough of your self-pity. Where is my lord?" Beel demanded, not content to be of comfort to the bleary-eyed archangel.

"The last I knew, he went to the Well."

Without an attempt at a farewell, Beel vanished. Raphael was left alone again, unsettled and unsure of where to turn. Too much time living up to the perfection that defined her had grown a monster inside, struggling to break free. Raphael's uncharacteristic outburst was evidence of that.

The shadow side of her inner being had shown itself, and the beautiful, flawless shell around her psyche had begun to crumble. Perhaps the change would help her face the incoming hordes, or perhaps it would consume her completely. For the first time in her everlasting existence, Raphael did not recognise herself or know how to move forwards.

Having already made it through the first layer of fire surrounding the Well's core, the Damned's energy form was frozen and splintered. The second sphere around the Well he now occupied was a contained blizzard throwing ice spikes the size of spearheads. The spikes sheared off frozen chunks of his frame that his Dark Light continually fought to heal and rematerialise. The progress was slow, but he was almost at the core. He gritted his teeth with determination, fighting the agony and gathering as much latent dark matter from the Well's surrounding area as he could manage. Sucking the red hues of Dark Light towards him, he collected just enough energy to fuel a concentrated firestorm at his back. His spine exploded like a jet engine. Propelled forth, he broke through the final layer of the Well.

The very essence of the Divine Mother surrounded him in the core. He was helpless in the face of her will as he was pulled to the very centre of the formless void.

No sound. No light. No escape of any kind.

He found himself paralysed as an intense energy from the Well began leeching his life force, bringing with it an unearthly, soul-wrenching pain.

The Damned's entire being was torn in every direction as a cacophony of voices and visions exploded into his mind. A merciless hurricane of fire and ice swirled into motion around him, slashing at his spirit and weaving through his frame. The force of the churning mass engaged a gravitational pressure that threatened to collapse his scattered mind.

Above him, Beel sensed her master in great turmoil. The dark angel darted at the Well only to be bounced off its outer wall, which had now become a barrier, locking the Damned within. All she could do was watch and wait.

*I will stay by your side, my lord, as you have stood by mine.*

In the Well, the Damned saw and heard everything all at once. The noise and clutter in his mind was unbearable. The Damned learned of Samael, the horror he presented for the humans. He felt his abominable power and its monstrous design. The dark angel could also see the greater threat of Michael at the helm, still to come. Then there was Abaddon, slaughtered by Samael himself. The Damned let out a scream in his helpless state. There was no sound. He saw Zelda's attack on Grace, leaving her victim to the Touch. He saw her decaying state and could do nothing.

Unexpectedly, the trap of the Well's void then began to send refreshing spasms of energy through his spirit. The Damned gathered his strength to escape.

*Universe, release me that I may save Grace and stop Samael. He will destroy everything. I can stop him. I know I can.*

It was futile. The Damned was unable to do anything before the Well had finished its energy transfer. His ability to portal had been nullified; even phasing to the surface was impossible. For him to take on the enhanced strength of the Well, he had to remain in his paralysed state.

He had to give up control.

The primaeval force that held him was one he did not know or understand. He could not be sure it would ever release him. The Damned resigned himself to the fact that Grace, Raphael, and Beel were on their own now. They were about to face down the heartless will of the Angel of Death, and they didn't stand a chance. The Damned made one last attempt to communicate should he not survive the Well, using the remaining reserves of his accessible Dark Light.

"Raphael. If you can hear me, go to Grace. Heal her. She has been poisoned by the Seven Sins. The earth needs her to survive. Cleanse her. Protect her. Be her guide. She has Gabriel's gift, and she is the key to winning this war."

Back in the shopping centre, the Damned's broadcast echoed in Raphael's mind clearer than her own thoughts. A glimmer of hope ignited a flash of brilliant green in her eyes as the archangel collected her Light power.

*Finally, a purpose.*

"I will guard her with my life, brother," Raphael replied with a soft smile. Racing off to Grace's location through an ethergate of flaming emerald, the archangel of the restoration class was charged with renewed confidence. There was nothing like fighting for the innocent to sharpen the mind.

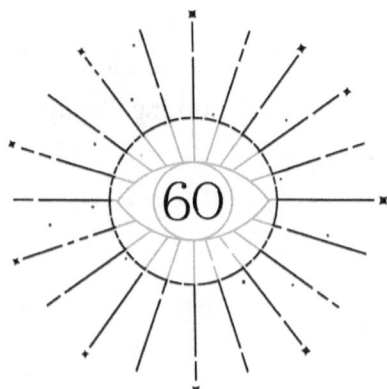

## 60

Back in Becontree Estate, the streets were overrun. Jack dusted himself off outside 68 Mayfield Road. Samael loomed large behind him. Struck by an unfamiliar, powerful presence, Jack swivelled on his heels to prepare for an attack.

Nothing.

Samael had warped behind Jack as he turned. Jack saw only the mob of touched prisoners and the humans fleeing to safety in the distance. The Angel of Death reached out and took hold of the back of Jack's skull, latching onto his soul.

"Resist me if you can," Samael croaked.

Arrested in a muscle-tightening hypnosis, Jack was rendered helpless, his eyes widening to maximum as his skin cracked open with dark lesions.

At that very moment, Grace shot up from the sofa in her living room and held her arms locked out straight, much to the surprise of Andy and Haylene, who jumped back to give her space. The cracks around Grace's chest and neck were retreating, leaving only a few wormlike discolourations around her eyes.

She was not awake. Eyes closed, breathing deeply, meditating, Grace had begun to meld with the otherworldly force dormant in her spirit. Andy and Haylene stared at each other and then back at Grace, sensing the need for stillness.

Grace's eyes suddenly snapped open, beaming bright gold. After a few seconds, the blinding glow began to dim and brighten rhythmically.

*Vaaum va vum. Vaaum va vum. Vaaum va vum.*

Landing just in time to witness the wonder of Grace realising her gift, Raphael was filled with a renewed vigour. The energy expulsion overcharged the appliances and electrical items throughout the flat, blasting sparks about the space.

Grace had established an unbreakable bond with Gabriel's Light. All ill effects of the touch evaporated in an instant, and her skin began to radiate warm luminescence like that of an angelic being.

Back at the Well, the Damned was still pinned by the swirling orb of fire and ice at its core. The dark angel held his arms crossed tight around himself, whipping his head back and forth to combat the extreme pressure. In the midst of his struggle, the stark realisation hit him that this could be his end, dissolved by the great earth mother.

*A fitting conclusion to my tormented existence. At least, in the end, I tried to help them.*

Slipping through the churning elemental winds surrounding him, the Damned heard a low, soothing voice reverberating from a distant place in the etherverse.

"There's no need to fight it anymore, brother. Let go of who you used to be, and step into who you must become." The firm, kind tone was unmistakable. It was Gabriel, the message either a weak remnant of his once eternal form or a lost echo guided by the cosmos as it gradually split apart.

In an eruption of all the colours of the rainbow, the Damned shot from the Well, propelled by the spirit of the Divine Mother within. Hurtling in a giant orange fireball, the dark angel was transported to Jack's exact location by the will of the Universe.

Jack's life force was already half-gone. His eyes were grey, rolling towards solid black, and his skin was littered with black crevices weeping dark ooze as he fell to his knees.

Materialising in the foetal position he'd held inside the Well, the Damned arose and marvelled at the eye-watering amber hue emanating from his hands, eyes, and hair. In an instant, he connected his increased power to Jack's spirit through a beam of amber Light directed at Jack's chest. Jack began to hyperventilate, his eyes flickering bright gold and back to black, the grip of the Seven Sins losing its hold. Samael stared at the Damned, appalled by his intervention.

"You! How?"

A huge gale whipped up above Becontree Estate as shards of lightning snapped all around Jack, Samael, and the Damned. The empowered dark angel's eyes cycled through their deep-orange glow to a searing, brilliant yellow. Coupled with the surge of power, a jarring emotion hit the Damned like a ten-ton truck as the being that haunted his mind overtook him. Holding the transfer of the Light to Jack, the Damned was lost in his mind, frozen to the spot.

Back with Grace, an awareness of her transformed self brought with it a sense of doubt as the golden pulse began to slow.

"I can't hold it in anymore," Grace said.

"Then give up control, Grace. Trust the power within you, and let go," Haylene said.

Raphael opened her palms and lent her nourishing emerald Light to help stabilise Grace's wavering energy field.

Grace crunched her eyelids closed. When she snapped them open, her eyes sockets were burning brighter than the sun. She spoke in a three-tonal voice that was not her own.

"Let go."

At that very moment, the illumination in Jack's eyes burst outwards, slamming into the Angel of Death.

"Let go," Jack boomed. The three-tonal voice Grace had manifested only seconds before sent a shock wave that shattered windows and exploded car tires nearby. The overwhelming beams from Jack's eyes pushed Samael back several metres, the Angel of Death's face awash with confusion. The aura of grey and gold around the massive archangel blinked intermittently, his Light force beginning to fail him. The blast left him surrounded by a throbbing force field of searing illumination.

Despite his immobilisation, the Damned's energy continued feeding Jack's force field in a symbiotic relationship with the human's spiritual aura. As remnants of the Seven Sins evaporated through Jack's pores in a hot black steam, the Light surrounding him was absorbed back inside his body, and he returned to normal.

Samael stood back to consider his next move, jarred by the experience and recognising a power in Jack that should not exist.

"Interesting. No matter. You are no match for death's grip,"

Samael growled.

Snapping out of his vision, the Damned warped next to Jack to stand between him and the Angel of Death.

"Leave the human, Samael, or I will end you."

"I would love to see you try."

Lashing out violently, Samael's tendrils wrapped around the Damned and held him fast, ready to turn him to stone. Jack made a run for the Range Rover, taking out two more touched humans with military efficiency on the way.

"You shall know death," Samael croaked as he moved towards Jack, reaching to regain his grip on the human. Jack's eyes glowed solid gold as he whipped around like a shot to stare directly at Samael's massive, outstretched hand. The force within Jack arrested Samael's movement, leaving the archangel helpless. The Damned braced himself and expelled an explosion of orange Light that singed Samael's tentacles, evaporating them in a grey mist.

Jack even moved like Gabriel, standing tall with outstretched arms and palms forward. He was again encircled by a glowing aura of energy. Warping behind Jack, the Damned released two amber beams from each of his bound fists. The Light fed into the orb around Jack as it grew in size, edging closer to Samael in his compromised position.

Back in the apartment, still upright with bright eyes, Grace lifted her arms into the same position as Jack, her palms open. As she hummed an otherworldly tone, Grace's palms and eyes burst with a dazzling golden energy.

"Ommm."

Moved by the great spiritual forces of the cosmos, Jack connected with Grace's tone.

"Ommm."

The resulting eruption of Light blew Samael off his feet and sent him flailing backwards through the air like a spinning plane. Twisting wildly, his form fractured and almost disintegrated. The monstrous archangel landed flat on his back in confusion.

Regarding his failing aura with horror, he darted his attention to Jack.

"But how? You are human!" Samael cried, a tremble in his voice. The hulking beast vanished in a sudden gust of grey-and-gold smoke.

Returning to himself, Jack fled for the Range Rover on instinct, clicking open the car and leaping to safety. Allowing his senses to catch up, he inhaled a huge breath while shaking his head and blinking. Jack had no understanding or real memory of the dramatic events that had just unfolded in the spiritual realm. The only evidence of his encounter was the cold fever rushing his body and the raw, red skin lesions around his eyes. Unable to pinpoint Lazaro or Dio in the chaos, Jack started up the Range and took off at speed. As he snaked through the narrow estate's roads, he dialled up a saved number on his phone through the vehicle's Bluetooth setting.

"Pick up, goddamn it," Jack pleaded.

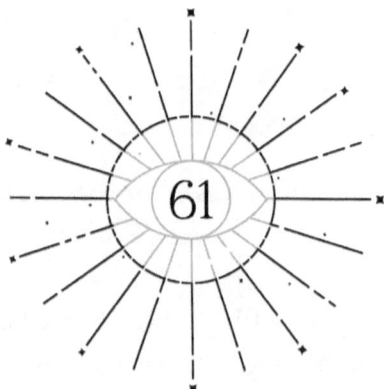

# 61

Hobbling through a weak ethergate, Samael dragged his right leg and held tightly to his right arm. The Light-energy connection around both his limbs was going haywire, and his formless appendages were without function.

The room he had escaped to was cold and dark and lined with blocks of limestone. The air on the physical plane was stale—not that this mattered to the Angel of Death. The space where he now cowered like a wounded animal was once a chamber of great power for him and his kin. The comforting memories were exactly what Samael needed to rebuild his confidence and recover his strength.

The Angel of Death was dumbstruck by the ignition of Light he had only barely survived. The force was nothing like he had experienced, even from his archangel kin. The most troubling element of his experience was the presence of the Damned and his elevated state. Samael had never known the dark angel to burn so brilliantly.

*What the hell is the Damned doing, coming to the aid of the humans?*

It was an unthinkable U-turn in the dark angel's allegiances. So many unanswered questions flooded Samael's mind that he could barely see straight. Compounded by his severe injuries, the dizzying state of consciousness Samael found himself in prevented his mind from sensing the towering archangel warping into the stone hideaway behind him.

The hulking figure crackled with zigzags of blue-and-gold lightning. His pitch-black mane billowed as the wild Light force surrounding him disrupted the ionic atmosphere of the room. Golden serpent eyes pierced the darkness and held fast to Samael's broken body—eyes that burned with hate.

"I thought you might crawl back here into your hole," Archangel Michael said. Samael whirled and glared up at his compatriot with the petulance of a scolded child.

"I can explain."

"I don't want to hear your excuses."

"I will not make excuses for my actions," Samael replied, defiant.

"You have failed me, with all the power I have given you. You are a great disappointment." Michael electrified his frame with stabbing blue spikes of energy that ripped through Samael like a Taser, further weakening him. "Where is Raphael?"

"That is not important now. I have experienced the emergence of a seer. She was channelling Gabriel's power somehow."

"Seers have come and gone throughout the ages without consequence, and Gabriel is no more. I have taken his power."

"You are mistaken. His power remains, and it is increased, bonded with a human and the Lord of the Damned."

"The presence of a seer is an unforeseen problem, but even a remnant of Gabriel's power cannot withstand my enriched form. As for the Damned, his time to face me will come, and I will dispatch with him as I did the last time. I will ask you again, where is Raphael?"

"She was hidden from my sight. Do not fret: I will find her and cripple her abilities. She does not have the conviction within her to be of any real threat."

"You are a fool. You have no idea of the threat she poses to my new world vision. I tasked you to eliminate Raphael as I dealt with Gabriel. That was the deal. You have failed in your responsibility, and you must atone."

"Atone? You are drunk on power, brother Michael. Ours was an equal alliance made on the condition that once the Seven Sins were unleashed, their power would be shared."

"I have changed the agreement in light of your failure. The great power I have given you can be just as easily taken away, and if you want to live, you will do as instructed."

"You wouldn't dare."

"You are welcome to test my resolve."

In that moment, Samael's heart began to turn away from Michael. The Angel of Death had never been a slave to anyone. Neither would he tolerate being chastised for doing his level best in spite of factors far outside his control. Michael's twisted reasoning was precisely why Samael withheld knowledge of the immeasurable Light energy that had torn his form to pieces. The sheer brilliance of this energy signature was one he recognized from before the birth of mankind.

The power of the Lightbearer.

Michael had lost his mind to the cancer of the Seven Sins—a risk he had known full well in deciding to dig up that ancient and rampant evil. The Seven Sins hungered to consume every ounce of goodness from any host, no matter how powerful. In the end, decay would win out.

All at once, Samael decided he would not be a casualty of Michael's madness. When more information about the Lightbearer's agenda in the present conflict was revealed, he would rethink his allegiances. For now, he played the dutiful servant.

"I will do as you see fit, brother," Samael said.

"That's the spirit. We can achieve so much more together, old friend."

Disappearing in a shard of regal blue and gold, Michael left to pursue the remainder of the first phase of his invasion. Samael knew that Michael would need to accelerate several other facets of the next wave due to the failure of his own scouting mission. Samael took heart from the fact that he had picked himself up from defeat before. Gazing around the inner tomb of the Great Pyramid of Giza, Samael connected with the story inscribed on the walls around him—fond memories of his finest hour.

The pictograms in the burial chamber detailed the Jewish Passover and the death of every Egyptian firstborn at his hand. In those times, the Angel of Death had been at the will of the Universe, serving a balance maintained by Gabriel. Samael may not have possessed Michael's power, but now that Gabriel was gone, he no longer had to toe the line.

*Michael may think he is in control, but control is often an illusion.*

With this thought, Samael settled onto his back, lying atop the sarcophagus encased below. Sucking up any and all life force from the bones of the dead for miles around, Samael vowed to find a way back to the power he rightly deserved.

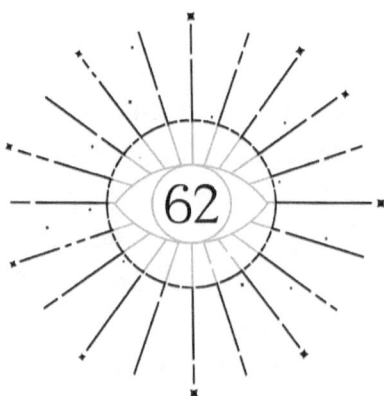

## 62

As the Light left Grace, an unseen force guided her body slowly back to its original sitting position like a leaf bobbing down a mountain stream. Her eyelids appeared heavy, her features had softened, and her skin was clear again, more nourished than before; and her eyes had returned to their normal forest green. Grace blinked and took in her surroundings. A soothing serenity had come over her.

Andy and Haylene both gawked at her with frozen, wide-mouthed smiles. Raphael stood admiringly with her hands on her heart.

"Mummy, you healed yourself and then turned into a giant fireball! That was so cool!" Andy said.

"It was phenomenal, Grace," Haylene added.

"You are the seer we have all been waiting for," Raphael said, barely believing her eyes and dropping to one knee in reverence.

"Oh, hello," Grace said, turning to Raphael.

"It is such a blessing, and a relief, that the Universe has finally sent you," Raphael replied.

"Who's there, Mum?" Andy chimed in.

"It's the archangel Raphael, Andy. She is the most honourable of all angelic beings and leader of the restoration class."

Both Andy and Haylene stared at Grace as if she had grown a second head.

"So, you do know who I am. You truly have tapped into the Light and all its gifts."

"I don't know how to explain it, but I just know things now. I know who I am and how to see the world as it really is."

A striking enlightenment had burst open in Grace's spirit. Tapping into the wisdom of the celestial planes, Grace was now fully aware of her part in the struggle to come. The angelic companions that she needed to commune with, and drive off, were clear to her. Her connection to every spiritual being hit her with a sensation that felt like her nerves and blood cells were escaping from her skin and bouncing off every ethereal power in the near vicinity. It was a perception beyond any cerebral understanding. With the realization of the deep reserves of Light power that coursed through her, Grace knew she had the capacity to match anything standing in her way.

"And this is just the beginning, Grace. I can help guide you. You are a healer, after all, just like I am," Raphael said.

"It's strange. I imagined you'd have wings and a halo, but I know now that all of that is a fantasy. All those images we have of your kind were created by man with all their limitations."

"Many things imagined by man concerning the spiritual realm venture far from the truth. Now that you have stepped into your gift, it is your calling to show them otherwise."

"Hang on. What? Angels don't have wings? Not even the cute baby ones with bows and arrows?" Andy interrupted.

"I'm afraid not, my love," Grace said to Andy.

"Aw. I wish I could see them like you can, Mum."

Grace's phone rang, breaking the atmosphere in the room. Shocked at the caller ID, Grace hurriedly answered.

"Jack?"

"Grace, listen to me. We need to get out of the city. Is Andy there? Is he okay?" Jack said.

"We're all fine. We heard what they were saying on the news, so we're staying inside."

"We have to move. I've seen what they were talking about firsthand,

and it's spreading fast. I don't know what caused all this, but it's worse than they're making out," Jack said.

"I think I know what started it all," Grace said.

"You've seen these things up close?" Jack said.

"You're not gonna believe this, but . . . two angels have appeared to me and warned me of a great evil," Grace said. After a long pause, she asked, "Jack? Are you there?"

"Grace, are you off your meds again?" Jack eventually replied.

"I knew you wouldn't believe me," Grace said, dipping her head with a heavy inhalation. "Well, it doesn't matter if you do or you don't. You'll see in time."

"Listen, forget that. We need to gather some supplies and get to a less populated area. I know an old safehouse where we can all hide out till I get my head around everything that's going on."

"Okay, we'll start packing up here," Grace replied.

"Good. Tell my little man I'm coming."

"I will, of course. Jack?"

"What is it?"

"Thank you for coming to be with us."

"No way I could leave you all behind. Just stay put, and I'll get to you as soon as I can," Jack said, ending the call.

Grace looked up to the ceiling as if to give thanks to the angels for bringing her husband back to her. A faint glow flashed across her eyes. Looking back to Andy, she stroked his cheek.

"Get ready, little man. Daddy's coming," Grace said as Andy beamed back at his mum with love emanating from his spirit.

Landing on the hexagonal stones of the Giant's Causeway, surrounded by an amber orb of flame, the Damned heard and saw everything.

The stones under his feet in the physical realm splintered, hissing and cracking, as red-and-golden fissures appeared across the full length of the causeway. The Well had transformed the Damned into a force that could walk between physical and ethereal worlds.

His empowered senses picked out golden spots of Light within the angelic ranks that remained after Michael's cleansing of the heavens. His newly enhanced telepathic abilities tuned into the movements of the twisted warrior and death classes. He could map out the battlefield of the next phase of Michael's advance in the blink of an eye. Shining brightest in his vision of the etherverse was the stunning Light energy at Grace's location.

A new seer had risen.

The damned and restoration classes were aligned alongside her.

Archangel Michael would soon meet his match.

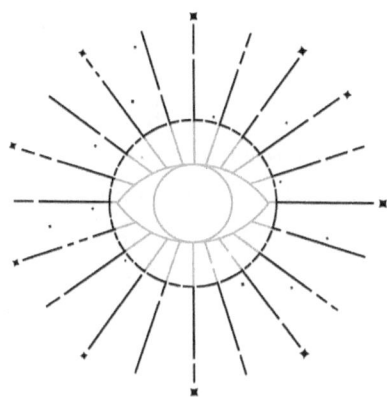

## ACKNOWLEDGMENTS

Firstly, thanks need to go to my partner, Jamie, who believed in this story from the start. Your encouragement and pep talks kept me going when I doubted my ability.

I'm also very grateful to Paulien Riesmeijer and Marie-Anne Kooij for being my proofreaders. Paulien, your critical eye and spot-on feedback were essential to this story taking its final shape. Marie-Anne, you kept going even though it wasn't your genre.

Koehler Books, thank you so very much for seeing the need for this story and backing me. Greg Fields, you are a wonderfully intelligent and positive mentor to me, and I am astounded you read the whole book. What a legend you are. Hannah Woodlan, you saved me from myself in the edit and were a gentle guide with such kindness in your feedback. I wish everyone had an editor as spot on as you. Lauren Sheldon, what an outstanding cover you crafted, and I'm excited to have you working with me on book two. Also, John Koehler, the big man, thanks for making the whole process informative and fun. Cheers, laddie!

I am also hugely thankful for my parents. Mum and Dad, you have always been there, cheering me on and helping make my dreams come true. Any child would be blessed to have parents half as caring and as wise as you are. Lastly, Grandpa Jimmy Smith, you were my Lightbearer and my hero when I was young. I hope that this book honours the way you lived—with wisdom, respect, and quick-witted stories that kept others smiling when times were tough.

www.ingramcontent.com/pod-product-compliance
Lightning Source LLC
LaVergne TN
LVHW091711070526
838199LV00050B/2359